To … tt

… s

Larson.

you guys.

Ardnas Marie

30 January 2022

Disturbance In The Darkness: A Fated Encounter

Ardnas Marie

This is a work of fiction. All the incidents, names, and characters are imaginary. Any resemblance to actual person, living or dead, is completely coincidental.

For more information on current and upcoming works, make sure to follow Ardnas Marie on

http://www.ardnasmarie.com
https://www.facebook.com/ArdnasMarie2742/

ISBN: 979-8-9853908-2-7

In memory of Larry Eber Taylor.

ACKNOWLEDGMENTS

I would like to thank my husband, Steven, for creating the book's cover and for creative input. I would like to thank Cathy Taylor for her patience while I finished the novel and for her continued support. Mostly, I would like to thank Lawrence Eber Taylor (Larry) or, as I called him, Grandpa Taylor. I read the first scribbled words to him. Though several people encouraged me to publish, it was Grandpa Taylor's feedback that cinched the deal. It was also his wish to see it published before his passing.

I would also like to thank everyone who bought the unedited version of this story. Very few knew I published unedited in 2019 at the dying request of Grandpa Taylor. I know several of you are waiting patiently for book two's release. I have attached a sneak peek, a teaser trailer if you will, of what's to come.

Real monsters don't need to hide in dark; they only need it to hide their monstrous acts.

—Ardnas Marie

PROLOGUE

1

Cheyenne rose, gasping for air. Her hair clung to her sweaty face and neck; she usually ran feverish during nightmares. She hooked the damp strands behind her ears and scanned the unfamiliar scene. The small room contained two nightstands and a bureau surrounding the bed and a large curtain concealed most of the wall opposite the bedroom door. Nothing about the bland room rang out to her.

She tossed the blankets to the side and pawed at the white undershirt she sported. "Well, this is new." It wasn't every night she dreamed about wearing men's clothing. She stood, tugging at the white shirt covering her otherwise nude body.

She exhaled and her breath turned to water vapors traveling through the cold air. Steam radiated from her body and the beads of sweat frosted to her face.

What's happening? None of this made sense. Did he kill somebody else?

She opened the closet, hoping to dress in something less revealing, to find a wall of red bricks. "What the hell?"

On the bureau, a pair of prayer hands, surrounded by photo frames, offered up a rosary.

Convinced he killed another innocent soul, she plucked one of the photos in hopes of learning whose life was prematurely taken, but it was empty. Her eyes skimmed the rest of photos. "They're all empty."

She focused on the wooden rosary wrapped around the prayer hands. Was God telling her to pray for what she did? She flipped the rosary and etched into the wood were three letters: D-E-D. Where the letters someone's initials or was it dead misspelled?

She closed her eyes, releasing the rosary. Did she finally succeed in taking her own life, ending the hell she had been living? She shook her head; she wasn't that lucky.

She pulled open the bureau's top drawer and not to her surprise, more red bricks. If dreams were symbolic, then what did the red bricks represent? The weight of her decision to swallow a bottle of pills? Perhaps. What made more sense was her decision to barricade herself from the world. That was until her best friend convinced her she could be saved. Her eyes fixated on the rosary. He was dead now and it was her fault.

If the room wasn't going to offer clues to where she was, Cheyenne thought the outside world might. She pulled back the curtains and surveyed a seemingly endless field of yellow calla lilies. "Where the hell am I?"

The giggles of a little boy emanated from the hallway.

Was *he* about to kill right now? Was she somehow thrusted into a nightmare yet to unfold?

"Hello?" Cheyenne followed the phantom laughter. "Little boy, can you hear me?" She entered the living room where the walls were covered with so many picture frames, it could be described as wallpaper. She stood in the middle of the room, staring at the empty frames. Did they represent lives taken too soon?

Behind her, the customed designed fireplace ignited into indigo flames, distracting her from the walls. The face of the fireplace was made from stone and recessed into the wall. On either side of the fireplace were two hand-carved benches molded into the walls, arching into tree boughs stretching over the elm mantle.

The fire snuffed out.

Her brows pinched inward. Weird, but what was normal about this . . . this . . . she hadn't yet decided what she wanted to call it.

She scanned the room waiting to hear the childish laughter. She spotted the front door. Maybe he went outside. She opened the door and more bricks.

Was she in purgatory for *both* their sins?

She shut the door and turned, noticing the bay windows. She pulled back the curtains. More lilies and in the distance a figure resembling a woman. She couldn't be sure; the figure was too far away.

The perfume of coffee lingered in the air.

She followed the fragrance into the dining room; it was barren. To her right, a sliding glass door framed the scene of children standing amongst the calla lilies. They were the same children who haunted her dreams, but none of them bared the marks which took their lives.

"They're all here."

Never have they all appeared at once, but this wasn't a normal nightmare. She searched for the little boy who never revealed his death to her. She spotted him sniffing a flower. He pulled it away from his nose and mouthed something to her. She didn't need to read his lips. She heard his message a thousand times over.

She tried to slide open the door, but there was no handle or mechanism to grip. She pressed her hands against the glass to slide it open, but the door did not budge. She looked back at the children and one by one, they vanished.

Beeeep, Beeeep, Beeeep. The coffee maker announced it was finished percolating.

She looked around the kitchen. “Hello?”

Like the rest of the home, it was vacant. The boy’s giggle never returned but, somebody was here. The coffee didn’t brew itself.

“Please come out; I won’t hurt you.”

She opened several cupboards until she found the coffee cups. Made sense they would be located above the coffee maker. She removed two and filled them. Whoever was here might reveal themselves over a hot cup of Joe. She left one cup on the counter and turned, grabbing the other.

A man grabbed her wrists and slammed her into the counter; her coffee sloshed, staining the white shirt, and blistering her breast. He was a giant of a man; Cheyenne was five-five. He could easily be six-five. His jaw length hair framed his face and clung to his five o’clock shadow. He flared his nostrils and furrowed his brow which darkened his green eyes.

She looked deep within his pupils and saw a glint of amber. She knew *he* had to be behind whatever this was. Was this man his next intended target? Why show her; he never revealed his victims before?

Saliva strung from the man’s lips. “If anything happens to my son, I’ll kill you.” He flung her by the wrists.

“Hmph!” Her back smacked into the breakfast bar and she collapsed to floor. He came at her and she curled into the fetal position, closing her eyes. She heard the snap of fingers and a familiar voice, echo, “Wake up!”

2

Cheyenne woke with the side of her face resting on the toilet seat and her finger in her mouth, purging her body of the pills she swallowed. The last thing she remembered was being in the kitchen eating handfuls of Tylenol for dinner and chasing them with Spiced Rum.

The loss of her best friend, her only friend, was too much. He died only a few days ago but his death left an unfillable crater. At least he gave that wretched bastard the finger before taking his own life. It was the ultimate 'fuck you' to that murderous abomination.

Her abdomen tightened. She hugged the toilet preparing herself for a violent heave. She hated throwing up. The acidic contents always filled her sinus cavities, and it didn't matter how much she blew her nose, there was always leftovers. When she inhaled through her nose, the vomit traveled from her sinus cavities into her throat via the nasopharynx, causing her to dry-heave.

She spit the last of the nasty taste from her mouth and flushed the toilet. Her head throbbed from the pressure of her violent heaving. She crawled on the floor, stopping in front of the sink.

On the floor in a puddle of her vomit, a message left for her spelled out in vegetables from yesterday's dinner and today's pills: Find JMD.

She pulled herself up the sink counter. "Whoever the hell that is." She stared at her mirror's reflection. Her long, wavy auburn hair matted with chunks of food embodied her misery.

She brushed her teeth and stripped out of her vomit covered clothes. Bruises covered her body in different stages of black, green, yellow, and purple. She turned examining her back. It was only a dream, but she felt the phantom pain digging into her love handles.

She took a quick shower and crawled between the sheets wearing a sports bra and panties. She glanced at the clock, watching the time flip over to three a.m. She pulled the string, clicking off the lamp. If she was lucky, she'd close her eyes and they'd never open again.

Cheyenne's closet door crept open and her eyelids rose.

"What do you want?"

One

The Captives

Jonny sat against the cool cast-iron bars keeping him prisoner. Straw blanketed the ground; it poked at his bare feet and it made his body itch. The dirt coating his naked torso turned to mud on his sweaty body.

The only light provided came from the dim bulb above the cage. It wasn't bright enough to illuminate the surroundings, only enough to cast shadows of the vermin accompanying him. It was torture . . . if only he could shatter it.

The odors were less tolerable. Jonny scrunched his nose. He could not remember the last time he or the other kid bathed. The dog manure and urine-soaked straw were last cleaned a month ago. None of that, though, masked the stink of death. The smell entrenched itself in his hair and clothes, haunting him everywhere he went.

He closed his eyes, listening to the slow, steady drips in the distant darkness. He counted the seconds between drips. One Mississippi, two Mississippi, three Mississippi, four. Three and half Mississippi's; the drips were slowing.

The sniffing, licking, and gnawing of the guard dogs and the squeaks of rodents fighting over scavenged food added to the already noisy night. To boot, his cellmate shuffled nonstop to find a comfortable position.

A vivacious roar from beyond the wooden walls carried the crowd's excitement and frustration.

"I'm scared, Jonny."

"I know, Al. Just do what I trained you to do."

Jonny touched his right cheek, feeling the swelling beneath the surface. He placed his face between the bars, spitting the metallic taste from his mouth. He grimaced and grabbed his right side.

"Did you win, Jonny?"

"Yeah." He leaned his head against the bars, shifting his eyes toward the single dim bulb, counting the drips in his head, feeling his hunger over the pain.

The wooden doors rattled with a loud bang.

Al's shadowy outline crawled to the far corner, gripping the bars. "They're coming for me!"

"Most likely."

The rattle and clank of chain links clearing steel loops overrode the other noises.

Al flinched with each click and clack.

The large wooden door slid partially open. The lamps outside cast their light momentarily into the barn.

He shifted his eyes toward Al. The crowd was energetic tonight. Their *Get up and hit him!* tantrums from the losing side, and the *YEAH!* screams from the winning team carried all the way from the compound.

Al gripped the bars even tighter, entrenching his head between his arms, and rocked. His voice quivered. "They're coming for me!"

"No," Jonny said. "We're getting another captive."

The insufficient light seeping through the doors did not

permit identification of the newcomer. The only thing revealed was the boy's petite frame.

Jonny did not require light to know who brought the new victim. The man always wore pointy-toed boots; he loved to kick the captives. The man was the bully holding the magnifying glass, taking pleasure in the suffering he inflicted. A lit cigarette always hung from his lips, and he kept a hunter's knife hidden under his pant leg.

The man booted the frail boy in the rear. "Go on, get over there." The man had a southern twang.

The new prisoner fell on the hard-dried dirt. "OW!"

The man shut the wooden door behind them. He turned and kicked the boy again, smacking his face into the ground. He laughed, grabbing the boy by his hair. He dragged him to the cage and slammed him into the bars.

"Stop it!" the childish voice bawled.

Jonny shook his head. The boy looked small, but his tiny voice confirmed his suspicions.

The man laughed, unclipping a set of keys from his belt loop. He squatted next to the boy, grabbing the padlock, and lunged his face at the child. "BOO!"

Jonny braced his right side and quickly jutted out his other hand, slapping the iron bars in front of the man's face.

The man fell backward, dropping his keys.

Al jumped. He raised his head from between his arms.

Jonny held his breath, hiding his pain behind bared teeth. "Congratulations, Lee. You've scared the shit out of a toddler."

Lee heel-dropped the bars. "Je vais te tuer!"

Jonny could not help but smirk.

"Je vais casser ton cou," Lee threatened.

Jonny leaned forward, clutching his side, spitting the metallic flavor from his mouth. "Le temps me dure."

Lee snatched the keys from the ground and unlocked the

padlock, keeping a vigilant eye on Jonny. He unthreaded the heavy steel chain from the cast-iron door, grabbed a handful of the toddler's hair and slammed the little boy's face into the bars.

"OW!"

Jonny flashed his hand forward, twisting the hidden nipple ring behind Lee's shirt.

Lee refused to release the boy's hair.

Jonny pulled, twisting the nipple ring toward the cage.

Lee fell forward, grunting. He pressed his torso against the prison, sandwiching the side of his face against two bars. "Avan la nwit dési."

Jonny twisted and pulled harder. He curled his swollen lip and narrowed his eyes. "What are you gonna do?" He gritted his teeth, twisting and pulling even harder, feeling the blood soak into Lee's shirt. "I've grown numb to your torture."

Lee begrudgingly relinquished the child's hair.

Jonny released Lee. He splinted his side, wincing in pain, and leaned back against the bars.

"Get in the damn cage!" Lee barked.

The small boy crawled toward the opening of his new home.

Lee kicked the boy again. "Get in there!" He grabbed the chain and wrapped it back around the prison door. "Fill him in."

The barn doors cracked opened and then closed behind Lee, shielding the world from them.

Al loosened his grip and crawled toward the newcomer. "Jonny, you got a death wish, do ya?"

Jonny leaned his head against the bars, focusing on the dim bulb. "I pray for death."

Al patted the child down, feeling his ribs and knobby knees and elbows. "You keep mouthin' off to Lee, you'll get your wish."

"Pfft! Mickey won't let him." Jonny retracted his knees to his chest, grunting in pain. "Every time he speaks that Louisiana French Creole bullshit," the left corner of Jonny's mouth curled up into a smirk, "I know I'm getting to him." He closed his eyes and tilted back his head. "Lee gets off on the fear he instills in us. No matter how much pain he inflicts, don't shed any tears. Eventually, he'll grow tired and move on."

Al touched the frail boy's face. "You feel small. How old are you?"

The boy swatted Al's hands away. "Five."

"You're a runt."

Jonny glanced at both boys' shadowy outlines. "Leave him alone. He's been through enough for one night."

"He's all skin and bones; he won't last."

Jonny sighed, tapping his head on the bars to the rhythm of the drips. "Knock it off, Al."

Al sniffed the air and then pushed the boy away. "Uh, he's pissin' himself."

Jonny stopped tapping. "I said knock it off!"

"I want my mommy," the boy cried. He turned and gripped the bars, attempting to squeeze through the small space. "Mommy!"

The cage was only two feet tall. Jonny had to shimmy around, grunting and grimacing toward the other two. He pushed Al away and pried the little boy's fingers from the bars. He placed the boy in his lap. "What's your name?"

"Ral—phie," he sniveled.

Jonny sniffed the air. He looked down at Ralphie's pants, barely making out the urine stain growing in radius.

Ralphie wrapped his arms around him. "I don't like the dark."

Pain radiated from Jonny's right ribs. He held his breath and hugged the child. "It's best that it's dark. You don't want to see what's in here." He rubbed the child's arms to warm him. "Is this your first time?"

Ralphie squeezed him tighter.

"Not so tight; I'm hurt."

Ralphie released him. "First time for what?"

"Listen to me. If they come for you, don't run. The punishment for running is worse than losing."

Ralphie licked the mucus from his upper lip. "Lose what?"

Frustrated, Al elevated his voice. "Didn't they tell you nothin'?"

"Just sit over there and shut up," Jonny said.

Ralphie's bony elbow dug into Jonny's right side.

Jonny held his breath and hoisted himself, cracking his head on the above bars.

The clangor scared Al back to the corner. He curled into a ball and rocked.

Unable to readjust, Jonny removed Ralphie's elbow from his side. "Why'd they bring you?"

"I don't know."

"What were you doing before they grabbed you?"

Ralphie repositioned himself, placing his back against Jonny's chest. "I was hungry, so I took some bread."

"Stole!" Al corrected. "You *stole* some bread."

Ralphie sat up, locating Al's shadowy figure. "I was hungry!"

"Al, I said shut up." He slid Ralphie off his lap. "It changes nothing."

Jonny's foot fell asleep. The cell imprisoning him wasn't long enough to allow him to stretch his legs. "When they come for you, you gotta be brave." He extended his leg as much as possible, drawing breath with each extension. He exhaled, bringing his knee back to his chest. "There'll be a crowd standing in a circle around you and another kid."

Ralphie started bawling. "I want my mommy."

Circulation still evaded his foot. He pulled Ralphie back and held him tight, already knowing the boy's fate. "They're going to make you fight that other kid. You fight him, and you win, you hear me?"

Al continued to rock in fear. "Yeah, 'cause you won't like what happens if you lose."

Jonny picked up a handful of urine-soaked hay and threw it at Al. "I said, shut up. I won't tell you again."

Ralphie crawled toward Al. "What happens if I lose?"

Jonny grabbed him by the shoulders, pulling him back. "You win so your mommy can find you."

Al stopped rocking. "Is that what you do?"

Jonny sighed, resting the back of his head on the bars. "No." He focused on the dim bulb. "I fight and I win because other lives depend on it."

Al crawled closer to them. "Then why do you want to die?"

Jonny closed his eyes; he wanted to forget. He wanted to forget what happened to him, what he did to others. Some part of him wanted to forget his promise. He opened his eyes, his voice gruff. "Mickey will never let me die."

Al sat next to him. "How long have you been a captive?"

"I was born a captive," Jonny said, rotating his ankle.

"Foot still asleep?" asked Al.

"Yeah, I never got the blood flow back."

Al crawled to Jonny's feet and massaged his calf and foot. "My mom used to do this for me when I was really little. It always worked."

Ralphie rested his head against Jonny's chest. "How old are you?"

"I'm ten, and Al's eight."

Two

The Encounter

1

Jonny twitched himself awake. The long hours and late nights had caught up to him. He remembered coming into the office to place an order with NAPA but couldn't remember if he actually did. He remembered the light being on and the blinds opened but neither were.

He propped his elbow on his desk, running his fingers over his stubbled face. He closed his eyes, shaking his head. He hadn't had a nightmare in decades. *Must be the weather.*

There was a light tap on the door. It cracked opened and light seeped in, spilling narrow streams over the oaken workspace of Jonny's desk. Long shadows of pencils, a desk lamp, and an old computer stretched across the desk calendar toward the drawn blinds. The soft, golden glow refracting off the desk gradually illuminated the wall of manuals and books behind Jonny's chair, then flowed around to the unkept, circular table in the opposite corner used as a pedestal for the old mini fridge.

"You awake?"

"Yeah." He leaned back in his chair and raked his fingers through his hair. "How long was I out?"

Steven Leary entered the office and opened the blinds to the glass wall, overlooking the shop floor below. "'Bout twenty minutes."

Thunder clapped nearby, shaking the rafters.

"Storms getting worse," Steven said.

"Why'd you let me sleep?"

Steven peered over his shoulder. "You needed a nap. Besides, I was stalling."

Jonny's eyes shifted from Steven to the glass wall. "Stalling?"

Steven pointed at the window. "Sandra's here."

"Am I in trouble?"

Steven chuckled. "Are you ever not in trouble?"

Jonny laughed. He thought about saying *only when I'm sleeping*, but the smartass remark didn't seem appropriate after waking from a nightmare. He stretched his arms over his head and yawned. "Does she seem upset or anything?"

"Nah. She's in a rather good mood."

Jonny exited his office, which was encompassed squarely in the center of the building. Positioned a few feet in front of his office was the customer service counter. He paused in the center of the customer's lounge and stared out the window.

The blackened clouds swallowed the sun and the streetlamps failed to power on. Rain pounded the windows, and it wasn't until the lightening flashed, he saw the flooded streets.

"Roseburg doesn't get thunderstorms like this," Steven said.

Lighting strobed, highlighting the swaying trees, and produced a small rumble. Another bolt branched across the apocalyptic sky like the roots of a redwood. Thunder quickly followed, quivering the shop lights.

“Yeah, I think we should close early,” Jonny said.

Steven pointed down the long corridor off to the side of the customer counter, rounding the restrooms to the shop floor. “She’s waiting for you in the garage.”

Jonny led the way, reaching the water fountain near the end of the hall. He spotted a plate of cupcakes on the workbench between two repair docks. He shifted his gaze to Sandra.

Sandra was showing another woman around the modest garage, both were drenched by the rain.

The stranger stepped away from a 1929 Rolls Royce Phantom and looked under the hood of a 1955 Chevy 3100 pickup.

“There’s my brother,” Sandra said.

The woman turned and followed her. She had long, wavy auburn hair and wore an unattractive long-sleeved yellow shirt, highlighting her small, but flabby belly. Her denim jeans stretched taut around her thick thighs and calves before flaring out around her ankles. She contrasted sharply against Sandra’s tall, gangly frame draped in a summer dress.

Jonny turned on his heels. “I’m going back to the office.”

“Jonathan Michael!” Sandra bellowed; he ignored her. She snatched a cupcake and aimed for his head, but socked his lower left shoulder.

The woman sprung forward, grabbing her plate of sweets, “Hey!”

Jonny whipped around, glaring at Sandra.

Sandra stole another cupcake, and the woman safeguarded the rest.

Jonny marched up to the stranger. Her brows were pinched inward and her lips slightly parted. “Miss, I apologize; my sister has wasted your time. I’m not interested in dating you.” He turned to Sandra. “Or anyone else you bring to my shop.”

Sandra smashed the chocolate cupcake into his face.

He pushed her away and wiped his face, slinging the frosting to the floor.

"Hey now," Steven said, rushing between brother and sister.

"What the hell is wrong with you, two?" the woman said with a Scottish accent. "I'm not here to date you." She focused on Sandra, saying, "If that's what you think, you are sorely mistaken."

Jonny stood at attention, staring at the woman. Her accent caused a vivid memory to flash in his brain: a bald woman wearing a hospital gown standing behind a glass window. Tears trickling down her cheeks. Smiling and pressing one hand against the glass.

"Haven," he said, involuntarily.

Sandra and Steven looked blankly at each other.

The woman caught his thousand-mile stare. Dark circles hung from his eyes and heavy red veins streaked noticeably through the whites of them.

"Cheyenne," she corrected. "My name is Cheyenne."

Her words broke his reverie. He continued wiping the chocolate residue from his mouth. "A Scot with an American name."

"My *athair* was an American; my *màthair* was not."

He raised an eyebrow. "What's *a-hair* and *ma-hair*?"

"Ah-her and maw-her are Scottish Gaelic for father and mother." Cheyenne pulled her sleeves up, stopping below her elbows. "I don't know what's going on but, I'm here because my car won't turn over." She looked at Sandra, passing a soft glare. "She said you're a mechanic and would fix it."

He continued to clean the frosting from his face. "My name's Jonathan, but I answer to Jon or Jonny all the same."

"Sandra said you would come by the house and check it out

if I baked some sweets."

The lightning struck close, followed by a deafening thunder cap.

Steven jogged to the wall and pressed a button. The enormous garage doors descended, blockading the rain from blowing inside the shop.

Goosebumps spread across Cheyenne's arms; her body trembled.

"I have towels in the office," Jonny said sniffing the air.

"No, it's okay. I should go."

He rubbed his nose. "It's fine, I don't mind."

She bit her lower lip and repeatedly glanced at the exit. She moved for the door. "Really, I should go."

"It's pouring cats and dogs," Steven said. "You'd be saturated before you ever reached the car."

The lights flickered, grappling to stay on.

Cheyenne closed her eyes and took deep, rapid breaths through her nose.

"You gonna be all right?" Sandra asked.

Steven grabbed a cupcake and took a bite. "You're afraid of the dark, aren't you?"

Cheyenne slowed her breathing and opened her eyes. She looked at Steven; he licked the chocolate frosting from his fingers.

"Or are you scared of the thunder?" he asked.

Cheyenne's eyes widened. She looked behind her, then around the shop, bending and stooping, searching under the workbench and cars. "Where'd your brother go?"

"Knowing him," Sandra replied, "he's getting us towels."

"Where?"

Steven pointed up at the glass wall. "His office."

She shook her head. "I shouldn't have come."

Sandra furrowed her brows. She scooped her ginger hair

out of her eyes and tucked the strands behind her ears. "I admit, it was wrong of me to use you as date bait, but my brother can fix your car. He's rough around the edges, but Jonny's a good guy once you get to know him."

The storm snuffed out the lights.

Cheyenne waved her hands out in front of her body, carefully maneuvering toward the exit.

2

Jonny stopped in the customer's lounge, pinching his nose; the fetid smell was getting stronger. He glanced at the ceiling lights; the generator should have kicked on by now. He returned to his office, maneuvering to his desk, and flung the towels earmarked for the women over his shoulder and opened the second drawer. He removed a large boxy flashlight and flipped the switch.

The bulb quickly dimmed to its demise.

He slapped the side of the flashlight in vain. Annoyed, he tossed the light on his desk.

Lightning flashed twice, faintly illuminating a petite figure standing barefoot on the desk.

Startled, he stepped backward, tripping on the rubber floor matt.

Another silent flash; the room was empty.

Jonny stood, shaking his head. What the hell did he see?

The thunderclaps from all three strikes collided together; the glass wall in the office shuddered.

He scoped the office. Where did it go? He moved swiftly to the glass wall, looking for Sandra.

Blackness shrouded the garage.

Jonny awaited the lightning on tenterhooks. He spotted a

faint amber glow and assumed Steven was using his lighter but when a second soft amber light followed suit, he knew his assumption was false.

Lightning flashed and the amber lights disappeared, but he spotted Sandra. Darkness returned and the amber lights with it.

Jonny bolted for the door.

Lightning struck, outlining the gaunt frame of a small boy standing in the threshold. The amber glow in the pits of his eyes out lived the flash into the darkness.

A warm whisper slipped into Jonny's ear. "Keep your eyes shut, no matter what." The warmth raised the hackles on his neck.

He whipped around but saw no one. He stormed the doorway. Again, no one.

The soft smacking of bare feet on tile escorted the high-pitched giggles down the hallway.

"Sandra!" He raced down the corridor to the garage and came to an abrupt halt.

The amber lights intensified in the dark void.

Jonny had the distinct feeling they were observing him. He only needed one more flash to reveal their source.

The halogen lights sparked to life, accompanied by the hum of oscillating fans.

Cheyenne stared back at Jonny. Her hands gripped her forearms.

"You all right, Jon?" Steven asked. "You look like you've seen a ghost."

Jonny nodded once, fixated on Cheyenne. How was it possible? He walked past them, glancing at Cheyenne's forearms. She embedded her fingernails into her flesh so hard the indents bled. He locked eyes with her.

"I should go," Cheyenne said.

Jonny nodded subtlety in accord. She knew; she had to.

"Well, wait, can you fix her car?" Sandra asked.

Jonny continued to the workbench and began putting his tools away.

Steven approached Jonny's side. "You sure everything's alright?"

He stared at Steven, clenching his jaw; his mind going a mile a minute.

"Dammit, Jonathan Michael! Are you going to fix her car or not?"

He continued to stare at Steven; his eyes turning venomous. "No."

"No? Why—"

Jonny's fist connected with the workbench. "You're not to associate with this woman ever again," he told Sandra.

Sandra marched toward him. "I'm not a child and I won't have you treating me like one."

Steven intercepted, holding her back.

"I'm your brother; I'm supposed to keep you safe."

She stood straight, forcing a sarcastic laugh. "I'm older than you." She double-tapped Steven's arm and he let her pass. She grabbed the plate of cupcakes, staring at them. "I'm supposed to protect you," she added, sotto voce.

He grabbed her bicep. "I can protect myself."

She jerked her arm free. "Who's going to protect you from you?" She walked away and handed Cheyenne the plate of sweets. "He hates cake."

Jonny focused his aggression on Cheyenne; his eyes pierced her through weighted brows. "You're to never come here again."

There was rage in his eyes. Cheyenne felt the hatred of his dagger stare trying to dig their way to the truth of her. The longer she stared into them, the more she saw the pain he hid. Whatever he witnessed tore open old wounds which never healed.

She gave Jonny the same nod he had given Steven. There was a familiarity to him she could not pinpoint. Almost as if she knew him. *Impossible, we just met.* She searched her brain's archives and couldn't recall a time their paths crossed. It didn't matter. She knew not to come. She should have run the moment she got out of the car. Why did she listen to *him*? Worse, Jonny knew. Somehow, he knew it was her fault. *What's he waiting for? Why doesn't he say anything?*

Sandra removed her keys from her pocket. "Come on; I'll take you home."

"The hell you will," Jonny said.

"Okay, okay, you guys," Steven said. He brought his hands together and stepped forward. "Why don't I take her home?"

Sandra shook her head. "Why?"

"Because you two are fighting, again." He pointed with his prayer hands at Sandra. "You don't want your friend to walk in the rain," he pointed at Jonny, "and he doesn't want you near her."

Jonny remained in a wide stance with flared nostrils, spearing Cheyenne with his glare.

Steven eclipsed Jonny's view of her. "I'll get her out of here," he said with stern tones. He looked over his shoulder at the women. "I have to pick my girlfriend up from work anyhow."

Cheyenne dumped the cupcakes in the garbage. "I can walk home."

"It's pissing rain outside," Sandra said.

There was a quick flash of lightning. The thunder made a low growl, gradually growing louder. The rumble vibrated the shop lights, causing them to flicker.

In between the lights flickering, Cheyenne spotted the two

amber dots above and behind Jonny. The shop lights returned to normal; he seemed unaware.

It was time to go. She darted for the exit.

Sandra grabbed her and pulled her back. “My brother is harmless. Please, let me take you home.”

Cheyenne locked eyes with Jonny; her body trembled, and her eyes welled. The first tear rolled down her cheekbone. “I need to go home.”

Sandra stared at her brother. “What the hell is going on? What did I miss?” She looked back at Cheyenne. “Why are you afraid of him?”

Cheyenne cleaned the tear from her face, keeping her eyes on him. “Please, I have to leave.”

Jonny’s upper lip curled. “Take her home, Steven.”

Steven tilted his head, narrowing his eyes. He pulled Jonny aside, waving the women away.

Cheyenne removed her flip-flops and snuck for the exit; Sandra pursued.

“Seriously man, what’s up?” Steven asked.

Jonny remained silent.

“Sandra’s right, what the fuck did we miss?”

Jonny had no explanation for what he saw or heard. Those lights and that woman were responsible. How?

“I know you’re not one to justify your actions, but that was unacceptable.” Steven closed the Rolls Royce’s hood and gathered the tools from his workstation. “That was a lot of animosity toward someone who didn’t deserve it. What the hell was that all about?”

Jonny paused and spun around. His eyes darted throughout the shop. “Sonofabitch!” He bolted for the exit.

Steven lunged, grabbing him.

Jonny turned; fist drawn.

Steven blocked his punch and pushed him. "They're already gone."

"Get the hell out of my way."

Steven pushed him back again. "Calm down."

"I swear to God," Jonny said, snatching a torque wrench from the workbench.

Steven took a step back into a cautionary stance with his hand reaching tentatively toward Jonny. "Whoa now, let's think about this."

Jonny huffed. "Get out of the way. You don't understand."

"I really don't."

The words knocked Jonny off balance. How could he make Steven understand? He studied Steven's countenance; his eyes wide and fixed on the torque wrench. Genuine concern painted his face.

Jonny looked down at the wrench he white-knuckled. He relaxed his stance and took a breath, lowering it. He was ready to bludgeon his childhood friend, a brother to him. He thought this part of him died.

"Look, they're gone. You don't even know where to find them."

Steven was right. Not only was Steven in the way, Jonny knew not where to search. His frustration returned twofold. "SHIT!" He assaulted the workbench several times, screaming, then flung the tool into the garage door.

"There's only one reason you don't want to talk," Steven said.

Jonny flexed his jaw feverishly.

Steven bobbed his head. "I'm right, it is your childhood."

"I'm sorry," Jonny said. He looked over his shoulder. "I don't want to talk about it right now."

Steven sighed through his nose. "That's your problem, you

never want to talk about it."

Jonny raked his fingers through his hair, pushing the long strands from his eyes. "I've spoken about it once." He glanced at Steven. "Now, I want to forget."

"We should close shop," Steven said.

"Yeah," Jonny said, retrieving the torque wrench.

3

Jonny stepped outside and noticed the streetlamps were on. He locked the shop doors, staring at Steven's reflection. "You didn't deserve—" He shifted his gaze to his own reflection and lowered his head. "I apologize."

Steven took a drag from his cigarette, blowing the smoke off to the side. "I appreciate that." He pulled his keys from his pocket. "I'll, uh, see you later."

They walked alongside the building, heading toward the back, and parted in awkward silence.

Jonny sat in his Jeep, hugging the steering wheel. He rested his forehead on his arms, mulling over the night's event. *How is she connected to those colored lights?*

His hip buzzed. He pulled his phone from his pocket, reading a text from Sandra: *What's going on with you? Are you ok?*

He honestly didn't know. He tossed his cell to the passenger seat.

If he wanted answers, he would have to interrogate Cheyenne. *Keeping Sandra away from her is going to be a challenge.* He lifted his head and glanced at his watch; it was time to get home to Jacob.

Three

Pressing Questions

1

Cheyenne slammed the front door behind her. She hurried through the house and frisbeed the dessert plate toward the kitchen sink.

The plate shattered against the cabinet and littered the otherwise spotless kitchen.

She tossed her keys on the nightstand and made haste to the master bathroom. She shut the door and leaned against it, rubbing her forehead.

"Dammit! I did as you asked! I befriended her!" She stepped to the sink, turning on the faucet. "Why do you do this to me?" She cupped her hands and stuck them under the water. She splashed her face and then glanced at the mirror, staring at her reflection. "Who is he and what do you want with him?"

Goosebumps saturated her body. She reached over and flipped off the light.

The amber lights slowly faded into focus behind her. The mirror reflected back its glow, dimly highlighting his claw reaching for her.

2

Jonny kicked off his work boots and unlocked the front door. "Jacob?" he said, placing his boots inside the shoe rack.

When Jacob didn't tackle him with a hug, Jonny went to the threshold separating the living room and dining room and peeked into the kitchen. "Anyone home?" He thought for sure Sandra would be chastising him the moment he walked through the door, but the house was quiet.

He turned around and made his way down the hall. He pushed open the first door on the left.

The toy chest lid was open, and Jacob's toys lay scattered about the room, the race car bed unmade.

"Jacob?"

The room resounded with silence.

He continued down the hall, passing Sandra's door and the laundry room on the right. At the end of the hall, the closed door to the bathroom.

Sandra sang "Landslide" over the soft-droning hiss of the shower.

Jonny halted. He would have cracked a smile if not agitated; Sandra never could carry a tune. Right now, she was safe; that's what mattered.

He veered left, poking his head into his room and sighed at the dirty clothes piled on the floor. *Gotta make time.*

The hissing of the shower stopped.

He stepped to the room directly behind him, knocking on the door. "GG?"

Sandra poked her head out of the bathroom. "They're in Portland, remember?"

He'd been busy at the shop for several weeks, relying on his grandmother to take care of Jacob. He rubbed his face with his palms. He'd forgotten all about the *Lion King* musical at the Keller Auditorium.

Sandra stepped into the hall, wrapped in a towel. "What's going on with you? What happened back at the garage?"

He combed his fingers through his hair. "I need a drink."

"Why are you walking away?" She grabbed his shoulder and jerked him back. "You always walk away."

He fell gently into the wall, leaning his back against it with his hands in his pockets, and stared blankly at the floor.

"I gave up trying to pry answers out of you years ago, because you were getting better. This is regression. I haven't seen you like this since we were kids."

Cold sweat beaded his forehead and ran down his temples.

"You weren't protecting me from Cheyenne. Something happened when the lights went out. What happened? What were you really protecting me from?"

His mouth opened but was silent. He looked at Sandra. "I saw—" his mouth closed, and he shook his head.

"You saw what?"

"I saw . . . nothing." He pushed off the wall. "I need a drink."

Sandra screamed in frustration and stomped into her room, slamming her door. She grabbed her cell from the vanity and texted Steven: *OTW?*

Steven: *Rounding the corner now.*

Sandra: *There's something seriously wrong with him. He's out back.*

3

Jonny stepped out the sliding glass door onto the back patio. He opened the beer fridge to the right of the door and grabbed the first bottle he could reach. He twisted the metal and chugged the bottle.

A familiar big block V8 rumbled up the street.

Jonny tossed the empty bottle into the recycle bin, reaching for another with his free hand. He closed the fridge and looked across the yard, considering the pergola and gas firepit. A warm fire seemed inviting, but he didn't want to hassle with the wet furniture.

He ambled to the handcrafted swinging bench his grandfather, Eber, built and hung from the support beams of the awning. He slid between the bench and the clematis flowers wrapping the wooden columns, making a point of brushing back the out-stretched vines. He needed to trim them soon, but he'd wait until the blooms died; they were too pretty for now.

He settled into the comforting creaks of the bench and focused across the yard, beyond the empty vegetable garden, to the small patch of yellow calla lilies against the fence. "Wish you were here." He raised his bottle toward the flowers and took a sip. He tilted back his head, closed his eyes, and waited patiently.

A metallic rattle and a high-pitched creak heralded a new arrival.

Jonny tapped the bottle's neck and sighed through his nose; he wasn't ready for this.

The squinch of heavy feet over wet terrain drifted around the left side of the house.

Jonny waited a few seconds and then glanced at the rose bush. "You don't have to hide. I heard the gate latch." He connected his lips to the bottle and slugged it straight back.

Steven walked around the roses and opened the fridge. “You want another?”

Jonny set his empty drink on the table and reached his hand out to Steven with a soft, slow nod.

Steven extracted two bottles and passed one to Jonny. “Some storm.”

“Hmph,” Jonny said. He twisted the cap from his drink. “Literally or figuratively?”

“Mind if I smoke?”

Jonny tossed the metal cap to the table in front of them “Go for it.”

Steven hammered a cancer nail out and pinched it with his lips. He lit it, taking a long, hard drag; he blew O-rings toward Jonny.

Jonny tipped the bottle upright and guzzled.

Steven turned his head, blowing the rest of the smoke off to the side. “We’ve been best friends for how long?”

Jonny jerked back his head. “Hmm.” Thinking that far back was a chore. “Since the sixth or seventh grade.”

Steven sucked on the end of his cigarette one last time. He put the cancer stick out on the bottom of his boot and exhaled off to the side. He wet his mouth and looked at Jonny. “Right now, I don’t feel like I know you.”

“I’m fine.” He connected his lips with his bottle and chugged.

“The hell you are.” Steven placed his half-smoked cigarette behind his ear and leaned forward, setting his beer on the table.

“Why are you so hard-pressed?”

“For starters, you’ve never allowed me to light up at your house, ever. I just blew O-rings into your face and nothing, not even a ‘fuck you’.”

Jonny tilted his head back and tapped his pointer finger on the neck of the bottle. *Steven's about to give one of his big-brother speeches.*

"You've been different since Cheyenne spoke."

Jonny took a swig of his beer. *Way to ruin a perfectly good buzz.* "I could have gone all night without you mentioning her." He tilted his beer to the side, gauging how much remained.

"I want to talk about the incident at the shop, about what bothered me the most."

Jonny's eyes landed on the lilies.

Steven used his chin and pointed to the flowers. "What do you think he would say about your behavior tonight?"

"He'd understand."

"Pfft! You wanted to hit that woman."

Steven's words were an insult.

Jonny whipped his head around. "I'd never hit a girl!"

"Your anger blinded you, or else you'd have seen she had all the signs of a battered woman." Steven reached for his drink. "She scanned the shop for the fastest escape. She wouldn't push her sleeves past her elbows. My mom would do that to hide the bruises." He took a drink. "She begged you for permission to leave."

Jonny interlocked his fingers and tapped his thumbs. Steven had something. Cheyenne's flighty behavior indicated possible abuse, but Steven lacked Jonny's clues. How could Jonny explain when he himself knew it sounded insane?

"You owe Cheyenne an apology."

He lowered his eyes; he wasn't so sure.

"What I don't get is why you were so threated by her. What happened?"

Jonny hated that question. Partly because he couldn't explain what happened, but mostly because it would exhume the past.

"Say something! We're worried about you. For Pete's sake, you pulled a wrench on me."

"You're right. I crossed a line tonight. I wish I could explain, but I can't. I'm begging you to let it go."

"Your childhood trauma is like a scabbed wound festering under the surface; it poisons you. Sandra told me that." Steven sipped his beer. "The only way to treat a wound like that is to drain it. Talk to me. Sandra did, that's how she healed."

Jonny listened carefully to his words and replied, "Some infections run deep; they scar you in ways you never thought. Just because you drain the toxins doesn't mean you were never poisoned." He finished his drink and focused back on the calla lilies. "Can we please change the subject?"

Steven returned to the fridge and pulled two more beers. He handed one to Jonny. "Who's Haven?"

Jonny twisted the cap from his drink and flipped it over the back of his knuckles. He only spoke of Haven to one other person. "Stays between us?"

Steven took a drink, nodding his head.

Jonny tossed the metal cap to the table and perched his left foot on top of his right knee. "She's Jacob's mother."

Steven coughed and gagged on the suds coming out of his nose. He gawked at Jonny, wiping the foam from his mouth and chin. "Well, you've kept that secret a long time."

Jonny let out a loud sigh. He took a sip. "I met her at the garage; I fixed her Geo." He stared at the flowers. "She was seventy dollars shy, so I told her to pay me when she could."

"Your norm," Steven said. "What'd she look like?"

Jonny's iconic side smirk appeared; it had been absent for weeks. "Like a young Ann Hathaway."

"Is she from around here?"

"London." He looked from the flowers to Steven. "Born in

Ireland, though. I could hear her Irish accent within her R's."

"Is she back in London?"

Jonny shook his head.

Steven rested his elbow on the armrest and propped his head on his thumb and pointer finger. "I remember the day your grandfather told us you'd become a father and would bring home a son."

Jonny shifted his eyes back to the lilies.

"Eber told us not to ask questions." Steven readjusted. "Obviously, something happened. You have your son; she doesn't."

He glanced briefly at Steven, then back to the flowers. His eyes watered, but no tears fell.

"You loved her." Steven sat straight. "What happened?"

"Maybe another night."

"Did she not return the same feel—"

Jonny pounded the arm of the bench.

Steven bit his lip and then exhaled. "All right, another night."

Jonny yawned. His buzz ruined by gloomy, untold memories.

"You haven't slept more than three hours in a night for several weeks. Hell, you fell asleep in your office today." Steven stood gathering the empty bottles. "Why don't you hit the hay? I'll clean up out here, then I'll head home."

Jonny stood and headed for the house.

"Can I suggest something?"

Jonny was tired and ready to go to bed, but Steven would not end the night without giving advice. It was usually sound, though.

"You haven't given yourself a day off in months. Come to Boomer Hill with us tomorrow. If you do, every day when I get off work, I'll help you at the garage and my days off, too."

His interest piqued, Jonny asked, “Who’s going?”

“Sandra, me, and Capri.”

Jonny rolled his eyes, but he needed the help. Graffiti customers were already trickling in for custom jobs. “I’ll take tomorrow off. Just keep your girlfriend away from me.”

“I can do that.”

Jonny walked up the single step and opened the sliding glass door. “You’re wrong, you know. He would’ve understood.”

“Ha! I don’t believe that for a second.”

“That’s because *you* don’t understand.”

Steven emptied his hands into the recycle bin. “Then make me understand.”

Jonny lowered his head, contemplating. “I saw lights.”

“What—”

Jonny slid shut the glass door. He was finished for the night; the day had worn him.

4

Steven took advantage of the golden opportunity to relight his cigarette. He looked to the stars, blowing the smoke from his lungs. Each star a perfect, fixed, twinkling white speck in the deep blue-black night sky. The temperature was already falling; it would be in the high sixties before long, despite the day’s high in the mid-nineties.

He pondered Jonny’s cryptic last statement of the night. He’d seen Jonny in distress before but never over lights. It didn’t add up. Jonny was full of rage which turned to fear once he realized Sandra was gone. He took another drag, shifting his gaze to the calla lilies.

The wheels on the sliding glass door rumbled and Steven turned exhaling. He half expected Jonny to step out and tell him to put out the cigarette.

Sandra stepped out onto the patio. "What happened?"

"Lots," Steven replied. "Where's he at?"

"In bed." She crossed her arms over her chest. "Did he say why he was an asshole toward my friend?"

He took another drag and put out the cigarette. "Sort of, but not really." He blew the smoke off to the side. "Before he went in the house, he said he saw lights."

Sandra's face wrinkled. "Lights?"

"He has dark bags under his eyes. He's tired and worn-out; his mind's playing tricks on him."

"Tired and worn out doesn't explain it." She bent down and picked a dead leaf from the clematis vine. "Something happened. I haven't seen him like this since he came home to us . . . before the therapy."

"His emotions are all over the place. Before you fish for more, I promised him it would stay between him and me."

"He's never confided in me." She turned to go back in the house. "He confided in our brother. When Dominick died, then it was our grandfather." She stopped and turned. "Now, it's you. Even after all we've been through."

Steven wondered if she was sad or jealous. "He's tired and worn out. The moment he realized he was letting go, he rebuilt his wall. Jon shut me out." Steven pointed to the yellow calla lilies. "The person he wants to confide in, isn't here anymore."

"That's my point. I'm here. I would understand."

"Would you? Jonny's a complex guy."

She sighed in frustration. "Is he going to be all right?"

Steven opened the sliding glass door, waiting for her to enter. "He'll be fine. He just needs to rest." He grabbed her hand. "I talked him into taking tomorrow off and to come with us." He rubbed his thumb over the top of her hand. "I need your help in keeping Capri away from him."

Sandra stopped in the doorway, reclaiming her hand. "Tomorrow's going to be interesting." She stared at Steven. "I convinced Cheyenne to do the same."

Four

Keep Your Eyes Shut

The metal-against-metal racket filled the stall. Jonny heard it a thousand times. The chain being pulled through metal loops. He hated the sound. He learned the small nuances, indicating the mood, the purpose of the visit: anger, pleasure, but worst of all, business; someone was about to fight.

Al scurried to the far corner, gripping the bars tight. He entrenched his head and rocked. "They're coming for me!" his voice trembled.

Jonny returned to his original spot in the cage, dragging Ralphie with him. "Wipe the tears from your face and remember what I told you."

The barn door slid open, highlighting two shadows.

"Is it them?" Al whispered.

Jonny ignored him. His concerns were for Ralphie. He pulled the child's face to his. "Keep your eyes shut, no matter what."

Al sniffed the air. "Is Mickey with him?"

"Yes," Jonny answered.

"Shut the door behind us," Mickey said.

Ralphie stretched his neck upward and covered his mouth with his tiny hand, whispering, “Mickey Mouse?”

Jonny closed his eyes, shaking his head at Ralphie’s childish question; *he’s too young.* “He owns you.”

Mickey stood in front of the cage. “Get the lights.”

Ralphie attempted to get a better look, but Jonny smothered Ralphie’s face into his chest. “Don’t look.”

There was a loud ka-thunk followed by an electrostatic hum which charged the barn lights.

Al continued to bury his head, rocking and muttering inaudibly.

Jonny blinked a few times until his eyes adjusted to the brightness. He finally got a good look at the child he coddled.

Ralphie had matted brown curly hair and freckles covering his arms and shoulders. His boney prominences protruded unnaturally. His height stunted, and his muscles atrophied.

Lee walked away from the beam housing the power and joined Mickey. He removed the cigarette from his mouth. “We should see what the little shit can do.”

Jonny kept his head down and looked through the prison bars at both pairs of boots. “You should let me train him, you dumbass.”

Lee kicked the cage, flinging debris in his face.

“Knock it off and open the damn cage,” Mickey said.

Lee unclipped the keys from his belt loop, unlocking the padlock. He jerked the chain and sparks flew from the door like a lighter’s flint.

Al death-gripped the bars and urinated himself. His chest heaved and his body trembled.

Ralphie lifted his head, but Jonny forced it down.

“Jonny, get out here,” Mickey said.

Jonny brought Ralphie’s face up to his. “Close your eyes and keep them closed.”

Jonny slid on his stomach, feet first, toward the opening. He kept his face toward the ground but his eyes on the Ralphie. When Ralphie opened his eyes, Jonny snapped his fingers. “Keep ‘em shut.”

Lee grabbed Jonny’s foot, dragging him out of the cage. “Stop wasting our fucking time!”

“Stand up,” Mickey said.

Jonny clenched his jaw, fighting the instinct to scream. He rolled onto his back, shifting his eyes from Lee to Mickey.

Mickey’s wavy hair stood nearly straight up, and his goatee came down to a sharp point. His body bore tattoos of Papa Legba, Damballa, and Baron Samedi.

“Stand up!” Mickey barked again. He placed his thumb over his right nostril, clearing his left.

Jonny did as he was told. He brushed the dirt and hay from his naked chest. “Well, if you cleaned this shithole, it wouldn’t stink.”

“I told you, he’s getting too big for his fucking britches,” Lee said.

“If you provided pants that fit, these wouldn’t be too small.”

Mickey raised his hand, muting the two. “I’m putting you back in.”

Jonny’s left foot slid forward. “I already fought! I fought twice!”

“You’ll fight again ‘cause I tell you to.”

Jonny clenched his fist. “Look at me! I’m busted. I can barely see out my right eye. I’m sure I have a broken rib or two. You haven’t fed me in almost three days. I haven’t had decent sleep in four, and you keep me locked inside a cast-iron tomb barely big enough for two people, let alone three.”

“Remember our agreement.”

“I haven’t lost yet, have I?”

“After Jonny wins,” Mickey said, “we’ll have the thief fight.

We'll see what he can offer."

"He's a runt. He'll die with the first hit," Jonny said.

Mickey glanced sideways at him.

Jonny stood his ground. "Let me train him before you kill him."

"Get the runt out," Mickey said.

Jonny placed himself between the cage and Lee. He walked backward and kicked shut the prison door. "I can train him."

"Lee, get the boy."

Jonny brought both arms up, protecting his sides. His fists balled up close to his face. "He'll die if you put him out there."

Lee laughed. "Don't start what you can't finish." He stepped forward and grabbed Jonny's wrist.

Jonny kicked Lee in the manhood; Lee's upper torso flew forward. Jonny brought up his left fist, connecting with an uppercut.

Mickey lunged, backhanding Jonny across the face.

Jonny stumbled to the ground, holding his right side.

Mickey kneeled over him and grabbed his throat. Jonny wrapped both hands around Mickey's wrist, feeling the oxygen seize in his lungs.

Mickey lifted him, slamming him against the cage. "Don't forget your place."

They stared at each other, neither wavering.

Jonny's face turned dark red, but he continued to glare at his nemesis, refusing to surrender.

Mickey slammed him again and released him in defeat. "Bah!"

Jonny rubbed his neck, coughing, choking, gasping for air.

Mickey stood. "Despite your bitching, you're still capable of fighting."

"Why doesn't he ever try that shit with you?" Lee asked.

Mickey smiled. He turned and stared inside the cage. "Al,

bring me that boy, and you'll not fight for a month."

Jonny continued to splint his right side. He turned his head, peering inside the cage with his good eye. "Don't you do it. He's lying, and we both know it."

"Not only will you not fight for a month," Mickey continued. "You'll get a steak and potato meal once a week."

Al raised his head, licking his lips. He released his grip from the bars and crawled toward Ralphie, who still obeyed Jonny's last command.

Jonny tracked Al with his one eye; his voice elevated and stern. "Don't you fucking do it!"

Mickey pressed his forearm against Jonny's head, grinding his face into the iron bars. He put his lips next to the Jonny's ear and continued his siren song. "I'll even let you sleep inside the house in a soft bed under warm covers."

"A shower, too?" Al asked.

Mickey grinned, whispering into Jonny's ear. "*Laissez les bon temps roule.*"

Jonny head-butted Mickey and crawled away.

Mickey grabbed him by the hair and slammed him into the cage. He delivered two hard blows to Jonny's right side.

Jonny squalled, reaching for his ribs.

Mickey looked inside the cage. "I gave you an order!"

Teary-eyed, Jonny flipped around.

Al jerked Ralphie by the arm, dragging him toward the open door.

Ralphie started to open his eyes.

Jonny's voice was coarse. "Keep your eyes closed." He took a deep breath and contemplated his next move.

Ralphie shut his eyes. "He's hurting me. Ow!"

"You don't have to jerk him!" Jonny curled his upper lip, repulsed by Al's betrayal. "He's too weak to put up a fight and you know it."

Mickey backed away, smiling in triumph.

Both boys neared the opening.

“Looks like Jon Boy has a trained pup,” Lee said.

Jonny darted his hand through the bars, grabbing Al’s arm. “I hope you die a long, painful death, you coward.”

“You’d do it, too.”

“Never.” He released Al, turning his back to him.

Al pushed Ralphie out of the cage.

Jonny grabbed the boy, tucking him against his left side. “Keep your eyes closed for me.”

“Don’t you think you’ve got enough to worry about?” Mickey asked. He snapped his fingers, pointing to Ralphie. “Why protect a kid you don’t even know?”

Lee reached for Ralphie.

Jonny smacked his hand away and rolled on top of the small boy. He hunched down, pinning his elbows on Ralphie’s sides, and latched onto the bars. He braced himself. “I’m sorry,” he whispered. “I’m sorry I couldn’t protect you.”

Lee swung his leg back, driving his pointy-toed boot forward into Jonny’s side.

“Again!” Mickey demanded.

Lee repeated his attack, kicking harder.

Jonny shifted his arm, struggling to protect his flank.

Al lay on the ground in front of him. Tears lined the bottom of his eyes. “He isn’t worth your life!”

Jonny glared at Al, flaring his nostrils and grinding his teeth. He held his breath, grunting with each impact, refusing to give Lee the satisfaction.

Lee delivered blow after blow, each harder than the last.

Jonny’s arm ached and grew tender; he did not know how much longer he could hold.

Lee drove the heel of his boot into Jonny’s back; Jonny collapsed, yelping in pain. Lee grabbed him by hair and tossed him off Ralphie.

Jonny winced, feeling the throbbing pain in his arm, side, and kidney. He closed his eyes, knowing the punishment was not yet over.

"Jonny?" Ralphie said.

Jonny opened his eyes. "Keep your eyes closed!"

"Shut up," Lee barked, driving the heel of his boot into Jonny's crotch.

He doubled over, clutching his groin, and buried his face in the straw, hiding his pain from Lee. The sickly feeling crept into his stomach. He coughed and dry-heaved.

Mickey kneeled next to Jonny, grabbing him by the hair and jerking his head up. "Al, you say Ralphie isn't worth dying for." Mickey released Jonny and his head plummeted to the ground. "He did something similar for you."

Al reached his hand out for Jonny. "He ain't worth it."

Ralphie lay on his back, keeping his eyes tightly shut. "Jonny?"

Jonny threw Al's hand off. "Everyone is worth it." He glared at Al and curled his lip. "Almost everyone."

"Open your eyes," Mickey told Ralphie.

Jonny lay on the ground, watching the helpless child.

Ralphie said nothing in reply; he only tightened his eyes.

Mickey snapped his fingers and pointed to Ralphie.

Lee lifted his foot and drove his heel toward Ralphie's skull.

"OPEN YOUR EYES!" Jonny said.

Lee halted; both men smiled.

Mickey patted Jonny's face. "*Prévisible.*"

"Fuck you," Jonny said, shrugging Mickey's hand off his face. He shifted his focused to Ralphie. "Open your eyes for me."

Ralphie picked himself up off the ground; his eyes remained squinted. "You told me to keep them shut, no matter what."

Jonny held his groin with one hand and scooted himself back against the iron bars. He took a deep breath, grimacing. His voice was soft-spoken. "I know I did."

Mickey backed away, smiling in triumph.

Lee raised his pant leg, removing his hunting knife. He smiled, licking the pointed end; he hovered over Ralphie.

Jonny's chest tightened and his bottom lip quivered. He stared at Ralphie's blurring image. "It'll be over soon."

"No matter what means—"

"If you don't open your eyes, they're gonna kill you." Tears dangled from Jonny's chin. He shifted his eyes to Mickey.

Lee stood behind Ralphie, wrapping his arm around the boy's chest. He brought his other arm up, holding his knife under Ralphie's chin. He pressed the blade firmly against his throat and smiled devilishly at Jonny.

"Ow, ow, OW!"

Red droplets appear beneath the blade.

"OPEN YOUR EYES!"

Five

The Darkness Within

1

"Hey, man, open your eyes!"

"RALPHIE!" Jonny fought against the weight pushing back on his shoulders. He let his body go limp. His eyelids rose and he saw two hazy silhouettes and when the massive paws lifted, he swung at their owner.

The figure grabbed Jonny's arms and crisscrossed them against his chest. "It's me, Steven."

He blinked his eyes a few times, bringing Steven into focus. He looked around; Jonny sat in the back seat of Steven's Challenger. He exhaled, closing his eyes. "I'm okay."

Steven released him. "You sure?"

He opened his eyes, bobbing his head. "Yeah, better now."

"That must have been one hell of a nightmare," Capri said.

Jonny curled his upper lip, resting his head. He hated the sound of her high-pitched voice. If you mixed the sound of her voice with her ignorance, it made for a character worthy of a SNL skit.

Capri tossed her hair over her shoulder. "Why can't we drive with the windows up? The wind is tangling my hair."

Steven ignored her and focused on Jonny. "You screamed his name."

Jonny cleaned the sweat from his forehead. "Where's Sandra?"

Steven sat forward in the driver's seat. He took a cigarette out and let it dangle from his lips, pointing out the window. "She wanted to invite a friend."

Jonny slouched in the back and stared at the car's ceiling. He rubbed his face with his palms and then raked his fingers through his hair. He stopped midway. Two nightmares in two days. He sat upright, cleaning the debris from his eyes. He blinked a few times, leaned forward, and looked out the front window. "Where we at?"

"At Sandra's friend's houses," Capri said.

"Which one?"

"I don't know. She didn't say."

"Steven?" Jonny asked.

"You've met her before."

Jonny pushed against Steven's seat. "I need some air."

Steven stepped out and raised the seat forward allowing Jonny to slide out.

Steven lit his cigarette. He took a drag and exhaled, batting the smoke away from Jonny. "You having nightmares again?"

"Hope not." Jonny took the bottom of his shirt and cleaned the sweat from his face.

Steven took another drag from his cancer stick, fixated on the round scars on Jonny's abdomen. "This wasn't the first, was it?"

Jonny shook his head. "The first was yesterday at the garage." He pointed to his sister. "How many times is she gonna ring the doorbell?"

Steven flicked the ash from his cigarette. "She's persistent, that's for sure." He rubbed the back of his neck, shifting the conversation back to Jonny. "You had a nightmare before meeting Cheyenne?"

Jonny focused his gaze to the Datsun parked in front of the yard. "That's what I said." He blocked the sun from his eyes. The duplex's paint peeled in several areas. There were two sets of steps. The steps leading to Sandra were dry rotted, but the steps leading to the neighbor's door were brand new.

Jonny looked around. He drove through this neighborhood to get to work. He looked back at the derelict Datsun. The weather strip around the windows grew green moss, pine needles covered the windshield wipers, and spiderwebs under the wheel well captured the warm breeze. The car's black exterior stained yellow from pollen dust.

"We're at Cheyenne's, aren't we?"

Steven raised his palms. "I invited you before I knew she was coming."

Jonny flexed his jaw. He glanced at Sandra texting on her phone. Did he drag her kicking and screaming, or did he camouflage his farrago of emotions to get answers? He locked eyes with Steven. "You'll help keep Sandra safe?"

Steven's brows came together. "Of course, but what makes you—"

"Keep your eyes open."

Jonny marched onto the porch and the steps groaned beneath his weight.

Sandra turned. "Dammit," she whispered beneath her breath.

Jonny took the last step slow, pointing to the door. "You sure Cheyenne's home?"

Sandra looked down at her cell. "She texted me before we left, saying she was ready."

He moved her to the side and knocked hard and loud.

She placed her hands on her boney hips. “Why were you so mean to her yesterday?”

He brushed his hair from his eyes and looked back at Steven. What could he say that wouldn’t cause more questions than he wanted to answer? Things she didn’t need to know. He tilted his head to the side; he needed to say something. “Didn’t you find her behavior odd?”

“What I find odd is how you can judge someone so harshly after a few minutes.”

He pounded on the door again.

“Are you upset she’s coming?”

Upset? Why wouldn’t he be? Cheyenne brought back his old life. He didn’t know how, but he had to pretend he didn’t feel betrayed to get the answers he sought. “I’ll tell you what. I won’t be mad if you stop trying to set me up on dates.” He checked the door; locked. “Besides, I owe her an apology.”

“Thank you.”

He stepped left of the door and leaned over the railing, looking down the side of the building. “I wouldn’t thank me yet.” He vaulted over the porch railing and peered through the first window he came to, but the white voile curtains obscured his view.

“Jonny!” Sandra ran down the steps.

He made his way down the building to an open window. He hoisted himself up, headfirst, into the window.

Sandra grabbed the belt loops of his blue jeans and tugged. “Jonathan Michael!” She gave another hard tug. “Cheyenne could be in the bathroom!”

Jonny needed to hurry. Steven ran toward them and he didn’t want to fight them both to enter the house. He used his foot and gently kicked her off, crawled the rest of the way through, and poked out his head. “You, okay?”

Steven helped Sandra off the ground. “Man, what the hell

are you doing?"

"Meet me around front; I'll unlock the door," he said, disappearing inside the house.

"Shit!" Sandra said. "What the hell is going on in his head?"

2

A mahogany bureau caught Jonny's attention. The antique bureau had bold flame grain fronts, acanthus columns, and the classical lion's paw feet. He ran his fingers along the grain, combing for telltale imperfections. The tool marks confirmed his suspicions; it was hand-carved.

He removed a photo from the bureau and blew off the dust, revealing a woman and a little girl pretending to have a tea party. The girl wore white pearls, oversized high-heels, a fitted red dress, and red lipstick. She was laughing. The woman dressed similarly, and she was smiling at the girl.

He, too, smiled.

Jonny sniffed the air. A distant memory flashed through his mind of a chair wreathed in flames. He rubbed his eyes, failing to smear the image away. He focused back on his agenda; he had answers to get.

He returned the photograph and gave the room a glance over. He assumed the room was being used as storage. There were boxes stacked on top of boxes. He took a step back, tripping over a box, and toppled into the wall.

That box wasn't there before, he was certain.

Jonny slowly opened the bedroom door and the hinges squeaked. Why wouldn't they, he was only trespassing?

Darkness greeted him, followed by the assault of rot, mildew, and ammonia. He pinched his nose and covered his mouth; his stomach curdled.

He stared at the door across the hall; could that be his destination? He waded over the pile of clothes between the doors in the short hallway. It was too dark, especially given the intense afternoon sun. A faint glimmer from the open doorway to his left stole his attention.

The bathroom grew mold from the grout and calking on the tile and tub, which contained standing water, long since browned, matching the ring it left around the rim. Used tampons decorated the wall in front of the toilet. The mirror lay shattered on the counter, around the elliptical hole where the sink should have been. A single lit candle projected a light show on the walls.

He glanced at the closed door; something wasn't right. He stepped out of the hallway and into the open layout of the kitchen and living room.

The scant light beaming around the kitchen's blackout shades highlighted the calamity of the kitchen.

Dirty dishes lay scattered on top of the counters and in the sink. Garbage overflowed the trashcan and several takeout containers and pizza boxes lay about the kitchen and living room, covered by flies.

Jonny was exceptionally neat; "clean freak" had been used to describe him, more than once. He washed dishes after every meal and took the garbage out every night, regardless of fullness; he hated lingering odors. He knew the taint filth left on a person. No matter how much they scrub, the odor always stayed with them. Cheyenne didn't seem dirty. She smelled of jasmine perfume, no excess of smells or odors. Was this even her house?

The curtains in the living room were not the white voile ones he had attempted to peer through earlier. They were old, thick, orange floral curtains with metal hooks. Crochet blankets covered the sixties vintage furniture. An oval, wood-cased tube television with a VHS player on top sat in the corner. The only sound he could hear came from the grandfather clock against the wall to his left.

He caught a hint of something burning. He maneuvered through the clutter, searching for smoke, or an ashtray, or any source of fire. The smell intensified into a revolting smell of burning flesh.

Jonny's intuition told him it was time to grab the others and leave. He raised his hand to unlock the front door.

"Jonny," a deep, rugged male voice called.

Jonny's heart revved, flushing his body with an icy heat. The pulse in his neck drummed in his ears. That voice, he had not heard it in years. He closed his eyes and turned to face the bastard.

3

Sandra slapped the front door and jiggled the doorknob. "Jonathan Michael! You better open this door!" She shouldered the door, yelling, "JONNY!"

Steven pulled her away. "Look, I gotta tell you something."

Sandra went to slap the door again, but Steven grabbed her arm and pulled her back.

"He's been having nightmares again."

"What?" She slapped his chest, pushing him away. "How could you not tell me?" She slapped him again. "HOW?"

Steven grabbed her hands. "He had one in the back of my car while you were ringing the doorbell. I'm surprised you didn't hear him yelling Ralphie's name."

"Yeah, I heard him yelling, but I thought it was because you told him about Cheyenne." She jerked her hands frees. "No wonder he's been acting weird. I gotta call GG."

Her phone powered down, displaying the charge symbol. "Give me your phone," she demanded, reaching for his pocket. Steven's phone had no dial tone. She hung up and tried again with the same result. Sandra stepped to the porch edge. "Capri, I need to use your phone."

Capri stepped out of the car and threw her phone at the seat. "Stupid phone stopped working," she slamming the door.

"Hey!" Steven said. "Don't slam the door."

"That's weird," Sandra said. "None of our phones are working."

"Why don't you guys just climb into the same window he did?" Capri asked.

"That's the smartest thing she said all day," Sandra said.

Steven pocketed his cell. "I expect comments like that from your brother, not you."

"And I expected you would have told me about his nightmares before now."

"He told me a few moments before crawling through the damn window."

She rubbed her forehead. "Please, just go get him."

Steven made his way around the building, and as he got close, the window shut. "Enough is enough. You've been in there forever." He tried to lift the window but it didn't budge. He cupped the sides of his eyes and peeked inside the room.

The outline of a tall figure ran out of the dark alcove into the kitchen.

4

Jonny focused on his breathing, slowing his heart. He opened his eyes and saw . . . no one.

Laughter traveled the home, echoing like an empty cave. The low-pitched chuckle flooded memories into Jonny's head, memories he worked hard to forget.

His ears were hot. He crushed his hands into fists. “Hello?” He waited for a few seconds, but the room was silent, save for the grandfather clock. He took a few steps forward, scanning the kitchen. “Hello.”

Tick-Tock.

Jonny stared at the master bedroom door. He sighed through his nose and approached the bedroom, reaching for the doorknob. He hesitated; Sandra was still outside. He took a couple of steps back, turned on his heels, and headed for the front door. He glared over his shoulder. What the hell was going on?

He went to unlock the front door and something grabbed ahold of his shoulder.

“JONNY!”

He whipped around, his left arm cocked and fist clenched, but again, saw no one. That voice, it couldn’t be, but it was undeniable. He stood motionless, waiting to hear something, anything.

The grandfather clock chimed.

Jonny flinched. He surveying the room, listening to the clock’s chime. He turned to the front door and wrenched on the locked knob. His hands would not cooperate. He struggled with the deadbolt and the lock on the doorknob. He yanked open the door, but the chain held it closed.

Sandra stood on the other side. “Are you okay? What took so long?”

He slammed the door and clawed the chain out of its groove. He tore open the front door and pushed Sandra aside. He rested his palms on the porch rail with closed eyes, trying to calm down, trying to rebury the dredged-up memories.

“Jesus, Jonny! What happened? Why in the hell did it take an hour for you to open the door?” Sandra asked.

He opened his eyes, white-knuckling the rail. “An hour?” He

released his grip. "I was in there maybe ten minutes, not no damn hour." He looked down at his watch to verify his claims, but the watch had stopped. He tapped the face and the watch changed from displaying 3:00 PM to 4:05 PM.

A firm hand landed hard on Jonny's shoulder. He spun with his fist drawn.

Steven blocked his punch and pushed him against the house. "Jesus Christ! What happened to you in there?"

The adjacent door jerked open. "What the hell's going on out here?"

Cheyenne's neighbor reeked of alcohol and cigarettes, and his potbelly hung over his jeans. The neighbor eyed the three of them and then to Steven's Challenger, where Capri remained. "Who in the hell are y'all dingleberries?"

Sandra approached the rail separating the two porches and extended her hand.

The man scoffed at her.

She withdrew her hand. "Well, we're here to pick up Cheyenne. Do you know if she's in?"

"That crazy screaming lady?" the neighbor said with a bit of a slur.

Sandra stepped back, and Jonny instinctively stepped in front of her.

The neighbor pointed to the Challenger. "Look, y'all look like friendly folk. You should stay clear of that psycho. Every damn day and night, she screams bloody murder, wakes everyone 'round here." The man pointed to his head, tapping his temple. "She's mental."

"Military man?" Steven asked, nodding his head toward the man's *Semper Fidelis* forearm tattoo.

"Marines," the man answered.

Cheyenne screamed and Sandra rushed for the door.

Jonny grabbed her and pulled her back.

The neighbor scoffed. "She's always screaming." He staggered back into his home mumbling, "I'm missing the game over this shit."

Sandra tilted her head, squinting her eyes. "What's wrong, Jonny?"

"It's not safe."

Cheyenne screamed louder.

Sandra pulled away from him and ran for the front door.

He lunged, snatching her arm. "Don't go in there."

"What do you mean, not safe; who's in there?" Steven asked.

"Something's weird about that house."

"LEAVE THEM ALONE!" Cheyenne screamed.

Steven rushed for the door, but Jonny threw his arm over Steven's chest.

"Dammit, Jon, move!"

"This isn't your dad beating you or your mom. This feels like a trap."

Steven pried Jonny off him. He furrowing his brows asking, "A trap?"

Sandra held Jonny's hand. "I love you, and I understand you're having a PTSD episode, but right now, she needs help." Sandra adverted her eyes to Steven, releasing Jonny's hand. "Hold him." She dodged Jonny's reach and ran for the door.

Steven put him into a bear hug, wrestling against his surge of adrenaline.

Jonny couldn't move his arms to stop her. "SANDRA!" He threw back his head, missing Steven. He lifted his leg and mule-kicked Steven's knee and they both went to the ground. He writhed wildly; Steven struggled to hold him. Jonny slipped free and punched Steven in the face. "You promised to keep her safe!" He leaped to his feet and charged through the door.

Six

The Wager of Life

1

Jonny came to an abrupt stop. This was not the same house he was in moments ago. The grandfather clock was stationary, the furniture brand new, the electronics all new. The curtains were again white voile. The floors were a waxed dark hardwood throughout the home.

He looked into the kitchen; polished. The tiny bay window in the kitchen beamed with light. Fresh potted herbs lined the windowsill. Green granite, matching the counters, crowned the island. Nestled in the corner of the kitchen, hid a small table for two.

Steven limped, rushing in behind Jonny. He stopped just past the threshold.

Jonny stood motionless, staring at the brightly lit alcove.

Sandra's voice drifted from the back bedroom: "You need to drink some more water."

Cheyenne's voice was softer but could be heard. "How d'you get in?"

Jonny shook his head. He had not imagined the pigsty.

Steven cautiously limped toward him. “You, okay?”

“I’m not sure.”

Steven dabbed his lip. “You still think it’s a trap?”

Jonny walked away without response. He didn’t need an assessment. He poked his head around the corner, peering into the storage room. His eyebrows furrowed and his head jerked back; the room remained the same.

He stepped to the side and pushed open the bathroom door; it was clean. The shower curtain had images of monkeys swinging on bamboo. The sink was a large, pearlescent emerald-glass bowl, behind which stood a faucet fashioned after an old well pump. He fancied it; he didn’t know why. The mirror was a large square, framed with real bamboo, and the cabinets painted brown with green trim.

The cracked bedroom door did little to muffle Cheyenne’s voice. “I’m fine. You shouldn’t be here.”

Jonny’s attention turned to the master bedroom. PTSD or not, he hated her. He hated how she made him feel, bringing the fucking past to the present.

Steven held out his arm, blocking Jonny from Cheyenne’s bedroom. “You, uh, want to wait in the car?”

He removed Steven’s arm. “No.”

Steven pulled him back. “You’re not going in there.”

Jonny stared at Steven’s busted lip. It was the first time he’d hit him. “I counted on you to help me keep Sandra safe and you let her run in here, blindly.”

“Protect her from what?”

“Don’t get in my way again.”

He removed Steven’s arm and pushed open the door.

Sandra disappeared into the master bathroom with an empty glass in hand.

Jonny shifted his gaze to the woman in bed.

Cheyenne wore a black sports bra and boy shorts

showcasing the dark purple ligature marks around her ankles. Bruises of all stages tattooed her entire body; the freshest injury adorned her shoulder.

Jonny tensed up. He glanced down at his own shoulder.

Steven brushed past Jonny. “Who did that to you?”

Cheyenne brought her knees to her chest, staring at the men. Her face exuded beads of sweat and her hair clung to the sides of her face. She locked eyes with Jonny. “You should all leave.”

“We will,” Sandra said from the bathroom. “I just want to make sure you’re all right.” She exited the bathroom with a cold washcloth in hand. “Here, let’s cool you off.”

Sandra spotted the men and waved them away. “You, two, leave.”

Jonny shook his head.

Steven grabbed Jonny’s arm and Jonny stared him down, removing Steven’s grip.

“We’ll be on the other side if you need us,” Steven said, refusing to back down.

Jonny shifted his gaze to Cheyenne’s battered body. He wasn’t heartless; she needed triage. He shifted his eyes back to Steven. “Right outside,” he said sternly.

Steven shut the door behind them and followed Jonny into the kitchen. “Maybe we should wait outside until Sandra’s done.”

Jonny shook his head. “Don’t push it.”

Steven motioned to the porch. “We’ll be right over there.”

Jonny narrowed his eyes. “I’m not leaving Sandra alone. It’s the last time I’m saying it.”

Steven signed. “I don’t want to leave Capri in the car.”

“She’s not a dog. She knows how to open the door and come in.”

2

Sandra patted Cheyenne's face with the cool cloth. "When Jonny was a child, he'd have nightmares. He was unawakenable and if you tried, he'd became violent in his sleep. Sometimes, he'd wake swinging. He hurt Dominick pretty bad onetime and Grandpa did the waking afterwards. Anyway, when he'd have a bad one, he'd drench the bed in sweat. Our grandmother would coddle him and clean his face with a cool cloth."

Cheyenne watched Sandra's eyes dart from one bruise to the another. "They don't hurt," Cheyenne said. She pushed Sandra's hand away and stood. "I'll be fine." She retrieved fresh undergarments from her bureau and stormed to her closet. "You didn't tell me he was coming."

"I didn't know either until Steven told me he invited him."

Cheyenne jerked a flannel shirt from its hanger.

"Look, Jonny never takes a day off, that's why I didn't ask him to come. How Steven convinced him is beyond me."

Cheyenne thumbed through her clothes, looking for jeans.

"My brother wants to apologize to you. Let him do that, and we'll leave."

Cheyenne stepped away from the closet. "Apologize? To me?"

"Yeah. He said he was an asshole toward you, and he needed to apologize."

Cheyenne shifted her eyes to the bedroom door. *Interesting.* "Your brother is an odd man."

Sandra grabbed the flannel. "I don't care about your bruises." Sandra furrowed her brows and shook her head. "I do, but I'm sure you'll tell me when you're ready. For now, it's ninety-six degrees out. Please put something cooler on."

The hair on Cheyenne's arms and on the back of her neck

stood on end. She closed her eyes, shaking her head. She grabbed a pair of blue jean shorts and a spaghetti strap shirt. “I should shower first.”

3

Jonny leaned against the kitchen sink with one arm crossed his arm over his chest, holding his bicep. His chin and nose rested on the thumb and forefinger of his other hand. He was on the fence. On the one side, he wanted to blame her. He had no other rational explanation for what he’d experienced a moment ago. Everything seemed to happen around her when he was alone. On the other, he sympathized. Nobody deserved to be a punching bag.

Sandra leaned across the island. “You, okay?”

He cleared his throat. “I’ll be fine.”

“Where’s Steven?”

“Babysitting his dog.”

“Seriously? What’s gotten into you?”

“C’mon, you know Capri’s refusing to get out of the car because there’s another female. Her jealousy and insecurities will push Steven out the door.”

“You think so?”

“Steven told me he’s tried breaking it off several times, but Capri cries it’s because of another woman.”

Sandra bit her lower lip, changing the subject. “Why’d it take you so long to open the door?”

Jonny slid his hand from his face and laid it across his other arm. “I swear, I was only in here for ten minutes.”

“Steven told me your nightmares are back.”

He looked up at her and leaned over the island, reaching for her hands. “Hey, I’m fine.” He pulled her toward him and locked eyes with her. "I promise. Steven and I talked last night, and he's right. I don't sleep enough, and I'm exhausted. I probably hallucinated yesterday." Jonny almost believed it. How else could he explain it?

She released his hand and stood straight. "Did you hallucinate after crawling into the window? It could explain why you're missing fifty-five minutes."

He returned to his leaning post and shrugged his shoulders. "I don't know. It all felt real, even last night."

"What felt real? Why won't you tell me?"

He ran his fingers over his stubble. "I don't know how to explain it." He pointed to Cheyenne's room. "My gut says she's hiding something."

"Everybody hides something," Sandra said. "Look at how much you hide, even from me. I don't see how that coincides with you hallucinating and having nightmares."

He wagged his pointer finger. "I said *probably* hallucinated."

Sandra grabbed her hips and sighed.

"I've never hallucinated before, not even after a nightmare. I only entertain the idea because of the lack of sleep."

She crossed her arms over her chest and scowled. "Stress can trigger PTSD and of late, you seem to have a lot of it. I understand you have deadlines and responsibilities at the shop, but you also have responsibilities at home. Your son being the most important."

"My son is the most important, but my responsibilities at the garage support him." He glanced down at his watch. "It's too late to go to the river."

Sandra tucked her hair behind her ears. "Would you be open to inviting Cheyenne over for a barbeque?"

He shook his head. "Absolutely not."

"You really don't like her, do you?" She walked around the island and hugged him. "Where did my baby brother go?"

He pushed her back.

"Really, where is he? 'Cause my brother wouldn't do nothing after seeing a woman bruised like that."

He stared at Cheyenne's bedroom door, clenching his jaw. Sandra was right, he wouldn't normally sit idle, but Cheyenne wasn't normal. Her bruises made her a victim, but somehow, he knew she was a danger to his family. He had a myriad question, and he knew only one person with the answers.

"Please," Sandra begged. "I need to make sure she's okay. If, after this, you're still uncomfortable, I will cut ties with her."

Jonny tapped his elbow, considering the proposition. He knew Sandra would make good on her word.

"I want to see if I can get her to open up and tell me who's abusing her."

This aligned with Jonny's agenda. Maybe he could make it work. It was a gamble. How could he ensure his family's safety? His son's safety?

"Call GG. If she's willing to take Jacob to the Fun Center for a few hours or to the movies, we'll barbeque."

"My phone's dead."

He pulled his cell from his back pocket and handed it to her. "GG has to agree to keep Jacob away." Jonny pointed to the master bedroom. "I don't want her near my son and you're not to be around her without me."

She hugged him tight. "I convinced her to wear cooler clothes. Do me a favor." She pointed toward the living room. "Go outside and stress to that idiot to keep her mouth shut."

"I'm not leaving you in here."

"I'll stand in the doorway so you can see me. I want to be here when she comes out."

"Stay where I can see you."

4

Cheyenne walked out of her room, braiding the tail end of her hair. She saw the spare room was open and closed it. She found Sandra leaning against the front doorjamb.

Sandra pointed to the bare walls. “You don’t have any family photos?”

Cheyenne shook her head. “When I came to America, I was a teenager, and I came alone.”

“That must have been scary, being young and alone. Why didn’t your parents come with you?”

Cheyenne could hear the other party members on the front porch talking about her bruises. She changed the subject. The less they knew about her, the better. She pointed outside, “Should I go out there or does your brother want to come in?”

“Jonny agreed to a barbeque since it’s late. He wants to invite you over.”

Cheyenne narrowed her eyes. “I thought he wanted to apologize?”

Sandra bobbed her head. “He does.” She slid her hands into her back pockets. “But he does things his way.”

“Meaning?”

“Jonny’s rough around the collar. He’s . . . emotionally damaged, but once you get to know him, you’ll see he’s an amazing father, brother, and friend.”

“Emotionally damaged?”

“I’m not trying to excuse him for his behavior. Jonny’s a complicated guy. He barricades everyone out, protecting his core.”

“Why does he keep others away?”

“He went missing when he was a child, gone for years. One

day, he showed up at our grandparents' house filthy and starved. His jaw, ribs, and fingers were all broken. When he was in the hospital, he was combative. He didn't trust anyone except one doctor. They had to put him in an induced coma so they could treat him."

"Are you telling the truth?"

"No one knows what happened. Still to this day, he refuses to talk about it." She ran her eyes down Cheyenne's bruised arm. "He would never admit it to you, but your injuries bother him."

Cheyenne glanced out the front door.

Steven and Jonny walked down the steps.

"I really believe the two of you got off on the wrong start. He's moody and unpredictable, but he's a really nice guy. I promise."

"Why do you advocate for him?"

"For years, our family worked with professionals to help him through his PTSD." Sandra looked out the front door. "He doesn't open up to me because he says he's protecting me. But I think it's because he doesn't know how." She used her head and pointed to Steven. "Steven kinda steers and nudges him in the right direction when he goes off course. Jonny's a stubborn pain in the ass, but he eventually acknowledges he's in the wrong. That's why I believe you two will get along. You just gotta be patient with him."

"Steven's his Jiminy Cricket."

"No." Sandra shook her head. "Our brother was his Jiminy Cricket. The rest of us are substitutes."

"*Was*?"

Sandra lowered her eyes. "Dominick passed three years ago."

Cheyenne lowered her eyes and bit her fingernail. There were so many unanswered questions surrounding Jonny. She turned her head, looking at the alcove. The biggest mystery was why *he* wanted Jonny.

She removed her finger from her mouth and walked to the front door. "If we stop by Sherm's, I can make homemade potato salad."

Sandra stepped onto the porch. "Thank you for giving him a second chance."

Cheyenne locked her house. She could see Capri from her peripheral.

Capri's eyes widened and her mouth dropped. "Why would you let someone do that to you?"

Sandra's head dropped forward into the cradle of her fingers; she rubbed them across her brow.

Jonny stopped talking in the middle of his conversation with Steven and pointed at Capri. "You should learn to keep your damn mouth shut." He turned to Steven. "Why are you even with that ditzy moron? I wouldn't care if the sex was good. If the brains don't match the beauty, it's not worth the hassle."

Steven put his cigarette out on the bottom of his boot, exhaling. "All right, settle down."

Sandra nudged Capri to the side. "I don't even know what to say to you right now."

Steven pocketed the butt, walking up the first steps. "Capri, honey, you're being insensitive."

Cheyenne removed her key from the deadbolt and turned. "It's okay, it's not the first time."

"Not the first time," Steven said. "There shouldn't be a time."

Cheyenne smiled. "You're a good man." She spotted the Dodge and walked toward the steps, pocketing her keys. "Is that a seventy-one?"

"Yeah, a seventy-one Challenger."

"I know it's a Challenger," she said. *Men never think women appreciate cars.* "It looks like an R/T addition."

Cheyenne caught the glance shared by both men. She recognized the look of mild astonishment on Steven's face; she'd found it on many men's faces at car shows. Jonny's look, though, she hadn't seen since leaving Scotland.

Steven joined Jonny, asking, "How do you know cars?"

She walked past both men, making her way to the trunk. "My *seanair* finds old classics, fixes them up, and sells them at auctions. He taught me some, not a lot."

"What does *shine air* mean?" Jonny asked.

Cheyenne ran her fingers along the black spoiler. *"Shen-er."* She glanced briefly at him. "Grandfather. In some ways, you remind me of him." She continued to run her fingers alongside the curve of the trunk, admiring the accented, black side stripe. She stopped halfway, never averting her eyes. "Is this Plum Crazy?" she asked, referring to the soft purple color.

Neither man answered.

She shifted her eyes to the wheels. The Challenger sported Mickey Thompson Sportsman Pro tires. The rims were stock steel with the classic chrome accent rings. She made her way to the front, admiring the insignia on the right side of the grill. She pointed to the hood. "What engine and tranny does it have? Is the suspension original?"

Steven grinned, elbowing Jonny in the ribs.

"It's a stock 426 Hemi, with a McLeod transmission. The suspension is an aftermarket racing kit," Jonny said.

"Why no roll cage?" she asked.

Sandra squeezed Capri's arm tight. She jumped up and down with glee. "Their first genuine conversation!"

"If I added a roll cage, then the rest of us wouldn't fit," Jonny said.

Steven pulled his car keys. "We ready to ride?"

Cheyenne pointed to Steven. “Your car?”

Jonny walked to the passenger side, opening the door. “I restored it.”

Goosebumps washed over Cheyenne’s body in waves. She looked to the duplex. Her neighbor walked out onto his porch holding a peach and sat down on the wicker chair.

Jonny sniffed the air, drawing Cheyenne’s attention. He looked back at her with an emotionless stare, combing her exposed flesh on which every hair stood alert. She felt naked, almost violated. She crossed her arms over her abdomen.

The neighbor took a bite of his fruit and began singing “Peaches” by the President of the United States of America.

All eyes turned to the porch.

5

The stray dog from across the street barked, but Sandra could not hear it. Capri’s mouth moved, but no sound came from her, either. The only sound Sandra heard came from the man in the wicker chair.

A memory flashed through her mind. Darkness surrounded her except for the glow of a lit cigarette; it illuminated with each inhalation.

She closed her eyes, taking slow, deep breaths through her nose and exhaling from her mouth. Her ears rang, and she heard her own breathing.

“I said, what’s wrong?” Capri said.

Sandra glanced at the man with uncertainty. “I hate that song.”

“I’m right here,” Jonny said, leaping onto the porch. “I gotcha.”

Sandra walked down the steps, looking back at the man; he

grinned at her.

6

Jonny raised the front seat forward, assisting Sandra into the car and waited for Capri to climb in before he pushed the seat back. He sat shotgun, unable to void himself of the putrid smell. He looked around; nobody else seemed to smell it. He rolled down the window in false hopes of fresh air.

The neighbor stepped to the porch rail, throwing his half-eaten peach across the yard. He grinned at the car, singing the chorus repeatedly, getting louder with each stanza.

Steven eased out of the driveway. “He’s really faschnickered.”

Jonny turned, reaching for Sandra’s hand. He squeezed it asking, “You alright?”

She took deep breaths and opened her eyes, squeezing Jonny’s hand, nodding.

Steven looked into the rearview mirror at her, wringing the steering wheel.

Jonny shifted his focus to Cheyenne’s arms. The hairs still stood on end. Goosebumps saturated every exposed part of her body. He had sweat rings under his armpits, around his neck, and down his back. How could she be cold?

Seven

Not His Eyes, Not His Voice

Jonny rummaged through the produce searching for firm, ripe Roma tomatoes. Had his work schedule not distracted him, he would have planted some a week ago. He placed two tomatoes inside the produce bag and then rubbed his fingers together. "Damn waxy film." He wiped his hand on his jeans and dove back in.

Sandra placed a head of lettuce and an onion in the basket. She pointed at the two bags of tomatoes. "You need all those Romas for burgers?"

He placed another tomato in the bag. "The steak tomatoes are for the burgers." He spun the bag and tied the top. "These are for marinara sauce."

"Store-bought tomatoes. Grandpa's rolling in his grave."

"Oh, don't I know it." He wiped his hands on his pants. "It's gonna take a shit-ton of fresh herbs to flavor those tasteless tomatoes."

Sandra raised an eyebrow. "A 'shit-ton'?"

Jonny's iconic side smirk appeared, but quickly vanished.

She raised her hands and plopped them down on the cart's

handle. "C'mon! Let yourself crack a smile. It's a beautiful day; I'm safe, you're safe, everyone's safe."

Jonny maintained a neutral face. "It's a unit of measurement; more than a ton but less than a fuck-ton."

Sandra laughed. "Which is bigger: a metric ton or a fuck-ton?

Jonny broke face and busted a gut laughing.

"There it is! I haven't seen that in a while."

Jonny calmed, but his smile remained. "What are talkin' about?"

"You being happy."

"I'm happy all the time. I just don't go around singing and dancing like a crazed person."

Sandra glanced at Steven and the women. "I gotta pee. I'll be back."

Jonny kept a close eye on her. She walked around the produce, making eye contact with Steven, pointing with her head toward Jonny. Steven gave a single nod and then spoke to the women, pointing at Jonny.

Dammit! He didn't need a babysitter.

Steven grabbed a watermelon on his travel and placed it into the cart. "Dessert?"

"Why not?" Jonny said, pushing the basket to the meat department.

"I'm surprised you agreed to bring her."

Jonny placed a pack of hamburger inside the basket. "I need your help at the garage. I didn't want us not going to Boomer Hill being an excuse you'd use for not keeping your promise."

Steven pushed the cart toward the hotdogs. "I'm touched and insulted at the same time." He halted. "Now why don't you tell me the real reason."

"It is the real reason."

"C'mon, man. You don't bring strangers to your house. The basis of our agreement solely rested on you taking today off. You could have easily stayed home, and binged watched *Archer* and I would have still helped."

Jonny placed a few packages of hotdogs into the cart. "Fine. I still don't like her, but something happened when I was inside her house that I can't explain."

"Try."

"So, you can be like Sandra and point to PTSD due to stress and lack of sleep? Cheyenne's hiding something and everything inside me says 'run for the hills'."

"But?" Steven asked.

Jonny sighed. "But I see her battered body and—" He lowered his head.

"And you feel like an asshat?"

He glanced up at Steven. "I remember how I found Sandra." Jonny shook his head. "I have to force myself to ignore my gut."

"If her bruises bother you, you're not ignoring all of your gut."

"They don't bother you?" Jonny asked.

"Of course, they do." He propped his foot on the undercarriage of the shopping cart. "The difference? I look at her and see a victim, not a perpetrator."

"I'm not treating her like a perpetrator."

Steven leaned against the handle. "You blame her for what may have been a figment of your imagination."

"I—"

Steven raised his hand, muting Jonny. "You haven't spoken to her to confirm your allegations, but you've proven to be a jackass."

Steven had him in a technicality; Jonny had nothing to counter.

Steven's phone buzzed.

"That's weird," he said, pulling the cell from his pocket. "My phone stopped working earlier."

Jonny pulled the cart toward him. "You were probably in a dead zone."

Steven returned his phone to his pocket. "The women are waiting by the car; I'm gonna go have a smoke."

"The neighbor," Jonny said.

Steven turned back around. "Cheyenne's neighbor? What about him?"

"Her mood changed when he came outside; she was quiet, reserved."

Steven bobbed his head. "What do you want to do?"

Jonny crossed his arms. "I don't know. This is more your area."

"My father was an abusive bastard. I could connect with her on that but, you have the gift of getting people to open up. If you can get over yourself, I think you should try talking to her first."

Check! Jonny had the in, he was looking for. He needed to downplay it. He shook his head. "I don't think—"

"I think if you knew her story, that gut feeling of yours would relax."

Jonny tapped his finger on the basket.

Steven pointed at the cart. "Don't forget the buns. I'm gonna go smoke."

With Steven inadvertently on board, Jonny could focus on his primary mission. He needed to get Cheyenne alone, though.

Jonny walked down the bread aisle. He tossed the burger buns into the basket and then bent down, snatching the hotdog buns from the lower shelf.

"Save her!"

Jonny rose and spotted a brunette boy with a freckled face clinging to his shopping cart. The child's irises were bright white and gazed into his. The boy couldn't have been any older than is son, Jacob.

The voice was a child's but the manner, the poise, the command, definitely not. Jonny had been unfortunate to meet enough children to differentiate them.

"You must save her," the boy said.

Jonny looked around for the parents, but there was no one else in sight. He dropped the buns into the cart. "Hey, buddy, where's your parents?" He walked to the front of the basket and kneeled. "Who needs saving?"

The boy let go of the cart and took a step back. "To get rid of him, you have to save her."

His eyes narrowed; he was unsure what the boy was saying. He held out his hand. "I won't hurt you, kiddo." He looked over his shoulder and then back at the boy. "Who is *he* and *she*?"

The boy continued staring at Jonny, his arms never leaving his sides. "Finish what you started."

A woman at the end of the aisle opened her purse. She and the boy had the same-colored hair. "Jackson, this way," she said, placing her phone inside her purse.

Jonny focused back on Jackson; he had to take a double look.

Jackson's eyes were now brown and shifted rapidly between the upper left and the center.

What the hell was happening?

The woman pulled her purse strap up her shoulder and walked toward them. "Sir, Jackson has nystagmus; he can't control his eyes."

"My apology; I didn't mean to stare."

The woman grabbed Jackson by the hand and drug him away.

"There you are," Sandra said. "We ready to checkout?"

He nodded, pushing the cart.

"I'm gonna get an ice cream, you want one?"

Jonny shook his head and made his way to the cashier, pondering if everyone was right about the lack of sleep. Again, he could not explain what he saw. Jackson had white eyes, not brown, and they were stock-still. Cheyenne was nowhere near this time for him to accuse her.

He pushed the cart up to the register and unloaded onto the conveyor belt. "Good evening, Kowanta, how's your day?"

Kowanta was GG's longtime friend. They met as little girls in Louisiana. She moved to Oregon five years ago, unable to shake her southern drawl.

She smiled. "I be doin' just fine, Mr. DeLuca."

"Please, Jonny, Jon, or Jonathan is fine." He bagged his groceries. "How are the grandkids?"

She pointed to the arcade games next to the ice cream counter. "Their uncle came up from Southern California to help celebrate the twins' birthday."

The uncle sported a mohawk which alternated between green and blue spikes. The twins fought over who was going to ride the horse first. The boy pushed his sister, and she fell on her butt, crying. The uncle picked her up, consoling her, and scolded the little boy.

"Not fond of the hairstyle, but he's good with all the kids."

"The kiddos still asking where their parents are?"

Kowanta's eyes watered. "I finally told 'em what death was and about heaven."

"What about the older grandkids? They helping out around the house?"

"The two oldest ones remind me of you. Maverick likes to

draw, and Maeve is learning the cello."

He placed his groceries in the basket. "Well, if either needs a lesson, you know where to find me."

She smiled. "I's couldn't afford to pay you."

He reached for his wallet and winked at her. "I'll do it for free."

She played with the St. Peter's necklace around her neck. "Who's the girl with your sister? The one with all them bruises?"

Jonny quickly searched the ice cream counter for Sandra; Cheyenne wasn't there. He handed her a hundred-dollar bill. "Sandra's friend." He placed his wallet back in his pocket and loaded the last of his groceries. "Sandra was alone with her?"

"No. Sandra walked up to that girl when I was ringing her out and merely stated you were about done." She placed the money inside the register and counted out his change. "Y'all should be careful, Mr. DeLuca." Kowanta held Jonny's money, playing with the necklace with her other hand. "That woman has a dark aura." She let her necklace go and handed him his money.

He smiled. "Keep it."

"Mr. DeLuca, I—"

"Call me, Jonny." He closed her hand around the money. "Buy the kids something."

She handed back the money. "But I's still haven't paid you for fixin' my van."

"Don't worry about it. Take care of your babies."

He pushed his cart toward Sandra, passing Jackson.

The boy approached him. His brown eyes continually darted to the left. "He says to finish what you started."

Eight

A Dream Realized

1

The earthy yellow of the house jumped out at Cheyenne as Steven pulled into the driveway. The white trim lining the roof, windows, and doors mimicked a fifty's vintage facade. She could tell the size of the house, but it hid its bulk behind architected modesty.

In the center of the yard, a whimsical, wishing well carved from an old tree trunk sat, surrounded by a cheery crowd of lavender lobelia flowers, barely visible over the tall, weedless grass.

Cheyenne fetched her groceries from the trunk and followed behind Sandra.

The herbs in the windowsill planters thrived in the sunlight. Cheyenne fancied the idea and would have to hang some in her windowsills.

Sandra unlocked the front door. "Gotta take off your shoes; Jonny doesn't allow them on the carpet."

Cheyenne slid off her flip-flops and left them next to the shoe rack by the front door. She stepped in a little farther, smelling aged vanilla and creamed sugar. She closed her eyes, filling her lungs with the sweet aroma. She imagined the little girl and woman from the photo she kept in the spare room on the bureau. The girl whisked a batch of homemade lemon curd while the woman added lemon zest.

"You're in the way," Jonny said.

She opened her eyes and stepped aside, allowing him to pass. She took a few steps forward. Family photos covered the walls, many of a little boy who had a striking resemblance to Jonny. There were a few photos of an elder couple. In one picture, they kissed.

The blanket of photos had an eerie Déjà vu feeling. Cheyenne recognized the layout of the photo frames but not the photos themselves. She knew she hadn't been there before nor in any other home with so many displayed memories.

Her eyes landed on a photo in a wood plank frame. Sandra was in the middle, Jonny was to the right of her, and another man was on her left. The man was dark-complected and sported a short afro. He dressed in a cassock with a white collar and a cross hung from his neck. The intense blue of his eyes contrasted his skin and complimented his features.

Cheyenne took a shallow breath and lowered her head.

"That's Dominick," Steven said. He shifted the groceries into one hand and reached for her bags. "He's their brother."

She passed her sacks to him. "He has a different father?"

Jonny stood in the threshold, leaning against the door frame which separated the living room and dining room. "Our mother was a Scarlet Letter," he said. "We all have different fathers." He stood upright, looking from Dominick's photo to Cheyenne. "Sandra wants you."

The hairs on Cheyenne's arms stood erect. She scanned the living room, fixating on the inglenook. On each side of the recessed area were two hand-carved benches molded into arching boughs over the mantle of the fireplace. Somehow, she knew this fireplace.

Goosebumps washed across her body in waves toward her face. She stared wide-eyed into the black abyss. *I shouldn't have come.*

Steven followed her gaze to the stonework around the firebox. On the elm mantel next to the urn, a wolf spider suspended down from the granite apron. "It's just a spider," he said.

"I know," she said, walking away.

Capri wrapped her arm around Steven's, watching Cheyenne enter the dining room and turn left, disappearing behind the wall. She tightened her grip around Steven, sneering. "She's after your attention and I don't like it."

Steven rolled his eyes. "Can you do me a favor?" he asked.

"Anything for you, baby."

"I need you to stop bringing up her bruises."

"I'm only making small talk. Besides, aren't you curious why she would let someone do that to her?"

Steven scoffed. "You seriously believe she let someone hit her?"

"You don't? I read an article where women hurt themselves or allowed others to hurt them to attract attention."

Steven balanced the weight in his hands. "I know there are women who do that, but I doubt Cheyenne is one of them. Now, I'm not going to tell you again, stop bring up her injures."

"Why do you care? You attracted to her?"

Steven rolled his eyes. "Jealousy is an ugly color."

Capri crossed her arms. "I'm not jealous. She's fat and ugly."

"Keep it up, and I'll call you a cab."

Capri plopped down on the sofa. "Fine, I won't even mention her or look at her."

"One more thing," Steven said. "If you don't want Jon jumping down your throat, I'd stay clear of him."

"What, you just want me to sit here?"

"Do whatever you want, just stay away from him and stop talking about her bruises."

"Maybe I should go home."

"Maybe you should," Steven replied walking into the dining room.

The fire poker fell smoothly across the mouth of the fireplace and whispers emanated from the black abyss.

Capri walked to the inglenook; soot sprinkled onto the hearthstone. She kneeled on the outer hearth, and crawled on her hands. She slanted her head, looking up to the damper.

2

Jonny kneaded the seasoning into the ground beef. He could not pry his thoughts from Jackson. The encounter disproved his theory of phenomenon only happening in Cheyenne's presence. Maybe he needed to get some rest. He hadn't hallucinated since he was a kid, not since the barn. This felt different. He recalled the fatigue and the confusion of those days. He was lucid at the garage, tired, but lucid. And again, at Cheyenne's house, though he couldn't explain the lost time. What if Sandra's right? Maybe it was PTSD . . . maybe.

The fetid aroma from Cheyenne's house permeated Jonny's nostrils. He wrinkled his nose, sniffing the air. He stared at the patty in hand and inhaled. His thoughts derailed into an acknowledgement; he had smelled this putrid scent many years ago. He took a slow, deep breath, closing his eyes and clenching his jaw.

The chair wreathed in flame imprinted his mind's eye.

His eyelids rose and he tossed the patty onto the platter. He pinched another serving of ground beef, glancing at Cheyenne; they were alone.

Cheyenne caught his stare and glanced away. The lack of jibber-jabber made the awkward tension between them more pronounced. She continued chopping the celery and gave the kitchen a once-over. The humorous notion hit her: at any other time, she would love this kitchen. "You have a lovely home, a lovely kitchen."

Jonny's eyes darted around the kitchen and dining room.

Cheyenne followed his eyes under the hanging cabinets of the breakfast bar and into the formal dining room on the opposite side. She read his face; he was mulling something in what she assumed was his shattered mind. Nodding in accord with himself, she wondered if he had a similar affliction to her own.

"Thank you," he said, resuming his task. "My grandfather was an Italian immigrant who loved to cook from scratch. He helped me, along with my brothers, remodel the kitchen to accommodate family gatherings."

"You have another brother?"

"Biologically, no. But I consider Steven a brother."

Cheyenne's eyes combed the golden-oak cabinets and the red marble counters. "I love how much counter space you have. Whose idea was it to line the entire kitchen with counters and cabinets?"

"My grandfather's. He, um, was a master wood worker. We cut and carved them out of recycled wood."

"You carved the cabinets?"

"Mm-hmm. Installed the lighting, too," he said, motioning under the cabinets to the recessed lights.

She turned around and pointed into the dining room. "And the table?"

"Out of East Indian Rose wood. Some of it went into the chess board in the hutch."

She looked at the large China hutch. "That, too?"

Jonny chuckled. "Goodwill provided it. GG, my grandmother, couldn't live without it. Caused a huge debate with grandpa. Grandpa used to cringe every time he walked past it."

She caught a hint of sadness in his story. His word choices lead her to believe his grandfather was no more. "You two were close?"

Jonny replied with a single nod. He remained quiet for a moment and then faced her. "I owe you an apology."

She scraped her celery into a glass bowl. "For breaking into my home?"

"And for the way I behaved last night. I was rude, and it was uncalled for."

She moved on to dicing the onion. "Where I come from there's a saying: *Maitheanas do nàmhaid, ach cuimhnich ainm a 'bhastard.* It means 'Forgive your enemy but remember the bastard's name'." She stopped dicing and turned to him. "I forgive you, but I won't forget it."

He placed the patty on the platter and grabbed the last of the beef. "Neither would I."

She scraped the onion into the bowl and then pulled back the tab on a can of olives. "You've been relatively mute since the store." She dumped a handful of olives onto the cutting board. "Penny for your thought."

He played with the meatball. "I thought I saw something."

Her knife paused. "What?"

He pressed the ground beef against his palm. “This boy, his eyes were white. His voice was, I don’t know, it was too mature. The weird thing, though, it was like he knew me.”

That wasn’t her doing, but she was interested. “What did he say?”

“It doesn’t matter.” He rounded the edges on the patty. “I’m sure I imagined the whole thing.” He faced her. “I’ve been excessively busy of late and haven’t been getting enough rest.” He added the last burger to the platter. “I’ve been seeing things, too.”

“Like what?”

“At my shop, I saw these amber-colored lights and shadows that spoke to me.”

She stopped prepping her potato salad. *He* fixated on Jonny, taking pleasure in toying with him. Jonny’s anger was raw, unfiltered. Did he really believe last night was a figment of his imagination? She recalled the dark circles around his eyes, highlighting the heavy red veins within them. She resumed chopping, glancing at him. He needed to know the truth; his life depended on it.

“What about you? You’ve been reserved since your neighbor walked out his house.” He pointed to her battered body. “Did he hit you?”

They silently stared at each other.

Jonny motioned to the scars coming up her back and to her shoulders. “He hurts you, doesn’t he?”

She shook her head. “Ryder gets belligerent when he drinks, but he’s harmless.” She went back to slicing the olives. “He hides a lot of pain.”

“Then who?”

She tossed the olives into the bowl.

He stood beside her. “I get it,” Jonny said, pumping soap into his hand. “You’re scared to talk, but there are places you can go and programs you can do to get help."

"It doesn't matter where I go, they will always find me."

Jonny's brows narrowed. "*They*?"

The sliding glass door opened, and Sandra poked in her head. "Grill's ready."

Jonny sidestepped to the breakfast bar, peeking between the bar's gap. He waved Sandra away. "Be right out."

Sandra smiled, shutting the door.

He returned to the sink, scrubbing under his nails. "I'm assuming 'they' refers to more than one person." He dipped his hands under the faucet. "If you're not comfortable talking with me or Sandra, GG's a retired state prosecutor. She also provides counseling at the church. She'd be able to help you better than anyone."

Her mind focused on the arduous task ahead. Jonny's astuteness made her realize she slipped. She stabbed her knife into a boiling pot of potatoes. She turned off the gas burner and then removed her crisped bacon from the paper-towel-lined plate. She set the bacon on her cutting board, butting the edge of the knife against the ends of the bacon.

"Do you really care, or are you being polite?" she asked.

He turned off the water and reached over her for the paper towels. "Look, setting our differences aside, nobody deserves to be used as a punching bag."

Cheyenne gave the bacon a rough chop. They made good stride, patching their differences, regardless of how miniscule. Had *he* not ruined their first encounter, would they have been friends? It didn't matter. She was about to add more pressure to their already fractured relationship. "I need to tell you something. Something I've not told anyone in a long time."

He removed the hotdogs from the fridge. "I'm listening."

Jonny had a temper and she feared his reaction. "I don't know what happened at Sherm's, but the lights and shadows at your shop were real."

His body stiffened. "Excuse me?"

Capri entered the dining room. The breakfast bar cabinets obscured her face. "What caused you to scream?"

Cheyenne rocked the knife on its point and froze.

"Shut up, Capri," Jonny said. He tossed the hotdogs to the counter. "You want to run that by me again?"

Cheyenne laid the knife down and placed her palms on the counter. She stared out the window above the sink.

"Well, are you going to answer him?" Capri asked.

Jonny glanced at Capri. He could only see her torso in the gap below the cabinets. "I can stir the pot on my own," he said. He focused back on Cheyenne. "Answer me. What happed yesterday?"

Cheyenne lowered her head. She balled her hands into fists. "Why are you doing this?"

Capri smirked, tapping her pointer finger on the breakfast bar. "It's fun watching you tremble."

Cheyenne turned and took a step to the side, looking around the breakfast bar cabinet; Capri wore a smile. "Please stop."

"Ignore that bimbo and answer me, please. What happened when I was in your house; who spoke to me? What were those lights in my garage?"

"Tell him why you don't share happy family memories; why you're alone."

Cheyenne snatched the knife from the cutting board and Jonny stepped forward to intervene.

"Aw, struck a nerve, did I?" Capri antagonized.

Cheyenne stepped around the suspended cabinets, safeguarding Capri's head from the kitchen light, and met her glowing amber gaze.

Jonny took a few steps closer.

Cheyenne turned so she could watch him. "Jonny, please, you don't understand."

He held out his hand. "Give me the knife." He was calm but stern in his demand. He stepped a little closer, watching the knife. "Give it to me before someone gets hurt."

Cheyenne stared at his overworked hand. His fingers had blisters and calluses. The first three fingers of his right hand were scared. She turned the knife around, handing him the handle.

"*Laissez les bon temps roule*," Capri said.

Jonny snatched the knife and stormed around the breakfast bar. "What'd you say?"

Cheyenne grabbed his arm, tugging him back.

Capri turned and walked away, heading out the sliding glass door.

Jonny went after her but Cheyenne held firm to his arm and jerked him back.

He flung her off and she flew backward into the stove. "Hmph!" The oven handle struck the middle of her back.

He tossed the knife on the bar's counter and stepped to her aid. "Sorry. I didn't mean to hurt you."

She stumbled to her feet, holding her back. "I need to go." She pushed his hands away. "It's not safe."

He glanced at the knife and followed her into the living room. "Not safe? You're the one pointing knives at people."

Cheyenne's eye landed on the fireplace. "You understand nothing."

She opened the front door and Jonny slammed the it shut. He towered over her, holding the door closed.

"Then talk. What happened yesterday, huh?" He rubbed his nose between his thumb and forefinger knuckle.

She turned around, briefly glancing at the fireplace. She shifted her attention back to Jonny.

His eyes narrowed, his nostrils flared, and his jaw flexed.

Jonny's enraged green eyes triggered an evocation; *If anything happens to my son, I'll kill you.* A dull phantom ache radiated across her love handles. The picture frames, the fireplace, Jonny, it all flooded back to her. Three years ago, her closest friend died and she spiraled. She had a bizarre dream she chalked up to her drug induced suicide attempt. But here she was, living it. Jonny the man in her dream. Her eyes targeted a picture of a little boy. His son, was he the boy giggling?

"I must leave!"

"Not until you answer my questions. Where did the lights come from?"

A thick, black brume slithered from the mouth of the fireplace.

She pulled and tugged on his arm, but she could not remove it. She pushed against his chest, but he did not budge. "Please! I need to leave."

He pounded the door next to her head with an open palm. "Answer me! What happened to me when I was inside your house?"

Her tears fell freely. "I don't know!"

"Bullshit!" Jonny punched the door. "What happened yesterday in my shop?"

Steven grabbed Jonny and pulled him back. He slid deftly between them and set a wide, staggered stance, maintaining a comfortable distance between himself and Jonny. "I don't know what your problem is, but you need to back the fuck off."

Cheyenne rushed out the house, tripping over a child sitting on the porch, removing his shoes.

"Ow!" cried the boy, followed by a sickening thud.

Jonny sidestepped Steven, but Steven repositioned in front of him. He grabbed Steven's shirt and brought his fist up. "If you don't let me go to my son, I'll knock you out."

"SANDRA!" a woman screamed.

Both men ran out the door. Jonny to his son, Jacob, and Steven toward Adélaïde, the DeLuca kids' grandmother.

Adélaïde was at the bottom of the stairs, holding Cheyenne's head. "She tripped over Jacob and smacked her head hard on the steps."

Cheyenne lay unconscious, her bare feet partially up the stairs.

Jonny picked Jacob up and examined him.

"I'm okay, Daddy."

He kissed Jacob's forehead and hugged him tight. He looked at Cheyenne's body. He shifted his stare to Steven. "I'll get Sandra."

Adélaïde brushed Cheyenne's hair from her face. "Why are her eyes wet? Why is she all black and blue?"

Steven stammered, lost for words.

"What happened?"

He shook his head. "I don't know." He embraced her aged hand. "We have a problem, though."

Adélaïde lifted her head. "You're not suggesting Jon did this?"

"Not at all."

Sandra ran out the front door and down the stairs. "What happened?"

Steven patted Adélaïde's hand.

She nodded. "Later, then."

Sandra peeled back Cheyenne's eyelids and watched her

pupils dilate. She checked Cheyenne's pulse and watched her breathing. She examined the back of her neck. "Did anyone see what happened?"

"She ran out the house and tripped over Jacob," Adélaïde said. "She was trying to avoid stepping on him, but she was off balance and fell, hitting her head on the edge of the steps."

Sandra palpated the back of Cheyenne's head; a bump had already formed. "How hard did she hit?"

"Pretty hard. I heard the smack from the Eldorado."

"You want me to call 9-1-1?" Steven asked.

Sandra shook her head. "No. She told me she never wanted to be a patient in our hospital or any other hospital."

"What?" Adélaïde asked. "She's so young. What if she has a brain bleed or worse?"

Capri stood in the entryway; her eyes brown.

"Steven, can you carry her to Jonny's room?" Sandra asked.

"Why does he have to carry her?" Capri asked, stomping onto the front porch. She crossed her arms. "She probably threw herself down the stairs for your attention."

"That's it," Steven said. He walked up the first step. "I can't take your jealousy anymore. You and I are done. Once Cheyenne is taken care of, I'll call you a cab."

"I'm not—"

"Shut up, Capri," Sandra said.

Steven scooped Cheyenne into his arms, asking, "You sure Jon's room is the best place?"

3

Jacob sat on the living room floor, playing with his G.I. Joe. He shifted his attention to the adults entering the house and going down the hallway. He leaned to the side, watching them disappear into his father's room.

"I don't know who she is, Sarge, but daddy says to stay away."

The crumbling of soot on the fireplace hearth drew Jacob's focus. He sat back on his butt, staring at the debris.

More soot fell from the flue.

He removed his G.I. Joe from the toy Jeep and carried him to the fireplace. He hugged Sarge and looked up the chimney. "Whatcha doin' up there?"

Nine
Investigation

1

Adélaïde stared out Jonny's bedroom window, supporting her chin and nose with her thumb and forefinger. Her other hand held her elbow from across her chest. Her boys bickered in the backyard. She couldn't catch everything, but the vulgar language she heard unnerved her.

Steven swung his fist and missed.

She lowered her eyes, absorbing the muffled hatred resonating through the double-pained glass. "Explain how one woman could tear those two apart."

Sandra removed the stethoscope from her ears, hanging it around her neck. "It's my fault."

Adélaïde stood at the foot of the bed. "Look at me."

Sandra did as commanded. "He's so upset with me. I forgot to call you and asked you to keep Jacob away from the house."

Adélaïde shook her head. "There's more to it than that." She returned to the window. "I just watched Steven swing at your brother. Steven's the calm, cool-headed of the two, Jon's voice of reason." Adélaïde recollected how Steven came to be a part of the family. Jonny refused to attend therapy with the psychiatrist. Out of the blue, he agreed to go if they adopt Steven. She turned, staring at Cheyenne's battered body. "How did she get those bruises?"

"We don't know."

"How do you not know? She's your friend, isn't she?" Adélaïde dismissively turned her eyes back to the window. She took a deep breath. "Did your brother hit her?"

Sandra stood defensively. "Of course not. How could you even think that?"

Adélaïde sighed in relief.

"Cheyenne's quiet at work. She always wears long sleeves, no matter how hot. People talk about her behind her back, and she always eats by herself. I tried for a long time to get her to talk with me."

"You obviously succeeded."

"Sort of. She was walking home from work in the rain. I pulled over and offered her a ride. She was hesitant, but got in. She told me her car was broken, and I told her about Jonny."

"Is she a nurse, too?"

Sandra shook her head. "She works in the ER as an admitting clerk." She walked to the window and wrapped her arm around Adélaïde. "He's different."

Adélaïde wrapped her arm around Sandra. "Which one?"

Sandra shifted her eyes to the lilies. "Jonny. I brought her to his shop yesterday. For a moment, I thought he had some interest in her."

"Still playing matchmaker?"

"He called her Haven."

"Who's Haven?"

Sandra shrugged. "Everything went awry when the storm took out the power." She walked back to the bed and sat on the foot end. "When the lights came back on, he was mean, rude, aggressive toward her."

Adélaïde continued to watch her boys; they stopped arguing and sat under the pergola.

"You're sure he didn't lay a hand on her?"

"He would never hit a girl, you know that."

Adélaïde walked away from the window. "If he didn't like her, why'd he bring her here?"

"Because of me."

"Jon doesn't do things without reason." She looked at Cheyenne. "Time to poke the bear."

"GG, Steven said Jonny's been having nightmares again."

Adélaïde grabbed her cross necklace. She lowered her eyes and exited the room. She entered the living room, where Jacob lay on the floor. "Why don't you go take a bath and get ready for bed?"

Jacob closed his coloring book. "Why's everyone fighting?"

"Because of a misunderstanding. Now go wash up."

She made her way out the sliding glass door and to the pergola.

Both men sat, neither spoke or looked to the other.

"You two are too old to be bickering like teenagers."

Steven stood. "You want my seat?"

"No." She focused on Jonny. "I want you to tell me the truth. Did you lay your hand on that girl?"

Jonny jumped to his feet, curling his hands into fists. "You tell her that crap?"

Adélaïde pushed them apart. "Sit, the both of you. He didn't have to tell me anything. The entire neighborhood can hear you two out here yelling and screaming at each other. Your son is in the house, listening."

Jonny locked eyes with Steven. "I never touched her."

Steven redirected his focus to Adélaïde and awaited her

cross-examination.

"We all know Jon's not a liar."

"He doesn't tell the truth either," Steven said. "Not the whole truth anyways."

She turned to Steven. "Why are you so convinced he hit her?"

Steven started to answer but she redirected him to Jonny. Steven shifted his eyes, glaring at Jonny. "I walked into the living room. Cheyenne was crying, begging for you to let her go. You stood over her, punching the door and yelling at her."

"Did you see him hit her?"

"No."

Adélaïde shifted her questioning to Jonny. "Who's Haven?"

His animus toward Steven showed on his face.

Steven relaxed back into his chair. "You can give all the nasty looks you want, but I didn't tell her."

Adélaïde drew herself to Steven, losing her prosecutor stance. "You know who she is?"

Both men stared at each other in dead silence; Jonny shook his head.

Steven broke eye contact and addressed Adélaïde. "Though he's being an asshole," Steven focused back on Jonny, "I promised I wouldn't tell."

Jonny nodded once at Steven and walked away.

"I'm not done," Adélaïde said.

He stopped and stared at the sliding glass door. "I know," he replied somberly, retreating into the house.

She took the now vacant seat, crossing her legs, and stared at Steven.

He avoided eye contact, cleared his throat, and straightened his shirt.

She propped her elbow on the armrest of the chair and cradled the side of her face into the L-shape of her hand. "You know you have to let him cool his head before you go at him like that."

Steven rubbed his temple. "I know. He's been a pain since yesterday. I let my frustration get the best of me."

"I know, I saw you swing at him."

"I should apologize, but . . . "

She looked at him incredulously.

"I will, I will," Steven said with a grin.

"You're with him all the time. What would cause him to shift drastically like this?"

"He's overworked. He doesn't give himself time off, and he doesn't get enough sleep. Just look at the yard. It hasn't been mowed in a while, he never planted the garden, the flowers need trimming . . . and his room? When have you ever known him to let his dirty clothes spill out of the hamper and pile on the floor?"

"Why do you believe his nightmares have returned?"

Steven brought his left leg up, resting his foot on his right knee. "He screamed Ralphie's name today in the back of my car."

Adélaïde wiped a tear before it fell. "If his nightmares have returned, maybe that's why he isn't sleeping."

"I asked if they returned and Jonny said he only had two. The one today in my car and yesterday when he fell asleep in his office."

"What happened when the shop lost power?"

"I really don't know. The lights came back on, and he was full of anger, rage. I distracted him so the women could leave and he pulled a torque wrench on me."

"He's scared. He always hides his fear behind anger."

"Yeah, I'd agree that. When he pulled the wrench on me, he looked frightened. I talked to him that night and he mentioned seeing lights."

"What sort of lights?"

"I don't know; he won't say."

"Something isn't adding up." She squinted her eyes, trying to fit the pieces together.

Steven shook his head, tapping his thumbs together. "Tonight's my fault. I pushed him into talking to Cheyenne."

"What do you mean?"

"Jon told me he hated her. He said he was forcing himself to hold back his feelings."

Her hand fell to her lap. "Him hold back?"

Steven bobbed his head. "Her bruises bother him. You can tell by his body language."

"You just said her bruises bother him. Your belief Jon hit her is counterintuitive."

"I know what I believe, but I know what I saw." Steven leaned his head back and stared at the stars. "I thought if he could get her to open up, his animosity toward her would dissipate." Steven pressed his lips together, feeling the bump Jonny gave him earlier in the day. Steven shook his head. "Never in a million years would I have thought I would've walked into the scene I did."

"If there's one thing I've learned," Adélaïde said, "you can't see an entire picture if you're only holding scraps."

2

First Sergeant stood on the lip of the tub, guarding the bathroom door.

"What do you look like?" Jacob asked. He scrubbed his hair, listening to the whispers coming from the air vent. He grabbed First Sergeant and held him in the air. "Like Sarge?" Jacob smiled. "Come out so we can play." He returned First Sergeant to his post. “I got a bedtime so I can’t play at night.” He dipped his head back, barely touching the water. “How come you hide in the dark?” Jacob sat back up. “I like playing hide-and-seek. What other games do like?”

3

Steven opened the sliding glass door; his stomach growled at the fragrance of hamburgers. He helped Adélaïde up the step, allowing her to enter first.

The chess board Eber and Jonny whittled together lay folded in the center of the dining room table. Steven knew all was water under the bridge.

“Smells good,” Adélaïde said.

Jonny removed the last cheeseburger from the skillet. “Want me to make you a plate?”

“We ate at Subway on the way home.” She kissed his cheek. “Portland’s a long drive. I think I’ll head to bed.”

Steven tapped Jonny’s shoulder with the back of his hand. He pointed to the dining room with his head. “Want me to make some coffee?”

“Yeah. I need to check on Jacob first.”

4

The light from the cracked bathroom door seeped into the hall, illuminating Jonny’s path. The fetid aroma, from Cheyenne’s home, still haunted him, growing stronger the closer he approached the bathroom door. He pinched his nose. The putrid smell was a reminder not only of his past, but of the woman lying in his bed. If not for Capri’s dumb ass, he would have answers.

The soft melody of Jacob's voice drew Jonny from his thoughts. He pushed open the door. "Whatcha hummin'?"

Jacob put soap suds around his G.I. Joe's face. "A song my friend taught me."

"Who's your friend?"

Jacob dunked his toy under the water. "Nicholas." He looked up at his father. "Daddy, do you and Uncle Steven hate each other?"

Jonny sat on the lip of the tub; his jeans soaking up the water. He held Jacob's face in his palm and smiled. "Hate's a strong word. We get frustrated with each other from time to time, but we never hate."

"Did you really hit the strange lady in your room?"

He leaned Jacob back and rinsed the remaining soap from his hair. "What have I told you about hitting girls?"

"Real men don't hit girls."

He helped Jacob stand and splashed the bathwater up his son's legs, rinsing the suds. He spun Jacob, rinsing his back.

"Why does Uncle Steven say you hit her?"

He grabbed a clean towel and wrapped Jacob's body. He plucked him out of the tub and dried him. "Sometimes, what we see is misconstrued."

Jacob cocked his head, "Mis-what?"

He grabbed Jacob's underwear from the counter. "Where are your pajamas?"

"It's too hot."

"Alright." He held the racecar underwear open and Jacob stepped into them. "Misconstrued means to misunderstand." He pulled Jacob's underwear up and kissed his head. "Go say goodnight and then hop into bed."

Jacob ran out of the bathroom.

Jonny uncorked the drain. "Jacob!"

Jacob popped his head back into the bathroom. “Yeah, Daddy?”

“I don’t want you singing or humming that song ever again.”

“How come?”

“Your auntie doesn’t like it.” He removed the toy from the bathtub and handed to Jacob. “Go say goodnight.”

Jacob snatched the G.I. Joe and ran out the door.

Jonny cleaned the mess in the tub and gathered his son’s clothes from the floor. His mind raced at what the lights could be and at what could have caused the shadow in his office.

Sandra knocked on the doorjamb. “Can I come in?”

“Yeah, I’m finished.”

She rubbed her hands down her quads. “Can we talk?”

He walked past her. “Not tonight.”

“I fucked up,” she said. “I forgot to call GG.”

He stopped in the doorway, clenching his jaw.

“I’m sorry.”

He stared at the floor. “I made it clear; I didn’t want Cheyenne near my son.” He made eye contact with Sandra. “I’m holding you to your word. Break it off with her.”

Jacob’s muffled voice crept out into the hallway; Johnny stopped to eavesdrop.

“Daddy doesn’t lie.”

Jonny pushed the door open and flipped on the light. “Who you talking to?”

Jacob sat in his race car bed, playing with his G.I. Joe. His eyes shifted to his closet. “Nicholas.”

Jonny grabbed the toy and pulled back the blankets.

“Just the sheet,” Jacob said, crawling under.

Jonny handed back the toy. “You and Nicholas go to bed.” He kissed Jacob’s head and turned off the light and left the door ajar. He entered the dining room where Steven awaited with the invitation of coffee and chess. He sat across from Steven and sipped his coffee.

"I've never asked before." Steven waved his fingers around the edge of the board. "What are the letters and numbers?"

A faint smile formed on Jonny's lips. "That's how I learned to play, by using grids to track the pieces. I'm teaching Jacob the same way."

"Why do you need the grid when you can see the board?"

"It was used for playing long distance; by mail. It always helped me. Gave me an extra layer to work with. Sort of a mental map." He pointed at the numbers along the side of the board. "The grid is numbered up and down, starting from the white pieces, one through eight. Then A-H from your left to your right."

Steven removed his cup from his lips, contemplating his first move. "I'm sorry I swung at you?"

Jonny took his shirt off, wiping the sweat from the back of his neck and underarms. "I'm not mad you swung at me. I'm pissed you think I hit her."

Steven opened the game by moving the king's knight from B1 to C3. "You, uh, gonna tell me what happened tonight?"

Jonny set his cup down, moving the king's pawn forward one. "Nope. If I had it my way, her ass would be at Mercy Medical and out of this house."

Steven moved his pawn from A2 to A3. "Did you at least find out how she got those bruises?"

Jonny grabbed his queen and lowered his head.

"Blindsided by your own agenda?" Steven asked.

Jonny moved the queen from D8 to F6. "From what I gathered; more than one person is abusing her."

Steven moved his pawn forward to H4. "What's happening to you? You're turning into a heartless prick."

Jonny moved his bishop from F8 to C5 and sipped his coffee. "She confirmed I didn't have a PTSD episode, nor did I hallucinate. What I saw was real."

"And what did you see?"

"It doesn't matter." He took another drink of his coffee. "When she wakes, I'll take her home and I won't ever see her again."

"It does matter." Steven drank the last of his coffee. He set his cup down and ran his middle finger around the lip of the cup. "Verbal abuse can be more damaging than physical abuse."

"Pfft! I didn't verbally abuse her."

Steven moved his knight within striking distance of Jonny's queen and released his fingers; the knight landed within Jonny's pawn's striking zone.

Jonny's fingers hovered over his active bishop. He moved his hand above his queen.

"What I saw when I walked into this house was abuse."

Jonny lowered his hand. "More coffee?"

Steven relinquished his cup. "If you were to walk in on me, or anyone else, treating Sandra in the same manner you did Cheyenne, what would your reaction be?"

Jonny sat down, handing Steven his cup; they locked eyes.

"I'm immune to your ugly stares," Steven said. "I also don't care if she validated you. Until you tell me what happened tonight and last night—"

"It has to do with the past." Jonny slouched back in his chair, staring mindlessly at the game.

Steven tapped his finger on the table. "How do lights, a lapse in time, and Cheyenne connect to your past?"

He shrugged his shoulders and shook his head. "She started to open up, but that bimbo interrupted us." He rested his elbow on the table and rubbed his jaw. He studied the board. “I lost the traction I made with Cheyenne and couldn’t gain it back.” He shifted his gaze to Steven. “I lost my temper, but I never touched her.”

“I want to believe you, but I know what I saw.” He sipped his coffee. “You never answered my question. Are you ever going to tell us what happened to you? Or who Ralphie is?”

“If you can ever beat me,” Jonny said. He moved his bishop to F2, capturing Steven’s pawn in front of Steven’s king’s bishop. “I’ll not only tell you who Ralphie is,” he tipped Steven’s king backward off the board, “I’ll tell you everything about the past.”

Steven focused on the medium round scars on Jonny’s chest, abdomen, and biceps. “Everything?”

“That’s what I said.”

Steven glanced at his watch. “It’s late. Rematch tomorrow?”

“It’s a date.”

Steven leaned back in his chair. “When I called Capri’s cab, I dumped her.”

“Thank God.”

“Thought that would make you happy.” He stood, downing his coffee. “Sandra said you can have her room; she’ll sleep with GG.”

It’s late, you take it. I’m gonna stay up and do laundry.”

5

Jacob used the sheet to clean the sweat from his face. “Hot.” He grabbed the glass of water from the nightstand his father always left.

The closet door crept open, and a tall shadow resembling Sarge exited.

Jacob put his water cup down and crawled to the end of the

bed. "Nicholas?"

The shadow marched to the bedroom door and disappeared into the hallway.

Jacob crawled out of bed and poked his head out, "Nicholas?" He looked into the living room.

Jonny's head was tilted back and his mouth gaped. The TV played Young Guns with volume muted and the subtitles on.

Jacob tiptoed past his aunt's bedroom, making his way to his father's room.

Cheyenne clutched the bedding, speaking Gaelic. "*Seanair stad.*"

"I'm not allowed around her," Jacob said.

Cheyenne thrashed in bed, moaning, "*Duilich seanmhair,*" repeatedly.

Jacob took a tiny step past the threshold. "I can? How?" He grabbed the doorframe and looked down the hall toward the living room. He turned back around, tiptoeing to the bedside. "What do I do now?" He placed his petite hand on Cheyenne's fist and looked back at the dark corner.

6

Jonny woke, rubbing his nose. He glanced at his watch; 3:10 AM. He sniffed the air, stood, and followed the rotting trail down the hall, poking his head into Jacob's room. Empty. He ran to his bedroom, refusing to enter. "Jacob, get over here?"

Jacob jumped, letting go of Cheyenne's hand.

Jonny sniffed the air; the smell was pungent.

Jacob stared at the dark corner and quickly grabbed her hand again.

"Right now!"

Jacob shook his head. "No, Daddy. Nicholas says you have

to come to me."

A dull amber light illuminated from the far corner.

Jonny stepped into his room, staring at it.

A second amber light appeared.

He grabbed Jacob.

Cheyenne immediately stopped thrashing and moaning and

Jonny became immobile, unable to release Jacob's hand. The stench overwhelmed his nostrils. Invisible flames lapped at his skin; he could feel heat washing over his body. The pain was unbearable. He screamed, but no sound vocalized.

Brutal visions of dead children sped furiously in his mind. They seemed so real, so tangible. He closed his eyes, but it only made them more vivid, more intense, more rapid.

The images stopped abruptly, and the pain dissipated. Ralphie faded into focus and whispered, "There you are."

"Stop it!" Jacob cried. "Stop it, Nicholas!"

Jonny shifted his eyes to Jacob and then toward the corner.

The amber lights shone brilliantly against the unlit corner.

Jonny attempted to move, but his body refused to cooperate. He tried to tell Jacob to run, but only unintelligible murmurs escaped.

A dark misty shadow catapulted from the corner of the wall with a triumphant cry: "JONNY!"

Ten

Escaping the Nightmare

Lee stood behind Ralphie, wrapping his arm around the child's chest. He brought his other arm up, holding his knife under Ralphie's chin. He pressed the blade firmly against the boy's throat and smiled at Jonny.

"Ow, ow, OW!"

Red droplets appear beneath the blade.

"OPEN YOUR EYES!"

Ralphie opened his eyes, struggling against Lee's arm.

Jonny knew he couldn't protect Ralphie from the horror surrounding them forever. Why today? He waited for the reality of the carnage to strike Ralphie.

The bodies of dead children hung upside down from the beams. The dripping sound came from one of the dead boys' slashed throats as it drained into a container. The two guard dogs chewed on the hands and ears of the deceased.

Ralphie's eyes widened, and his jaw dropped. He stopped fighting and turned around, reaching for Lee to hold him. "Mommy!"

Lee knocked him to the ground.

"Ralphie, look at me, not at them," Jonny said.

"Stop coddling him," Mickey said.

"I want my mommy!"

"LOOK AT ME!"

Ralphie did as Jonny demanded. The wet patch in the center of his pants grew and ran down this leg.

Jonny held his right side and readjusted. He grimaced and grunted with the slightest movement. "I know you're scared but everything's gonna be okay."

Lee threw his blade at Jonny and it landed next to Jonny's foot. "Shut up."

Jonny did not flinch. He turned his head and spit the metallic flavor from his mouth.

"Find your happy place."

Jonny furrowed his brows. He did not recognize the voice. He rolled his head against the bars, facing his captors.

Mickey stood motionless, his fingers on a half-extracted Lucky Strike. Lee crouched fixed near Jonny's feet. His outstretched hand inches from the knife in the ground.

"Go to the place that makes you the happiest."

The mature voice came from Ralphie.

Jonny closed his eyes. Must have taken too many blows to the head. He turned around and looked inside the cell.

Al, too, froze in time; his head lowered.

"Al, say somethin'."

Al scurried toward him on his hands and knees. He reached the iron bars and jerked up his head. "Go to your safe place."

Jonny fell backwards. He flipped over and looked at Ralphie.

"Remember your happy place. Your safe place," the voice said again from Ralphie.

Jonny splinted his side and stood.

The dead children pointed to the barn door. The boy whose

blood dripped into the container was the last to point. His dead eyes opened, and the voice spoke. "End the nightmare."

Jonny ran to the door, grunting in pain with each breath. He slid open the door and the night lamps blinded him. He shielded his eyes and ran out.

"There you are," a man said.

Jonny lowered his arm. He stood in an exam room where a man in a lab coat sat next to a desk. On the desk, a pencil and paper.

"Have a seat, Jon."

Jonny cautiously made his way to the desk and sat in the empty chair. He looked around the room, confused. How was he here and not outside?

"You're a fast learner. You learned sign language, fluently, in a matter of months."

Jonny picked up the pencil. The paper contained multiplication problems. His eyes narrowed. This was a memory from when he was seven. He began answering the math problems. "Doc?"

"Yes?"

"You told me isolation would cause my mind to play tricks on me."

"If you allow it. Have you?"

"I don't think so. I practiced sign language, imagining conversations with my brother and sister."

The doctor removed the pencil from Jonny's hand. "I want to challenge your intellect." He placed a board in front of him asking, "Have you ever played chess?"

He shook his head. "Am I going crazy?"

The doctor placed the pieces on their appropriate squares; Jonny helped.

"Is this the place you feel the safest?" asked the voice escaping the doctor. It opened the game with the king's knight at C3. "Concentrate. Where do you feel the safest and go there?"

Jonny pinched himself. "Ow."

The voice chuckled. "You make this real. Now close your eyes and go to the safest place you can think of."

"I've gone insane," Jonny said, closing his eyes. "I've let the darkness take hold." He took a few deep breaths and slowly exhaled.

"You got to save her."

Jonny opened his eyes. He stood in the bread aisle of Sherm's. Jackson stood before him; one eye brown, the other white.

Jonny looked around and then at himself. "This isn't right." He touched his body. "I was an adult when this took place."

"You're not concentrating," the voice said.

He looked back at Jackson. "This is her doing."

Jackson interlocked his fingers, resting his hands in front of his navel. "It's my doing."

Jonny balled his small hands into fists. "Where's my son?" He swung at Jackson and went through him, falling to the ground. "Who are you? What are you?"

"Escape the nightmare and reunite with your family."

"Are you the shadow, from my shop?"

"No."

"The amber lights, then?"

"No. Now, concentrate."

Jonny closed his eyes, took a deep breath, and exhaled.

"He's coming," a young, panicked female said.

Jonny knew the voice and opened his eyes. "Sandra?"

He surveyed the new room. Drawings of space rockets covered the blue painted walls.

Someone wrapped their arms around him, holding him against their body.

A young Sandra shut the bedroom door. “Dominick, you gotta get him to stop crying.”

Jonny looked at the dark complexion holding him. “Dominick?”

Sandra crawled onto the bed. “Stop crying.”

“I’m not crying,” Jonny said.

Sandra clapped her hands. “This isn’t your happy place,” the voice said, escaping her mouth.

“Why don’t I remember this?”

“Perhaps you were too young.” It pointed to Dominick. “Now, do as your brother says.”

“Let’s play a game, Jonathan. Close your eyes and match your breathing to mine.”

Jonny closed his eyes and focused on Dominick’s rhythm. He took several deep breaths, not once feeling pain from his right side.

For the first time, he felt relaxed. Wind caressed his face, the sun warmed his skin, and he smelled wheat.

“Jonny?”

He opened his eyes, but the intensity of the blue sky forced them shut.

“Jonny?”

He shielded his eyes and squinted them open. “Mama?”

Eleven

Vindication

1

Cheyenne moaned, groping the back of her head. "Ow." She remembered little after running out the door. She sat up, scanning her surroundings. A lamp on each side of the bed illuminated the room and a gentle breeze, coming from the partially opened window, played with the curtains. A bureau against the wall, opposite of the bed, displayed younger photos of the DeLuca family and a younger Steven. Amongst the photos, a wooden rosary encircled ceramic prayer hands.

She pulled back the blankets and sighed. At least that part of the dream didn't ring true. What else was different? She opened the closet. A small part of her expected a red brick wall but the closet was normal and organized. The clothes hung straight on the hangers and separated by type. Jeans hung on the left side and shirts hung color coded on the right. Dress clothes hid behind the shirts in plastic bags. A small safe sat on the floor next to dress shoes.

She spotted several canvases with realistic paintings. The one in front was of an old man and a preteen, fishing the river in the woods. They sat on a fallen tree which created a bridge to the other side. Floating the river, a red rose. She flipped to the next painting. It was painted in a bird's eye view of a funeral. Her eyes focused first on the raindrops falling toward the man hugging a casket covered by the American flag. He held a single white rose in one hand and a bottle of beer in the other. On the ground next to his chair, another bottle of beer. Amazed by the depth of details of both paintings, she flipped to the next.

Cheyenne gasped. It was a painting of a single, giant, yellow rose. The artist went into a lot of details to not only showcase the beauty of the flower, but the imperfection, too. The edges of a few petals fringed brown, the green leaves partially eaten, and the thorns, not all pointy-sharp. The most astonishing detail was the illusion of the rose being 3D. She heard of this rose before; her best friend described it to her in detail.

She flipped to the next canvas. It was a painting of a woman lying in a hospital bed with oxygen in her nose. The detail that went into painting the woman . . . she looked lifelike, as if she was there in person. Cheyenne searched for the artist's telltale signature; a single rose painted somewhere within the story they told. She found it, in the reflection of the dying woman's moisten eyes. Holding a single pink rose was Jonny. The painting made Cheyenne emotional. The woman did not smile with her dried, cracked lips, but with her eyes. Was it Jonny's presence that made her happy or the rose? Maybe both.

Cheyenne flipped through the rest of the canvases, paying no attention to the art, searching for the artist's name. She flipped back through the first three. Everyone one of them had the same initial.

Her mind's eyes flashed back to the night she tried to overdose on pills and alcohol. On her bathroom floor, a message spelled out in her vomit: Find JMD.

"Find Jonathan Michael DeLuca."

She spun around, locating the window. In her dream, there was an endless field of yellow calla lilies. What's out there now? She drew open the curtains and honed in on the lilies. Other than needing to be mowed, nothing about the back yard stood out.

She grabbed the wooden rosary from the prayer hands and skimmed her thumb over the letters: D-E-D. She didn't know if this was one of Nicholas's games but she knew it was dangerous to stay.

The walls carried a child's muffled voice down the hall.

Was he the owner of the laughter from her dream? She tiptoed down the hallway and stopped in front of Jacob's room.

Jonny slept in Jacob's bed with his arms out to his sides; his legs draped over the foot end. A light saber and a glow worm highlighting his body.

"Daddy says violence isn't okay."

The child's dialogue stole her attention. At least it wasn't laughter. She continued down the hallway, focusing on the conversation.

"If you know, how come you want to hurt them?"

She closed her eyes and leaned against the wall, mouthing, *please God.*

"It looked like they were hurting."

She rounded the corner, spotting Jacob on the floor near the fireplace with his G.I. Joe.

He stopped pushing his toy Jeep and looked at her. "Are you cold?"

Numb to the goosebumps, she fixated on the fireplace.

"Want a blankie?"

Her eyes welled; *this can't happen again.* She bolted for the door.

Jacob stood hugging his G.I. Joe. "I tried to take your

nightmare away."

She froze with the doorknob in her hand.

"Did Nicholas hurt you like daddy?"

She faced the child. Tears tickled down her face; her eyes darted toward the hall. "What do you mean 'like daddy'?"

Jacob stepped forward, handing his toy to her. "Sarge can keep you safe."

She kneeled in front of him. More tears wetted her cheeks. She feigned a smile. "Such a brave gentleman you are."

The side of Jacob's mouth curled into a half smirk, enhancing more of father's features. "I'm gonna grow up to be brave like daddy."

She glanced at the firebox. "You said Nicholas hurt your daddy, how?"

"He tried to dig into daddy's chest." Jacob pointed at one of her bruises. "Nicholas gave him a bruise like yours."

Cheyenne ran for Jacob's room and tapped Jonny's face. "Wake up!" This was her fault. She knew better.

"It doesn't work," Jacob said, hugging his toy.

She looked over her shoulder. "How long has he been unresponsive?"

"What does that mean?"

She closed her eyes and rephrased. "How long has your daddy been sleeping?"

Jacob stepped further in. "The man covered in light said daddy would be okay if I put light around him."

"Man covered in light?"

"He was outside the window when Nicholas hurt daddy. The man told me to open the curtains and let the moonlight in."

Cheyenne turned her attention back to Jonny. She needed to focus and ask questions later. She shook his shoulders without success.

"The light man touched daddy's head and daddy fell down."

She wound her hand back and slapped Jonny across the face. "Wake up!"

"What the hell are you doing to him?" Adélaïde asked.

Jonny's hands jetted around Cheyenne's throat. He rolled off the bed, landing on top of her.

Adélaïde tugged on his shoulders. "Jon, wake up."

Cheyenne reached for his face but could barely swat at him; his long hair dangled in front of his closed eyes.

"Go get Steven!"

Jacob ran into Sandra's room. "GG needs help!"

Steven hared out of the room and pushed Adélaïde aside. He wrapped his arms around Jonny and jerked back, "Wake up!"

Jonny held firm to Cheyenne's throat.

Adélaïde reached for Jonny's hands, failing to pry them loose.

Cheyenne grabbed his hair and pulled.

Jonny opened his eyes and released her. He fell backwards on top of Steven, staring at Cheyenne.

She wheezed, taking a deep breath. She coughed, struggling for more air.

Adélaïde aided Cheyenne, helping her up. "You must understand. When he has nightmares, it's hard to wake him."

Jonny stared at his hands. "I'm sorry." His eyes shifted to Cheyenne. "I'm sorry."

Cheyenne batted Adélaïde off her. She stumbled to her feet.

Jonny shrugged Steven off him and sat on Jacob's bed. He lowered his head, staring at his hands. "I'm sorry."

"Go wake Sandra," Adélaïde said to Steven. She followed Cheyenne into the living room. "Wait, a minute!"

Cheyenne targeted the front door.

Adélaïde hurried in front of Cheyenne and blocked the door with her body. "He didn't mean to hurt you. Let Sandra triage you before you leave."

Cheyenne massaged her throat, coughing. Her throat was raspy but she could utter, "I'm fine."

2

Jacob handed his father the G.I Joe. "Don't be mad at me, Daddy."

Jonny lifted his head. "Why would I be mad at you?"

Jacob rubbed his nose with his tiny fist. "I told the lady what he did to you. She got sad and tried to wake you up."

Jonny ran into the living room. "Where she at?"

Sandra pointed to the door. "She wouldn't let me check her."

Jonny hurried out of the house. He didn't care he was in his boxers without a shirt to cover his scars; he needed her. He ran to the sidewalk, yelling, "WAIT!" He grabbed her arm and spun her around.

Cheyenne brought up her free hand.

He blocked her swing. "I'm sorry I hurt you." He released her. "I—I—" he stuttered, lost for words. He never laid a hand on a woman until now. Why did it have to be her?

3

Her eyes searched his body. A myriad of round scars adorned his flesh. She didn't notice them when she was focused on waking him. "You have nothing to be sorry about." She turned back around, and he stepped in front of her. "It's my fault," she said, walking around him.

He blocked her path.

"What do you want from me?" she asked.

"The truth."

He deserved to the know the truth, but the courage she mustered yesterday had vanished. Her sorrow lodged in her throat and welled in her eyes. "You have a beautiful family." She exhaled, cleaning her tears. "They aren't safe if I stay."

"I'm aware."

They stared at each other. Both, waited for the other to make the next move.

"You and I are a lot alike," he said. "We both have secrets neither want to discuss. Yesterday, you almost told me yours."

She cleared her throat and stood tall. "Almost doesn't count." She stepped past him.

He stood aside. "They think I hit you."

Cheyenne faced the house where his family watched from the porch. "He never hit me!"

He shook his head. "I need you to make them understand."

"How's that my problem?"

"You knowingly endangered my family. It's the least you can do."

"Pfft. You knowingly endangered them when you invited me. So don't give me the guilt trip bullshit."

"You wouldn't risk coming unless there was a way to make it safe."

"It's too dangerous." She walked backward, pointing at his bruised chest. "As you're aware."

He raked his finger through his hair. "Did you get what you were after? If not, you came for nothing."

He offered a second chance; she didn't know if she'd get another. She glanced at his family, weighing the risk.

"What is it?" Jonny asked.

"What is what?"

"What are you after?"

Her focus toggled between Jonny's eyes. He's smart. "The truth, like you." She stared at the morning sun. "When I say I need to leave, you let me go."

He nodded in agreement.

She pointed to Jacob with her head. "You're to keep your son away from me and out of the house."

"Done. Anything else?"

"Afterwards, you and your family are to stay far away from me, including Sandra."

He extended his hand. "Deal."

They walked toward the house together. Jonny raised his arm in front of Cheyenne and she halted. "Jacob, why don't you and First Sergeant go play in the backyard until breakfast is ready."

Jacob walked to the edge of the porch and handed Cheyenne the G.I. Joe. "Here, Sarge will keep you safe."

She smiled and handed the toy back to Jacob. "I'd feel better if Sarge kept you safe."

Jonny picked Jacob up, kissing his head. "Coffee anyone?"

4

Jacob walked toward the pergola, stopping in the middle of the yard. "You came back." He ran to the end of the fence where the yellow calla lilies grew. "Thank you for helping me last night." He scratched his head. "What's your name?" He was quiet for a few seconds. "I'm Jacob." He cocked his head. "How do you know my name?" He paused. "Yeah, we can be friends." He looked down at Sarge, asking, "Are you like Nicholas?" His brows furrowed. "You know him? Are you his friend, too?" Jacob lowered his eyes, "He is a liar." He held out his toy. "This is First Sergeant, but I call him Sarge. He's a marine like

Uncle Steven." Jacob smiled. "Why are you bright?" Jacob's jaw dropped and his eyes widened. "Wow! Can I touch them?"

5

Jonny placed the clean clothes in the laundry basket in neat stacks, separating Jacob's clothes from his own. He set the laundry basket aside and snatched a white undershirt.

"There's been quite the debate around here," Adélaïde said, "surrounding you and what happened yesterday. We all heard Jon's story, what's your tale?"

Jonny slid his arms through the shirt. "In her glory days, GG was a well-respected State Prosecutor. If you lie, she'll know."

Cheyenne sat down. She glided her fingers over the table. "This table is beautiful."

"My husband, Eber, was a carpenter and an artisan of wood. He and our three boys made it out of East Indian Rosewood."

Jonny pulled a chair out for Adélaïde, then sat next to her and across from Cheyenne.

"Where do I start?" Cheyenne asked.

"Did Jon hit you?" asked Adélaïde.

Jonny sighed. "I can't believe this is still a question."

Adélaïde patted his hand.

Cheyenne's eyes shifted to each person in the room. Anticipation grew the longer she remained silent. "He never hit me."

"My apologies," Steven said.

Cheyenne stood. "I should go now."

"What are the lights?" Jonny asked.

This wasn't part of the deal. Did he lie to her and set her up?

"Where do the lights come from?" Jonny asked.

Was this his intended goal the entire time? She locked eyes with him. "You're playing a dangerous game."

"You would've left already." Jonny opened his hand to her seat. "I only want the truth."

She scanned the room; everyone looked puzzled. She slid back into the chair, landing her eyes on Jonny. Tricked by this asshole. She intertwined her fingers, resting her forearms on the table, and relaxed against the chair. "I believe your fist-pounding, tough-guy persona is an act to hide the fragile little man you are." She glared at him. "That's the truth."

The room echoed in silence.

Sandra sat next to her. "I'm team, Cheyenne," she scooped her ginger hair behind her ears, "but provoking my brother won't solve anything."

"Let her speak," Jonny said.

"Capri said something to him, and it hit the root of him. He went after her with a knife." Cheyenne's focus shifted to Adélaïde. Her wrinkled hand blocked her parted lips. Cheyenne refocused her attention on her foe. "I feared he'd plunge the knife in her back. So, I grabbed his arm. When he turned around, murderous intent filled his eyes."

Jonny closed his eyes and slowly leaned back in his chair.

"What did Capri say?" Adélaïde asked.

Neither one answered.

"What happened when you grabbed Jonny?" Steven asked.

Jonny nodded, giving her the silent okay.

Cheyenne found it humorous he thought she need his permission. "He flung me into the oven door."

"Lie," Adélaïde said. "You told us he didn't hurt you."

"No, I said he didn't hit me."

Jonny patted his grandmother's hand.

"When Jonny realized what he did, he became apologetic."

"When I came into the house," Steven said, "I heard pounding, Jon yelling, and I saw you sobbing and begging. What caused you to be afraid of him?"

Cheyenne stared point-blank at Jonny. "I'm not afraid of you."

"You were cowering by the front door," Steven argued.

Cheyenne shifted her focus to Steven. "The moment he began apologizing, I saw that man you all love so much." She planted her eyes on Jonny, "I saw the man, you desperately want to be."

"If not him, then what were you afraid of?" Steven asked.

Cheyenne lowered her eyes, refusing to answer the question.

"No wonder Jon disdains you," Adélaïde said. She looked at him. "She reminds you of you."

Jonny furrowed his brows. He tilted his head down and to the left. He glanced to her. "The lights. You're afraid of them."

Her eyes welled and her chin trembled. So, that was his goal, to expose her secretes. She needed to tell him the truth if she was going to keep the little boy safe. "Your son is your weakness."

Jonny sat upright in his chair.

Tears dangled from her chin like stalactites. "He'll be your undoing."

The coffeemaker stopped percolating.

Goosebumps spread across Cheyenne's body, and Jonny sniffed the air.

The coffee pot shattered, spraying the kitchen with coffee.

Cheyenne and Jonny locked eyes. "It's time for me to go."

"Let me dress and I'll take you home," Jonny said. "Go wait outside, please."

Cheyenne excused herself and disappeared into the living room.

"What the hell," Sandra said. She grabbed a towel from the laundry basket. "What's going on between you two?"

Jonny shook his head. "Nothing. We were having a conversation."

She mopped the coffee. "Weirdest fucking conversation I've seen."

"I'll get dressed and head into town for a new coffeemaker," Adélaïde said.

"Don't worry about it," Jonny said.

Steven stood in the living room's threshold, preventing Jonny's departure. "I'm surprised you didn't go ballistic on her when she mentioned Jacob."

"Wasn't necessary."

"What do you think she meant?"

Jonny grabbed the laundry basket. "Doesn't matter. I'm taking her home, out of our lives." He pushed past Steven and went to his room. He dressed and grabbed a flashlight from the nightstand. He instinctively checked to make sure it worked. He entered the hallway and pulled the string to the attic.

If he didn't grab the hidden coffeemaker before he left, Adélaïde would run into town for a new one. It would ruin the surprise and waste money. He would rather give her the present early.

The attic was dusty and dark. Most of the junk belonged to Adélaïde. She sold her home after Eber passed and refused to get rid of his belongings.

Jonny placed the flashlight inside the attic. He hoisted himself up, knocking the flashlight over with his toes. "Shit!" He stood to retrieve it, having to hunch lower as the roof tapered down. He palpated the floor for the light.

Whispers rose from the far end of the attic; a dark silhouette stood behind some boxes.

He waited a moment for the amber lights to appear; they did not. He turned the flashlight on, but it did not illuminate. He pinched his nose. The musty aroma of old boxes gave way to the revolting scent of decay.

Loud scrapes of cardboard over wooden planks changed the attic atmosphere.

He glanced up, and the silhouette was gone. He focused on the flashlight, pounding it on his right palm.

The creaking of the wooden planks approached him.

He pounded the flashlight harder and faster. "C'mon, you piece of shit!"

Light emanated from the flashlight; a dense, black mist stood beside him.

He extended his arm, but the light snuffed out.

A scuttle ran across the floor.

It was time for Cheyenne to get the hell away from his house. He snatched the hidden coffeemaker and made his way down the stairs.

Jacob stood at the bottom of the stairs. He held his G.I. Joe up in the air. "My friend said he needed to give you light."

Jonny picked Jacob up and kissed his head. "Strange enough, I needed light." They entered the kitchen, and Jonny kissed Adélaïde's cheek. "Happy early birthday." He handed her the new coffeemaker. "Now the coffee will be ready when we get up in the mornings."

6

Jonny refused to apologize for what any normal person would do. She said she was after the truth; what truth? He drove slower than the speed limit, hoping to gain some ground. With the Jeep's top off, Cheyenne's hair danced about. It made it difficult to read her expressions.

Cheyenne held her hand out the window, moving it delicately through the wind, pretending to be a maestro.

Jonny turned up the radio. "You like Ramin Djawadi?"

She brought her hand inside and closed her eyes.

He slowed the car but did not stop. She couldn't ignore him forever. "How long did you live in Ireland?"

She stared at him; her brows pinched together. "Three years. How did you know?"

"I can hear the accent change within your R's." He looked at her body. "How d'you get all those bruises?"

She looked out her window. "I fell down the stairs."

He frowned.

"You're used to getting your way, aren't you?" she asked.

He ignored her question and asked his own. "How d'you get the scars on you back?"

She cocked her head. "How d'you get yours?"

His side smirk made an appearance. He stopped at the streetlights and focused on her. "Why are you afraid of the amber lights? What are they?"

Cheyenne looked out her window. She chewed on her fingernail. "Why don't you talk about your past? Who kidnapped you?"

The car behind them honked.

He shifted into first gear. "Is that what Sandra told you?"

"Weren't you?"

He paid attention to the traffic. She's smart. Have to give her something to get something. "No," he finally answered. "I volunteered to stay under the condition they freed my brother and sister." He glanced at her. "I will not answer any follow-ups."

"Fair enough," she said.

"Who's the woman and little girl dressed as socialites?"

A weak smile formed on her face. "My *seanmhair* and me when I was seven." Her smile faded.

"What is *shenver*?"

"Shen-uh-ver and it means Grandmother."

"Where is she now?"

Cheyenne pointed to the sky. "In heaven."

"Why do you always refer to your loved ones in Gaelic?"

She fidgeted with her fingers. "Out of respect. I sometimes try using the American words but it feels unnatural." She chewed on her fingernail again.

Jonny removed her hand from her mouth. "That's a nasty habit."

"What did Capri say to you; I didn't recognize the language."

He pulled up behind her broken-down Datsun and put the Jeep in park. "*Laissez les bon temps roule.* It's Creole. It means 'Let the good times roll'."

"Why did it anger you?"

He closed his eyes, shifting in his seat. "Nothing good ever came after those words."

"Part of your past?"

He opened his eyes, refusing to answer.

"Your *seanmhair* has an accent. Where's she from?"

"Natchitoches, Louisiana." He stared at her house. "What truth are you seeking?"

"It doesn't matter." She reached for the door. "You have a beautiful family. Endangering them to learn my secrets is foolish."

He grabbed her arm.

She stared at his massive, over-worked hand.

"How do you know Mickey?" he asked.

She shook her head. "Never heard of him." She opened the

Jeep door.

He pulled her back in; he needed answers. “When I broke into your house, what happened to me in there?”

She removed his hand. “I don’t know; it’s never happened before.”

“That night in the garage—”

“Your intuition is right. You and your loved ones should stay far away.”

He stared at the marks he left on her throat. “I’m sorry I hurt you. I didn’t mean—”

“I don’t hold any grudges or ill will toward you.” The hairs on her arms stood on end. “It’s time I left.”

“Every time you get goosebumps, I smell burning, rotting flesh. Where does it come from?”

She averted her eyes to Ryder; he stood on his porch. She took a deep breath, stepped out of the Jeep, and looked back inside. “Bathe your son in light; keep him away from the shadows.”

Twelve
Family Failings

1

Jonny dried his hands and exited the bathroom, tossing the spent paper towel into the wastebasket. He found Sandra in his office talking on the work phone.

"My brother walked in. I'll call you back later." She hung up the phone and intercepted Jonny with a hug.

He kissed her cheek. "Who was that?"

"Capri."

He rolled his eyes.

"I made you tuna salad sandwiches with extra dill relish."

He unwrapped the plate and took a bite. He winked at her. "Wouldn't eat it any other way."

She sat across from him. "Capri's sad Steven broke up with her. She doesn't understand why."

He picked up a chip. "Besides being a complete moron? Her hair wasn't red enough."

"Huh?"

He popped the chip in his mouth, "Capri's not his type."

She caressed the woodgrain on his desk. "I have a sensitive

question to ask."

He tossed the sandwich to the plate and leaned back in his chair, interlocking his fingers behind his head.

"What happened the other day when I brought Cheyenne here? Why'd you become so hostile toward her?"

He repositioned, keeping his fingers interlocked, and rested his forearms on the desk. He looked down at his hands, tapping his thumbs together. "When I came up here for the towels," he paused and pointed at the corner of his desk. "Ralphie's dirty bare feet stood right here."

"You hallucinated Ralphie? What's that got to do with her?"

Jonny shook his head.

She sat forward. "Who *is* he?"

Jonny pressed his lips together, resting back in his chair.

She drew in a large breath, throwing her hands in the air. "Why won't you tell me? Why won't you tell me what happened?"

He pounded his desk with the side of his fist. "All I want is to bury the past." He pushed the food away. "But you and everyone else keep it at the surface!" He stood. "I've got work to do."

"What about your food?"

"I've lost my appetite."

"Wait!"

Sandra wrapped her arms around him. "I don't know what's so horrible you can't tell me." She squeezed him tight. "There isn't anything you could do that would make me think less of you."

He hugged her, kissing the top of her head like he would Jacob. "I endured things and did things to keep you and Dominick safe from them." He squeezed her. "Horrible and unimaginable things."

"What you did or what you endured?"

He rested the side of his face on her head. "Yes."

"Yes, what?"

He held her at arms-length. "It's my burden and my burden alone."

Sandra gave the silent nod. "I got to go," she said.

"I've gotta get back to work anyhow."

"Don't forget, today's Jacob's last day at preschool. You need to pick him up at one."

"I won't," he said. "Steven is only working a half shift at the VA. He should be here in an hour or so."

Jonny did not have time to paint the 1968 Mustang waiting for him in the paint booth. He began stripping the paint from a black 1970 Cougar Eliminator. He grabbed his sander and made a quick examination of the car's body. He grabbed the rusted metal above the rear passenger wheel; the metal crumbled in his hand. "What a shame." He returned to the black cat's hood, put on his respirator, and started sanding.

2

Cheyenne slid on her oven mitt and opened the oven door. She grabbed the glass pan and her cellphone rang. She placed the lemon bars on the stovetop and sidestepped to the island, picking up her phone. "Hello?" She closed the oven door, narrowing her eyes. She touched the base of her neck. "Um, have you tried calling his shop or Sandra's phone?" She listened to the man on the other end. "Um, what about Steven, their family friend?" Cheyenne held the phone with her shoulder and untied her apron, tossing it on the island. "No, please don't do that." She blew the air out of her cheeks. "I'll—I'll have to call a cab, but I'll be there." She hung up the phone, turned the oven off, and walked into her room. She grabbed her wallet and keys from the nightstand and turned.

Ryder grabbed her by the throat and slammed her into the wall.

She held onto his wrist, staring into his amber pits, gasping for air.

He leaned forward, sniffing her face. “You smell like fear.” He licked the rogue tear from her cheek and grinned. He pressed his lips against her ear, “Tastes like fear.” He picked her up and tossed her across the room.

Cheyenne bounced off the front of her bureau and fell to the floor. She crawled, struggling to breathe.

He kneeled and grabbed her hair, jerking back her head. “Bring me his son.”

3

Jonny finished sanding the front of the Cougar. He glanced at his watch; twelve-thirty. “C’mon, Steven.” He closed shop and waited in the customer lounge. He glanced at his watch and then looked out the window, crossing his arms.

4

Cheyenne’s cab arrived at Fullerton Elementary. “I’ll be right back.”

“I’ll only wait five minutes,” the cabby said.

Cheyenne grabbed the glow necklaces out of her purse and snapped them. She searched the halls for the office, connecting two glow necklaces together. She followed the signs and entered the office. She spotted Jacob sitting in a chair against the wall. She kneeled, placing the necklace around him.

Jacob raised his head, sniveling.

"What happened to your lip?"

"He picked a fight with three boys," said a deep voice from behind.

She handed Jacob the glowing necklaces. "Put them on." She stood and turned around, extending her hand. "I'm Cheyenne Tàillear, and you are?" She looked at his gray hair. It did not match the wrinkle-free face.

The tall black man embraced Cheyenne's hand with a firm but gentle shake. "Principal Lysander." He returned his hand deep within his dress slacks. "Jacob started a fight and refuses to say why."

Cheyenne stared at Jacob. "Just like his *athair.*"

"Excuse me, Mrs. Taylor?"

"Miss Tàillear," she said. "When his father doesn't want to answer, he becomes mute."

"I can only release him to a family member. The problem is your name isn't on the list. Jacob claims you are related. How?"

Cheyenne glanced down at Jacob.

He stared at her, wiping his nose on his sleeve.

She pressed her lips together, contemplating. "I'm his *piuthar màthair.*" Cheyenne closed her eyes. "Um . . . his aunt on his mother's side."

"I'll need you to sign him out, Miss Tàillear."

Cheyenne followed behind the principal. "You called Jonny's shop, and he didn't answer?"

The principal handed her a pen. "The line has a busy signal, it never rings." He gave her the sign-out sheet. "We tried several times. Sandra's phone goes straight to voicemail, as did the family friend."

Cheyenne signed the paper. "What of the *seanmhair*? Uh, I mean grandmother?"

"Adélaïde already told us she would be unavailable today

and to call Jonathan."

"We must go. My cab said he would only wait for five minutes."

The principal stared at Cheyenne's throat. "Is there a reason you're reluctant to take your nephew?"

Cheyenne picked Jacob up and held him on her hip. She faced Principal Lysander. "We have an understanding. I stay out of Jonny's life, and he stays out of mine."

5

Jonny closed shop and ran to his Jeep, slamming the driver door. He revved high and dropped the clutch hard, heading for Fullerton Elementary. He ran the yellow light and sped even faster until he reached the school zone. Typically, a fifteen-minute drive, he made it in six. He parked crookedly and sprinted into the office. With labored breathing, he said, "I'm here to pick up Jacob DeLuca."

The blonde behind the counter lifted her head. "Someone already picked him up."

"Was it my sister?"

Principal Lysander came out of his office. "I'll handle this, Mrs. Morales."

"Who has Jacob?"

The principal extended his hand. "Hi, Mr. DeLuca, nice to see you again."

He accepted the principal's hand. "Call me Jonny."

"I've tried calling your shop since eleven, and all I've gotten is a busy signal. I tried your cell and home phone; both went to voicemail. Your sister's and Steven's phones went straight to voicemail."

"Who-picked-up-my-son?"

Principal Lysander handed him the sign-out sheet. "Miss Tàillear was reluctant to come until I told her I would have to call child services."

He snatched the paper from the principal, reading Cheyenne Tàillear. He slammed the paper on the counter. "She's not on the list!"

"If not for her, your son would have gone to the state."

He ran to his Jeep. He reversed out of the parking lot, debating which home to go to first. She wouldn't take Jacob to her house. Not after the warning she gave.

He sped home and jumped out of the car, leaving the door open. He grabbed the doorknob and then stopped. He took several deep breaths and calmly opened the door.

The curtains in the living room were open; the midday sunlight filled the room. The lights throughout the house were on.

He heard talking coming from the bathroom and stepped into the hall, eavesdropping by the door.

6

Cheyenne rinsed the washcloth in cold water. She wrung it out and continued to clean Jacob's lip. "Are you going to tell me why you were fighting?"

Jacob crossed his arms. "I didn't start it."

She pulled him forward and cleaned his face. "Tell me what happened."

Jacob shook his head.

She sat on her knees, holding his hands. "You've put me in hot water with your *athair* once he finds out I picked you up." She lifted Jacob's tiny chin. "The least you can do is tell me what happened?"

Jacob flinched his head back. “What’s a-her?”

“*Ah-her*,” she said. “It’s Gaelic for father.” Cheyenne raised an eyebrow. “Tell me what happened?”

He swung his feet. “I was talking with my friend, Angel, when Billy and his friends came up to me. They were pushing me and calling me Snow.”

“Snow?”

“Like Jon Snow,” he said.

“Tsk, tsk, tsk. Shame on their parents for lettin’ ‘em watch that show.”

“They called me a ‘motherless bastard’. So, I punched Billy in the nose and kicked Sam in the gut. Their friend pushed me to the ground and started hitting me.”

“I lost my *màthair* when I was five.” She wiped his tears. “Your *màthair* may not live with you, but you have one, everyone does.”

“Everybody asks daddy who my mommy is, but he never tells them.”

Cheyenne continued to clean his lip. “Have *you* asked him?”

He stared at her.

She rubbed his cheek. “Maybe he’s waiting for you to ask?” She rinsed the washcloth in the sink.

“Are you gonna tell daddy I got into a fight?”

She left the washcloth in the sink and sat on the edge of the tub. “I think it’s best you tell him rather than him find out from somebody else.” She rested her forearms on her knees. “Tell your daddy the truth. I’m sure he’ll be understanding.”

Jacob shook his head. “Daddy said violence is never okay.”

She frowned. “There’s a difference between protecting yourself and fighting just because.”

He touched his lip. “It feels swollen.”

She slid to the floor and sat on her knees in front of him. “Jacob,” she paused, biting her lower lip, “how did you know my phone number?"

"Angel told me it."

Cheyenne squinted her eyes, shaking her head. "Your friend?"

"He's the one who saved daddy from Nicholas."

"Has Nicholas shown himself to you?"

Jacob rubbed his lips together, playing with the fresh bump. "I think he looks like Sarge."

Jonny stepped into the bathroom and saw Jacob covered in glow necklaces. "Who's Nicholas?"

Cheyenne jumped to her feet. "I should go."

"He's the one hurting Cheyenne, Daddy."

Jonny grabbed Cheyenne by the elbow; he fixated on her bruises.

Jacob slid off the toilet. "Angel says to trust Daddy, he'll protect you."

Her stare, toggled between Jonny's eyes. "No one can protect me." The peach fuzz on the sides of her cheeks rose. "I need to go." She walked out of the bathroom and down the hall.

He poked his head out of the bathroom doorway. "If you wait a second, I'll take you home."

She stopped and turned.

Jonny smelled the air.

"You need to keep your son away from me. Keep the glow sticks on him until I'm long gone."

Jonny replied with a single nod. *Maybe I misjudged her.* He rubbed his chest. No, no, he didn't.

He attended to Jacob. "I heard you tell Cheyenne what happened." He kissed Jacob's forehead. "I'm proud of you for sticking up for yourself."

Jacob stared at his hands, playing with his fingers. "Who's my mommy?"

He cupped Jacob's face. "Go on into the living room. I'll be there in a minute."

Jacob slid off the toilet seat. "She's a nice lady. She needs your help."

"Go on, I'll be there in a second." Jonny glanced at his watch and exited the bathroom, taking a detour to his room. He found his cell lying on the bed where he'd tossed it this morning. He picked it up and saw five missed messages from Jacob's school. He sighed through his nose and opened the closet door, unearthing the safe. He ratcheted through the combination and pulled out a single box.

Inside were several photo albums, hundreds of loose photos, videos, a box of ammo, and a gun.

He returned the gun and ammo to the safe and locked it. He grabbed the box and entered the living room.

Jacob sat on the floor, playing with his G.I. Joe.

Jonny sat on the couch, placing the box next to him. He pulled out a photo album. "Jacob, come sit on my lap; I want to show you something." He wrapped his arms around Jacob, holding the photo album in front of them. "Your mother's name is Haven Marie O'Sullivan."

Jacob leaned against his father's chest, nestling his head under Jonny's chin. "She's pretty."

He kissed the top of Jacob's head. "Yes, she was."

Jacob tilted his head back, asking, "Where is she now?"

"When your mother found out she was pregnant with you, she also found out she was very sick." Jonny felt his throat hardening. He coughed, failing to dislodge the lump.

Jacob took the album from his father's hands and set it to the side. "But where is she now?"

Jonny's chest heaved.

Jacob turned around in Jonny's lap and hugged him. "It's okay, Daddy."

"She's in heaven." He wrapped his arms around Jacob, hugging him. "Your mother wanted you to know she loved you. She documented every day she had left just for you."

"How come nobody else knows about her?"

"Several reasons," he said. "The doctors told us it would be a difficult pregnancy; she knew we would be in and out of the hospital. The likelihood you would be born before the sickness took her wasn't probable. Your mother didn't want people to be excited and then sad if we lost you." He smiled, kissing Jacob's nose. "She was always thinking about others, like you." Jonny placed his forehead against Jacob's and gazed into his hazel eyes, Haven's eyes. "Your mother requested to undergo heavy treatments after you were born. I took you to the hospital every day to see her. We stood behind a large glass window like the one in my office. She would always put her hand against the glass, crying, wishing she could hold you."

"Why couldn't mommy hold me?"

"You were born early and, at first, sickly. She didn't want to risk it."

"I'm sorry you miss her, Daddy."

Jonny's stomach growled. "I'm hungry, you hungry?"

"Nuh-uh." Jacob stared at the box containing his mother's memories.

"Do you have questions about your mom?"

Jacob shook his head. "Not about mommy."

"You can ask me anything, even if it's not about your mom."

Jacob shifted his eyes to his father's dirty face and tried to clean the grease from his stubble. "Angel wants to know why you refuse to help Cheyenne."

"Who's Angel?"

"Our friend. He helped us when Nicholas tried to hurt you.

He held Jacob's hands. "What happened after Nicholas

attacked me?"

"Angel stood outside your bedroom window when Nicholas tried to hurt you. He's the one who told me to open your curtains so the moonlight would scare Nicholas away."

"The amber lights."

"Those are his eyes," Jacob said. "He's afraid of the light, that's why he hides in the dark." He touched Jonny's chest. "Angel wants to keep us safe. He wants to keep Cheyenne safe."

The one thing Jonny wanted, the one thing he requested, was to keep Cheyenne away from Jacob. And now this . . . thing is interacting with him. Jonny's brows betrayed his consternation. "What is Nicholas?"

Jacob leaned forward, cupping his hand around his mouth and Jonny's ear. "Evil."

7

Sandra straddled Steven's lap in the back seat of the Challenger. He helped fasten her bra and ran his hands down the sides of her body. "You still look as beautiful as you did when we were teenagers."

Sandra pulled her dress down over her head. "Do you think Jonny knows about us?"

Steven buttoned the front of her dress. "Nah. Why?"

She pulled her hair out from under her dress. "Today, he said Capri wasn't your type because her hair wasn't red enough. I played it off as if I didn't understand."

He wrapped his hand around the back of her head, bringing her in for a kiss on the lips. "If your brother knew about us and if he had an issue, don't you think he would've said something?"

She rolled her eyes. "You know him; he's calculating. He reveals nothing until he's certain he's gathered enough intel." She ran her fingers through Steven's chest hair. "I don't think he would say anything to either of us." She plucked a gray hair. "Does he ever talk to you about his one-night stands? Who the women are and where he takes them?"

"Your brother is a private man when it comes to his sex life."

"Pfft! He keeps his entire life private."

Steven frowned. "What happened to him is a little different. Nobody wants to feel vulnerable. Regarding his one-night stands, he tells me with whom and where but never the details. I'm sure he only tells me that much for security purpose." Steven tapped her hip. "What time is it?"

Sandra crawled off his lap and pushed the seat forward. She opened the door and stepped out, straightening her dress.

Steven stepped out of the car and pushed the seat back. He grabbed his cell from the passenger seat and powered on the phone. "Shit!"

"What?"

"It's one-thirty."

8

Jacob lay on the floor surrounded by photos, watching a home movie. Haven, four months pregnant, spoke to her stomach. She had long brunette hair which she kept in a messy bun. Though she was not feeling particularly well, she wore a smile.

Jacob took a bite of his sandwich. "She sounds like Cheyenne when she talks."

Jonny shifted his focus from the photo album. "Your mother is Irish; Cheyenne's Scottish."

Jacob looked back at his father. “Their Rs are the same.”

A prideful smirk formed on Jonny’s lips. He winked. “Yes, they are.”

Sandra walked through the front door spotting a younger Jonny and Haven on TV. “Is that his mother?”

Jonny closed the photo album and put it back inside the box. He marched toward Sandra; red faced with flared nostrils. He did not take his eyes off her. “Jacob, I have to go back to work.”

“Is it okay if I keep watching the movies?”

“Of course.” He faced Jacob. “Your mother made them for you.”

“Jonny, I—”

He raised his hand. “Save it. You and Steven knew I had to pick him up from school.” He grabbed his work boots. “If GG isn’t home before you have to go to work, call me and I’ll come home.”

9

Jonny closed the Jeep door and sauntered up the stairs, halting at Cheyenne’s front door. He closed his eyes a moment, loosing himself in the rich tone of her vocals. She’s talented, for sure. He was there on business, not pleasure. “Sergeant Mackenzie,” he shouted.

Cheyenne stopped singing. She removed the knife from the lemon bars and maneuvered around the island. She peered out the front door, tightening her grip around the knife.

“I didn’t want to just walk in,” he said.

“How do you know Sergeant Mackenzie?” she asked

"Anyone who's watched 'We Were Soldiers' has heard Sergeant Mackenzie."

Why was he here? She waved him in, returning to the lemon bars.

Jonny followed her into the kitchen and stood at the island. "Never heard it sung by a woman before."

"Every year, on this day, we'd have our family reunion. There'd be more food than anyone could eat. At the end of the night, we'd be drunk on Dark Island Reserve and King's Ginger singing Sergeant Mackenzie."

"Why?"

"To honor those who served. We lost a lot of family to military services."

He eyeballed the lemon bars.

"Have one with me, won't you?"

"Yes, please."

She grabbed for the powder sugar.

"None for me."

"I thought my seanair and I were the only ones who didn't eat powdered sugar with them."

He took the plate from her. "You sing beautifully. Did you sing professionally somewhere?"

She shook her head. She was not sure if he was making small talk or if he was trying to ease into the real reason he came.

He examined the lemon bar and broke a piece of the crust, tasting it by itself.

"It's a shortbread cookie crust," she said. Cheyenne opened the cupboard and stood on her tippytoes stretching for two glasses.

He chuckled and stood behind her, grabbing the glasses. "Why put them up there if you can't reach them?"

"I had a stepstool, but it broke." She opened the

refrigerator. "Milk or water?"

"Milk," he said.

"My seanmhair and I created the crust recipe together because I hate graham crackers."

"So do I," he said.

He was overly friendly; she didn't like it.

"Cut the crap. You don't like me you never have."

Damn right, he thought. "I don't trust you and I think you'd agree, I have good reason."

She bobbed her head. "I told you to stay away. You know it's not safe. So why did you come?"

He took a deep breath. "Last night, I found Jacob holding your hand while you slept. When I grabbed him, I couldn't move, couldn't talk. I felt like I was on fire." He crept forward. "I saw horrible images of dead children flash through my head. I couldn't make out who they were, that's how fast they flashed."

Cheyenne scanned his exposed dermis. He didn't have any marks or bruises. She sat at the table. "You should go."

He ignored her. "I saw them in the corner of my room. The amber lights. The burning feeling, I felt all over me, doesn't compare to the pain I felt when that thing tried to burrow into my chest."

She stared at his chest. "You should go and never come back."

"This morning, that thing tried to attack me in my attic." He walked to the table, grabbing her by the wrist. "Jacob tells me it talks to him. Tells him to sing the one song that gives my sister anxiety attacks."

Cheyenne jerked her wrist free of his soft grip. "I'm sorry for the pain I've caused."

"Since you've come into my life, my past . . . "

"Your past, what?"

He stepped away. "What is it and how does that thing know so much about my family?"

Cheyenne shrugged her shoulders. "I don't know why, but he's fixated on you. He'll use anything and anybody against you.

"Years ago, I dreamed I was in your home. I was wearing nothing but a white shirt. I walked out of your bedroom and entered the kitchen, where you were making a fresh coffee. I pulled two coffee cups out of the cabinet and when I turned around, you grabbed me."

His brows furrowed.

"In my dream, you slammed me against the counter." She rubbed the phantom pain in her lower back. "You told me you'd kill me if something happened to Jacob."

Jonny pulled his keys from his pocket. "Do you believe I would?"

Cheyenne met his stare. "With no hesitation."

He nodded several times. "Then we understand each other?"

She acknowledged him with a single nod. "If you fix my car, I'll leave, and you won't see me again. I'll pay you whatever you want."

"I'll fix your car if it's fixable, for free." He spun the keyring around his finger. "It's the real reason I came over." He walked to the island and finish his milk. "You stepped up when the rest of us failed my son, when I failed him. You didn't have to, but you did."

Cheyenne's forehead wrinkled. "I don't understand."

"There isn't a dollar amount I can give you that would show my gratitude. What I can give you is what you asked the first time we met and that's to look at your car."

She shook her head. "No, I don't understand *you.*" She walked to the island, grabbed his glass, and rinsed it. "Right now, you're this nice, gentle person; I don't feel I should trust."

She turned to him. “I mean, how long do I have before you’re an asshole again?” She opened the dishwasher and then stood still, holding the glass. Her eyes squinted, and she glanced at him. “You’re afraid your past is going to be revealed. That’s why you didn’t finish what you were saying a minute ago.”

He headed for the front door. “It might be a couple of days before I can come get your car, but I will.”

Cheyenne trailed him. “This morning, I thought we’d finally bonded and understood each other, made peace. You tricked me with your lies.”

He glanced over his should. “I didn’t lie. I told you the truth.” He crossed the threshold. “I’ll come for your car in a few days.”

She stormed to the door. “Don’t bother. I have enough shit in my life. I don’t need yours, too.” She slammed the door, resting her back against it. The gall. She was stupid to think they could be friends.

The hairs on her arms crawled.

“Jonny!” She jerked open the front door in time to see the Jeep drive away.

Ryder stepped in front of her view. His hand shot forward, latching around her neck. He threw Cheyenne back inside and shut the door.

Thirteen

What's eating you?

1

Jonny unlocked his office and heard a low beep emanating from the phone on his desk. He turned the light on and grabbed the handset, slamming it on the receiver. He went to the glass wall and scanned the shop.

2

Steven bent under the hood of a 1970 Buick Gran Sport GS 455. He unbolted the carburetor, setting it next to the air intake. He turned, reaching for a larger socket.

Jonny's knuckles tagged him behind the square of his jaw.

The whack of ligaments and bone rang in Steven's ear and a sharp tear radiated above the impact; Jonny had connected with a haymaker. Steven went down to one knee, barely holding himself off the spinning pavement. He had seen his share of fights and could take a punch, but it helped to see it coming. He stood and swung in a single deft motion.

Jonny stepped outside Steven's swing and brought his hand up under Steven's jaw, flinging him upward onto his back, and pinned him on the workbench.

Steven got his forearm under Jonny's chin and pressed it against Jonny's Adam's apple. "What the fuck, Jon! Why you trying to knock me out?"

He let Steven go and walked away. "You, dumb fuck!" He spun around, taking a single step forward with his fist drawn. "I should have knocked you out!"

Steven stood, spitting blood from his mouth.

"Because you wanted to get your dick wet, I almost lost my son!"

"What gave us away?"

"Pfft!" Jonny turned away. "I almost lose Jacob, and you're worried about how I found out." He shook his head. "The only ones who thought your relationship was a secret were you two."

"Wait, what? How d'you almost lose Jacob?"

Jonny leaned against the workbench and exhaled. "Sandra didn't connect the phone to the receiver when she finished setting up the rendezvous point with you. The school was trying to call." He rubbed his forehead. "You two always shut off your phones when—" He forcefully pushed off the workbench and headed for the paint booth. "They were going to call child protective service to take him."

"I'm sorry. You have every right to be upset."

Jonny faced him. "You damn right I do!"

"What about your cellphone?" Steven asked.

Jonny furrowed his brows.

Steven closed the gap between them. "The school would only call me or your sister if they couldn't get ahold of you. Where was your cellphone?"

Jonny ignored the question and headed for the paint booth.

"Hey! I'm talking to you! You forgot it, didn't you?" Steven followed close behind. "What's eating you, Gilbert Grape? This isn't solely about Jacob. Something's had you preoccupied for a year now."

Jonny stopped, turning his hands into fists.

"You've been working nonstop since your grandfather passed, hardly eating, hoarding money, spending less time with Jacob."

Jonny faced Steven. "I'm a failure! Is that what you want to hear?" He pounded his fist against his chest. "I have bills to pay and mouths to feed. I can't spend time with my son because I can't afford to hire employees." Jonny widened his stance. "And yes, I forgot my phone because I was too busy proving, to you, I didn't fucking hit that woman, nor was I having a PTSD episode."

"Well, I'm glad it's our fault you fucked up today."

Steven's statement rang true and Jonny relaxed his stance. He raked his fingers through his hair with a deep sigh.

"Don't use Sandra and me as an outlet for your mistake. You're the reason the school couldn't get ahold of you."

Jonny bobbed his head. "You're right."

"You sucker punched me, asshole."

"My apologies."

"It's the second time you've socked me. Brotherhood only counts for so much. Next time it comes to blows, it comes to blows. You read me?"

Jonny acknowledge him with a single nod. "I'm stressed and Cheyenne—"

Steven spotted Jonny buckling under his burdens. He pointed to the office. "Want to sit down, like adults, and talk about what's bothering you?"

"I suppose you want to hold hands and sing, kumbaya?"

"Whatever gets you talking."

They went to the office, and Steven pulled two bottles of water out of the refrigerator. He handed one to Jonny.

Jonny sat at his desk, staring at the sandwich from earlier.

Steven slid the plate closer to him. “You’ve lost a lot of weight.”

Jonny took a bite and tossed the sandwich to the plate. “I know I’m difficult, but I appreciate you and I’m grateful for what you have done for me and my family.”

“Now who’s singing kumbaya?” Steven asked.

A weak smile formed on Jonny’s mouth. He opened the drawer and pulled out a bottle of Tylenol. “For your jaw?”

Steven held out his hand.

He handed Steven two tablets, and then popped two into his mouth, guzzling the water. He tossed the bottle into the wastebasket, shooting a three pointer.

Steven wheeled his chair further away, tossing his bottle into the wastebasket. “You may beat me at chess, but I always win at basketball.”

“And baseball,” Jonny said.

“And football,” Steven said.

Jonny tapped his finger on the desk.

Steven scooted the chair back. Jonny’s tapping was a telltale sign he was contemplating something.

“You knew grandpa had stocks and bonds?”

Steven shook his head. “Eber only talked finances with you and Dominick.”

“To make a long story short, Grandpa’s accountant embezzled my grandparents’ entire life savings, and GG doesn’t know.”

“How you gonna tell her?”

He stared blankly at his desk, shaking his head. “I don’t think I can.”

“What about the money she got from selling her house?”

"The government took it. Paid their back taxes and the debt their accountant racked up in their names. The hospital took the rest." He took another bite of the sandwich. "I took a second mortgage out on my house and a business loan out on the shop to cover the rest of the money they owed and to match the amount they sold their house for."

"Did Eber know?"

Jonny crammed the rest of the sandwich in his mouth. "Grandpa knew; he's the one who told me. I told no one what I did to save them until now."

Steven stood and retrieved another water. "GG was a prosecutor. You don't think she could've handled this in court?"

"It's not about that. I put them through hell when I came back."

Steven stole a chip.

Jonny slid the plate toward him. "They never gave up on me. They both put in long, hard hours to raise us kids. They spent tens of thousands of dollars trying to provide me with the best psychiatrists. Had it not been for them, there's no telling how I would've turned out."

"I get it, I do." Steven took a drink. "You wanted to prevent them from worrying and stressing. You wanted to take care of them like they did you."

Jonny walked to the glass wall, soaking in the shop's emptiness. "I let all my employees go to save money. I'm behind on the shop payments." He turned, resting his back against the window. "With the economy on the down, people all over are losing their jobs and can't pay."

Steven stood beside him. "I know you're prideful, like Eber."

Jonny closed his eyes. "I won't take your money."

Steven leaned against the glass, crossing his arms. "I spend ninety percent of my time at your place anyhow. So, how's this for a compromise? I'll move in, help pay half the mortgage, utilities, and buy all the groceries. I'll give you an interest-free loan to help get you caught up on the shop payments."

Jonny tilted his head back. He swallowed, mulling over the offer. He shook his head.

Steven sighed, rubbing the back of his neck. "When I came back from my second tour in Iraq, you helped me through my darkest days of PTSD. You remember what you told me?"

"Family helps family; that's how we stay strong," Jonny said.

"Are we not family?"

Jonny bobbed his head, staring blankly at the ground. He pushed off the glass. "Let me think about it. Right now, I gotta paint the Mustang. Francis will be here in the morning to pick her up."

Steven trailed Jonny. "Is there anything else you want to get off your chest?"

"Not at the moment."

"What about Cheyenne? You've been moody since meeting her; your emotions are all over the place."

"Because of her, I don't sleep." He glanced over his shoulder. "Sometimes less than an hour."

3

In between coats, Jonny helped Steven work on a 2000 Dodge Ram 1500, replacing the differential. When it was time for him to cure the Mustang's paint, he set the timer on the control panel for forty-five minutes and then helped Steven rebuild the Ram's transmission.

Jonny rubbed his eyes and splashed cold water on his face. He grabbed some paper towels and dabbed his face dry.

Steven stood outside the bathroom door, holding two cups of coffee. "Thought you might want some wake-up fluid."

Jonny took a drink, pointing to the halogen light. "Thought you said you replaced it."

"I did. But even the new bulb doesn't work. I think the storm the other day did something."

Jonny yawned, fighting sleep.

Steven stared at the water droplets remaining on Jonny's face. "Maybe we should go home and get some sleep."

Jonny took another drink. "I'll let the Mustang cool for another twenty, and then I'll polish it. Francis will be here at seven."

"I know you got deadlines, man, but you gotta sleep."

"I told you, when I close my eyes, I don't sleep."

"I can finish the transmission," Steven said, "if you want to work on the black cat."

The next few hours flew like minutes to Jonny. He finished polishing the Mustang and stood back, inspecting his work for imperfections.

"Hey, Francis is here for the pony," Steven said.

He continued to inspect his work. "I'm almost done. Let him know I'll be out in a minute."

Francis walked around the Mercury Cougar Eliminator. The front half of the car and most of the back half was sanded.

"She's a beauty, isn't she?" Steven asked.

Francis scratched at the rust on the hood. "I knew guy in Prague, Oklahoma, who found one of these rare cats."

Steven popped the hood so Francis could inspect the cat's dark heart; she sported a 428 Super Cobra Jet and dual-quad carburetors. "Yeah, Jonny had to talk the owner into keeping her black."

Francis dusted his hands. "Does the owner not know what he possesses?"

"Nah. He's a young kid who probably thinks it's a chick magnet."

Francis chuckled. "In my day, they were." He glanced at his watch.

"Jonny's almost down; he's inspecting his work."

Francis surveyed the yard. A few classics were waiting to be worked on, along with several newer cars. "How about you? You own a classic?"

Steven pointed to his Challenger. "Jonny has one, too." He pointed to the storage shed in the far back of the yard. "When he became a father, he locked her away."

Jonny walked outside, wiping his hands clean. "Sorry to keep you, Francis." He extended his hand.

"No worries," he said, shaking hands. "Troubles getting out of bed this morning?" he asked. "Your eyes are bloodshot."

Jonny faked a laugh. "No. Had a family emergency yesterday, put me behind. I worked all night to make sure your car was ready this morning." He waved Francis to follow him. "Let's go check out your car."

Steven put away the tools and cleaned up while Jonny finished with his customer.

They came out of the booth and Jonny had Steven bring the Mustang out front.

Francis handed over his ID and credit card.

"From Florida," Jonny said. "Why not have someone down there paint the pony?"

"I grew up in Tri-City," Francis said, taking his ID. "We come for Graffiti every year. Last year, a friend of mine had a mural done on his El Camino. All I could do was admire the details and fine lines. He gave me your card, highly recommending you."

Jonny signed the invoice and relinquished it to Francis. "Thank your friend for me."

Steven handed Francis the keys. "She's ready for ya."

"Gotta lock the till in the safe," Jonny said, "then I'll be ready."

Steven escorted Francis out and shook his hand. Then he headed to the shop floor, shutting and locking the garage doors. He entered the office to find Jonny fast asleep. Steven gave a childish giggle and whipped out his cellphone.

Jonny's head tilted back with his mouth gaping; a low, raspy snore escaped. His arms hung lifelessly to each side, held out slightly by the arms of the chair.

"These are gold," Steven said. He returned his phone to his pocket with a self-satisfied smirk. He patted Jonny's cheek to revive him. "Hey, Jonnnnyyy . . . wake up, buddy. C'mon, wakey-wakey."

Jonny smacked his lips in his slumber but did not respond.

"Well, shit. I hope you appreciate the crap I do for you." He brought Jonny's arm over his head, slinging Jonny over his shoulder. Steven carried him out of the office and found Kowanta standing outside, waiting for the shop to open. He unlocked the doors, allowing her to enter.

"Oh, my! Is he okay?"

"Yeah, just pulled an all-nighter. Have a seat, I'm just gonna put him in the car."

"Do you need help?"

"I think I can manage."

Kowanta paced the floor, waiting patiently for his return.

Steven jogged back. "What can I do for you?"

"I finally got the settlement from my daughter's car accident, and I wanted to pay my bill in full."

"That's great." Steven waved her to the office. "Did they finally settle, or did they fight you in court the entire time?"

"Some witnesses came forward with actual video of the accident and proved the officer caused the crash that killed her." Kowanta opened her purse and pulled out her wallet. "The state settled and offered me a huge dollar amount."

Steven opened the safe, pulling the books. He sat down and opened the records. "How much, if you don't mind me asking?"

"More than I can spend in my lifetime. I have an appointment with a lawyer to set up college funds for the grandkids. From there, I'll go to work and finally give my notice."

"It's a shitty circumstance, for sure. I'm glad things are looking up for you, though."

She peeked inside the record book. "What's all them names in red?"

"Those are people with outstanding balances."

"There's so many! What about them highlighted in blue?"

"Those are accounts that are over a year old that have never made a payment."

"Oh, dear! There are more of them than the other. How does he stay open?"

Steven smiled. "I work for free."

"Why doesn't he turn people away?"

Steven ran his finger down the list of names, searching for hers. "Jonny believes the economy will get better one day. When it does, he believes the community will remember who helped them when they were down on their luck."

She handed Steven the four hundred dollars she owed. "He's hoping it'll increase his business."

Steven counted the money and handed back a twenty.

She pushed his hand away. "He gave me money the other day when he came to the store." She stood, sliding the purse strap up her shoulder. “What if he loses the shop?”

Steven sighed.

“I’s really do have more money than I can spend. Let me pay those customers’ bills.”

Steven walked to the safe. “That’s a conversation for you and him.”

“Prideful like Eber.” She smiled. “Mr. DeLuca’s a good man; I’ll think of somethin’.”

4

It was 8:45 AM when Adélaïde heard the recognizable rumble of Steven’s Challenger. She peered through the front door’s sidelight; Steven focused on pulling Jonny’s unconscious body from the car. Her left hand covered her mouth, and her right shot instinctively for the doorknob. “What happened?”

Steven motioned her to calm. “He’s all right; he’s just a little tired, is all.”

She eyed the fresh bruise on Steven’s face. “What happened to your jaw?”

“A misunderstanding.” He focused back on Jonny and pulled him out of the front seat. “We pulled an all-nighter finishing a few work-orders; he fell asleep in his office.”

She held the front door open and Steven lugged him up the stoop.

“Do you have him?” she asked.

“Yeah, I have him.”

She hurried ahead of Steven and opened Jonny’s bedroom door. She pulled back the blankets and caught his head as Steven lay him down.

Steven stretched; his hands braced against the small of his back. “He’s gained some weight since our college party days.”

Fourteen

Jonny Talks

1

A youthful Jonny splinted his right ribcage, wheezing and limping down the hallway toward the front door. His jaw and nose were broken, his right eye swollen shut. Bones on three of his fingers on his right hand protruded through the skin. He held onto the doorknob, listening to the high-pitched scream of a man in the background.

The pipedream of freedom now lay beyond two inches of dry-rotten pine. All that remained was to twist the piece of tarnished brass. Jonny closed his eye. The ethereal nature of his freedom weighed upon him.

The door burst open, knocking Jonny to the floor. A man engulfed in orange flames charged clumsily through the doorway.

Jonny crawled, wincing, wheezing, crying in pain.

The man grabbed him by his injured leg; Jonny moaned. The fiery man flipped him onto his back.

He kicked the man's kneecap and he collapsed onto Jonny's legs. The intense heat bled through his jeans.

The man ablaze grabbed hold of Jonny's cracked ribs with his sizzling hand and pulled himself up. He reached for the Jonny's shoulder, crawling the rest of the way up his body.

Jonny woke, screaming. He sat up in bed, his breathing labored. He rubbed his face with both hands.

"Daddy?"

He looked to the foot of the bed; Jacob's left eye was hazel and his right, amber.

"Are you going to save her or me, Daddy?"

Jonny rubbed his eyes, and when he opened them, Jacob was gone. He crawled out of bed and walked toward the living room.

The living room was now the barn in which he was held captive. At the far end, Jacob sat restrained to a chair. On the complete opposite side was Cheyenne. She, too, was restrained to a chair.

A deviant chuckle echoed within the air. "Who's it going to be?" it asked.

They both burst into flames, Jacob screaming for his father.

2

Jonny sat up, screaming, "JACOB!" He plopped back in bed wiping the sweat from his brow. He stared at the ceiling, his chest heaving.

Steven barged in. "You alright? I heard you screaming."

Jonny pulled back the blankets and stood.

"Jesus, you're drenched." Steven glanced at the bed. "You haven't had a nightmare make you sweat this bad since you were a kid. You sure you're alright?"

Jonny removed his wet clothes. “How did I get home?”

“You fell asleep in your office, so I drove you.”

Jonny pulled a fresh pair of boxers from his bureau. “Jacob, where is he?”

“With Sandra and GG.”

“How long was I out?”

“Maybe six hours. Did you get any real sleep?”

“It was a nightmare inside a nightmare.” Jonny retrieved a shirt and grabbed a pair of pants. “The second, involved Jacob.”

3

Jonny showered and then tasked an oscillating fan to dry his bed. He joined Steven in the dining room for coffee.

Steven finished the last funny in the newspaper and tossed it to the table. He looked through the gap below the breakfast bar cabinets. “I made you shit on a shingle; it’s in the microwave.”

Jonny removed the plate from the microwave and sat across from Steven. He took a bite and slid the plate away.

“I know,” Steven said, “it’s not Sandra’s sausage gravy.”

Jonny stared mindlessly at the stale bread smothered in poor man’s gravy. “Sandra told you who Mickey and Lee were, yes?”

Steven settled back into his chair. “She told me what they did to her but not who they were.”

“They kept me locked in a cast-iron cage. They’d starve me for days before Lee would bring me rotten food covered with maggots.” He shifted his eyes to Steven. “I’d eat the maggots, so the spoiled food wouldn’t poison me.” He pointed to the plate. “It may not be Sandra’s gravy, but it tastes better than maggots.”

“Glad I can raise the bar.”

Jonny chuckled, “Smartass.”

“Do what I can.”

Jonny pointed to the bruise on Steven’s face. “How’s the jaw?”

“Sore.”

“We good?” Jonny asked.

“Water under the bridge. I meant what I said, though. Next time, we go to blows.” Steven tapped his thumb on the table, changing the subject. “How long have you known about me and your sister?”

Jonny smirked. “Since we were kids. I came home early from one of my shrink visits and heard you two up in the treehouse. She was crying as she told you what that sick sonofabitch did to her.” He sipped his coffee. “That’s when I knew she had feelings for you.”

“Why didn’t you tell us?”

“Why hide your relationship to begin with?”

“You. Sandra didn’t think you’d approve.”

“Why the string of side girlfriends?”

“To throw you off, but I never slept with them.”

A faint smile formed on Jonny’s lips. “Even when you guys thought you were being subtle, it was obvious. I know she loves you and you her.”

Steven wagged his pointer finger. “I don’t just love her; I’m in love with her. There’s a difference.”

“Semantics, I see how you are with her.”

“Do I have your permission to marry her?”

Jonny chortled. “You don’t need my permission to marry my sister.” He followed Steven into the kitchen. “Hey?”

Steven turned around.

Jonny held out his hand. “I’d be honored if you married her.”

Steven grabbed Jonny’s hand and pulled him into a hug.

"Means a lot to us."

Jonny filled both their cups. "I know you'll take good care of her."

Steven relaxed back into his chair, slouching. "You think you'll ever marry?"

Jonny grabbed the newspaper, reading the front page. "Nah. I'm too much of an asshole."

"You can be . . . but, we've all seen a softer side." He sipped his coffee. "Even Cheyenne stated as much."

Jonny turned the page, sipping his coffee.

"Those photos of you and Haven also show a kinder you."

Jonny's eyes peered over the newspaper.

"Just a heads up, GG found the photos of Eber touching Haven's pregnant belly. she's pissed, to say the least."

"I was hoping to explain some things to her before she looked at those."

Steven pulled a photo album out of a drawer and handed it to Jonny. "What made you finally tell Jacob about his mother?"

Jonny opened the album to the first page. "Cheyenne." He stared at a photo remembering the day. "She knew I was waiting for Jacob to ask me."

Steven raised a brow. "When was she alone with him?"

"Jacob got into a fight at school yesterday. She was the one who picked him up. Some kids were making fun of him for not having a mother. Cheyenne—" Jonny stared at another picture.

"Cheyenne, what?"

Jonny turned the page. "She was good to him. She handled the situation nicely."

The impact of the statement jerked Steven's head back. A closed-lip smile formed on his face. "Never thought I'd hear you give her a compliment."

Jonny averted his eyes from the pictures. "I may be stubborn, but not so much I can't acknowledge a good deed."

"So, tell me what happened."

"Jacob told her I never talk about Haven. Cheyenne told him it was because I was waiting for him to ask." He brought his cup up to his mouth. "It's true, I was."

"It's eerie how well she can read you."

"Nothing has changed; I still hate her." Jonny touched the bruise on his chest. The not knowing fed his hatred toward Cheyenne even more. "I think the amber lights are something sinister."

"What makes you think that?"

"Jacob says they're eyes and they talk to him."

"What?" Steven leaned forward, resting his arms on the table. "Why didn't you say something before now?"

"Because, when he'd talk to it, I thought he was talking to his toy." Jonny took a drink. "Jacob calls the lights Nicholas, but there's something else he sees that's talking to him."

"What?"

"I don't know but he calls it Angel. Even weirder, when we were at Sherm's, this boy came up to me. His irises were white, and he kept telling me to save her."

"Save Cheyenne or someone else?"

"At the time, I didn't know. But I think he was talking about Cheyennc."

Steven took a drink of his coffee. "What are you gonna do?"

Jonny locked eyes with Steven. "Keep Jacob away from her. She even told me yesterday to keep him away."

Steven frowned. "Don't you want to figure out what the lights are?"

"Among other things but, the risk isn't worth it." He folded his hands together and rested them on the table. "The other night, Jacob was holding her hand. I grabbed him and I saw dead children. The images came one right after the other." He snapped his fingers. "Like you'd see when flipping through pages with your thumb. It happened so fast; I couldn't tell you what the kids looked like."

"What did you do? What did Jacob do?"

"I was paralyzed; I couldn't move. I couldn't talk. It was like I didn't have control of my body. All the while, I felt like I was on fire." He grabbed his chest. "When I thought I couldn't take any more pain, I saw him. I saw Ralphie.

Steven rested his chin on his thumb and his index finger on his upper lip.

"When I saw Ralphie, the pain went away." Jonny was reluctant to say anymore; he already said too much. If he stopped now, Steven would badger him for more. He sipped his coffee contemplating. What the hell? "Ralphie spoke to me. He said, 'There you are'."

Steven stood and refilled their coffee. "Who is Ralphie? He clearly means something to you, or you wouldn't be plagued by him." He handed Jonny his coffee. "Maybe Jacob sees Ralphie. Could Ralphie be the angel?"

Jonny's eyes moistened. He lowered his head speaking somberly. "I hope so." He blinked, releasing his sorrow. He wiped his sadness away asking, "Can we change the subject?"

Silence fueled their conversation for several minutes. Steven drank the last of his coffee and pointed to the smothered toast. "You know, you could save money if you bought cheaper food."

Jonny grabbed the plate and forked a bite into his mouth. He bobbed his head and took another bite. "As far as the groceries go, you said you'd buy them."

Steven sat tall. "So, you're gonna allow me to help you?"

"Under two conditions. One, when you and Sandra have sex, you gotta make sure your door is shut, and Jacob can't be home." He cut a piece of the toast, mopping the gravy. "I'm not ready to explain to him what sex is."

"What about tired sex? I mean, sometimes we just wake up and—"

"I don't need to hear the details. Just, make sure your door is shut at night."

"And the second?" Steven asked.

Jonny swallowed. He took a drink, rinsing his mouth. "If you're gonna help pay my debt on the shop, then I want us to become fifty-fifty partners."

Steven relaxed back in his chair. "You worked hard to buy the place." He tapped his right thumb on the table. "Are you sure you want to relinquish half, 'cause you don't have to."

"You're a brother to me; you always have been. But I can't take something for nothing. You've always been good with money and our customers. Most of all, I trust you." He extended his hand. "Do we have a deal?"

Steven wrapped his hand around Jonny's. "I know it was a difficult decision, but I'm glad you didn't let your pride stand in the way."

The front door swung open and hit the wall. Both men ran into the living room, finding Jacob struggling to carry two bags of groceries.

"Here, let me help you," Jonny said.

Jacob desperately tried to lift the bags higher. "No, Daddy. I'm trying to work on my muscles."

Steven laughed. "Adorable."

"Well, go put them in the kitchen," Jonny said with a smirk.

When all the groceries were in, Jacob sifted through the bags. "It's not in this one, either."

Jonny grabbed the bag from him. "What are you looking for?"

"My night lights; I need my night lights."

Jonny unloaded the contents of the bag onto the counter.

"Hey, Jacob, you want to come to the shop with me tonight and learn what I do?"

Jacob paused and looked up at his father. "REALLY?"

The corner of Jonny's mouth lifted upward. "Yes, really."

Jacob went back to rummaging through the sack. "Okay, let me find my night lights."

Adélaïde opened the photo album and handed it to Jonny. "Tomorrow, we need to talk."

He looked at the photos of his grandfather holding Jacob as a newborn. "Jacob, go play in your room; the adults have to talk." He stared at Haven's picture, waiting for Jacob to exit the dining room. "What do you want to know?"

"Who is she? Where did you meet her? Why couldn't we have met her?"

He shook his head. "There's no romantic story. She was a customer I had a one-night stand with."

She smacked his chest. "We taught you better than that!"

"Grandma, I have one-night stands all the time, I just don't tell anyone about them."

Adélaïde broke eye contact and lowered her head. Her shoulders slumped and a heavy sigh escaped her parted lips. She massaged her temples, shaking her head. She targeted Steven. "Did you know about his lecherous behavior?"

Steven nodded. "Sure. So did Eber."

"Did you love her?" Sandra asked.

"I didn't at first; I admired her bravery." He stared at her photo. "Haven had breast cancer, and she didn't want anyone to know she was pregnant. The doctors told us the likelihood Jacob would be born before she died wasn't good." Jonny cleared his throat; damn lump. "The more I spent time with her, taking her to her appointments, watching Haven talk to her belly, the more I loved her." Jonny focused on GG. "Grandpa found out when Dominick brought him to see the oncologist. We happened to be there, waiting when they arrived."

"What did Eber say?" Adélaïde asked.

"Grandpa saw me holding Haven's belly. He told me he'd never seen me that happy, and he thanked her."

"How long did they know before you brought Jacob home?" Adélaïde asked.

"Haven was six months. Grandpa told her he had cancer, too. She agreed to allow him over to visit, to make videos, and to take pictures for Jacob."

Adélaïde grabbed her cross. "That's why he postponed his radiation treatments."

"Why wouldn't she let us know about Jacob? Why didn't you at least tell us about her?" Sandra asked.

"Haven didn't want people feeling sorry for us. She didn't want people to tell her she was making a mistake by having Jacob instead of the treatment. She didn't want—"

"And what did you want?" Adélaïde asked.

"Understand, she chose Jacob's, your great-grandson's, life over her own. What I wanted was for her to be comfortable and happy." He held Adélaïde's hands. "If that meant keeping everyone else in the dark while she and I dealt with the shitty circumstances of seeing the pregnancy to term while planning her funeral, then so be it."

Adélaïde walked away. "There's too many damn secrets in this house."

Fifteen
Jacob's Plea

1

Jacob mumbled staring out the car window. "Nope, not that one. Not that one." He touched the glass with his finger. "That one. Daddy, we should check on Cheyenne and make sure she's all right."

Jonny turned in his seat. His eyes combed over Jacob in a moment of fatherly pride. Jacob's desire to protect Cheyenne fed Jonny's desire to protect him. *That . . . thing will not come near him again.* "How'd you know she lives there?"

Jacob withdrew his stare from the window and shrugged his shoulders. "I don't know, I just do."

Steven nudged Jonny with his elbow. "Should we turn back and check in on her?"

Jonny glanced at Steven and shook his head subtly, pointing at Jacob with his eyes. "Maybe on the way home."

"It might be too late," Jacob said.

Jonny faced forward, catching Steven's concern; a discussion was coming.

Steven pulled into the parking lot. He pointed to the

package at the front door. "Must be the Ford's new rear axle."

Jonny pulled the front seat forward allowing Jacob to climb out. "Have to replace the whole axle?" He took Jacob by the hand and walked toward the front door.

"Yeah, the customer let the bearing go too long. Driveshaft scored into the differential housing. I ordered a new ring and pinion set as well; metal shavings chewed 'em all to hell."

Jonny handed the door key to Jacob and bent down on one side of the axle. "Hold the door open."

Steven bent down on the opposite side. "We should've stopped and made sure Cheyenne was okay."

There it was: the conversation Jonny foresaw. "Don't get me wrong, Steven, for a split second I agreed with that logic."

"But?" Steven asked.

Jonny came to a stop. "When I dropped her off, she told me to surround Jacob in light and to keep him away from the dark."

Steven redistributed the weight in his hands. "What does that have to do with stopping?"

Jonny shook his head. "I don't think it's a coincidence Jacob wants night lights now."

They continued to their destination, hauling the heavy axle next to the Ford.

"Whatever that woman has attached to her is a danger to Jacob, to my family." Jonny peeked over Steven's shoulder, locating Jacob. "As long as Jacob isn't near her, he's safe."

"Her life has no value, then?" Steven asked.

Jonny frowned. "I didn't say that. One day you'll have kids of your own and you'll understand. Your child's life is always paramount." Jonny stretched his back. "I'm gonna take Jacob to the office, give him an overview of the place."

Jonny snuck up on Jacob, tickling his sides; Jacob squalled. Jonny lifted him, nibbling on his belly, and carried him into the office.

Jacob pointed to the wall at a picture of a car drawn in crayon. There was a stick figure under the car and a smaller stick figure, standing on a ladder, under the hood. "Hey, I drew that."

Jonny winked. "I keep all your drawings. That one happens to be my favorite."

He carried Jacob to the glass wall and pointed at the three hydraulic lifts where Steven was preparing the Ford for its axle transplant.

"That's where we work on all the cars," Jonny said with a prideful smile. "We do everything from a simple oil change to overhauling engines."

Jacob pointed to an area nestled off to the side, asking, "What's that, Daddy?" He pressed his cheek against the glass, trying for a better view.

"It's called a paint booth. It has a built-in heating system so I can cure the paint afterward."

"Wow! What are you going to teach me today?"

"I'm gonna show you how to sand the paint off the cars and remove any rust. Then, we'll prep and ready the cars for airbrushing."

"What's airbrushing?"

"An art." Jonny looked around his office smiling. He had worked hard to build his business and even harder to obtain his customers. "One day," he said carrying Jacob out of the office, "all of this will be yours."

They walked through the shop and out the opened garage doors. He set Jacob on the gravel lot. "This is a nineteen-seventy Mercury Cougar Eliminator. This beauty is the rarest of the Cougar family and was nicknamed the Black Cat."

Jacob pointed at the raw metal. "Why isn't this black?"

"We have to sand the back half to match the front before we

can restore the color."

Jacob pointed to the rust above the rear tire. "How do we get rid of the rust?"

"You know what we call rust?"

Jacob shrugged his shoulders.

"The iron worm."

2

Steven sifted through the tools on the workbench, determining which ones he needed to install the new axle. Jacob's laughter caught his attention and he peered out the garage door.

Jonny kneeled next to Jacob. He placed his mouth next to Jacob's ear; a trait Eber had when he taught.

Jacob giggled some more, pushing his father; Jonny fell to the gravel, playfully. Jacob sat on his father's stomach, tickling his underarms and ribs. "Tickle, tickle," Jacob said through his giggles.

Steven couldn't help but smile.

"Can't remember the last time I heard my grandson laugh."

"He's always the happiest with his son," Steven said.

Adélaïde stood behind him, watching father and son. "I came to apologize to him; I was out of line."

"It's water under the bridge to him, you know that. I know you don't accept Jon's explanation, but he took responsibility for his actions." Steven glanced at her. "Jacob has made him a better man." He pointed outside. "Look at them?"

Jonny held Jacob and picked himself off the ground. He leaned Jacob backward and nibbled on his stomach.

"Jacob is the best thing to happen to him," Adélaïde said. She lowered her head, gripping her necklace. "I was hurt." She glanced at Steven. "Eber never hid secrets from me and to find he hid a secret this big. I blamed Haven for his betrayal. I let my mind go down the rabbit hole wondering if he ever cheated on me. I know better; he would never cheat on me."

Steven hugged her. "Nobody likes being excluded. You gotta remember, they kept everyone from the truth. Eber happened to show up at the right place at the right time. They gave Jacob the opportunity to know Eber through those photos and videos. Their intentions were never to hurt you."

"I'm aware," she said, stepping outside.

Jacob let his body go limp, hanging his arms beside his head. "I surrender, Daddy." He pointed. "Do it to GG."

Jonny flipped Jacob upright and planted him on the ground. He kissed Adélaïde's cheek. "What brings you here?"

"Can we talk?"

3

Jacob listened to Steven explain what they were going to do and how they were going to do it. Steven was in the middle of explaining why they were putting in the new axle when Jacob walked away.

"Hey, I thought you wanted to help me fix the truck?

Jacob wandered to the hallway. He looked up at the burnt-out halogen light.

Steven trailed him and followed Jacob's gaze to the rafters. "Whatcha looking at?"

"How come the light isn't on?"

Steven picked him up and carried him back to the shop floor. "Not sure. Hasn't worked since the storm."

Jacob rested his head on Steven's shoulder. "Uncle Steven, Angel says we need to check on Cheyenne."

"Who's Angel?"

"My friend." Jacob wiggled free. He looked up at the glass wall. "I tried to tell Daddy we needed to help her."

Steven kneeled. “What makes you think they’re talking about Cheyenne?”

“They’re not. They’re talking about my mommy.”

Steven’s brows furrowed and his head tilted slightly to the left. “How do you know that?”

“Angel told me.”

Steven held Jacob’s hands. “What makes you think something happened to her?”

Jacob stared at the light swinging from the ceiling. “Angel told me. He says we need to help her, save her.”

Steven squinted his eyes. “From what?”

Jacob whispered into Steven’s ear, “Evil.” He leaned back and looked up at his father’s office. “If we don’t help her soon, Angel says she might die.”

“Your daddy told me she said to keep you away from her.”

“Because she thinks that’ll save me, save Daddy.”

“Will it not?”

“Angel keeps me safe. He’ll keep us all safe.”

“Who and what is Angel?”

“A bright light and he’s our friend.”

From Steven’s peripheral, he saw the office go dark. He handed Jacob a wrench. “Untighten all these bolts; I’m gonna go talk with your dad.” Steven intercepted Jonny by the water fountain. “I think we should check on Cheyenne. Jacob’s saying she might die.”

Jonny raked his fingers through his hair and acquiesced with a reluctant nod. “You go. We’ll stay here.” He shifted his gaze to Jacob. “If she acts like she’s scared, leave.”

Steven furrowed his brows.

“Trust me,” Jonny said.

Jacob set the wrench on the ground and ran to the men. “Angel says to be careful, Uncle Steven; Nicholas likes to play games.”

“If you need me,” Jonny said.

“I’ll call ya,” said Steven.

4

Cheyenne lay on the sofa in the dim nightlight cast from the range hood in the kitchen. The streetlamps outside projected dancing shadows of the trees on the walls. The serene quiet, in which she wallowed in her misery, was broken by the low rumble of a familiar V8. What part of *stay away* didn’t Jonny understand? She forced herself off the couch and limped to the door, ensuring it was locked, then she hurried to the kitchen for a knife.

The shadows on the walls slid together toward the alcove of the rooms. Two faint glints shone near the ground, at the head of a large vein of smoky black, and slithered out into the kitchen.

“Don’t even think it,” she said, turning the knife toward her abdomen. “I’ll do it,” she closed her eyes, “and you know it.”

Nicholas stopped. He erected himself into the semblance of man and faced her.

Three heavy blows rattled the front door.

Nicholas marched toward the living room.

She sliced her palm and he looked at the blood seeping from his hand; his eyes glowed hot.

“Consider it a warning.”

Cheyenne eyed the jiggling doorknob and flinched when the door was rapped upon.

“Cheyenne, it’s me, Steven. You home?”

Her eyes moistened; another innocent life. She looked to Nicholas. “Who’s it gonna be, him or us?”

Nicholas went for the door and Cheyenne sliced her forearm

and when that didn't stop him, she sliced her outer thigh.

Nicholas bled from the cuts on his forearm and thigh but did not stop.

Steven pounded the door again. "If you're home, please answer the door."

She started to stab her abdomen but spotted the lighter on the island and grabbed it instead. She flicked the flint and placed her palm over the flame.

Nicholas grabbed his hand and looked back at her.

She removed her hand. "No more! I won't let you take any more lives."

He hissed at her and crawled to the floor, dissolving into the shadows.

A piece of paper slid under the front door followed by heavy footsteps descending from the porch.

She waited until she heard Steven crank the Challenger over before she put the lighter down. She took a deep breath and let her shoulders deflate. She took a stance against Nicholas and won; she couldn't believe it.

She wrapped her hand with a towel and applied pressure. If she had cut it any deeper, she would need stiches. The other two cuts were superficial and already stopped bleeding. She grabbed the letter, opened the front door, and stared at the stars. She had always known Nicholas was afraid of light, but the fire stopped him in his tracks. Did she have a new tactic she could exploit?

The creaking wood plank of the deck derailed her train of thought. She looked to the left; Ryder glared at her with burning amber pupils, his arm already crossed low over his belly. He flung his arm up, dragging his fist across her face, sending her sprawling back over her threshold.

She crawled backward to the couch, pulled herself up, and wiped the blood from her nose.

Ryder slammed shut the door; she turned to run. He grabbed Cheyenne by her braid and reeled her back. He picked her up and hurled her into the grandfather clock.

She collapsed to the hardwood in a cascade of glittering glass shards, eviscerating her hands and knees upon landing. She looked up at the amber eyes striding toward her.

5

Steven's failure to bring back news of Cheyenne's safety put Jacob in a foul mood. He pushed against Steven's legs trying to get him to go back. When Steven went to pick him up, Jacob stepped away.

"You have to go back," Jacob pouted.

"Nobody's home," Steven said.

Jacob crossed his arms over his chest. "She needs us!" He stomped to the hallway and sat on the floor, under the broken light.

Steven kneeled in front of him. "She wasn't home, buddy. I don't know what else you want."

"I'm not talking to you until Cheyenne's safe."

"Let him be," Jonny told Steven. "He'll be fine in a few hours."

Jacob gave Steven a raspberry and then sat with his arms crossed and his lower lip puckered.

All night, Jonny bounced between working on the Cougar and helping Steven. He approached Jacob at one point, asking, "You ready to be a big boy and help?"

Jacob shook his head, never verbally acknowledging his father. He sat against the wall, pouting for another hour. He finally stood and entered the paint booth.

Jonny shut off the music and removed his respirator.

Jacob lowered his head and mumbled, "I'm hungry."

"Okay, I'll finish painting tomorrow." He unzipped his jumper. "You ready to apologize to your uncle?"

Jacob kept his head down and crossed his arms, shaking his head.

"Hey, I love you," Jonny said.

Jacob ran to his father, crying, and Jonny picked him up. Jacob hugged him tight. "I love you, Daddy."

"If Cheyenne wasn't home, there wasn't anything Steven could do. Now, dry your tears and apologize to him."

Jonny carried him out and they joined Steven. "Ready to call it a night? Jacob's hungry."

"Yeah, this is as good a spot as any."

"Don't worry about cleaning up. I'll come back later tonight and finish," Jonny said.

Jacob held his arms out to Steven and he took Jacob without reservation. Jacob kissed and hugged him. "I'm sorry, Uncle Steven."

"Me, too, buddy."

Jonny locked the doors while Steven secured Jacob in the car seat. They loaded up and headed home. When they rounded the corner toward Cheyenne's house, Jacob glued his face to the window.

"We have to stop to make sure she's okay!"

Jonny looked at Steven. "It's late; we're not stopping."

Jacob kicked the back of the seat. "But, Daddy, she's gonna die!"

"Don't be kickin' the seat," Steven said.

Jonny rubbed his forehead. "I said, not tonight."

Jacob folded his arms over his chest and puffed out his lower lip. "She's gonna die!"

Jonny continued to rub his forehead. Jacob had become entangled despite his efforts. What was worse, Jacob knew more about what was going on than him. The feeling of failure rooted itself into the pit of his stomach. It powered the anger boiling inside him. “Her lights are off, she’s probably in bed.”

Steven glanced into the rearview mirror. “I’ll drop you and your dad off, and then I’ll go back and check on her, again.”

6

Cheyenne lay on the kitchen floor in the fetal position, holding her stomach. She stared blankly into the darkness, weighing herself down to the bottom of self-pity. She was so far gone, she never heard the Challenger’s arrival.

There was a loud knock on the front door. “Cheyenne, it’s me, Steven.”

She struggled to pick herself up, but she knew she had to; Steven was innocent. She crawled to her hands and knees, grabbing the lighter from the floor. She stood and hobbled on broken glass to the cabinet under the sink where she removed a tin canister.

Ryder came out of the bathroom, his eyes still amber.

She doused herself with the contents of the canister. The fumes burned her eyes and airway. She coughed and gagged, struggling to breath. “So, help me God—” She went into a cough fit, almost dry heaving. She fought for a breath and finished her threat. “—I will light us both up if you go after him.”

He ignored her and stomped across the disheveled home, crunching on broken glass.

Cheyenne flicked the lighter.

He ceased and looked into the kitchen.

The blows to the front door were more forceful. “Open up, Cheyenne.”

"You've taken everything from me," Cheyenne said. "Robbed me of my life. Why do you want them so badly?"

7

Steven walked around the house, peeking through the windows. Her curtains were all drawn, and the lights were off. The only thing he saw was his own reflection. He went back to the front door and pounded harder, elevating his voice. "I'm not leaving until I know you're safe!" Steven rapped on the door. "Cheyenne, answer me!"

8

Cheyenne hobbled to the front door and rested her forehead against it. "Go away."

The doorknob jiggled. "Jacobs convinced someone is trying to hurt you, and so am I."

"Really, I'm fine." She turned around and slid down the door, muffling her cries.

"Then why are you sitting in the dark, crying?"

She tilted her head up. "I'm in mourning. So, please let me grieve."

"Sorry for your loss. What happened?"

Dammit. Was Steven kneeling on the other side of the door? He was used to playing big brother, wasn't he? He needed to leave. She would not allow him to haunt her, not tonight.

"C'mon, Cheyenne, talk to me."

She focused on the amber eyes. "I won't let you have him."

Who's in there with you?" he asked, jiggling the doorknob again.

"Steven, please, I'm on the phone. "My seanair passed away.

Now leave me be."

"I—I'm sorry to hear that. You sure you want to be alone?"

"Everyone grieves differently. I just—Yes, I want to be alone."

"Okay. If you need anything we'll be here for you."

Cheyenne waited patiently for the V8 to fade into the distance. She lifted herself off the floor and made her way into the kitchen. She stood in the puddle from the canister and eyed the lighter in her shaky hand. "I'm tired." She flicked the flint and looked to Ryder. "I don't want to do this anymore." She closed her eyes and dropped the lighter.

Sixteen

Angelic Salvation

1

Jacob hotfooted it into his father's room and pulled on Jonny's arm. "Wake up, Daddy! You gotta go save her. Wake up!"

Jonny sprung to the side of the bed. He was disoriented and his response was more knee-jerk than consciences thought. "It was a bad dream."

Jacob grabbed him by the hand and tugged. "No, Daddy, she needs help."

Half asleep, he followed.

"He's gonna hurt Cheyenne, we have to save her!"

Jonny rested his face in his palms. First dreamless sleep in several days, ruined by the woman who caused his dreams. He grabbed Jacob's shoulder and kneeled. "Why are you so certain she's in danger?"

"Because she won't do what he wants." Jacob jerked his dad's hand, dragging him. "Nicholas is hurting her!"

He picked Jacob up and headed for Jacob's room.

Adélaïde opened her bedroom door. "For crying out loud, it's

3:30 in the morning." She turned on the hall light. "What's going on?"

Steven stepped out his room with Sandra standing behind him, holding onto his arm. "What's going on?" he asked.

Kicking and pushing off his father, Jacob cried. "Daddy's gonna let her die; we have to save her!"

Jonny held him tighter and tighter.

"Is he still talking about that woman?" Adélaïde asked.

Jonny frowned. "Her name is Cheyenne."

"Please, GG, we have to go save Cheyenne; he's hurting her!" Jacob wiggled free of his father and shot his eyes to Steven. "Uncle Steven, you gotta believe me; we need to save her."

Jonny lowered his head, rubbing his brows. "That's enough!"

"Jonathan Michael!"

Jonny whipped his head and looked up at Jacob.

Jacob's determined countenance framed his luminescent white eyes. "GO-SAVE-HER!" His tone was commanding, far too mature for his tender age.

Sandra's trembling hand covered her gaping mouth. She focused on Jonny. There were only two people who called him Jonathan; she was one of them.

Jonny kneeled next to Jacob. Everything made sense now. The voice from his dream telling him to find his safe place, Jackson from Sherm's, and the so-called Angel Jacob interacts with.

Jacob's eyes faded back to their comforting hazel color.

"We gotta go save her. Please, Daddy, please!"

Jonny cupped both hands around Jacob's face and nodded, whispering, "Okay." He kissed Jacob on the forehead, wrapping his arms around him. "Okay."

"Daddy, I can't breathe."

Sandra pushed passed Steven and approached Jonny with open arms.

Jonny brought his hand up, shaking his head. “You got any more of those glowsticks?” he asked Jacob.

“YES!”

“Get dressed and grab all you have.” Jonny shifted his gaze to Steven. “You get dressed, too; you’re coming with me.”

Adélaïde followed Jonny into his room. “You don’t mean to go there now?”

Jonny snatched his sweatshirt and sweatpants from the bureau. “I do. I don’t know why, but I have to.”

Adélaïde walked down the hall to Jacob’s room.

Jacob sat on his bed, snapping glow ropes and connecting them together. “Don’t worry, GG. Angel says he’ll protect all of us.” He jumped off his bed and ran into the living room. He stopped in the middle of the room, staring at his aunt.

Sandra sat on the sofa, hugging a pillow.

Jacob placed his hand on top of hers. “Angel says not to be sad.”

She feigned a smile. “I’m not sad, sweetheart.”

He hugged her. “Angel says everything is going to be all right.”

Jonny kissed the top of Sandra’s head. He sat beside her and put on his shoes. “You alright?”

She bobbed her head. “I’ll be fine. You?”

“Yeah.”

Jacob handed his father three of the glow ropes. “Angel says to put them on.”

Jonny put one over his son’s head. “I want you to wear them.”

Jacob removed the glow rope and put it over his father’s head. “We all need to wear them.”

"We ready?" Steven asked, grabbing his keys from the end table.

"We'll take the Jeep," Jonny said. "I don't want her to know we're coming."

Steven kissed Sandra on the lips. "We'll be back."

Sandra followed them to the front door, locking it behind them. She entered Jacob's room, sat on the bed, and picked up his pillow, squeezing it tight. "I miss you."

Adélaïde stood in the doorway, "Do you want to talk about it?"

Sandra shook her head. "I want to be alone."

"I'll make some coffee," Adélaïde said. She walked into the living room and stared out the window, fiddling with her cross. "Keep them safe, Eber."

2

Jonny parked a few houses from Cheyenne's, surveilling the duplex. Cheyenne's well-lit neighborhood was stagnant save for the relentless bark of a large dog somewhere on the block. Her porch light shone on the emptiness of her front yard and patio.

Cheyenne's front door opened, and Ryder stepped out and shambled back to his home.

"He has to be the bastard beating her," Steven said, through gritted teeth.

"Not him," Jacob said leaning forward. "Nicholas is the one hurting her. Angel says the neighbor is a puppet."

"Does Nicholas possess people?" Jonny asked.

Ryder stopped in his doorway, and turned a glinting amber eye in their direction. Cheyenne's porchlight snuffed out, followed quickly by pops and electric sizzle of the streetlamps blowing out, until the once stadium-lit street was pitch black. The amber glint of Ryder's eye was replaced by the glint of the doorknocker and announced by its slam.

Jonny doubled checked Jacob's glowsticks.

"I'm fine, Daddy. Angel says he won't let anything happen to me."

Jonny stepped out and grabbed Jacob, carrying him on his hip.

"What's the plan?" Steven asked.

"Grab her and take her back to my place."

They jaunted across the street.

"And if Cheyenne refuses?" Steven asked.

"I'll take her against her will."

Steven halted. "Whoa now."

"It's not the first time I've been instructed to save her." Jonny planted Jacob on the ground. "I don't know why, but I have to."

Jacob held Steven's hand. "Don't worry, Uncle Steven, she won't refuse."

Steven leaped up the stairs and opened the door. He felt for the light switch and flicked it up and down, but the house did not illuminate.

"Where's your lighter?" Jonny asked.

"Sandra asked me to quit, so I threw it away."

Jacob pushed his way inside the house. He flicked the switch and the house sparked to life.

Both men stared at the boy.

Jonny snatched Jacob's hand, pulling him back.

The living room was a calamity of tattered cushions and overturned furniture. A piano keyboard protruded from the shattered grandfather clock. A yellow smear on the kitchen wall highlighted the puddle of lemon bars and broken Pyrex below. The open cupboards were baren, their contents strewn over the counters and floor. A dull red trail of footprints led from the kitchen to the front door, to the master bedroom.

"You smell that?" Steven asked.

"I do," Jonny answered. "Smells like—"

"Paint thinner," Steven said.

They made their way through the carnage to Cheyenne's room. The door was closed and blood smeared the crowning of the doorframe and on the doorknob.

Jonny faced Jacob. "I don't want you to see this."

Steven held Jacob back.

"She's alive, Daddy."

"She could be severely hurt." He looked to Steven. "I don't want him to see."

Steven lifted Jacob and held down his head, whispering, "We came as you asked. Now, do as we say."

Jacob wrapped his arms around Steven's neck. "But—"

"Keep your head down," Steven said.

Jonny rapped the door. "Cheyenne, it's me, Jonny."

There was no reply.

He peered over his shoulder.

Steven angled Jacob away from the door and motioned with his chin for the go-ahead.

Jonny cracked the door. "Cheyenne, I'm coming in." He glided his hand on the wall, searching for the light switch. He flicked on the ceiling light.

Cheyenne's bedding strung across the floor; the white, cotton sheets were stained red. Her body lay supine with her head hanging off the foot of the bed. Her clothes were mostly ripped from her body and the cord from the lamp was wrapped around her neck.

Jonny rushed to her and removed the cord. He placed two fingers on her neck, feeling for life.

"Is she?" Steven asked.

"It's faint and she's burning up." He removed her hair from her face and smelt his fingers. "She's covered in paint thinner."

Her bottom lip was split, and her nose bloodied. There was fresh bruising on her cheeks resembling a shoe print.

"That sonofabitch tried to kill her," Steven said, setting Jacob down and running out of the room.

"Dammit, Steven!" Jonny rushed to Jacob, blocking his view of Cheyenne.

"Daddy, the neighbor didn't hurt her."

"I know. Steven is blinded by his anger." Jonny looked over his shoulder at Cheyenne. He was stuck in a hard spot. He needed to cool Cheyenne and wrangle Steven. "Close your eyes." He carried Jacob passed Cheyenne and set him down in the master bathroom. "Turn on the shower, cold water only, and then sit on the toilet with your eyes closed."

"Daddy, Angel says everything is gonna be alright."

Jonny pointed to the toilet. "Let me know when your eyes are closed."

Jacob turned the bathroom light on. He pushed back the curtain and turned on the shower. He ran to the toilet and yelled, "Ready!"

Jonny carried Cheyenne into the bathroom, laid her in the tub, and positioned her so the water would miss her face.

"Angel says this isn't your fault."

The lights in the house pulsed to darkness.

Jonny stood, flicking the light switch up and down.

"Angel says, go get Uncle Steven."

Jonny removed the glow ropes from around his neck and placed it around Jacob.

Jacob gave the lights back to his father. "Angel says you need it. He says he'll protect me." Jacob took his glow ropes and placed one around Cheyenne's neck and then handed the rest to his father. "Angel says to take them."

Jonny grabbed them. "You stay here until I get back." He ran out the bathroom, through the house, and into the neighbor's house.

Ryder's house smelled of booze and cigarettes. It was dark, but the layout mirrored Cheyenne's. Jonny followed the thwacks of fists on flesh coming from the back alcove. He focused into the darkness and made out Steven's figure in the back bedroom sitting on top of Ryder, delivering two lefts and a right.

Ryder laughed, choking on blood and broken teeth.

Jonny pulled Steven off. "He's not himself, remember? Look at his eyes."

The amber pits grinned intensely at them as blood dripped down along his cheeks.

"Those are what I saw in the shop," Jonny said.

Ryder laughed; his eyes bled black. He rolled onto his hands and knees, convulsing, and vomited a thick black sludge.

A long, gangly claw birthed from the puddle of mist-shrouded dregs. A second, equally putrid, arm breached, and together, the two drew the thick pile of black deposit out of view into the shadows. The last of the pour from Ryder's mouth strung to the vile figure. He gave one last violent heave, pouring the final drop into the shadows and collapsed to the ground.

The thick black dreg sprouted more limbs.

Jonny pinched his nose, but the rancid smell of burning flesh was overpowering.

The shadow creature scurried up the wall to the ceiling and ran behind them. It dropped to the floor, making a moist splat and slowly unfolded. The creature's silhouette stood taller and brawnier than any man they had seen. The creature eyed

Jonny and the glow of its amber pits intensified. "*Laissez les bon temps roule.*"

Jonny's nostrils flared. He turned his hands into fists and rushed forward.

Steven wrapped his arms around Jonny's chest and stomach, fighting to hold him back.

Jonny ripped one of the glowsticks from his neck and flung it at the creature.

It hoisted itself up to the ceiling, uttering an ear-piercing yowl. It glared at both men and stampeded across the ceiling and out the front door.

Jonny pried at Steven's grip. "It's going after Jacob!"

They sprinted back to Cheyenne's house and into the empty master bathroom.

Panic set in Jonny's chest. "JACOB!"

Steven checked the closet. "Jacob," he said pushing the clothes to one side.

Jonny searched under the bed. Nothing, no one. He sprung to his feet. "JACOB!" he heaved.

Steven returned from the closet. "Did you hear that?"

Jonny put up his hand. "Shhhh."

Muffled voices emanated from the alcove along with the sound of shuffling boxes.

Both men walked to the alcove.

The door to the storage room was closed, but a bright white light illuminated through the cracks of the door frame.

Jonny opened the door, shielding his eyes. "Jacob!"

The light dissipated.

"We're behind the boxes, Daddy."

A fortress built from the boxes sat in the center of the room. Jonny removed the top box and handed it to Steven, working his way down. He lifted Jacob out of the barricade. The feeling of relief subdued the anger he felt for failing to protect Jacob from Cheyenne's current state. He hugged him tight. "I told you to stay put."

Steven continued to remove the boxes so he could reach Cheyenne. "How'd you move her and these boxes?" he asked.

"I didn't, Angel did."

Jonny caressed his son's face. "Where did the bright light come from?"

"Angel said he needed to surround us with light. He said the light would bounce off the mirrors inside the box." Jacob pointed to the open box next to the bureau. "He surrounded us with the mirrors and then placed the heavy boxes around them."

"I love you so much," Jonny said.

"Don't be scared, Daddy. Angel's one of the good guys." Jacob pushed off his father's shoulders and wiggled free. He crawled between Steven's legs to Cheyenne. "Angel was trying to heal her."

Jonny helped Steven move the last of the heavy boxes. He stepped forward, crunching glass; he lifted his foot.

"She has glass in her body," Jacob said. "I've been pulling them out."

Jonny picked up his son and handed him to Steven. He raised his sleeves and bent down, scooping Cheyenne into his arms. He tossed her torso up, aiming for a better grip. The glass in her back dug into the meat of his arms. His face grimaced. "Let's go," he said.

Steven led them through the house.

"Let me go first," Jonny said. "If that thing blitz attacks us, I don't want Jacob getting hurt."

Jacob wrapped his arms around Steven's neck, whispering in his ear. "But Angel protects me."

"He's a father, he'll always worry about your safety."

Jonny snuck out the front door, scanning the early morning

dawn. He walked down the porch steps, searching for the creature. He waited by Cheyenne's car, motioning for Steven.

Steven crept out onto the porch and down the steps to Jonny.

"He's not here, you don't have to worry," Jacob said.

"How do you know?" Jonny asked.

Jacob let go of Steven's neck. "You can smell him; I can feel him."

"Feel him how?" Steven asked.

Jacob shrugged his shoulders. "I don't know. It's like the creepy feeling you get when you're being watched."

They made haste to the Jeep. Steven took the keys from Jonny's front pocket and unlocked the vehicle. He secured Jacob in his car seat and then helped with Cheyenne.

"Should we seatbelt her in?" Steven asked.

"We're not far from the house," Jonny said. He looked to Jacob. "Can you hold her head if we lay Cheyenne on her side?" He removed his sweatshirt and balled it into a makeshift pillow, placing it between the car seat and her head.

Once they had her situated, both men jumped into the Jeep and sped down the road.

Jonny glanced into the rearview mirror at them.

Jacob pulled the glass fragments from her shoulder and back. "You're gonna be alright," he said. "Daddy's gonna save you now."

3

Adélaïde opened the front door. "Sandra, they're back. Somethings wrong!"

Sandra jumped from Jacob's bed and ran out the door and down the porch steps. "Is she okay?"

Jonny carried Cheyenne inside the house. “I think so.” He hauled her into his room and placed her on his bed.

Sandra followed in shortly with her stethoscope and sphygmomanometer. She placed the cuff around Cheyenne’s upper left arm. “God, she’s burning up! GG, can you get me the ear-thermometer out of the medicine cabinet? Steven, get me all the ice packs out of the deep freezer.” Sandra pumped the cuff and placed the stethoscope in the crook of the elbow inside Cheyenne’s bicep. She listened for Cheyenne’s pulse, focusing on the gradually falling gauge needle. She removed the cuff from Cheyenne’s arm. “She’s 100-over-55, but we need to get the rest of her clothes off!”

Jonny stepped back from the bed.

“Stop being a damn man about this and help me get her clothes off!”

“Here,” Adélaïde said, handing Sandra the tympanic thermometer.

Sandra put the thermometer in Cheyenne’s ear and pushed the start button; it beeped, displaying 104. “GG, get a sheet and soak it with cold water and bring it to me.”

“I got the ic—” Steven stopped at the foot of the bed staring at Cheyenne’s nude body.

Sandra stood, snatching some of the ice packs from his hands. “Christ! Yes, she’s naked. Would you two stop acting like a couple of virgins and help me cool her off!”

Jonny followed Sandra’s lead and placed the rest of the ice under Cheyenne’s armpit, ribs, and groin.

Adélaïde returned with the sheet and Steven helped cover Cheyenne’s body.

Sandra retook Cheyenne’s temperature. “GG, have we still got any of grandpa’s Tylenol suppositories?”

“Let me go check.”

“What else can we do?” Steven asked.

"Nothing right now. Cheyenne's vitals are fine. I just need to get her temperature down."

Steven pointed to Jonny's arm. "You're bleeding."

"Yeah, cut myself on the glass in her back." He touched Cheyenne's neck, examining the ligature bruising. His lip curled, his brows narrowed, and his nostrils flared.

Violence against anyone, particularly women, upset Jonny. There was something different about this.

Sandra laid her hand on top of his. "What happened?"

He pulled the sheet over Cheyenne's neck and balled his hands into fists. He walked to the door saying, "Get her temperature down, and then we'll explain."

4

Jonny peeked in Jacob's room. Jacob's butt was up in the air and his torso buried inside his toy chest. "What are you doin'?"

"Looking for my lightsaber!"

"When you're done, come find me."

Jonny continued his path to the living room, where Steven awaited him.

"Jon, I know you saw what I saw."

He acknowledged Steven with a bob and continued into the kitchen. He pulled two coffee cups from the cabinet.

Everything was calming down, and Jonny had time to ruminate. What the fuck was it and how did it know so much about the past?

Steven retrieved the creamer. "What are you gonna tell them?"

"The truth." Jonny grabbed his coffee and headed for the sliding glass door.

Steven followed.

"I need to be alone," Jonny said, sliding shut the door.

5

Using tweezers, Adélaïde pulled glass fragments from Cheyenne's feet. "We should call the police."

Sandra secured another Band-Aid on Cheyenne's back. "And tell them what? A little boy who speaks to the afterlife told us that someone was trying to kill her?"

Jacob ran into the room, holding his lightsaber in one hand and glow sticks in the other. "We have to surround her with light."

"Why don't I take those," Steven said. "I need you to go take a bath and get into some clean clothes."

"But Daddy wants to talk to me."

"Your daddy needs some alone time. Go bathe, and when he's ready, your daddy will come to you."

Sandra wrung one of the washcloths and handed it Steven. "Wash the blood off her back. If you find any more glass, pull it out." She turned Jacob around. "Go on, do as your uncle told you." She walked to the bedroom window and focused on Jonny.

"We saw . . . something," Steven said. "I think he needs time to process."

"What did you see?" Sandra asked.

"I don't even know what to call it."

Adélaïde fidgeted with her necklace eyeing Cheyenne's comatose body. "She can't stay here. Nothing good will come of this."

Sandra walked out of the room, making her way outside. She stood next to Jonny and admired the yellow lilies. "GG is convinced it's grandpa."

Jonny tossed his cold coffee. "There's no harm in it."

"The type of bruising around her neck, you've seen it before."

He turned and hugged Sandra, resting the side of his face on the top of her head. "Yes."

She wrapped her arms around his waist asking, "You scared?"

" . . . Yes."

Seventeen

The Barter

1

Jonny exited the bathroom, slinging his towel around his neck. He entered the living room, drying his head, to find Jacob lying face-down in his coloring book with a crayon still resting gingerly in his fingers. A low raspy snore, which Jonny could identify since Jacob's infancy, emanated from his parted mouth.

Sandra stood in front of the bay windows, with her arms wrapped around her midsection, staring blankly at the yellow lilies. Steven approached her, handing Sandra a cup of hot tea.

Jonny picked Jacob up and sank into the couch, stroking Jacob's head. He was exhausted and keeping him close seemed a good idea. Jonny doubted he would return to the same dreamless sleep he had before three a.m. but, he would take any amount of peaceful sleep he could.

"There's fresh coffee," Adélaïde said entering the living room. "You want me to make you a cup?"

Jonny was too tired to review the details over coffee. He

already explained to Sandra what happened. “I’m good, GG.” He wrapped his arms around Jacob. “Later when the stores open, I’ll buy more glowsticks and candles.”

Adélaïde sat next to him. “Why do we need those?”

“It’s afraid of the light.”

Jacob’s tiny fist rubbed his nose. “His name is Nicholas.”

“Shhh. Go back to sleep,” Jonny said.

Jacob lifted his head, yawning. “But you wanted to talk to me.”

Jonny placed his hand under Jacob’s shirt and softly rubbed his back. “I want you to sleep, we can talk later.”

“Who’s—”

Jonny placed his finger to his lips, silencing Adélaïde. He continued to rub Jacob’s back with one hand and Jacob’s face with the other.

Jacob’s body went limp and his mouth gaped.

Steven leaned against the wall by the bay windows. “How’d you know to throw the glowstick at that thing?” he asked.

“Cheyenne told me.”

Sandra set her teacup in the windowsill and sat on the floor in the middle of the room. “When did she tell you that?”

Jonny closed his eyes, resting his head against the couch. “I believe that thing is attached to her somehow.” He opened his eyes halfway. “When I broke into her house, it taunted me.” He closed his eyes; his voice was getting softer. “The night she hit her head, it attacked me in my room; Jacob saved me. He knew to draw back the curtains to let the moonlight in.” Jonny’s eyes opened only a quarter of the way. “It attempted to attack me again in the attic. Luck was on my side and my flashlight happened to turn on.” His eyelids shuttered and his speech slurred. “The other morning, when I dropped her off, she told me to bathe Jacob in light.”

“She can’t stay here,” Adélaïde said.

He reached for her hand. “I don’t know why, but—” he yawned, fighting the Sandman. “—I have to.”

Jonny felt his hand sliding off of hers but fighting it was futile. His head grew cumbersome under his debility and gravity pulled it back as his vision faded black.

2

Adélaïde took the blanket from the couch and covered them both. “Let them sleep,” she said.

Steven pulled the handle on the couch, raising Jonny’s feet. “That thing spoke to him. It said Loss or Lass.”

Sandra bulged her eyes at Jonny. He failed to mention the phrase. Did he lie? No, he intentionally omitted it because that’s what he does . . . protects. Her tears burned her eyes. How would that abomination know to say the phrase? Was this somehow her fault? Was God punishing her for hating him? For blaming God for what they went through as children? She blinked and her sorrow trickled down her face. “*Laissez les bon temps roule*,” she said.

Steven’s brows furrowed. “Those were the exact words.”

Sandra stood and headed for the hallway.

“I never taught your mother to speak Creole. How’d you know to say that?” Adélaïde asked.

“It was in a bad dream.”

“What does it mean?” Steven asked.

“Let the good times roll.” Sandra wiped the tears clean. “I need to lie down.”

3

Adélaïde poured coffee into two cups and creamer into one. She listened to Steven's tongue jumble the creole phrase.

"Loss lay tong Rolaid."

She giggled under her breath, hearing the frustration in his voice. "Steven, sweetheart, it's okay."

"Anyways, the phrase made Jonny lunge for that creature. I think it has something to do with his past." He frowned. "With their past."

She ruminated on his statement. There was truth in Steven's epiphany. Sandra knew the phrase, too, and it made them both upset. It was pointless to probe Steven on the matter; she would have to investigate another way.

"Steven, tell me what happened." She turned, offering his cup. "Everything."

"Well, when we got there, the neighbor was leaving her house. We went in and found Cheyenne . . . " He paused and raised his cup to his lips, then lowered it without a sip. "When I saw her like that, I saw my mother. I remembered my father."

Adélaïde squeezed his hand. "I'm here."

"I ran next door and beat his face in. Didn't even faze him; he just laughed." Steven sipped his coffee. "Jonny had to pull me off him, had to point out his eyes."

"His eyes?"

"Yeah, they were glowing, golden . . . " Steven stammered searching for the right word. "Lights. Like candles or embers." He pushed away his coffee. "That thing poured out of his face."

"What did it look like?"

"It was dark. All we had was a dim wall plugin. But it ran up the wall like a lizard, crawled across the ceiling and transformed into a man."

Adélaïde clutched her necklace and crossed herself. "Evil has many forms. It hides who it really is." She collected their cups, "Where was Jacob?"

"Jonny left him with Cheyenne."

She stopped pouring coffee and turned around. "He left Jacob?" She set the coffee pot down, "With her?"

Steven bobbed his head. "When we returned to Cheyenne's house, they weren't where we left them. We found them in another room which radiated a blinding light."

Adélaïde returned to her seat, sipping her coffee. "Where did the light come from?"

He shrugged his shoulders. "We don't know. Jacob said Angel wanted them there."

She tapped her cup and smiled. At least Eber was there to keep them safe. "Eber was always fond of Jacob." Her smile vanished and her face hardened. "She can't stay, she'll be the end of him."

Steven stood, yawning. "Jon will never let anything happen to his son."

"She'll be the end of Jonny," Adélaïde said.

Steven narrowed his brows and frowned at her. "Not likely." He yawned again. "I'm going to go lie down."

"Get some rest, I'll clean up in here."

Adélaïde placed both cups in the dishwasher. She put her hands on her hips and sighed. Cheyenne needed to go. The church would know what do. She picked up the phone, pushing the talk button.

"Put the phone down."

Adélaïde turned and saw Jacob, his irises white. She smiled, setting the phone back on its base. "Eber? Eber, I've missed you."

Angel pulled out a barstool and climbed up. He leaned over,

kissing her cheek. “He must save her.”

She pulled away, angry. Eber would say such a thing. “Why him? That boy has gone through enough.”

“That boy is a man now.” Angel grabbed her cross. “God does not give us more than we can handle.”

She retrieved her necklace, asking, “Did he ever tell you what happened?”

The white eyes stared deeply into hers. “Not everything, I'm sure.” He patted the barstool next to him and she sat. “His past will continue to haunt him until he can forgive himself. The more you and everyone else push him, the more he'll withdraw.”

She cupped Jacob's face. “Then tell me what happened?”

Angel removed her hand. “Sometimes, not knowing is better.”

She held his hand in both of hers. “He's having nightmares again. Please tell me how to help him.”

“When he's ready, he'll come to you.”

Adélaïde stood with her back toward Angel. She closed her eyes and sighed. “Do you think he'll ever be ready?”

The lack of reply caused her to turn around; she found herself alone. She entered the living, finding Jacob asleep on his father's lap in the same position he had been in when she left.

Jonny leaned forward with his eyes closed. “RALPHIE!”

Jacob woke and wrapped his arms around his father's neck. “It's okay, Daddy.”

Adélaïde rushed to them and tugged on Jacob. “Let go!” If Jonny went violent and hurt his son—she couldn't finish the thought. “Eber, please help!” She let Jacob go and patted Jonny's face. “Jon, sweetheart, wake up.”

“Open your eyes!” he yelled.

She grabbed Jonny's hands, ready to shield Jacob if

necessary.

Jacob whispered into his father's ear and Jonny opened his eyes.

Adélaïde looked at Jacob, her mouth hung low. No one had ever woken Jonny from a nightmare. Not without the violent tantrums or pinning him down until the nightmare played out. "What did you say to wake him?"

Jacob wiped the exuded beads of sweat from his father's face. "I didn't say anything, Angel did."

Eber heard me. A faint smile formed on her lips but vanished quickly. She stared at Jonny, waiting for the 'I'm okay' nod.

Jonny ran his hand down the back of Jacob's head. He glanced at Adélaïde saying, "I'm okay, really."

"I'll get you some water," Adélaïde said.

4

Jacob brushed his father's sweaty hair out of Jonny's eyes. His stare ping-ponged around Jonny's face and then, veered off to the scars on his chest. "Daddy, what are your nightmares about?"

Jonny relaxed into the couch. His nightmares had vanished almost a decades before Jacob was born. How much did he witness? "The same monsters I've dreamed about since I was a kid."

Jacob rubbed the circular scars on his father's chest. "Did your monsters give you these?"

Jonny normally gloated about how fast Jacob could put two-and-two together but this time, Jonny found himself off-base. He bobbed his head and pointed to his biceps, "And these, the ones on my back, and on my legs."

"How'd they make them?"

There was a lot he wanted to tell and teach Jacob, but the horrors of his past didn't make the list, at least not at this stage of Jacob's life. Jonny shook his head. "One day, I'll tell you, but today is not that day."

Jacob looked into his father's green eyes. "I have nightmares, too."

"Oh, what about?"

"You finally find happiness, and Nicholas takes it away."

Jonny furrowed his brows. Nicholas was a new thing in their lives. Why was Jacob dreaming about him? Moreover, what made Jacob think he wasn't happy? "What makes you think I'm not happy?"

Jacob fidgeted with his fingers.

Jonny glanced to the threshold of the dining room and living room and saw Adélaïde watching them. Depending on how he answered, there would be a discussion later.

Jonny pinched Jacob's chin, tilting his head up. "You can tell me; you're not in trouble."

"Auntie Sandra and GG say you're always worried about something and that you worry you're failing all of us. Uncle Steven says you fear you're failing as a daddy the most."

Jonny's callused thumb caressed Jacob's cheek. "Those are natural concerns. They don't make me sad; they make me aware of why I work so hard to provide for my family."

Jacob looked toward the hallway. "Angel says, go to her."

Adélaïde stepped forward. "Don't!"

Jonny planted Jacob on the floor and approached her. He grabbed his water and kissed her cheek. "I have to."

"I don't want that woman here."

Jonny did not stop walking. He glanced over his shoulder. "I know."

5

Jonny sat on the edge of the bed, setting his water on the nightstand. He felt Cheyenne's forehead and then grabbed the thermometer. He took her temperature: one hundred degrees. He tossed the thermometer to the bed and pulled the sheet away from her throat. His rough fingers skimmed the marks.

"You said you've seen those before."

Jonny jumped. "Jesus, you scared the piss out of me."

"Move," Sandra said, "I need to check her vitals."

He switched places with her.

Sandra checked Cheyenne's blood pressure, pulse, respirations, and temperature. She removed the melted ice packs and touched the marks on Cheyenne's neck. "Where have you seen these?"

Jonny stared at the ceiling; his Adam's apple dropped and then rose. "That sonofabitch was always trying to find ways to torture me."

Sandra scooted to his side and wrapped her arm around him. "Please, tell me what happened."

Jonny escaped Sandra's embrace and sat on the floor. He rested his back against the bed and relaxed his elbows on his knees, turning his hands into fits. "When I was six, they took me to New York to train; I trained with a guy named Flynn for two years. The night I was supposed to return, I saved a boy and girl."

"Was the boy Ralphie?"

He shook his head. "I never knew his name, but apparently, he was an important kid. Mickey found out what I did, and had Lee suspended me in the air for several days." He looked at his scars. "After the first day, my body went numb; I couldn't feel the pain anymore. After the second day, they added weight, and the hooks pulled at my flesh. For a moment, I could feel my skin tearing before I would go numb again."

"Did Mickey choke you?"

He shook his head. "Not me; the girl I thought I rescued. She sacrificed herself so the boy could get away."

Sandra crawled to the floor, sitting in front of him. "Did Mickey kill her in front of you?"

He shook his head. "New York is the headquarters. The people they worked for ran an underground sex trafficking for children and illegal sex clubs. The girl was a part of it."

"How do you know?"

"She told me."

Sandra grabbed his hand. Her voice trembled. "Did he make you choke that girl?"

He shook his head.

Sandra's body deflated.

"She was thirteen and looked like you, except she had green eyes. Her name was Annika."

"Jonny, what happened to the girl?"

He looked to the ceiling and swallowed. He closed his eyes, and tears ran down his cheeks. "That's enough for now."

Sandra stood to her feet. "You always do this. You stop just before unveiling what happened."

Jonny erupted from the floor and elevated his voice. "Sometimes knowing is worse than being in the dark." He clawed a white undershirt from his bureau. "Consider yourself lucky." He bumped into Adélaïde outside the room. He looked at her, then to Sandra. They hadn't conspired together to extract information out him since he first arrived home. Eber had put a stop to it.

Jonny scowled, sighing out his nose.

Adélaïde raised her hand.

He stepped away, putting on his shirt, and entered the

living room.

"Jacob, get your shoes on."

He dropped his crayon and skipped to the shoe rack. "Where we going?"

Jonny grabbed his work boots and put them in the shoe rack and then grabbed his flipflops. "To the store."

Jacob opened the front door and skipped to the Jeep. He talked to himself carrying on a conversation about the duck pond.

Jonny inspected Jacob's seatbelt. "Does your car seat feel a little too snug?" He loosened the shoulder straps giving a finger's width room.

"Angel says I'm gonna be tall like you."

Jonny smirked.

"Daddy, how tall were you when you were my age?"

He tussled Jacob's hair. "Taller than you."

"Whoa, you were a giant!"

Jonny chortled. "I was always freakishly tall for my age." He jumped into the Jeep and drove to the Dollar Tree.

6

Jacob clung to the front of the shopping cart while Jonny pushed it down the aisle. He allowed Jacob to grab all the glow sticks and candles from the shelves and then they traveled to the next aisle.

Jacob jumped off and ran toward the groceries.

Jonny searched for matches. He crawled down on his hands and knees, finding them on the bottom shelf in the far back. He grabbed the last two boxes and sauntered after Jacob.

Jacob came, running, around the corner, tossing a loaf of bread into the cart.

Jonny smiled. "Okay."

Jacob hitched a ride on the front of the cart. "Daddy, Angel says we need to pick up some clothes for her."

Jonny had no desire to return to Cheyenne's place, but Jacob saw too much of a woman's body already. He counted his blessings Jacob never raised questions; he was too young for the birds and bees.

Jonny pointed to the loaf of bread. "Before or after?"

"After!"

Jonny paid for his merchandise and wheeled the cart outside, still with Jacob clinging to the front. He placed one foot on the undercarriage of the shopping cart and pushed with his other foot. He lifted his accelerator into the air, allowing the cart to drive freely.

"Wee!" Jacob said, giggling.

Jonny dropped his foot and pushed off the ground, catching Jacob's infectious laughter.

They neared the Jeep and Jonny slowed the ride. He handed Jacob the bread and pointed to the car seat. He loaded the rest of his purchase in what he would consider the trunk and drove to the duck pond. He parked and glanced into the rear-review mirror. "Is Angel with you?"

Jacob unclipped his seat belt. "He's always with me."

"Can you ask him a question for me?"

"Angel says he can hear you."

Jonny gazed at the morning sun. "Can you heal the marks on Cheyenne's neck?"

Jacob leaned forward, hugging his father. "If I do this, you have to do something for me."

Jonny turned and stared into Jacob's white eyes. He gave a single nod, agreeing with the terms.

Angel crawled into the front passenger seat. "In order to help save her, you have to gain her trust. You've done some damage, so it won't be easy."

Jonny lowered his gaze. "What is it you want me to do?"

"You're not going to outwit her; she's smarter than you. You need to be honest with her; you need to tell her."

Jonny jerked his head up. "I get anxiety and panic attacks trying to tell the ones I love, and you want me to tell someone I abhor."

Angel smirked. "Abhor is a strong word, don't you think?" He grabbed the bread and jumped out the Jeep. "Besides, we both know it's not her you abhor." He handed a few slices out to the homeless. "How many mental tally marks have you given toward your similarities; five, ten, fifteen?"

Jonny followed beside him. "I stopped counting."

"If you loathe her, then her persecutions won't matter. You need only tell her, no one else if you choose."

"Why does she need to know about my past?"

They stopped at the waterfront and Angel tore a piece of bread, tossing it to the ducks. "You're not ready to know the truth, none of you are." He threw another piece. "I'll wait until the end of the day for your answer."

Jonny snatched the other half of the bread from Angel and plucked it apart for the ducks. "Do you know who GG thinks you are?"

"I do," Angel answered. "But like you told Sandra, there's no harm in it." He handed Jonny the loaf of bread. "To try and get Cheyenne to open up, you might introduce her to Dolores."

Jonny did miss her and he could see Cheyenne warming up to her, but there was a reason he hadn't seen Dolores since Jacob was born. Besides, another concern nibbled at his thoughts.

"Is that thing always with her?" Jonny asked, tossing a piece of bread.

Angel fed a duckling from his palm. "No, but he's never too

far away."

Jonny kneeled and petted the duckling in Angel's hands.

"You are Nicholas's target. Everyone else is just a means to get to you, even your son."

"How does he know so much about me, about the past?"

"Like I said, you're not ready to know the truth." He put the duckling down. "Life is like a chess game. You move your pieces to achieve an end goal. You can't lose sight of the goal."

Jonny knew it was Angel's way of saying, *Figure it out on your own.* He stood tossing the bread to the ducks. "Can I have my son back? I was looking forward to spending time with him here."

Jacob's eyes faded back to their hazel selves. "Give me a slice, Daddy."

Jonny smiled. He removed a slice of bread and kneeled behind Jacob. "Tear a small piece and roll it into a ball. Lay it flat in your palm and the white goose will eat it from your hand."

Jacob did as his father instructed. "That tickles," he giggled.

Jonny nibbled on Jacob's neck, picking him up.

"I surrender! I surrender!"

He turned Jacob around, tossing him in the air.

Jacob laughed. "Do it again, Daddy! Do it again!"

He tossed Jacob several times and then held him in the air, spinning around in a circle, smiling. He cradled Jacob, pretending to be dizzy and fell to the ground.

Jacob sat on his father's stomach, reaching for his dad's neck. "Tickle, tickle, tickle."

The ducks and geese surrounded them, all trying to get the bread laying on the ground.

Jonny sat upright, catching his breath from his laughter. "Let's finish feeding our friends."

Jacob sat between his father's legs and threw a piece of

bread at the wildfowl.

Jonny drew his left knee up, perching himself up with his right hand. He looked across the shimmering water to reflect.

Jacob rested against his dad, holding a duckling. A low audible growl came from his stomach.

"You hungry?" Jonny asked.

"Uh-huh."

"Okay, let's go."

Jacob handed the homeless man the rest of the bread. He returned to his father, grabbing his hand. "Can I watch more of mommy's videos when we get home?"

Jonny picked him up. "Of course. You never have to ask permission." He secured Jacob in his car seat and then hopped into the driver seat. He glanced at Jacob through the review mirror. "I agree to the terms."

Eighteen

Dolores

1

For several hours, Jonny sat on the floor resting his arms on his knees, fidgeting with the wooden rosary. How would he tell her? He wasn't sure he could. He was already drenched in sweat from the mere thought. He glanced at the motionless body in his bed. Why did she have to know? They weren't friends. He closed his eyes and leaned his head back and focused on quelling himself.

The crunch of the carpet fiber buckling under the weight of feet pulled him from his meditation. He didn't need to open his eyes to see who entered. Sandra was the only person in the house who avoided tiptoeing. He always associated it with being a graveyard nurse giving three a.m. pills.

Jonny hefted himself up off the floor. He grabbed the prayer hands and extracted a wad of cash.

Sandra wrapped her stethoscope around her neck. She pulled the sheet over Cheyenne's throat. "I finally got her temperature stable."

He counted the hundreds in hand. "That's great."

"I hope you're not mad about the shirt."

He stopped his count. "What shirt?"

"While you were gone, I dressed her in one of your undershirts."

He peered over his shoulder. "White?" He turned round. "The last conversation we had, she told me about one of her dreams."

"What was it about?"

He leaned against the bureau, crossing his feet. "She told me she was in my room before ever stepping foot into my house. She walked into the kitchen wearing nothing but a white tee-shirt; I was there."

Sandra scooted to the foot of the bed.

"Cheyenne said I hurt her, threatened to kill her if anything happened to Jacob."

Sandra wrapped her arms around her stomach. "What did you say to her?"

He scoffed. "She won't be happy to see me when she wakes."

"Jonathan Michael! What did you do?"

He ignored the question and handed her some money. "I was going to grab some of her clothes while I was out, but the thought of sifting through her underwear drawer made me uncomfortable."

Sandra took the money and counted it. "This is your vacation money."

He nodded. "You know her sizes, right?"

She handed back the money.

Jonny pushed her hand away. "Buy Cheyenne some clothes, so when she wakes, she's not wearing my undershirt."

Sandra set the money on the bed. "You've got a big heart. I'll buy her some clothes, but I'll use my own money." She paused in the doorway. "That money is for you and Jacob."

He retrieved the money and tucked it in his front pocket.

Sandra leaned against the doorjamb. “Steven said that monster spoke the words.”

He glanced at his sister and bobbed his head.

“What does it mean?”

Jonny stared at Cheyenne. “I don’t know, but nothing good ever came after those words.” He focused back on Sandra. “It seems to know a lot about us.”

“Maybe when she wakes, we’ll finally get some answers,” Sandra said. She pushed off the doorjamb saying, “If I’m going to buy her clothes, I should do it now before I head to work.”

Jonny waited until Sandra left and then pulled the sheet away from Cheyenne’s throat. His breathing echoed in his ears, drowning out his thoughts. He rubbed his fingers over the marks and closed his eyes, remembering the girl he spoke about, remembering Annika.

2

Annika already bared two strangulation marks. Her tears cut a path through her dirt-stained face to the end of her jaw.

Lee held her shackled hands in front of her, snickering at a young Jonny.

Mickey walked into the room from behind Jonny, holding a length of barbed wire. He took up position behind the girl.

Annika begged, but no sound came from her mouth.

Mickey brought the barbed wire up and around the girl’s head.

The words sliced through the loud drumming in Jonny’s ears: *Laissez les bon temps roule.*

3

Jonny reopened his eyes, clenching his jaw. He covered the marks and returned to his sitting position on the floor. He tilted his head back and closed his eyes.

"Deep in thought?"

Jonny's brows furrowed; he didn't hear him coming. He glimpsed at Jacob's pale eyes; they were at once unnerving and comforting. "How are you so quiet?"

Angel sat Indian style in front of him. "You gave me your answer rather quickly. Curious, what made you agree?"

Jonny gripped the rosary, kissing it. "When I was playing with Jacob." He pulled the rosary over his head and handed it to the puppeteer.

Angel took it and stood. He placed it back over Jonny's head. "You keep it." He sat, crossing his legs again. "You were playing with your son . . . "

"I thought with all the horrible and sinful things I've done; I didn't deserve the happiness and joy playing with Jacob brought me." He stared blankly at the body in his bed. "From the moment we met, everything she's done has been to protect us." He drifted his gaze back to the puppet master. "She'll never know what it's like to have the joy of children, to have a family, to know what love feels like."

"You know nothing about her nor her past, so why should any of that matter?"

Jonny sat cross-legged. "You were right about our similarities, but the difference, I escaped my nightmare and had my family to help me through the aftermath." He pointed to Cheyenne. "She continues to live her nightmare with no one to help her."

"Have you really escaped your nightmare, or have you let it fester inside you?"

Jonny's eyes narrowed.

"Everyone has a backstory. Some, like yours, are graphic and painful; some, like hers, are . . . unbelievable. The lucky ones are those who have nothing interesting happen."

Jonny brought up his knees and rested his elbows on them. He rubbed the stubble on his upper lip with his forefinger.

Angel stood, placing his hand on Jonny's shoulder. "You're hoping if you do this, it'll atone for what you did." He walked to the foot of the bed and turned. "There's a reason for everything." He peeked over his shoulder at Cheyenne. "God doesn't give us more than we can handle."

Jonny continued to massage his upper lip while staring blankly at the floor.

"The only one holding you responsible for your actions is you," Angel said. "Are you sure you can do what I've asked of you?"

Jonny shook his head.

"Are you sure you want me to do this?"

He stared into the white eyes controlling Jacob's body. "Yes."

"Leave us and close the door. No one is to enter."

Jonny shut the door behind him and guarded the entrance.

A bright light gradually pierced through the doorjamb, floodlighting the hallway.

Adélaïde turned the TV off and walked the hall. "What's going on?"

Jonny stood in the middle of the hallway. "Go back into the living room."

Steven walked out of Sandra's room; his hair disheveled. Blanket indents were forged in his chest, and the right side of his face redden from the pillow. "That's the same light."

The light intensified; they shielded their eyes.

Adélaïde held out her hands and waved them side to side, maneuvering her way to her boys. "I don't like this! I don't want her here!"

Jonny pushed them into Sandra's room. "The light is my doing, not hers." He kissed Adélaïde's cheek. "Did you not raise us to help those in need?" He clutched her necklace. "Are you not a devout Catholic?"

With everyone in Sandra's room, no one paid attention to the light dissipating.

"It's done," Angel said, entering the room.

"What's done?" Steven asked.

Angel ignored the question and addressed Adélaïde. "You will stop your nonsense."

She placed her hands on her hips.

"Nicholas is tied to Jonny's past in ways none of you will understand. This is one case you will not win. Like it or not, Cheyenne stays," he pointed to Jonny, "until he fulfills his part."

Steven kneeled eye level. "How are they connected to him?"

"You've always been a good friend and brother to this family. When the time is right, you'll know the truth." Angel grabbed Jonny's hand. "Come with me."

Adélaïde stepped to follow but Steven pulled her back. "Whatever he's about to tell him, it's not for us."

4

Steven put the keys in the ignition and pulled out of the driveway. "Why we going to the shop?"

Jonny rolled down his window and rested his arm on the door. "To bring Dolores home."

Steven smiled. “It’s about time. You want some help?”

“Nah, I can handle it.” He stared at Cheyenne’s open front door as they drove by. “In a few days, we need to tow her car to the garage. I promised her I would take look.”

Steven smirked. “For hating someone as much as you do, you sure have had a lot of private talks with her.”

“It’s not like I had much of a choice. Cheyenne is the only reason Jacob wasn’t taken.”

“Touché.”

They drove the remaining two miles in silence. Steven pulled around back and Jonny jumped out. He locked the gate behind Steven’s car and met him by the back door. He unlocked the door asking, “While I’m taking her out, could I get you to spray the clear coat on the Cougar?”

Steven put his hand on Jonny’s forehead. “You feelin’, all right?”

“Yeah, why?”

“Meticulous Jonny is allowing someone else in the paint booth.”

He swatted Steven’s hand from his face. “The Cougar is going to be the last car I do. I’m gonna close the shop.”

“No, no, no! I said I would help get you caught up!”

The side of Jonny’s lip curled upward. “He’s right, you’ve always been an excellent friend to me.” He unlocked his office. “I didn’t mean for good.”

Steven sighed. “Pro tem?”

Jonny opened the safe and recovered out a set of keys. “Yes,” he said. “I can’t be here while trying to figure out how to save her.”

“What about graffiti? Your customers are already pouring in.”

“I’m going to post an announcement on our social media accounts.

"Are you sure? Graffiti is your money maker."

"Money will never be more important than a life," he said, walking past Steven.

Jonny made his way to the storage container outside and unlocked the box, opening both doors. "Hey there, Dolores; it's been a while."

Whimpering came from beneath Dolores's belly.

He walked alongside the covered vehicle, cocking his head. He stooped down and looked under the car.

Floundering through its own mess whimpered a puppy. It spotted Jonny and whimpered more, dragging itself toward him.

Jonny searched the container for the entrance point. He settled on a small hole rusted out of the back corner. He scooped up the puppy and went back inside the garage.

"Hey, Steven!"

Steven stepped out the paint booth. "Aww, where did you find the dirty ball of cuteness?"

"Under Dolores." Jonny carried the puppy to the bathroom sink. "Can you get me a few towels from the office."

"Gonna clean him?"

"Yeah, looks like the mother gave birth under Dolores, and this poor guy has been crawling in the muck."

"How old do you think he is?" Steven asked.

"His eyes are open; maybe two to three weeks." He turned the water on, setting the temperature to warm. He washed and rinsed the puppy, paying close attention to the ears, nose, eyes, and mouth.

The puppy whimpered and barked.

Steven set a stack of towels on the toilet. "I didn't know how many we'd need."

Jonny washed the puppy's belly. "I think he's a she." He held the puppy in the air, verifying the sex.

"It's a girl, all right," Steven said. "Whatcha, gonna do with her?"

Jonny glanced her over. "I think I'll keep her, maybe give her to Jacob." He looked to Steven. "Animals are good at sensing danger and stuff. Maybe she can sense Nicholas coming before I can."

"It'll be a little bit before that, I would assume," Steven said, "but yeah, I'm sure we can train her." He pointed to the puppies back leg. "Whatcha gonna call her, Tiny Tina?"

The puppy's back left leg appeared twisted backward.

"That's probably why the mother left her," Jonny said. He grabbed a fresh towel and handed it to Steven. "Nah, not Tiny Tina. I'll let Jacob name her."

Steven swaddled the puppy with the towel.

"New plan," Jonny said. "I'm faster at airbrushing, so I'm gonna finish the Cougar, and I'll let you and the pup freshen up Dolores. When the Cougar's done, we'll head to the store for puppy supplies."

He turned the light off. "Come on, lets hurry, it's getting late, and I'm getting tired. I want to try and sleep some tonight."

Nineteen

Bait and Switch

1

Cheyenne stirred to the scent of men's cologne, Jonny's cologne. “Fucking A.” She sat up, rotating her head and neck, stretching her arms above her head; her body did not ache. She removed the glow ropes from her wrist and neck, blew out the candles, and tiptoed into the living room. If she was stealthy enough, she could escape scot-free.

Free, was she really? She would always be burdened by his deeds, always tiptoeing through life afraid to love, afraid to experience life as long as she lived.

The dining room light highlighted Jacob's sleeping body on the living room floor. A puppy lay curled up in a ball, tight against his body. Another makeshift bed laid emptied on the other side.

Oil and fresh garlic seasoned the air.

She veered course to the kitchen, escaping no longer desirable.

Jonny stood in front of the stove in his boxer-briefs, stirring ingredients in a giant pot, humming Moonlight Sonata.

Cheyenne knew he had scars but she never noticed them all over his back and legs.

She didn't notice any ticks of hostility and advanced forward, tugging the bottom of the undershirt; she felt exposed. She opened the cupboard above the coffee pot, looking over her shoulder.

He continued to hum, dumping chopped onions into the pot.

She poured coffee into two cups, and clinked the pot into the base of the coffee marker.

"You're awake," Jonny said.

Cheyenne turned and assumed a wide stance. She glared at him with pursed lips and balled fists.

"Of course," he said. "Your dream." He took a few steps back. "Sandra was supposed to have changed your clothes." Jonny returned to the stove, removing ten pounds of tomatoes from a giant pot of boiling water. He placed them into several bowls of ice water. "I can give you a pair of sweatpants until she comes home." He pointed to her lower half, "That way, your lady parts aren't peeking out."

"Why the hell am I here?" She took a step forward. "You brought me, didn't you?"

The garlic and onions were done sautéing and he covered them with a lid, turning off the stove. "Jacob insisted."

She took another step forward, elevating her voice. "How dare you use that little boy as an excuse to torment me."

He closed the gap between them, baring his teeth. He bent down face-to-face. "I'd never—" He stopped and stood erect, walking to the coffee she poured. "Jacob knew you were in trouble." He turned, bringing the cup to his lips.

"You hate me so much, why not finish what Nicholas wouldn't?"

Jonny's left eye squinted and his head slanted. He sat his

cup on the counter. "I don't want to hurt you."

She pounded his chest. "Bullshit!"

He grabbed both her wrists and spun her around. He held Cheyenne tight against his body, pinning her arms against her chest and covered her mouth with his free hand. "It's four-thirty in the morning. My family's sleeping."

She headbutted his chest, screaming under his big paw.

He dragged her through the dining room. "If you're gonna make a ruckus, we can go outside."

She twisted and flung her body, failing to break free from his secure grip.

He kept his hand clasped over her mouth and his other hand firmly around both her arms. He pressed his mouth to her ear. "Open it!"

She tagged his lips with the back of her head.

He jerked her head to the side, speaking through clenched teeth. "So-help-me-God, you better open the door!"

Cheyenne jerked her head side to side, shaking his hand free of her mouth. She scowled at him. "I can't reach it. You need to free my arm."

Jonny released one of her arms and she immediately went for his hair; she gripped tight, pulling forward.

Jonny grunted. He unlocked the sliding door and flung it wide. He carried her out, shutting the door behind them. He brought them to the pergola and pried her fingers from his hair. He pushed her to the ground and walked away.

Cheyenne sprang to her feet and charged him, shoving his back.

He whipped around. "Come on! Get it out of your system!"

She rushed him punching and slapping his chest.

He grabbed her forearms. "All that pent up anger and that's all you got!" He flung her to the ground. "Fuckin' hit me!"

She stood beating his stomach and chest with the side of

her fist, kicking his legs.

He grabbed her again. "Nicholas has taken your life away, taken your loved ones."

Cheyenne jerked her hand free and delivered a stinging blow to his face. "Why didn't you just kill me?" She went limp, retracting her hand to her chest.

Jonny let her fall to the ground. He raked his fingers through his hair. "We're a toxic mix, you and I."

She rubbed her hand, feeling the burning remnants of her last strike. "You should've finished me off," she said between sobs. "If I die, he dies."

"So, that's why you're still alive." He walked to the pergola and removed the blanket from a chair. "I've taken enough innocent lives." He handed her the blanket and when she didn't take it, he wrapped it around her. He walked back to the pergola and lit the gas firepit.

Cheyenne stood, wrapping the blanket around her. "Why wouldn't you hit me?"

"I've never hit a girl in my life." Jonny lowered his head. "Except for when you tried to wake me."

"That doesn't count," her teeth chattered. "You were asleep; you didn't know what you were doing."

He waved her over.

"I want to die." Her body shivered and her arms went slack. "I thought if my dream came true—" She lowered her head and dropped to her knees.

He stood next her and stared at the calla lilies. "The moment I saw you were wearing my white shirt, I asked myself why you didn't run for the door."

She stared up at him.

"I didn't understand why you'd try and provoke me with such violence." He looked down at her, holding out his hand. "Listening to you talk confirms my suspicions."

Cheyenne buried her face into her palms.

He kneeled and removed her hands, forcing her to acknowledge him.

Her chest heaved; she could barely catch her breath. “I’m sorry.” She wrapped her arms around her stomach and continued to sob. “I thought . . . I thought . . . I thought—”

“I know,” he said. “You thought I’d end your life for you.” He pulled her up by the shoulders and then scooped her into his arms. “Let’s get you warmed up.” He laid her down on the reclined lounge chair and sat at the bottom, warming his hands, listening to her cry. “Ever since you stepped into my life, memories I’ve worked hard to bury have been dredged up.” He peeked over his shoulder. “I hate you for it.”

She shivered.

He slid back, wrapping his arm around her.

She pushed him away.

“Don’t be stupid,” Jonny said. He forced her against his body. “You’re freezing.”

She laid her head on his shoulder, wrapping her arm over his body, siphoning his heat.

2

An hour had gone by, and Jonny remained silent convincing himself to befriend her. He didn’t know if Cheyenne was quiet because he was, but she laid on him sniffling. He hated it when people felt sorry for themselves. She brought her sorrow upon herself; she’ll get no sympathy.

He gazed into the fire seeing the chair wreathed in flame. “I close my eyes at night, and I relive the past all over again.” He yawned. “I’ll help you get rid of Nicholas, then I want you out of my life, my family’s life.”

Why would he volunteer to help? Was his past that horrible? She thought about her friend who died three years ago. Back then, he was her only friend. He, too, believed she could be saved and it cost him his life. Jonny had a young son, a family he worked hard to support. She would not be responsible for their lives, too.

Jonny's arm went slack and slid off her body, followed shortly after, by a slight snore resonating from his mouth.

Cheyenne relaxed to the rhythm of his heart, succumbing to the weight of her eyelids. Her arm twitched settling across his abdomen.

3

Sandra unlocked the front door and entered. The fresh smell of Italian cooking filled her lungs.

Steven stood in the bay windows, sipping coffee. “Morning, babe. How was work?”

“Long.” She wrapped her arms around him, resting her head on his back. “They fired Cheyenne today. It was her second time as a no-call-no-show.” Sandra nuzzled into Steven's back, closing her eyes. “Probably a good thing, though, with that thing attached to her.” She yawned, ready to hit the hay. “Cheyenne not only put the staff at risk, but all the patients' lives, too.”

Steven caressed Sandra's arm, sipping his coffee, observing the backyard. “She has to eat, too, and last I knew, it required moolah.” He brought Sandra's hand to his lips, kissing her fingers. “What would you do if the roles were reversed?”

Sandra shrugged her shoulders. “I don't know, probably kill myself.”

Steven pulled her around. “Excuse me?”

Sandra stretched her neck to kiss him; he pulled away. "What? I wouldn't want to be responsible for the loss of another life."

"Cheyenne's your friend, right?"

"Of course."

He set his cup inside the windowsill. "Nobody hates her more than Jon." Steven pointed out the bay window, "But if he can find a way to overcome his hatred and lend a hand, I think we should do are part to help rescue her, too."

"How long have they been out there?"

"Don't know. They were out there when I woke, and I've been up for at least an hour."

She tapped Steven's butt. "I'm gonna take them a warm blanket." She grabbed the vacant blanket from the floor and looked back at Steven. "I never said I didn't want to help her."

4

Cheyenne used her finger and drew a circle around the scars on Jonny's chest.

"Brought you guys a blanket."

"Shhh," Cheyenne said.

Sandra spread the blanket over them. "How long has he been out?"

"For a while."

Sandra turned off the firepit and pulled a chair close to him. "Never thought I'd see the day you two got along."

"I wouldn't say we're getting along. More like we're tolerating each other."

Cheyenne moved his arm and slid off the lounge chair. She brought the small blanket he had given her and wrapped her lower half.

"Shit! "I was supposed to have changed your clothes."

Cheyenne dragged another chair over, sitting on the other side of him. "I wasn't nice to him at all when I woke."

"He told me you might be pissed at him."

Cheyenne rubbed her hand, feeling the bruise forming. "I kicked, punched, and slapped at him. Not once could I get him to raise a hand to me."

Sandra inhaled sharply, pressing her lips together. "That's not the man my brother is. He watched men beat and rape our mom. He was so little; I don't know if he even remembers." She brushed his hair from his eyes. "I want to scream at you and ask why you'd want him to hurt you." She looked to Cheyenne. "But it seems the two of you have overcome whatever it was, so it doesn't matter."

"Your brother seems different from the last time we spoke."

Sandra brought her chair closer to him and held his hand. "When they rescued you, you had three ligature marks on your neck. They bothered him." Sandra looked to Cheyenne. "My brother asked Angel to heal them."

"He said something to me, and I don't think he meant to say it."

"What did he say?" Sandra asked.

"He had taken enough innocent lives."

"He chooses his words carefully. He's never spoken to anyone about what happened." She shifted her eyes to Cheyenne. "He's going to open up to you."

"Doubt it."

Sandra stood. "You don't understand. Those marks on your neck reminded him of something. He tried to tell me, but he couldn't." She scrubbed her face dry and narrowed her eyes. "Don't ever hit my brother again."

5

Jonny brought his hand to his face, scratching his jawline. "What time is it?"

"Almost nine," Sandra answered.

He sat up, rubbing his eyes. "How was work?" He tossed the blanket aside and stood stretching.

"Busy; we're short staffed."

Steven carried out the puppy and set her in the grass next to the pergola. "Why'd you guys sleep outside?"

Jonny grabbed the blanket, covering his sister. "I didn't mean to fall sleep." He pointed to the puppy. "She kept me up all night. When Cheyenne woke up, we came out here to work out our differences."

"So, you're good now?" Steven asked. "No more nasty looks or trash-talkin' each other?"

Jonny looked to Cheyenne, putting the ball in her hands.

Cheyenne picked up the puppy, fiddling with the back leg. "We have a better understanding of each other, at least. Eventually, we'll get there." She returned the puppy to the grass. "Where'd she come from?"

"We found her at the shop yesterday," Steven said.

Sandra headed for the house, waving Cheyenne to follow "I have clothes for you."

"Is it all right if I take a shower?" Cheyenne asked Jonny.

He nodded his head.

Steven bagged the puppy's poop. "Did you get any restful sleep?"

"No," Jonny answered. He rubbed the back of his head, squinting his eyes at the lounge chair. "Except when I fell asleep out here. It was the best sleep I've had in days."

6

Adélaïde stepped out of the shower, wrapping a towel around her body and placed her shower cap on the bathroom counter. She sat at her vanity and opened a jar of face cream, dapping her fingers inside. She rubbed her face, spotting Eber in the mirror, standing in the closet behind her. She turned around, but the closet was empty. She looked back at the mirror and saw him. "Eber?"

Eber smiled. "I miss you, Adélaïde."

"I wish I could feel your touch one more time." Adélaïde said. She turned around and found her closet door shut. She looked back into the mirror, and the closet door was open. She held tight to her cross. "Eber?"

Adélaïde's reflection lunged out of the mirror and grabbed her by the throat. "He can't save her, none of you can."

Adélaïde pulled back, failing to free herself from her alternate self's iron grip. Her reflection came with her, catching its hips on the mirror-side of the vanity's desktop.

The vanity toppled over, mirror and all, onto Adélaïde. Its weight and that of her assailant dug into her stomach and legs.

Adélaïde was pinned to the ground. Her throat struggling to pass air under the pressure of her reflection's steadfast stranglehold. She could not scream, only small squeaks and gasps.

My kids . . . I need to . . . get to . . . she dreaded what might happen if she did not act. She had a sudden and desperate epiphany. *It's still in the . . . I'm . . . she's in the . . .* Adélaïde reached under her bed for the nightstick she kept. She stretched her arm, elongating her fingers, but it stayed out of reach. She wiggled her body and stretched her arm back under the bed.

The reflection released one hand from Adélaïde's throat, clawing at her arm.

Adélaïde wheezed, struggling to reach the nightstick.

The reflection laughed; its eyes fading to amber.

Adélaïde poked her reflection in the eye, digging her thumb in deep. She snatched the nightstick and swung, shattering her vanity mirror and the reflection into fragments.

She pushed against the vanity, grunting but was unable to move it. She tilted back her head, eyeing the closed bedroom door. "HELP! I NEED HELP!"

Cheyenne burst through the door. "What are you doing on the floor?"

"Get the vanity off me."

Cheyenne kneeled beside her and held her hand. "But your vanity isn't on you."

Adélaïde gawked at her legs and then at the vanity against the wall, where it had resided since the day she moved in with Jonny.

Twenty

The Folly of Arrogance

1

Cheyenne walked into the dining room tying the end of her braid; Sandra sat reading at the table and drinking hot tea; Steven studied the chessboard, contemplating his next move; and Jonny toiled at the counter next to the stove.

Cheyenne removed the lid to the giant stockpot, smelling the magic simmering inside. The flavors from the garlic and shallots now mingled with several pounds of skinned Roma tomatoes.

Jonny held a tomato upside down and pinched the frilled edge of the skin to the blade with his thumb. He peeled back the skin as deftly as curling wrapping ribbon. He placed it inside the pot and pointed his knife at the fresh herbs on the cutting board. "You mind chopping some herbs?" he asked annunciating the H.

Steven snapped his fingers at Sandra, motioning into the kitchen.

Cheyenne lined the herbs and removed a knife from the woodblock. "How fine do you want them?"

The tomato Jonny handled refused to detach its skin. He worked his knife as not to take the meat with the flesh. "Rough chop, they'll render down as they cook."

"Most people don't know to cut an x in the bottom of the tomatoes," Cheyenne said. "Where'd you learn to make marinara sauce?"

He lifted the lid and placed the tomato inside. "My grandfather was an Italian immigrant." He picked up the final tomato. "Cooking was one of the first things we bonded over." He smiled. "That and cars."

"I miss his fresh mozzarella," Sandra said sitting at the breakfast bar.

Jonny looked back at her and winked. "We'll have to make Caprese salad soon."

Sandra smiled.

Cheyenne scraped the herbs into the pot and stirred.

Jonny turned his attention to the stove. He stood behind Cheyenne, wrapping his hand and around hers. "You want to carefully fold in the ingredients," he said. He manipulated her hand, gingerly folding the herbs. "You don't want to smash or bruise the tomatoes."

She followed his instructions incorporating the rest. "Do you puree the tomatoes at the end, then?"

He took the wooden spoon from her, dipping it in the pot and bringing it back out. He blew on what little liquid he had and slurped it into his mouth. He dipped the spoon back in. "No," he replied. "The tomatoes will melt if you give them time, enriching the flavor of the garlic and herbs." He brought the spoon to Cheyenne's mouth.

She blew on the tiny pool of sauce and then sipped the marinara; her eyes widened.

"Does it need anything? More herbs, garlic, salt, or pepper?"

Cheyenne shook her head. "Nah."

"Then, it's perfect."

"You guys sure did hash out your differences," Steven said.

Sandra slapped Steven's chest, shaking her head.

Cheyenne wrapped her forearms around her midsection and walked away.

"It's your turn," Steven said.

Jonny sat down at the dining room table, examining the board. He moved his king's bishop and then picked up the newspaper.

Sandra followed Cheyenne into the living room. "Are you okay?"

Cheyenne could still feel Jonny's warm breath on her neck. "It felt like he was trying to seduce me."

"Far from it." Sandra sat next to her. "Our grandfather did bond with him over marinara. Grandpa held Jonny's hands, teaching him how to work the knife, how to keep his fingers from being cut while chopping." Sandra tucked her hair behind her ears. "Grandpa would always whisper into our ears when he would teach us things like it was a big secret. He's not flirting with you; he's trying to bond with you. I promise."

"How's Adélaïde?" Cheyenne asked. "I noticed she wasn't here when I came out of the shower."

"GG spends most of her days at the church. Helping with the soup kitchen and marriage counseling."

Sandra seemed oblivious. Did Adélaïde not tell them? The DeLucas were overprotective of their own. Cheyenne was certain she wouldn't be there if Adélaïde told them about Nicholas's assault. "How come you and Jonny don't attend church?"

"I've never attended." Sandra looked to the pictures on the wall. "I blame God for what happened to us, for what happened to Jonny." She removed a photo of both her brother's; they wore choir gowns. "Jonny stopped going when

Dominick died."

Cheyenne lowered her eyes. "How come?"

"Dominick was working for the church when he passed. They still haven't told us how he died, and they haven't allowed us to bury his body." Sandra handed the photo to Cheyenne.

She avoided the photo and walked away. "What kind of work was he doing?"

"None of us know. It's this huge mystery surrounding the church."

Jacob blasted through the sliding glass door. He held the puppy in his arms like a baby. "I have the perfect name for her!"

The women conjugated into the dining room. Cheyenne studied the board next to Steven and Sandra returned to her book.

Jonny looked away from the newspaper. "What'd you come up with?"

Jacob handed the puppy to Cheyenne. "Meet Phoenix!"

Cheyenne petted the puppy. "Beautiful name for a beautiful girl." The puppy licked her face. "How'd you come up with it?"

Jacob pulled a chair out and stood on it.

Jonny peered over the newspaper. "We sit on our butts, not our feet." He glanced at the board.

Steven moved his queen's knight.

Jacob sat down, reaching for the puppy. "Angel said daddy gave Phoenix a second chance at life when he saved her."

Cheyenne found herself distracted by the game.

Jonny moved his bishop, capturing Steven's pawn.

She looked back at Jacob and smiled. "A very fitting name then."

"Daddy's gonna give you a second chance at life, too."

Jonny snatched the pawn and paused, shifting his attention

to Jacob and Cheyenne.

Cheyenne envied the boy's reckless hope. The last time she had hope, it ended the same it always did, in death.

"Checkmate," Jonny said.

"Can I play?" Cheyenne asked.

Sandra closed her book around her finger. "You sure you want to play him? Not even our grandfather could win against Jonny."

Steven and Cheyenne traded places.

Jonny realigned his pieces. "That's not true, Grandpa bested me before."

Cheyenne placed her pieces on the correct squares. She smiled at him. "It'll be something else we can bond over."

She opened the game by moving her white pawn to E4. He followed suit by scooting his black pawn to E5. She jumped her knight to F3, and he moved his knight to C6.

Jonny went back to reading his newspaper.

Cheyenne scoffed under her breath and brought her bishop out, landing it on C4. "Your turn."

He moved his other knight to F6 without look away from the newspaper, gaining control of the board's center.

Cheyenne frowned. She pushed her active knight forward to G5.

Jonny set his bishop on C5. He licked his finger, turning the page.

Her knight captured his pawn at F7.

He answered with his active bishop to F2 and locked eyes with her. "Check."

Sandra looked away from her book. "I told you."

Cheyenne looked around the room. Nobody cared about the game except for Steven; he watched intently. Cheyenne furrowed her brows.

Jonny continued to read his paper.

"He said 'check', not checkmate." Cheyenne's king knocked the bishop from the board.

Jonny folded the newspaper and turned it over. He moved his knight from F6 to E4, putting her back into check.

Cheyenne's king retreated to E1.

He smirked and brought his queen out to play, advancing her to H4; he winked at Cheyenne. "Check," he announced for a third time.

"You should give up," Steven said. "He's just toying with you."

She quickly shifted her king to E2, and he followed, positioning his queen at F2.

"Che—"

Cheyenne's hand darted out, side-stepping the king to D3.

His knight countered from E4 to C5, "Check . . . times five," he said, winking at her.

She shuffled her king to C3.

"That's a bad sandwich to be in," Steven said. He pointed to the board. "You've cornered yourself. She's in checkmate, right?"

Jonny followed with his queen to F4. He released his piece, glancing at the board. His left eye twitched.

"No." Cheyenne smirked, spotting Jonny's mishap. "I still have options."

"He's winning, though," Steven said.

Cheyenne raised an eyebrow at Jonny. "He was."

"Well, don't you sound smug," Sandra said.

Jonny tossed the newspaper aside.

Steven pointed to her king. "He's chased your king all over the board; you can't move your king anymore without putting yourself in check."

"We all make mistakes," Cheyenne said, locking eyes with her adversary.

Jonny leaned forward; his eyes darted around the board. “Mistakes can make things interesting.”

Jacob put the puppy on the floor. “To infinity and beyond!”

Sandra closed her book. “I think Jacob’s right. You’re going to make him capture all your pieces before admitting defeat.”

Cheyenne sighed. “But he hasn’t beaten me yet.” She marched her pawn from D2 to D3, and Jonny forwarded his queen to F2. She followed close behind; her active knight charged from F7 to G5.

He shifted his rook from H8 to F8.

She followed quickly, pushing her queen from D1 to H5. “Check.”

Sandra stood and walked around the table asking, “Is she beating you?”

Jacob crawled into Steven’s lap.

“Like she said, ‘check, not checkmate’.” Jonny winked at his opponent but this time, it did not go unnoticed.

He moved his pawn forward to G6, her queen danced to H6, and he followed with his rook from F8 to F6.

Cheyenne floated her bishop to F7. “Check.”

He glanced at her; Cheyenne winked.

Jonny’s cocky smile made an appearance. “I haven’t made a crucial mistake since I was a kid.” He analyzed the board, smiling. He eliminated her bishop with his rook.

She captured his rook with her knight. “Couldn’t see past your ego?”

Jonny shunted his king from E8 to F7, dismounting the knight. “My apologies, I underestimated you.”

Her queen flounced his pawn at H7, putting him in check for the third time. “That was your first critical mistake.”

He dispatched his king to F6, and she summoned her knight from B1 to D2. He led his pawn from D7 to D6, and she took aim at his queen, sliding her rook from H1 to F1.

"I'm not going to lie," Sandra said, "I'm kinda rooting for Cheyenne to win."

Steven squeezed Sandra's leg. "C'mon now, it's just a game."

Jonny retreated his queen to F5, next to his king.

Cheyenne quickly took his pawn at C7 with her queen.

He dispatched his knight to D4. "Who taught you to play?"

She repositioned her pawn from G2 to G4. "I had no friends growing up."

His king slunk to G5.

"My seanmhair taught me how to cook, dance, play the piano, cello, and to sing."

"Jonny plays the cello, too," Sandra said.

"Check, by the way." Cheyenne teased as her knight leaped to F3.

He advanced his king to G4, taking her pawn.

She called her lone pawn from H2 to H3. "Check."

Jonny's king slew the pawn.

"My seanair taught me about cars, motorcycles, and chess." Cheyenne shot her queen to H7. "Check."

Jonny smiled and his head bobbed. He looked away from the board. "To the bitter end?" he asked.

She smiled back. "To the bitter end."

His king fled to G2, and she flanked the king with her knight at H4, putting him back into check.

He thwarted Cheyenne's rook with the king; she retaliated, wiping out Jonny's queen with her knight.

"She's really going to defeat you," Steven said.

"Maybe," Cheyenne said. "The game isn't over yet."

Jonny avenged the queen with his pawn, taking her knight at F5.

Cheyenne's queen rushed forward to H2, and he followed behind, stepping his bishop forward from C8 to D7.

They locked eyes, and Cheyenne smirked. She slid her

bishop to G5 opening the path for her rook to his king. She released her game piece and knocked Jonny's king over. "Checkmate."

Sandra covered her mouth, failing to conceal her glee. "Oh my God! She beat you!"

Jonny leaned back in his chair, nodding his head.

"No," Cheyenne said. "You let me win."

Jonny cocked his head to the side and furrowed his brows. "No," he said.

She stood. "Your head wasn't in it. Your knight could have put me in check at any moment, but you never capitalized on it."

"My apologies," he said. Jonny opened his hand, palm side up, toward the board. "Would you like to play again? You'll have my full attention."

Steven glanced at his watch. "You told the kid he could pick the black cat up by three."

Jonny's smirk was still present. He redirected his attention to Steven. "What time is it?"

"Five after two." Steven grabbed Sandra's hand and they headed for the living room. He turned saying, "You still gotta get dressed."

Jonny pushed his chair under the table. "Relax, I only need a shirt."

Phoenix hobbled to the sliding door and scratched the glass.

Cheyenne opened the door. "Rain check?"

"You'll have my undivided attention," Jonny said.

2

Jacob pushed one of the dining room chairs to the stove and stood on it.

"Son, what are you doing?"

Jacob grabbed the wooden spoon, removing the lid from the pot. "You keep underrating her." He turned, glancing at Jonny. "You need to open your eyes."

Jonny reached for the wooden spoon and Angel smacked his hand with it.

Angel dipped the spoon into the pot. He brought it back out, blowing on the sauce; he tasted it. "Store-bought tomatoes?"

Jonny took the spoon from him. "I didn't have time to plant anything in the garden this year." He tasted the sauce. "Trying to wash the waxy film off these tomatoes was a bear."

Angel wafted the air from the pot to his nose. "It was a nice touch, teaching her how to fold and not stir."

"I wanted to do it with Jacob, but she's definitely the type who likes to take part in the kitchen."

Angel grabbed the spoon and returned it to the pot. "Being open and honest with her is a good thing. Telling her how she brings your past to the present and how that makes you feel, will make telling her what happened easier." He faced Jonny. "But next time, less aggression."

Jonny loaded the knife and cutting board into the dishwasher. "Her and I are too toxic together. I don't know how I'm gonna hold up my end of the deal."

Angel frowned. "Sometimes during a chess game, one has to sacrifice key pieces in order to win the game." He hammered the wooden spoon against the pot. "You need to decide what aspects of your life you're willing to sacrifice." He grabbed Jonny's shoulder. "You have to do this; her life is dependent upon it."

Jonny leaned against the counter, contemplating.

"Like you told Cheyenne, Nicholas has taken everything from her. That makes her emotionally fragile." He relinquished the wooden spoon and pointed to the pot. "Teach your son."

3

Cheyenne carried Phoenix in and set her on the floor. She started putting away the chess game, but quickly abandoned the idea, watching father and son.

Jonny stood behind Jacob, holding his hand. He bent slightly, putting his mouth next to Jacob's ear. "You want to fold the sauce like this."

Cheyenne lowered her head.

"I told ya, he wasn't flirting," Sandra said. She walked into the kitchen. "Jonny, put this on," she said, tossing a shirt.

Jonny turned, catching it. He slung it over his shoulder and returned to Jacob. "Want to taste?"

"Yeah!"

Jonny dipped the spoon inside the pot and blew on the sauce until it cooled then, handed it to him.

Jacob attempted to place the entire spoon into his small mouth, smearing sauce on both sides of his face.

Jonny lifted him off the chair and took the spoon from him. "Put the chair back."

Jacob did as he was told then he helped Cheyenne put the game away. "Daddy?"

Jonny side-stepped to the dining room, tucking his shirt. "Yeah?"

"Would it be alright if Cheyenne took me to buy your birthday gift?"

Jonny paused. He looked from Jacob to Cheyenne.

"GG's at church, Uncle Steven's going to the shop with you, and auntie Sandra going to bed."

Jonny tightened his belt and then removed his jeep keys from his pocket. He hesitantly handed Cheyenne the keys.

Jacob jumped up and down, clapping his hands. "Yay! Let me get my piggy bank!"

"What about the sauce?" she asked. "I can stay and watch it."

"It has to simmer all day. I've turned it down and it should be fine until I get back."

Cheyenne's eyes narrowed and her forehead wrinkled. Not even eight hours ago, they were yelling and screaming at each other. She assaulted him. "Are you sure?"

"Let me know how much he spends so I can replace his piggy bank."

She caught a glimpse of the fear he attempted to hide. Why is he handing over Jacob, the most precious thing he cares for? "Are you comfortable with me taking him?"

He stopped in the living room archway and peered over his shoulder. "No."

Jacob ran into the dining room. He jumped up and down, shaking his piggy bank. "C'mon, Cheyenne! Let's go!" He grabbed her hand and dragged her into the living room, passing Jonny.

"If you don't have shoes," Jonny said, "you can wear my flipflops."

"These ones," Jacob said, pulling out the flipflops. He slipped his tiny feet inside his own flipflops and jerked opened the front door, pulling her out with him.

Cheyenne spotted the 1971 SS Chevelle parked next to Steven's Challenger.

Steven pushed off his car. "Is Jon on his way out?"

"He's getting his shoes on," Cheyenne said, pointing to the Chevelle, waiting for Steven to answer the question posed by her face.

"That's Dolores," he said. "She belongs to Jon."

She helped Jacob fasten his seatbelt. "Why Dolores?"

"Because, I painted her cranberry red," Jonny answered, "and the lead singer of the Cranberries was Dolores." He moved Cheyenne out of the away, double-checking Jacob's car seat. He loosened the strap crossed over his shoulder. "Tomorrow, I'll buy you a new car seat." He kissed Jacob's forehead. "Be good and mind her."

"You remember what day tomorrow is, don't you?" Steven asked.

"It's hard to forget."

"What's tomorrow?" Cheyenne asked.

"The day my brother died."

Twenty-One
Toll of Bedeviling

1

Cheyenne and Jacob waited to checkout at the bookstore. No surprise the store was going out of business. Books were all but extinct thanks to the complacent masses' growing demand for increased entertainment from decreasing effort. Even with everything marked fifty percent off or buy-one-get-one, business was less than booming.

Jacob found several books he wanted, but nothing for his father. He offered Cheyenne his money.

"I'll buy them for you," she said. "Your money is for your father's birthday gift."

Jacob pointed to the hairs standing up on her arms. "Are you cold?"

"Something like that," she said, rubbing her arms.

"Can I go play hop-scotch over there?" he asked, pointing to the children's area of the reading lobby, adorned with a cartoon-city themed hop-scotch court.

"Stay where I can see you."

Jacob skipped away watching a man, wearing a grey suit

and a small cloth hat, sit down with the Wall Street Journal. He completed half the hop-scotch court before kneeling to tie his shoe.

"Embracing the light, are we?" Angel rose and sat adjacent to the man and got comfortable. His bright white eyes met the man's amber ones.

Nicholas tossed the newspaper aside and removed the Kippah from the Jewish vessel's head. He twirled the religious symbol around his finger, slinging it to the table in front of them. "Hmph. It's darker in here than you'd expect."

"Oh, not so dark inside Jonny, huh?"

"Give me time, and he'll be consumed with darkness."

"He may hide dark secrets, but Jonny doesn't let them turn out the light; I've made certain of the that."

Nicholas's eyes glowed a bit brighter. "You can't keep them from me."

"Cheyenne's doing a pretty good job by herself." Angel crossed his legs and laid both hands on the armrest. "She even managed to provoke you to the point of almost killing her." Angel smiled. "Tell me, when you were choking her, could you feel your life slipping with hers?"

Nicholas laughed with low devilish tones. "Her attempts were futile." He kept his eyes on Cheyenne. "I was able to give granny a glimpse. The ol' ball and chain believes her departed is gonna save them." He looked to Angel. "Snuffing the old bitch won't be hard; they'll think she had a heart attack."

Angel looked to Cheyenne. "Jonny," he said, staring back at Nicholas, "will stop you."

Nicholas scoffed. "That little bastard you possess has more balls than his daddy." He interlocked his fingers and rested them on his lap. "Jonny's scared." He used both index fingers and pointed to the boy's body, taunting, almost singing, "I know his weaknesssssss." He grinned. "Fear is a beautiful thing."

"If the boy is such a weakness to his dad, then why did he allow her to take him?"

Nicholas's eyes glowed hot.

Angel scooted to the edge of the chair and leaned on the armrest. "Fear begets vigilance." He looked over his shoulder, not much time; Cheyenne made it to the cashier. "Adélaïde," he turned back around, "her frail figure houses a palpable vigor." He smirked and the boy's face mimicked his father's. "As for Jacob," he leaned back in his chair, "he's under my protection; I'll obliterate you."

"If you could obliterate me, why wait?"

"You cannot taunt me. I have my orders."

Cheyenne grabbed her bags and headed toward Jacob.

Nicholas snatched the newspaper from the coffee table. He lowered his eyes, keeping them out of sight.

Jacob jumped from the chair, running to Cheyenne. He wrapped his arms around her thighs and stared up at her. "I know what I want to get daddy for his birthday."

She threaded her fingers through his dark brunette hair, pushing the strands up and away from his eyes. "What?"

He grabbed her hand, leading her out the store. "Follow me!"

2

Jonny slammed the tow truck door and proceeded to guide Steven back. "Woe!" he said. He snatched the cables from the tow bed and crawled under the front of Cheyenne's Datsun.

Steven watched Jonny from the side mirror. From the corner of his eye, Steven saw the neighboring door open. He jumped out of the truck and made his way to the rear.

Ryder leaned against the railing. His face was black and blue, he wore a Steri-Strip across the bridge of his nose, and his front teeth were missing.

Steven wrestled with a mixture of shame and male pride.

"Heya, fellas," Ryder said.

Jonny jumped to his feet.

Ryder pointed to Cheyenne's open front door. "Have you seen my neighbor?"

"Did I beat him that bad?" Steven asked.

"I don't think he ever knew what was happening when it was happening. That thing possessed him; he was never in control."

Steven took a few steps forward. "What happened to ya?"

Ryder lifted his hands and shrugged his shoulders. "I can't remember. I must have gotten shit-face-drunk and fallen or something." He chuckled. "It wouldn't have been the first time."

Jonny hopped the stairs and extended his hand. "We haven't formally met. I'm Jonathan but I answer to Jon or Jonny all the same." He used his thumb and pointed over his shoulder. "And that's Steven, my best friend and soon to be brother-in-law."

Ryder wrapped his hand around Jonny's. "You can tell a lot by a person's shake. Yours is a firm, sturdy shake. A sign of a good man." He released Jonny's hand and removed a pack of Lucky Strikes from his breast pocket. "I'm Ryder," he said sliding a cancer stick out and handing it to Jonny.

"No thank you, I don't smoke."

Ryder struck a match and lit the tobacco end while sucking on the filter end. He blew the smoke and pointed to Cheyenne's house. "Have you seen her?"

Jonny batted the smoke away from his face. "Cheyenne was attacked a few nights ago and too afraid to be alone. For now, she's staying with my family."

"Attacked?" By who?"

"Guy named Nicholas. You know him?"

"Never heard of him. I'm glad to hear she's okay. I was worried with her front door wide open, and her house trashed the way it is."

"We'll let her know," Jonny said. "For now, we're here to tow her car to my shop.

"I'll let you get back to it," Ryder said, pinching the cherry from his cigarette.

"I'm gonna go find the keys and lock up her house," Jonny said to Steven.

3

Jonny scanned the disarray searching the floor for the house keys. He flipped the couch upright and kicked around the debris. Each step crunched the glass-littered floor. He stared at Cheyenne's bed, envisioning the cord wrapped around her neck.

He rubbed eyes. "Damnit, she's alive; stop it." He searched the nightstand, pulling the drawer open. Jonny pocketed her keys and continued to rummage. He pulled out the loose papers, discovering an address book. Only one name and phone number attached to an address in Shetland islands, Lerwick Scotland was written down. He used his cellphone and snapped a picture. He closed the book and replaced everything he removed.

Jonny eyed the room, grabbing things he thought she might need. His hands were getting full, so he set everything on the bed and went to the kitchen for a bag. He stopped in the alcove, eyeing the sink in the guest bathroom. He found himself still drawn to it but the why eluded him.

"You need help finding her keys?" Steven asked.

"Nah, I found them."

Steven looked around the floor at the blood and broken glass. "Before she returns home, I feel like we should clean the place."

Jonny could not look at the bloody footprints without seeing Cheyenne and the cord. "Not today," he said, rubbing his eyes. "Is the car hooked up?"

"Yeah, we're ready to roll."

Jonny locked her house, abandoning the items he collected; he wasn't mentally ready.

4

Jonny opened the driver's door and pulled the hood-release. He examined the engine playing with the spark plugs. The wires and rubber hoses all but crumbled when he touched them and he wiped away thick sludge from the dipstick. He crawled partially under the car and pulled the oil plug.

Steven finished playing secretary and assisted with the Datsun's engine. "You, uh, look at the engine?"

Jonny pushed himself out from under the car and grabbed a towel from the workbench. "Yeah, I saw it," he said, cleaning his hands. He tossed the rag back to the bench and returned to the engine.

"You know, pinning won't fix that, right? Steven asked. "You have to replace the whole engine head."

Jonny stared at the cracked head, crossing his arms over his chest. "I need to prolong fixing her car as long as possible."

"Prolong?" Steven rubbed his hands together, scrubbing the greasy dirt from his fingers. "You can't even fix it. A new engine will cost more than the car's worth."

"Something is telling me she's gonna run. If Cheyenne knows her car can't be fixed, she might leave sooner." He glanced at Steven. "I know I would."

"What are you going to do?"

Jonny stared blankly at the engine, shaking his head. "I don't want to stop her." He shifted his gaze to Steven. "That thing her and Jacob call Nicholas, in my dream, it basically told me I had to pick."

"Pick what?"

"Who to save." Jonny's eyes moistened. "Jacob or her."

"There's no doubt in my mind who'd you choose. It would be the guilt, though, for not saving them both, that would eat at you.

"For the first time since I escaped, I'm afraid."

"You know, I would never let anything happen to your son?"

Steven's assurance did little to quell Jonny, but Jonny bobbed his head because he knew what Steven spoke rang true.

"If you're worried, why not let her leave?"

Jonny shut the hood and leaned against it. "Angel keeps telling me I have to save her, but I don't know why."

Steven rocked side-to-side. "Angel did say she's tied to your past."

"I don't know how, though." He paced the floor. "I remember every detail. Hell, when I close my eyes at night, I'm standing inside my own dreams watching it play over as if I was at the movies."

"Hmm," Steven said. "There's something in your dreams you're missing then. If your past comes to you tonight, keep your eyes open."

Jonny needed air. He stood outside the garage doors. A single grey cloud caught his attention; it's gonna rain. It didn't matter the rest of the sky was clear and the sun was bright; it's Oregon. If there's a single grey cloud, it rained in that one spot.

"When I found her keys, I found an address book. It was completely empty except for one name."

Steven joined him, placing a cigarette between his lips. "Who was it?" he asked searching his pockets for a lighter.

Jonny snatched the coffin nail from Steven's mouth and broke it into several pieces. "You quit, remember?"

"Been craving one and when Ryder lit up, I remember I had one inside the pencil drawer in the customer service desk."

"There's gum in my desk if you need it," Jonny said.

"Whose name was in the address book?"

"Seanair. I assumed her family was gone. Now, I think Cheyenne ran away to protect them. I found it odd how she hardly spoke of them, but now, I think that's how she copes."

"It couldn't have been an easy decision, I'm sure," Steven said.

"Sandra told her I was kidnapped. I know why she lied but the truth is, I agreed to stay as long as my siblings were freed." He shook his head. "So no, it wasn't an easy decision."

"What do you mean, 'freed'?"

"This isn't about me, now focus," Jonny said.

"According to Angel, it has to do with your past. So, in a-around-about way, it is about you." Steven removed his keys from his pocket. "Napa left a message, said our supplies were ready for pickup. I'll leave you to your thoughts."

Jonny pulled out his wallet.

"I got it," Steven said.

5

"Daddy! Daddy!" Jacob shouted, running into his father's arms. "I got you the best gift ever."

"I'm sure you did." Jonny picked Jacob up and kissed his head. He pointed at Cheyenne's feet with his head. "See you bought new shoes."

"I'm no fashion queen, but your oversized flipflops didn't go well with the dress." She hiked her dress a little, pointing her toe. "But these generic white shoes can go with any outfit."

Jonny pointed to the Datsun.

Cheyenne's eyes lit up. "Can you fix it?"

Small rain drops kissed the graveled parking lot in random splats, gradually increasing in tempo.

Jonny carried Jacob to the wall, allowing him to press the button, shutting the garage doors.

Jacob wiggled free and spread his arms out to his sides and ran, making airplane noises.

"I take it, your car has been sitting for a while."

"A year or so," she said.

Jonny winced in disbelief but did not press the matter. "I have to replace all your hoses, they're weathered. I'm in the middle of the oil change. The oil is old, burnt, and turned to sludge. Before I put in the fresh oil, I'll have to do an engine flush."

"So, it won't take long?"

Jonny popped the hood. "Not that simple." He pointed to the crack. "You have a major crack in the engine head."

She bent forward, looking at the crack to which he pointed. "But it can be fixed," she said.

Cheyenne was not like most girls. She knew a thing or two

about cars, but how much? “Before I pin it, I need to figure out what caused the crack to begin with.” He pointed to the water pump. “If the pump is faulty, then the coolant can’t flow through the system and cool as designed. If your coolant is low or you have a leak in the cooling system, and you drive, the engine will overheat, causing the head and block to crack again.”

Cheyenne leaned back, dusting road grime from her hands. She started to wipe them off on the dress.

“Here.” Jonny retrieved a towel from the workbench. “Don’t mess up your pretty dress.”

The hairs on her arms stood straight up; he sniffed the air.

Jonny spun around; his eyes ping-ponging the garage. “Jacob!”

A loud pop bounced off the walls and the lights died.

Jacob’s lack of response spiraled Jonny into panic. “JACOB!”

Cheyenne placed her hands out in front of her body. “Jonny—”

“Ssshhh,” he told her, listening.

“Daddy?”

Jonny searched the shop, looking for the amber eyes. “Where are you, Son?”

“By the water fountain.”

Cheyenne maneuvered through the shop, bumping into things.

Jonny made his way toward Jacob, leaving her behind. He continued to scan the shop and spotted them; the amber eyes observed from the far corner. Jonny charged for the water fountain.

Nicholas slithered across the wall.

Cheyenne screamed, “Run, Jacob! Run!”

Jacob remained rooted.

Jonny rushed to Jacob's aide, but Nicholas was much faster, and he knew it. A novel terror filled his chest.

Cheyenne stepped on the creeper, and it slid out from under her foot, causing her to face plant. She swiftly stood to her feet and continued toward the boy, clouting her shin, but she kept advancing.

Jonny watched Jacob turn in slow-motion toward him and then toward Nicholas's fast-approaching shadow. I'm not going to make it, Jonny thought. "No, No, No, No, NO!"

Cheyenne twisted her ankle. She hobbled on her other foot. "RUN!" she screamed.

Nicholas's shadowy silhouette leaped from the wall toward Jacob, far beyond Jonny's outstretched fingers.

Jonny's heart plummeted from his chest. "JACOB!" The word escaped his heaving chest in an unrecognizable screech, echoing off the walls.

A bright beam of light dropped from the broken halogen above the water fountain, crushing Nicholas into the floor, squalling in pain, in a whoosh of black dust.

Jonny rushed to Jacob's side. "Are you hurt?" he asked, inspecting Jacob's body.

"I wasn't scared, Daddy, and . . . " Jacob paused, looking up at the light, "and you shouldn't be either. Angel says he won't let Nicholas hurt me."

6

Steven parked in the front of the shop, noticing the power outage. He set the Napa order on the counter and unlocked the office. He opened the breaker box, flipping each breaker.

7

Jonny stood, holding Jacob tight, and stared at the halogen light as it died.

Jacob pointed to Cheyenne. “She needs you, Daddy.”

Jonny could care less what Cheyenne needed. He needed to know the threat was gone, he needed to make sure Jacob was safe.

“Go-to-her.”

Jonny did not need to look at Jacob’s eyes to know Angel controlled him.

“How’d you trip the breaker?” Steven asked, walking down the hall.

Jonny handed Jacob to him. “Keep my son safe.”

Cheyenne could only take one to two hops at a time. The hopping motion caused her foot to throb and ache, almost worse than applying pressure. She ran out of objects for balance. She looked to her car, estimating it to be ten hops away. She held her breath and hopped as fast as she could. By the fourth hop, the pain radiated up her leg and she involuntarily rested her foot on the floor, causing unbearable pain. Off-balanced, she quickly lifted her foot and tumbled forward to one side.

Jonny caught her and scooped her into his arms. He carried her over to the workbench, struggling to clear a space big enough to set her.

Steven lent a hand. “Is anyone gonna tell me what the hell happened?”

Jonny set her on the bench. “Nicholas paid us a visit,” he said reaching for her injured ankle.

Cheyenne swatted at his hand. “No! It hurts too much.”

"I won't hurt you; I promise." He squatted reaching for her foot.

She flinched. "Ow," she cried in false pain.

He brushed her hand away. "Do you trust me?"

"No. No, I don't."

He sighed and looked to Steven. "You remember where the first aid is?"

"Yeah, in the office, behind the door," Steven answered.

Jonny used his chin and pointed. "Jacob, go with your uncle." He waited until they were out of earshot and then cleared a spot next to Cheyenne, hopping onto the workbench. "When I was a little boy, I climbed an old oak tree to save a cat. The cat didn't need saving. I know that now, but when you're that age, you don't know any better. Anyways," he said, coughing. "I climbed this tree, and that damn cat kept going higher and higher. I climbed so high, the last branch I tried to pull myself up on broke under my weight. As I was falling, I had to have hit a dozen of those damn branches.

"My brother, Dominick, found me later clinging onto a branch afraid of falling. He tried to climb the tree, but Dominick couldn't get a good grip and kept sliding down."

Jonny massaged his throat, clearing it.

Cheyenne heard the lump in his throat. She didn't understand why he kept trying to clear it, obviously it did little to dislodge it.

"Dominick had to have spent an hour trying to persuade me to jump. He said he would catch me, but I told him I was too afraid. He asked me if I trusted him, and I said no, even though I did." Jonny slid off the bench and stood in front of her. "That's how strong fear is; it can be paralyzing."

"Is that true?" she asked.

"Every word."

"How'd you get down?"

"Dominick told me to close my eyes and to let go. He promised he would catch me in his arms like in the movies." Jonny chuckled a little. "He didn't catch me, I landed on him."

"You and your brother were close?"

"The three of us were. We all traveled through the same hell. Sandra and I have our moments, but there isn't anything we wouldn't do for the other."

Cheyenne frowned. "Sandra warned me to never lay a hand on you again."

"I would say it's because I'm her baby brother, but I think you know why she's protective over me." He squatted. "I'm asking you to close your eyes and trust me. I promise I won't hurt you, but if you watch, you're going to be anticipating pain, making things worse."

Steven handed the first aid to Jonny and he set it on the floor beside him. "Please, Cheyenne, your foot is already swollen."

She drew in a deep breath, closing her eyes.

Jonny untied the strings and carefully unlaced the shoe. He gently slid the shoe from her foot.

The swelling turned her sock into a tourniquet.

He removed his knife, "Okay, hold still." He pulled the top of the sock away from her flesh; his blade cut the fabric with ease. He slid the sock off her toes and opened the first aid kit. He carefully wrapped an ace bandage around her foot and ankle. "Open your eyes," he said.

"Did it hurt?" Jacob asked.

Cheyenne looked down at his handy work, shaking her head. "Not at all."

Jonny placed the first aid on the bench next to her. "I doubt you'll be able to drive the Jeep." He handed Cheyenne her shoe and sock. “Steven can take you guys home.” He stroked the back of Jacob’s hair. “I’ll see you at home.”

She returned the Jeep keys to Jonny. “Thank you for trusting me with your son.”

Jonny didn’t trust her, he trusted Angel. Instead of correcting her, he ignored her statement and addressed Steven. “I’ll lock up, and then head home.”

Steven picked Cheyenne up and carried her to his car.

Jonny followed them, locking the door behind them. He sat at his desk, staring at the phone, doing nothing for several minutes except listen to the clock tick. Finally, he took his cellphone out and dialed the number from Cheyenne’s address book.

He listened to the phone ring several times. He rested his elbow on the desk and raked his fingers through his hair waiting for the machine’s greeting to end followed by the beep. “She’s at 4151 Hourglass Way Street, Roseburg, Oregon.”

Twenty-Two

Deaf Ears, Blind Eyes, Fading Light

1

Cheyenne lay awake in bed staring at the light show the candles projected on the ceiling. The adrenaline surge from Nicholas's encounter had not waned. She rolled over, exhaling, unable to oust Jonny's panicked voice from her head.

She removed one of the candles from the nightstand and hobbled to the bureau. She combed over the family photos displayed in a gentle arch, focusing on a picture of the three siblings; Dominick held Sandra's legs and Jonny held her torso. Sandra posed, her hand placed on her hip and the other under her head.

Cheyenne touched Dominick's face, such an unforgettable face. She looked to another, where Dominick held Jonny in a headlock, giving him a noogie. There was a third when they were all younger in a swimming pool. Sandra sat on Steven's shoulders and Dominick on Jonny's, each holding fun-noodles, ready to do battle.

The whole bureau was an exhibit of happiness, sprinkled with wide smiles and bright eyes. Even Jonny smiled. Where were all of those smiles now?

The photos brought back too much; she had to walk away. She used the wall to help limp down the hall and into the living room.

"Le temps me dure."

He's dreaming again. She kneeled beside Jonny's makeshift bed, remembering what happened last time she tried to wake him. She'd have to be careful this time. "Jonny, wake up."

"Je vais vous tuer tous les deux."

"You're dreaming, wake up."

"Keep your eyes shut, no matter what!"

"Ever since you came into his life, his nightmares have returned."

Cheyenne looked to the dark figure sitting on the couch. "You sound like his echo."

The lamp turned on and Adélaïde crossed her arm over her chest. She sat on the couch, bouncing her foot on her knee.

"Ralphie!"

"How do you know Debra?"

Cheyenne's face wrinkled and she shook her head. "I don't know any Debra's." She focused on Jonny. "I have nightmares, too. The dead, mostly children, come to me and show me how they died. When I wake, I bear their marks."

Adélaïde pursed her lips, enhancing the wrinkles around her mouth. "Is that why you're always bruised?"

Cheyenne nodded, leaning forward, hovering her hand over his chest.

Adélaïde clutched her cross. "Don't you dare touch him!"

She retracted her hand and rocked back on her knees.

Adélaïde released her necklace, resting her arm across the other. "You should be in church, repenting for your sins."

Jonny raised his arm, thrusting his hand forward; Cheyenne dodged. "*Laissez les bon temps roule.*"

"What are my sins?" Cheyenne asked, lowering his arm.

"Whatever you did to have a hellish demon attach itself to you."

"You religious nutbags are the same."

"Excuse me!"

"You all blame the victims."

"How are you the victim?" Adélaïde asked.

"The same way it's always the woman's fault when she's raped. You think I sought to be plagued by Nicholas? He's been attached to me since I was little, since before I can remember. What could I have possibly done to bring this upon myself? You tell me since you and God are so close! Ask him for me! Ask him what atrocities has this little girl committed in his eyes!" Cheyenne took a deep breath and looked away. "God turned his back on me long ago."

"God does not turn his back on those who ask for forgiveness. It is you who have turned against God."

"In my experience, people who claim to be devout Christians always point the finger. Except for one. He became my closest friend. Not only did he make me believe I could be saved, he convinced me I was worth saving."

"Then go to him."

Cheyenne stared at Adélaïde through watery eyes. "Nicholas went after him and my friend killed himself."

"Which makes you responsible for your friend's death."

The weight of the statement landed in Cheyenne's chest. Her sadness lodged itself in her throat.

"I won't let you be the death of Jon or anyone else in this house."

Jonny's face grimaced and his breathing labored.

Cheyenne's chin quivered, and she inhaled sharply. "Yesterday, I couldn't see his face, but I didn't need to. I heard it in Jonny's voice. He was terrified he was about to lose his son and so was I." Cheyenne wiped her nose. "When everyone leaves to pay their respect to Dominick, I'll leave." She wiped the falling tears from her face. "I won't be responsible for Jacob's life or anyone else's anymore."

Adélaïde smiled. "They all mourn Dominick differently." She sat on the edge of the couch. "Sandra and Steven will eat at Dominick's favorite restaurant for brunch." She pointed at Jonny. "None of us knows where he goes, but he'll disappear first thing in the morning and won't be back until supper."

Cheyenne cleared her throat and wiped her face. She leaned forward, placing her hand on the ground. "When Jonny slept next to me, he didn't have nightmares. If you want his nightmare to end, I think I have to lay next to him."

"What makes you so sure?"

"Because when I fell asleep next to him, I didn't have nightmares either." She hovered her other hand above his chest. "I just don't know why."

Adélaïde marked to her room, "Be gone in the morning," she huffed.

Cheyenne placed her hand on his chest, sliding her fingers upwards.

He grabbed her hand, pulling her up. "Haven."

She rested her head on his chest. "My name is Cheyenne."

2

Jonny blinked his eyes open, looking around the living room; he was alone. There was a sadness, heaviness, in his walk to his bedroom; his head hung low, his shoulders slumped, his stride lacked luster. He raised his hand to knock on the doorframe but saw his bed empty. He opened the closet and, pulled his black dress shoes from the shoe rack, letting them dangled from his fingers as he rose. He grabbed one of the suits cloaked in a pale plastic and removed his undergarments from the bureau.

He bumped into Sandra going to the bathroom. She scanned the contents in his arms. "You want me to go with you this time?"

"No." His voice was barely a whisper.

She embraced him. "Where do you go?"

He kissed her hair, resting his cheek on her head. "Nowhere."

"I'll use grandma's bathroom," she said. She pulled away, and the scruff on his face clung like Velcro to her hair.

He shut the bathroom door, locking it. He hung his suit on the towel bar and laid his shoes and undergarments on the toilet lid. He gazed in the mirror, raking his fingers through his hair; it was longer than he preferred. The grey near his temples was giving away his age. He moved his hands to his face, feeling the whiskers along his jaw and chin. He opened the mirror and removed the shaving cream and razor.

3

Jacob stared out the bay windows, tugging on his pajama bottoms, releasing a wedgie. "Why do you think she's out there by herself, Sarge?" He raised his free hand, holding onto nothing. He looked up, talking to no one. "Why is she sad?" He set Sarge in the windowsill. "We should ask her." He lowered his hand and ran outside to the pergola. He bent down to look up at Cheyenne's face. "Why are you so sad?"

Cheyenne lifted her head, cleaning her cheeks. "I need to be alone."

"Nah, uh!"

"Please, I don't want to be bothered." She rested her head back on her knees, turning away from him.

Jacob wrapped his arms around her. "We can listen."

She lifted her head wanting nothing more than to tell the child to bugger off, but it was the last time she would see him.

"You're my friend," Jacob said. "Friends are supposed to help each other when they're sad." He climbed onto the chair with Cheyenne and held her. "You'll feel better if you talk, that's what GG says."

Cheyenne relaxed and embraced him back. She said nothing for a long time and when she did, her voice quivered. "Why didn't you run like I said, shouted, screamed?"

"Angel told me not to."

Her brows furrowed. "Who's Angel?"

"My friend, and he wants to help you."

"Who is he and where did he come from?"

"He says you're not ready."

"What does he look like?"

"He's a bright light with feathered wings."

Cute, an Angel.

Sandra exited the sliding door and approached them. "Go inside, Jacob; we'll be leaving in a few minutes." She sat down opposite of Cheyenne. "It seems it's going to be a sad day for everyone." She brushed her ginger hair behind both ears. "I'm going to apologize ahead of time. Jonny is more than likely going to be in a foul mood and might take it out on you and the rest of us."

"Pfft. What else is new?"

Sandra fought back her tears. "Today is the anniversary of our brother's death."

"Am I to tiptoe around him? He's not the only one whose lost someone near and dear."

"I know he can be a bastard, but he has a good heart, good

intentions." She stood. "And once he considers you family, there isn't anything he wouldn't do for you."

4

Jonny walked out of the bathroom, showered and shaved, and stopped at the end of the hallway, watching Jacob in the bay windows.

Jacob grabbed Sarge from the windowsill and stared outside. He raised his hand, holding onto the air, and looked up saying, "But she's not alone." He sat on the living room floor next to Phoenix. "Daddy, Cheyenne's sad; she shouldn't be alone."

Jonny did not respond. He stood in the bay window, observing the scene: Sandra walked toward the house and Cheyenne pulled her knees to her chest.

Jonny entered the dining room. "Leave the door open," he said.

Sandra slid the door back open. "While you're gone, Steven and I are going to take Jacob out for brunch. GG said she would be home later."

He nodded, sliding the door shut. He continued his pilgrimage, past Cheyenne to the yellow calla lilies. He pulled out his pocketknife and cut two flowers from their stems. He lay one of the lilies next to Cheyenne's feet and walked away.

5

Jonny drove through the countryside. The shrubbery was greener this year and there were more wildflowers than usual; it lightened his mood.

He drove for almost thirty minutes on washboard roads before turning off the dirt road onto a long, narrow, unforgiving driveway. There were dried potholes, some so deep he almost scrapped the bottom of Dolores. The extreme potholes, he drove around, nearly putting his Chevelle in the ditch. The hedges terminated abruptly, exposing a poignant homestead. He came to a stop and placed the shift lever in park. He leaned back into his seat, staring out the driver's side window.

There was an open field. The grass was overgrown and full of weeds. The blackberry bushes grew wild, choking out the smaller trees and shrubs. Honeysuckles grew up the rusted clothesline pole, which were missing two of the four lines.

He faced forward looking out the windshield, clenching his jaw.

A house obstructed his view. Part of the roof was collapsed and the exposed wood charred. The rest of the roof was missing its shingles. The gutters were filled with years of neglect. Amongst the debris, an abandon bird nest. The formerly white wood siding struggled to shield the house from the elements. Dry rot embedded into parts of the wood beams on the porch holding the remaining roof. The wooden porch itself was weathered, rotted, and dilapidated. Weeds grew between each wooden plank. The four wooden steps leading to the porch were overgrown by aster flowers. One of the front windows was broken and long, black streaks stretched toward the roof. The other windows were intact but filthy. The grass in front of the house stood nearly to the window seal.

Jonny grabbed the lily from the passenger seat and stepped out of the car; the wind kissed his face.

He closed his eyes and inhaled the fresh air, catching the scent of a distant memory. He could hear children laughing. He tilted his head up allowing the sun to warm his face.

"Come and get me," he heard in his head.

Jonny opened his eyes, looking over the open field. The blackberry brambles once again shrubbery, which framed the manicured lawn. He saw his siblings as children, turning Jonny's younger self in a circle, his eyes blindfolded.

"Polo," Sandra said.

Young, two-year-old Jonny ambled with his hands out in front of his body. His childish voice calling, "Marco."

Dominick stood behind him, whispering in his ear, "Polo."

He smiled at the memory, walking around his Chevelle. His gaze landed to the clothesline and his smile flattened. He saw his mother's backside; she hung bedsheets. A gust of wind blew the sheet from her hand, and Dominick ran after it, helping their mother clip the bedsheet to the line.

Jonny stared at the house and curled his lip. The home was pristine. Mickey leaned on one of the wooden beams. He had a fresh tattoo on his chest of Papa Legba. He drank from a bottle of Rum, watching them.

Jonny lowered his head, clenching his jaw. He bent under and an old oak tree; the present fading into focus. He cleaned the debris off a picture of Dominick and laid the lily on top of three withered flowers from past years. He sat on the dried dirt and relaxed against the tree trunk, pulling the hidden rosary from his shirt.

6

Jacob flung the front door open, running inside the house. His arms went slack and he stopped in the middle of the living room. His G.I. Joe hung at his side. "She's gone, Sarge."

"Watch out, buddy," Steven said, carrying in several bags.

Jacob slipped off his shoes and ran down the hall.

Sandra closed the front door, clutching her purse. She snuck into Adélaïde's bathroom and sat on the side of the tub. She opened her purse and pulled out a rectangular box. She set her purse on the floor and read the directions.

Jonny arrived home early. His bladder full, he headed for the bathroom. He reached for the bathroom doorknob but halted.

"Humpty Dumpty had a great—" Jacob girded down; bloop "—fall."

Jonny chuckled and went Adélaïde's bathroom.

Sandra gasped, clutching the box against her chest.

Jonny zoomed in on the box. He shut the door and sat next to her.

"I'm scared," she said laying her head on his shoulder. "What if I am?"

He leaned his head against hers.

"What if Steven leaves me? What will I do? With our shitty upbringing . . . what if I'm not any good?"

He took the box from her. "I was scared, too." He wrapped his arm around her. "Steven isn't going to leave; he's in love with you." He kissed her head. "When we were kids, you took care of us. You made sure we were fed, bathed, and nursed us back to health. You, not Debra. When I brought Jacob home, I was lost. I had no idea how to take care of him. You taught me how to change his diapers, make his bottles, and how to bathe him." Jonny walked to the door, holding onto the doorknob. "So, if you are pregnant, you're gonna be a damn good mother."

"Thank you." She tucked her hair behind her ears. "What's the truth behind Haven?"

"She was a one-night stand; we were both drunk."

"Is that why you don't drink outside the house anymore?"

"Partly." He sat down on the toilet. "Dominick and I were at the shop going over the piano and cello duet we were to play at church. Haven came in crying, breaking the news about her cancer and the pregnancy. She told us this was the second time the cancer returned." Jonny tore some toilet paper and blew his nose. "She was Catholic, too, and didn't want to make the decision of having treatment or having an abortion on her own." He glanced at Sandra. "Dominick helped counsel us. Haven grew up in an orphanage and didn't want our child growing up in foster care. If I wasn't going to raise the baby, she wanted to abort. She didn't want anyone to know. She didn't want everyone pitying her, trying to convince us we were doing the wrong thing. Most of all, she wanted to spare everyone the grief if we lost the pregnancy."

"Haven seems like she would have been good for you."

"She was good for me. So good, I purposed to her." He lowered his head. "But she turned me down."

"Why?"

"She was dying." Jonny opened the door. "I wish you could have met her."

7

Jacob sniffed the lily his father left for Cheyenne. His white irises stared blankly at Cheyenne's empty chair, and his fingers twirled the stem.

Jonny stepped onto the pergola and tucked his hands in his pockets.

Angel handed him the flower. "Your son told you she shouldn't be alone. I told you she was emotionally vulnerable."

Jonny snatched the lily. "Jacob told me you used him as bait." He tossed the flower and kicked the chair away. "If you were alive, I would have killed you!"

Angel laughed. "Anger is blinding. I did it to show you."

Jonny signed through his nose. "To show me what? How fucking powerless I am to protect my son? Why would you show me that?"

"To break the barrier holding you back."

"What barrier? The fear of losing Jacob?" Jonny asked.

Angel snapped his fingers, pointing to Jonny.

He did not find amusement in Angel's gesture. "Hold me back from what?"

"From saving her." Angel glanced up. "You still have not fulfilled your end of the bargain. You may hide your feelings from the others, but not from me. You're treating her like the enemy. You want her gone, save her."

"I could let it end. I could let her die," Jonny said.

Angel's eyes turned platinum. "Is there not enough death on your conscience?" Angel shoved Jonny backward, toppling him to the ground. He sat on Jonny's chest and smacked his face. "Jacob has told you; I protect him, I won't let anything happened to him! Now, I'm telling you; you have nothing to fear! Now do what you promised!"

"Why does her life matter to you?"

Angel stood. "It matters to God; therefore, it matters to me."

Jonny rubbed his cheek. "Why did Cheyenne leave?"

"Oh, you noticed her missing?" Angel held out his hand. "I didn't think you cared."

Jonny stared at the tiny hand, hesitating to grab it; he wanted to smack it away. Regardless who controlled it, it belonged to Jacob. Jonny took his hand and stood. "I care but I care about my family's life more."

"If you want to know the reason she left, you should ask GG."

Jonny stood tall and his lips parted.

"GG will come around, but you have to be firm with her." Angel picked up the lily. "You need to get your head on straight." Angel handed the flower to him. "Bring Cheyenne back."

Jonny headed for the sliding glass door.

"GG's home," Angel said. He pointed toward the roses. "Use the gate."

8

Jonny's hand hesitated to knock on Cheyenne's front door. How was he going to bring her back? He knocked and waited a few seconds and then rapped again. He turned the doorknob; it was unlocked.

"Hello, Cheyenne?" He sniffed the air, it smelt of bleach. He took two steps in; his senses on high alert. "Cheyenne?" He cautiously made his way to the master bedroom.

Cheyenne lay in bed in the fetal position.

"Cheyenne, it's me, Jonny."

She did not stir.

He rounded the foot of the bed and turned on the new lamp, discovering an empty bottle of pills. He picked the bottle up reading Unisom. He tossed it and shook her. "Wake up, Cheyenne."

Cheyenne's hand slid off her wrist, exposing crimson streaks flowing onto the ensanguined sheets.

He smeared the blood with his thumb and quickly, more blood replaced it, making it difficult to determine how deep the cut.

He turned her other wrist over; it was cut free. Inside her palm rested the blade. He removed the razor and chucked it across the room. "FUCK!"

Twenty-Three

Turning Point

1

Steven refereed Jonny and Adélaïde, focusing closely on the former. He wanted to believe Jonny would never hurt her, but Jonny hadn't been himself in pert near a week. Hell, Jonny slugged him twice, the first time, Steven sort of understood but the second, completely unwarranted.

With Sandra focusing on Adélaïde, none of the adults noticed Jacob sneaking in with Sarge. He covered his ears licking the snot from his upper lip.

Jonny crumbled the suicide letter and threw it across the living room. "She did it because of you, GG! You!"

GG reached for him; he backed away. "I did it to protect you—

"I'm a grown ass man!"

"—and this family. I never thought she'd try kill herself."

Steven placed his hand against Jonny's chest, keeping a safe distance between him and Adélaïde.

Jonny glanced at Steven and took a small step back. He sighed, raking his fingers through his hair.

Adélaïde pointed to the floor. "You've been through enough!"

He ripped his hand from his hair and pointed down the hall. "And Cheyenne hasn't? You ever stop to think she's here because," he beat his chest with a closed fist, "I want her here!"

"That woman isn't your responsibility!"

"And neither are you, yet here you are!"

Adélaïde gasped, reaching for the nape of her neck.

Sandra wrapped her arms around Adélaïde. "He's angry; he didn't mean it."

Jacob hurled Sarge at the adults. "Stop it!" He pushed against the air, sobbing. "No, you can't take control!" His little chest expanded and expelled air, struggling to supply sufficient oxygen between sobs.

Jonny squatted next to Jacob and handed Sarge to him. "Hey, calm down and breathe. GG and I are okay."

Jacob beaned his father in the face with his toy. "You're a horrible person!" Jacob could only manage two or three words between his sobs. "She did it—because you're—mean to her, because GG's mean—to her, and because me—and Angel made her—sad."

Jonny reached for Jacob. "Calm down, everyone's okay. Tell me how you made her sad."

Jacob swatted at his father, still hyperventilating. "No! You, you never—listen!"

Jonny grabbed Jacob's wrist. "Calm down."

Jacob pulled out of Jonny's soft grip. "You're . . . mean; I hate you!"

Jacob ran down the hallway and crawled up Jonny's bed. He wrapped his arms around Cheyenne crying into her shoulder. "I care about you."

Jonny did what Angel told him to do; be firm with GG. They were both headstrong but his last words tasted sour. He couldn't apologize because she would take it as being right and further her attempts at getting rid of Cheyenne. Was Cheyenne's life less important than his? Angel didn't seem to believe so.

Jonny's argument with Adélaïde wasn't why he stood hushed in his room. He never yelled or cussed in front of Jacob. How much did he see? Did Jacob act out because of the adults' behavior or Cheyenne's failed suicide attempt? Both?

He sat on the side of the bed, nestling Sarge between Jacob and Cheyenne. "You said some pretty hateful things out there." He petted the back of Jacob's head. "Hurt my feelings."

Jacob rolled over pushing Jonny's hand away. "You were mean to Cheyenne."

"You're right. I was ugly toward her, because I was afraid." He wiped the tears from Jacob's face. "I owe her an apology."

Jacob sniveled, licking the mucus from his upper lip.

Jonny cleaned Jacob's nose, wiping the snot onto his pants. "Our friend slapped some sense into me and now, I'm trying to be a real friend to her."

Jacob tucked Sarge inside Cheyenne's arm then turned around and hugged his father. "Sorry I hit you."

Jonny kissed the top of Jacob's head, inhaling his scent. "I love you so much."

"Love you, too, Daddy."

Jonny sat against the wall at the head of the bed. He pulled Jacob into his lap and wrapped his arms around him. "Why do you think you made Cheyenne sad?"

Jacob sobbed into his father's chest.

"Hey, what's wrong?"

"She tried to kill herself because of me, because of Angel."

"Hey . . . shhh . . . shhh . . . shhh." Jonny put his hand under Jacob's shirt and softly rubbed his back.

After a few minutes, Jacob stopped crying and relaxed into his father's body, wiping his nose on Jonny's shirt. "She thought Nicholas was going to kill me, and she blames herself." He sniveled. "She's my friend and I hurt her."

Sandra knocked on the doorjamb. "Dinner's done."

Jonny used his head and waved her away. "I thought Nicholas was going to hurt you, too." He lifted Jacob's chin. "You didn't hurt her, I did. You tried to warn me not to leave her alone and I didn't listen. If anything, you tried to help her." Jonny pulled his shirt to Jacob's nose. "Blow." He cleaned the runny mucus from Jacob's face and then kissed his nose. "Let's go eat dinner so Cheyenne can rest."

"Can Sarge stay so he can protect her?"

Jonny stood, holding Jacob on his hip. "Somebody needs to stay and watch over her. I think Sarge is the best person for the job."

2

They gathered around the table, holding hands; Adélaïde led them in prayer.

"Dcar Lord, we thank you for the bounty we are about to eat. We thank you for watching over our family and keeping us safe from harm. We thank you for giving us the strength to forgive and move forward, the strength to change what we can, accept what we cannot, and the wisdom to know the difference. In Jesus's name, amen."

Jacob kept his eyes closed. Remnants of salt-stained streaks still visible on his cheeks "Dear God, please watch over Cheyenne. She's lost and needs our help. Please help take her pain away and help us get rid of Nicholas. In Jesus's name, amen."

Jonny opened his eyes, and winked at Jacob. "Amen," he said.

Jonny swirled his fork inside the mound of spaghetti, listening to forks clang plates. He wondered, did Jacob's nurturing nature come from his teachings or did Jacob inherit it from Haven? He brought his fork to his mouth and then lowered it. "You know, your g-pa use to ask the Lord to watch over those who were lost and hurting."

Jacob brought his fork to his mouth, but the spaghetti slid between the fork's prongs; he had not yet mastered the stab-and-twist.

Adélaïde lowered her iced tea. "Yes, he did. Every meal, in fact."

Sandra started laughing. "You guys remember that one time when grandpa said grace and asked the Lord to forgive him for," she deepened her voice, "my gluttonous ways as I'm about to devour this meal."

Jonny feigned a smile while everyone else laughed. Cheyenne's suicide letter was vague: *GG's right. As long as I'm alive, everyone around me is dead.* He remembered a time in the ring when a similar notion struck him, while standing over a lifeless young body. Now, as then, the thought twisted his stomach and hollowed his chest. Did he contribute to her downward spiral? If he had merely paid attention to Cheyenne earlier. If he had spotted the signs, he would have stopped her . . . wouldn't he? The more he dwelled, the less certain he was. It should never have fallen to Cheyenne; she didn't deserve this. A final selfless sacrifice to save the DeLucas, and to a greater extent, the world from a foul, shadow-dwelling demon. She didn't deserve his chastisement, his scathing glares, his callous disregard. She had sacrificed herself time and again for others. She deserved more; she deserved better.

Jacob struggled to kept the spaghetti on his fork. “Daddy, Angel says to go to her; she’s awake.”

The room went silent and everyone stared at Jonny.

He laid his fork down and cleaned his mouth.

Sandra stood. “Maybe I should make sure she’s feeling alright.”

“I’ll go,” Jonny said. He walked around the table and grabbed Jacob’s hand. He placed his mouth next to Jacob’s ear and whispered, “Like this.” He placed a spoon in Jacob’s right hand and grabbed Jacob’s left hand, twirling a mouthful of noodles against the spoon. “Now, it won’t fall.”

3

Jonny paused a foot from his room. He didn’t know what to expect but he steeled himself for the worst. He tucked his hand inside his pockets and entered.

Cheyenne fixated on the photo she held. Her face red and full of tears. “You-son-of-a-bitch!” She stumbled toward him, dropping the photo. She clenched her fists and beat his chest. “Why do you keep bringing me here?”

He allowed each strike to land unchallenged. With any luck, she would beat the guilt out of him and refuel her desire to live.

She reached up, striking him across the face. “Why can’t you just leave me alone?” She struck him again and he bit his lip. She raised her hand a third time and Jonny spun her around, pinning her against his chest. “Let me go!”

He squeezed her tighter, lifting her bandaged wrist in front of her face. “You’re a part of this family now. What you do to yourself, you do to us.”

Steven and Sandra stood in the doorway. Sandra advanced but Steven pulled her back.

Cheyenne cried harder and her knees buckled.

Jonny guided them to the floor, against the foot of the bed.

She rested her head on his chest and wrapped her arms around him. "I can't do this anymore. I don't want to do it anymore."

He brushed her hair away from her face. "Shhh, it's okay. You won't have to do it alone, not anymore." He caressed her back, hoping it would calm her like it does Jacob.

Jonny's touch and the pills took their toll on Cheyenne. Her eyelids closed and her body relaxed into him.

Sandra picked the photo up from the ground and sat on the foot of the bed. "Why'd you bring this?"

Jonny leaned his head against the bed, shifting his eyes toward Sandra. "You've been inside her house. Did you see any other photos?"

Sandra shook her head.

"That photo means something to her. Right now, she needs to be reminded of it."

"Want some help putting her back to bed?" Steven asked.

"Yeah, my foot's trying to go to sleep; I hate the pins and needles feeling."

Sandra stepped out of the way, placing the picture on the bureau. "Be careful, Jonny."

He looked to Sandra, pulling the blankets over Cheyenne. "Excuse me?"

Sandra drew the curtains open and lifted the window. The cool breeze blew her hair from her face. She glanced at the lilies. "I know you, Jonathan Michael. I know you're going to try and save her." She turned staring at both men. "Somebody needs to. Be smart about it." She kissed Steven. "I'm going to bed."

Jonny followed her to the door. He kissed her cheek whispering, "I promise." He shut the door and leaned against the bureau. His eyes danced among the DeLuca photos, landing on Cheyenne's picture.

"I can see the wheels turning," Steven said. "Want to include me?"

"I'm used to doing stuff like this on my own."

"Like you told Cheyenne, you don't have to do it alone anymore."

Jonny bobbed his head.

"What intel do we have on Nicholas?" Steven asked.

Jonny removed his shirt and wiped the sweat from the back of his neck and underarms. He tossed it into the hamper and stood in front of the window. "We know he's afraid of light."

"Yep, and he can possess people," Steven said. "But, can he possess everyone? If not, what's the criteria?"

Jonny shrugged his shoulders. "I don't know, but it's a damn good question." He pointed with his head toward Cheyenne. "When Nicholas is around, she gets goosebumps and becomes flighty and I smell burning, rotting flesh."

"We've seen him transform and we know he's fast," Steven said. "GG told us Nicholas posed as Eber and then again as her reflection, attacking her."

Jonny furrowed his brows. "Yeah, but the way she described it, it sounded like it was in her head. If GG really broke her mirror, it wouldn't be whole right now."

"It doesn't seem we have enough to come up with a concrete strategy," Steven said. "We need reconnaissance."

"The person to provide intel is laying right there," Jonny said pointing to the bed.

"You're not gonna get anything from her now," Steven said. "She's checked out. She needs a reason to give us intel."

"Angel said she'd be more open if I told her about my past."

"No man, you don't get it. She needs a reason to live. She needs someone to give a shit about her, otherwise—"

"I care about her! I give a shit!"

"Then take the initiative and *show* her you give a shit."

4

Phoenix sprung, ridge-backed, to her miraculously unhindered feet. She curled her lip in a deep, vicious growl, pacing in front of the fireplace.

Jacob dropped his crayon and crawled toward the fireplace, stopping an armlength away. His face wrinkled with hate. "We already told you, Cheyenne doesn't belong to you anymore." He leaned toward the blackness, whispering, "Daddy's gonna save her."

An arm, shrouded by a black veil, jutted out from the fireplace. Sebaceous fluid oozed and dripped onto the floor from the long claw-like fingers. The hand smoked and sizzled from the light of the room; it reached for the Jacob's throat.

Jacob did not flinch.

Phoenix leaped from the floor, pouncing the arm. She sunk her needle-sharp teeth, growling and shaking her head back and forth.

Nicholas made a low caterwaul, flinging the puppy across the room.

Phoenix landed with a grunt and rolled.

"We're not afraid of you!"

Nicholas's arm swung back around for Jacob.

Phoenix lunged and latched onto the hand, sinking her teeth deeper.

Nicholas slung his arm, but Phoenix held on, ripping small

chunks away with her rear claws. Nicholas retracted his arm inside the black crevice, squealing in pain.

Phoenix detached from the hand and paced the front of the fireplace, growling.

Adélaïde ran out of the dining room pulling Jacob away. She held him tight and stared wide-eyed at the fireplace.

He hugged her. “Don’t say anything to daddy.”

Twenty-Four
Burying the Hatchet

1

Cheyenne woke to a low raspy snore. She heard it first two days ago, when she fell asleep outside. She rolled over and saw Jonny sleeping with parted lips. What was he doing in bed with her? It explained why the dead did not visit. Did he, too, make the connection between them and their nightmares?

She laid her head on his chest; her ear suction cupped to his warm, tacky skin. Hidden within the muffled yet amplified snore, was the slow soothing lub-dub of his heart. She outlined a scar on his abdomen with her finger, exploring her way down his ribs to another.

"Mmm . . . that tickles," he said, removing her hand. He blinked opened his eyes, staring at the ceiling. "How do you feel?"

She shrugged her shoulders. "How'd you get them?" she asked.

He looked at her, raising an eyebrow, and tapped her back. "You tell me about yours, and I'll tell you about mine."

Cheyenne rolled up off his chest and drew her knees to rest her head.

"I didn't think so," he said. He tossed the blankets and went to the window.

"Why'd you sleep next to me?"

He glanced over his shoulder. “In case you woke again and tried to finish what you started.”

So, he hadn’t made the connection, but stop her? It was for the best, surely, he knew it. She lowered her head rubbing her wrist. “It’s not the first time I’ve tried killing myself, it’s not even the second.”

“What number are you on?”

The crude question belied the concern in his voice.

“Sixth. I take sleeping pills to sleep deeper. This time, though, the intent was to OD but there was only one pill left. That’s when I decided to cut my wrist.”

“But why take your life after I told you I’d help?”

She hugged her knees, turning her gaze toward the closet. She bit her lower lip, replaying the moment Nicholas catapulted for Jacob; Jonny’s shrill cry rang in her ears. “The thought of Nicholas . . . I don’t want to be responsible for Jacob’s death.” She rotated her head, staring at his back. “Sometimes, when I sleep, the dead come to me.”

“You’re afraid my son will haunt your dreams.”

Cheyenne closed her eyes. “It’s more than that. They show me how they died.”

Jonny looked over his shoulder. “Show you? How?”

“It depends. Some grab my hand and lead me through their final moments. Others . . . ” she paused looking at her mark-free body. “They’re angry, almost . . . violent about how they reveal their death.”

“Violent how?”

“Like they’re seeking some kind of justice or vengeance. I feel their deaths and bare their marks when I wake.”

Of course, there was the one who never touched her nor showed her anything; the gaunt boy and his one cryptic command.

“The other night when you slept in the living room, you

called out a name. Ralphie. Who is he?"

Jonny did not answer. He folded his arms and propped himself up on the windowsill.

She took the hint and removed the bandage, assessing the damage to her wrist.

"How is it?" he asked.

"It'll scar."

He glanced at her, talking over his shoulder. "I lost hope once and tried to kill myself." He focused back out the window. "A man named Lee had his way with me."

"He raped you?"

The breeze swept through Jonny's shoulder length hair.

"Raped, violated, molested, sodomized." He lowered his head then looked over his shoulder. "They're all words describing a horrific act."

Cheyenne crawled out of bed, putting a little pressure on her bruised ankle and blew out the candles. "How old were you?"

He looked to the lilies. "Six."

She limped around the bed. "How does a six-year-old know how to kill himself?"

"When you grow up in the environment I did, you just know. Jonny glanced at her. "I tried to OD on Lee's cocaine. The ironic thing," he said turning around, leaning against the window, "my attempted overdose landed me in the hands of the man who rescued me."

"You were six when you were rescued?"

"I was ten. The planning took four years."

She picked up the photo of her seanmhair and clutched it to her chest. "Who's Debra?"

Jonny stood beside her, staring at his photos. "The woman who gave birth to me."

"Your màthair."

He lifted a photo from the bureau of him and Adélaïde. He was dressed in a graduation gown holding his diploma. Adélaïde wore a navy-blue pencil skirt with a white silk blouse. Her hair draped to her shoulders. Her gaze not on the camera but fixed on Jonny.

"I don't even remember what Debra looks like. Once in a dream, I thought I heard her voice." He handed Cheyenne the picture. "GG's my mother."

Cheyenne placed the photos back on the bureau. "Aren't there any photos of Debra?"

He opened the bureau's top drawer and pulled out clean underwear and an undershirt. "My grandfather disowned her. Destroyed any memory of her."

Cheyenne limped to the bed and sat down. She tapped her temple and pointed to Jonny. "He didn't destroy all memories of her."

Jonny lowered his eyes and silently removed a pair of pants and a shirt from the closet. "Did you leave any clothes here?"

"Yes, but the bag is in Sandra's room. Why?"

Jonny grabbed his keys from the nightstand. "I want to take you somewhere." He stepped past the threshold of his room and stopped.

Adélaïde stood on the other side, eavesdropping. She embraced him. "I'm sorry. I just—"

He bent down kissing her cheek. "I know, you just want to protect me."

Steven walked out his room and pointed to the bathroom. "Either of you about to us it?"

Adélaïde pointed to her room. "You can use my bathroom."

"Is Sandra awake?" Jonny asked.

"Yeah."

Cheyenne limped to the hall. "The clothes she bought me are in the mall bag next to her vanity."

Steven disappeared into the room and reappeared handing Cheyenne the bag.

"Can you do me a favor?" Jonny asked Adélaïde. "Can you make some tuna salad sandwiches for me and pack them in a cooler with drinks?"

"Extra dill relish?" she asked.

"I wouldn't eat it any other way."

Jonny pointed to his room. "You can dress in there. I want to leave soon; it's gonna be a long drive."

2

Cheyenne went outside and found both men under the hoods of their American muscle. She took each patio step one at a time and stopped in front of the Challenger, examining the engine.

"A beast, ain't it?" Steven asked, with a prideful grin.

She bent forward, getting a better look at the chrome headers. She stood erect, making her way to the Chevelle Super Sport. She leaned inward, inspecting the bright orange engine block flanked by the polished valve covers.

Jonny put his hands inside his pockets, gazing under the hood.

"LS5?" Cheyenne asked.

A partial smile formed on the corner of Jonny's lips. "You know your engines; I'll give you that."

Sandra stepped out on the porch wheeling an ice chest and holding a blanket.

Steven carried the ice chest to Jonny's car. He glanced at the Chevy's big block. "So, what do you think?"

Jonny chortled.

Cheyenne shifted her eyes between both men. "I'm not

getting in the middle of whatever debate is going on between you two."

Sandra smacked Steven's rear. "These two have been dick-slapping each other since they were preteens."

Steven set the ice chest down and wrapped his arm around Sandra's waist. "Hey, babe, you're supposed to be on my side."

"Let me guess," Cheyenne said. "You think your Hemi is better, and he thinks his 454 is better?"

"Not only do I have a 454," Jonny said, "I have a three-speed Turbo Hydra-Matic transmission, quadrajet carburetor, cowl induction, 450 pounds of torque, and over 500 horsepower."

Cheyenne looked under Dolores's hood again. "What type of suspension do you have?"

"The front suspension has coil springs, and the rear has trailing arms with coil springs."

"Gees, you don't have to be an arrogant ass about it," Sandra said. She puffed out her chest and deepened her voice. "I have horsepower and coil springs der-de-der!"

They all laughed.

Steven carried the ice chest to the trunk. "Pop it open, Jon."

Cheyenne walked to the driver's side of the Chevelle. "It doesn't matter what you have under the hood," she said. "It matters if the driver can handle the beast." She wiped the dust from the door and looked inside.

The interior was black, the front seats were buckets, and the back, a bench seat. There were no rips, stains, or fading.

Jonny stood beside her, sliding his hand out his pocket and relinquishing the keys. "Start her up."

Sandra gripped Steven's bicep, holding her breath.

"Calm down," Steven whispered.

Cheyenne stared at the keys.

"Go on," Jonny said. "Start her up."

Cheyenne took the keys. She opened the door and eased into the driver's seat. She inserted the keys into the ignition but waited to ignite Dolores. Cheyenne placed her hands on the steering wheel, examining the dash. All the dials, odometers, and radio were all faithful homages. Her eyes explored downward to the horseshoe shifter. She wrapped her hand around the lever and smiled. Her fingers glided back to the ignition and she closed her eyes.

The start motor whirred, followed quickly by a loud growl, settling into the gentle purr of a two-ton jungle cat being scratched behind the ears.

She pressed the gas pedal, clearing the engine's throat and swaying the vehicle beneath the torque. She eased off the gas and Dolores returned to a tectonic rumble. Cheyenne appreciated the sexy 'blub-blub' of American muscle.

Jonny rested his arms on the roof of the car lowering his head inside the window. He tapped the roof with his thumb. "My grandfather and I restored her together."

"How bad was she?"

"Dolores was nothin' more than a rusted frame." He opened the door and held out his hand.

Cheyenne handed back the keys.

Jonny hugged his sister. "We'll be back around supper."

Sandra held her breath, squeezing him tight. She slowly exhaled. "Be careful and don't do anything stupid."

He released her and reached for Steven's hand.

Steven pulled him inward, hugging him. "Don't worry about your son, I'll take good care of him."

"I know you will." Jonny removed his cellphone from his back pocket, placing it in Steven's hand. "I need to be alone with her, uninterrupted."

"What if there's an emergency?" Steven asked.

"Everything will be fine," Jonny said, sitting down. He

turned over the engine and gripped the horseshoe. “You ready?”

“I don’t even know where we’re going,” Cheyenne said.

3

Jonny sprinted up the on-ramp of the northbound I-5 and merged, widening the throttle.

Cheyenne closed her eyes, listening to the symphony of the valves and pistons. “You tryin’ for a speeding ticket?” She opened her eyes and looked at him. “Or are you showboating?”

Jonny applied more pressure to the gas pedal. “It’s been a long while since I’ve opened her up.”

She laughed. “What’s your definition of ‘awhile’?”

He slowed the car. “The day Jacob was born.”

Her smile faded.

“Steven and I, along with my grandfather, use to go to Kent, Washington. It’s the closest NHRA track. We used to drag race. Sometimes we’d race, but mostly drag.”

“Who’s better?”

“Straight drag, hands down I am. Race wise, I might be ahead the first laps or so, but once Steven gets the track memorized, there’s no stopping him.”

Cheyenne looked ahead, fidgeting with her fingers. “Where are you taking me?”

He glanced at her then back to the road. “Where I survived for the first ten years of my life.”

Cheyenne’s forehead wrinkled. “Why?”

He winced, pursing his lips to the side.

She rolled down her window, midway. “You’re not a hard man to read.”

He glanced at her, sliding his hand up the steering wheel to the twelve o'clock position.

"Anytime you make that face, you're contemplating whether or not to tell me." She stared out the window. "Just before you unveil your thought, you take a deep breath through your nose and slowly release the air the same way."

"Our relationship needs patching. I figured I'd be the bigger person and empty my skeletons first."

"Why me? Why not Steven or Sandra?"

He remained silent, staring straight ahead.

Cheyenne propped her elbow on the door. Her thumb pressed against the side of her mouth. She stared pensively out her window to the horizon. "It's because my opinion carries no value to you."

He continued staring forward. "That's not why." He glanced to her. "Your opinion has value." He paid attention to the road, a red Honda hopscotch through traffic. "Depending on what it is."

She pulled her hair inside the car and rolled up the window. "Not to ruin the good thing we got going on, but what game are you playing?"

"No game," Jonny answered. "I'm going to save you."

"Hmph. The only person you'll end up saving is Jacob."

He stared at her, glancing at the road periodically. "Do you bring up my son just to piss me off?"

Cheyenne rested the side of her head on the window. She looked to the floorboard, fidgeting with her fingers, and then glanced at him. "If you were trapped in a room with all your loved ones and me, and Nicholas tells you he's going to kill Jacob unless you kill somebody in the room. You'd pick me because I'm nothing more than a headache to you, and you care nothing for me."

Jonny tightened his jaw.

"The next day, Nicholas comes to you and says the same thing. You're a practical man, and you'd pick Adélaïde because she's old and has lived a long life. Again, Nicholas comes to you the next day, giving the same spiel you pick Steven, the next day, your sister."

Jonny locked eyes with her. "That's not why I'd pick you." He glanced at the road, tapping his brakes. "I care about your wellbeing."

"Pfft! Enlighten me."

"I'd pick you because you've already told me if you die, Nicholas dies."

"I've taken that off the plate," she said. "I'm one of the people in the room who can die."

Jonny bobbed his head. "It'd be difficult, but I'd still pick you first because I have no emotional connection." He paused, changing lanes, allowing the ambulance to pass. He glanced back at her, "Only a moral one."

"Like I said, you care nothing for me."

Jonny furrowed his brows and let out a defeated exhale. He put on his blinker, merging into the right lane. "Is that what Nicholas did to your family?"

She saw the blue sign for the rest stop. "How much farther? I've gotta pee."

"We're going to Tillamook County to a long-forgotten town." He veered off the I-5, pulling into the rest stop.

"What's the name of the town?"

He shifted the horseshoe into park. "Idiotville."

Cheyenne scrunched her nose. "Nuh-uh. You're so full of shit."

"I shit you not," he said removing the keys from the ignition.

She opened her door and started to step out but he grabbed her, pulling her back.

"For this to work, we have to set aside our differences. We

both have barriers up, unwilling to let others in, but we need to be open, at least with each other."

She removed his hand and lowered her head.

"What happened to your family?"

Cheyenne planted one foot on the ground. "Nicholas killed 'em in front of me one at a time." She wiped her face and exited.

4

Jonny educated Cheyenne on the history of Idiotville and Ryan's camp, nestled deep in the difficult terrain of Oregon's Tillamook State Forest. After the two-decade long Tillamook Burn, lumber mills in the area had no forest to log. Men would hike for days to salvage usable wood from the still-glowing forest, only to return covered in soot and choking on ash with meager hauls of charred lumber. They were lovingly referred to as "idiots" and thus the name of the town was decided, or so one tales goes.

"The place is still hard to get to, even with the highway through there. It's why Mickey and Lee could do what they did for so long."

"Sandra said you didn't like the marks around my neck." Cheyenne tore a piece of her sandwich. "She said it reminded you of something."

Jonny met her stare.

"You said, open and honest. You go first," she challenged.

He inhaled and exhaled slowly through his nose. "Mickey and his brother Lee . . . " He wiped away the fresh sweat already beading on his brows and took another deep breath. "They liked finding new ways to torture me."

Cheyenne took another bite of her sandwich.

"I rescued this girl and boy once, or so I thought." His ears began to drum. "The girl looked just like my sister, red hair, freckles, except, this girl had green eyes instead of brown."

Jonny took a swig of water and fumbled to replace the cap.

"Unburdening yourself isn't easy," Cheyenne said. "There's no judgment here; take your time."

He gave her the silent nod, finding some comfort in her words.

She took the cap from his hand and removed the bottle from his lap. "When you want more, let me know."

"They wanted me to rape that girl. I was eight years old. Every time I'd refuse, they'd strangle her with a cord until she passed out. This went on for a lot of days." He propped his elbow on the door, resting his head against a clenched fist. "Lee would pierce my body with hooks and suspend me in the air over the girl's naked body. Each night, he added more and more weight to me. My skin would rip against the hooks." He stared at Cheyenne, glancing at the road. "One day, just before she passed out, she looked at me, begging."

She handed Jonny his water. He guzzled half the bottle and handed it back.

"What'd the girl beg for?"

"Her life."

Cheyenne took a bite of her sandwich. She pointed to his lunch in the dash. "You want me to open your sandwich?"

Jonny shook his head, finishing his anecdote. "The next day, Mickey brought in a string of barbed wire. He stood behind the girl and looked at me with a wicked grin."

Cheyenne's hands dropped to her lap. Her mouth parted; she was transfixed.

"Mickey brought the barbed wire up over her head, and I grabbed it just before he could cinch it around her throat."

Cheyenne scrutinized his hand. "Is that how you got the scars on your fingers?"

"No."

"What happened to the girl?"

Jonny locked eyes with her. "Do you really want to know?"

She stared out her window in silence for a long time. Jonny thought he had his answer but then she turned back around. "Yes."

"I told Mickey she had to be checked for diseases before I would do the deed. It was meant to buy me more time." Jonny sat quietly for a second, waiting to see if Cheyenne had any follow up questions. "I took the girl to the man who saved me. I explained to him what was going on and told him I couldn't do the deed."

Cheyenne wrapped her sandwich and tossed it to the dash. She held up his water and he shook his head.

"My friend knew the girl. She belonged to a man named Ludvig. He's a powerful man who operates illegal fight clubs, sex clubs, and sex trafficking rings."

Cheyenne put the cap back on her water. "What did you do?"

"The girl told me it wasn't rape if she consented, and she told my friend she would make sure Ludvig knew we saved her life."

Jonny slowed the car, eventually coming to a dead stop in Portland traffic. His attention on Cheyenne, Jonny finished his narrative.

"Because I knew I wouldn't be able to perform, my friend gave me something he called trail mix."

"What's that?"

"A combination of E and Viagra."

"Sexstasy?"

Jonny nodded. He turned on the blinker and took the exit onto the 217 North.

"I don't know which of us had the shittier stick growing up," Cheyenne said.

He flipped his blinker on, easing into the left lane, following the signs for the US-26 Westbound for Seaside. "I was reunited with my family. Yours was taken from you," he said.

"Your past has stained you," she said.

"And your past didn't stain you? You hardly speak about your past and when you do, it's brief." Jonny stared at her. "That, tells me you hide some dark secrets. Secrets always leave stains."

Cheyenne looked out her window, chewing on her fingernail.

Jonny reached over and removed her hand from her mouth. "That's a terrible habit. Do you know how many microorganisms are under fingernails?"

"Is that a true story?"

"Yes."

"You're really not trying to fool me or trick me?"

"No." He slowed the Chevy allowing the cars from the on-ramp to merge. "If our first encounter had been different, I would assume we'd be friends instead of foes." He glanced at her. "I treated you unfairly, damaged your trust."

Cheyenne stared at her hands, fidgeting with her fingers. "I ran away when I was thirteen. My uncle Rory lived in Ireland; he helped me." She paused. "How'd you know I lived in Ireland?"

"Haven was from Ireland. You say your R's the same way she did."

"Uncle Rory helped me move to the States. He rented me a one-bedroom shack and paid the rent for three years. On my eighteenth birthday, he sold his farm and gave me the money to live on."

"What happened to him?"

"He was diagnosed with liver failure."

"Is there any of your family members still alive?"

"Just my seanair." She fidgeted with her fingers. "I lied to Steven. When he came to my house to check on me, I told him my seanair died and that's the reason I was crying. I needed him to leave before Nicholas killed him."

"I'm sure Steven forgives you." He glanced at her. "Remind me, seanair is father?"

"Grandfather," she corrected. Cheyenne rested her head on the window. "He's a lot like you. He thinks he knows what's best for everyone, hot-tempered, and thinks he can save me."

Jonny slowed to match the traffic ahead. "Why isn't he in your life now."

"It's best he thinks I'm dead, safer for everyone."

Jonny flashed the car in the right lane, allowing it to pull in front of him. "Sounds lonely," he said.

"Even though I had my grandparents, I've always been alone." She brought her fingernail to her mouth and Jonny pulled it away. "I've never been to school, never had friends; except for one, never been kissed or made loved to." She lifted her head. "I used to bring books to the park and pretend to read. I would listen to the children play, and I would dream." She took a drink and then replaced the cap. "One day, I was listening to these two boys play hide-and-seek. Since I didn't know their names, I called the boy who counted, Seek and the other who hid, Hide. I closed my eyes, listening to Seek count to ten and ask if Hide was ready."

Jonny observed her closing her eyes.

"Hide yelled 'no'. Seek went back to counting. He counted to three before asking if Hide was ready. 'Yes', he yelled. Seek opened his eyes. 'I can see you', he shouted."

Jonny grunted a laugh.

"Aye, I laughed, too." Cheyenne opened her eyes; her chin quivered. "Nicholas killed those boys."

Jonny hid his emotion in the webbing between his thumb

and index finger.

"He kills everyone around me, especially those I become attached to and care about."

Jonny reached for his water.

"You think you're gonna save me, but you're gonna get you and your family killed." She removed the cap and handed him the bottle. "If we're friends like you say," she rested her head on the window, closing her eyes, "then you'll let me die."

Twenty-Five

The Past Comes a Haunting

1

Jonny slowed to a crawl as the paved road transitioned into graveled washboard. Dolores vibrated violently, waking Cheyenne from her slumber.

She sat up, looking around. Sun rays beamed through the surrounding Douglas Firs. She turned in her seat, staring out the back window at the cloud of dust. She turned back around and saw an old, rickety, wooden bridge. "Jonny, stop! It won't hold!"

"It'll be fine."

She grasped her seatbelt with one hand and the door handle with the other and closed her eyes. The crunch of gravel was blasted away by the deafening metallic cadence of Dolores marching across diamond-plated steel and the strained groan of bowing planks. Cheyenne flinched with each clank. Dolores dropped suddenly; Cheyenne screamed and braced back in her seat, flailing her arm forward in a misguided attempt to prevent the dash from caving in her face.

"Relax. The erosion created a little ditch at the end of the bridge." He pushed down her arm. "Open your eyes."

Her eyelids rose but she did not find comfort. Yes, they made it over the bridge, but they were going uphill on a weather-damaged road on the side of a cliff with no safety rails. She looked down out her window and could only see the plunge to her death.

"What are you afraid of?" asked Jonny. "You tried to take your own life."

She frowned at him. "You weren't scared when you attempted suicide?"

"I was scared shitless." He turned right onto more of the same road. "My apologies for assuming."

"I'm scared each time I attempt suicide. I assume everyone is. There's a brief moment of clarity. Your body floods with adrenaline and rationality kicks into overdrive."

"What makes you go through with it?" he asked.

"The same thing that always does." She stared at him. "I'm one life compared to the many Nicholas will take and with that tidbit, the world would be better off without me." She saw Jonny's eyes moisten. "Why does that make you sad?"

"You're braver than me, a true heroine." He locked eyes with her. "Admirable trait."

For thirty minutes, they drove on narrowing side roads and, several times, Cheyenne closed her eyes and held her breath.

"Where are we?" she asked.

Jonny turned left onto a neglected driveway. "We're here." He eased into each pothole successfully avoiding scraping the bottom of Dolores.

Cheyenne pointed to a vast pothole, entrenching her head. "Watch it!"

"I see it."

"If you were going to go off-roading, you should've brought the Jeep." She stared at the road ahead. "How often do you come here?"

He maneuvered over another pothole. "Once a year. Today, makes twice."

Movement in Cheyenne's periphery drew her attention outside her window. Obscured amongst the weeds and wildflowers stood a decapitated body. The headless corpse trod forward, exposing its small stature. His petite fingers intwined sticker-bur-matted hair of the head he carried. The glazed eyes blinked, and he raised his free hand pointing to the end of the driveway.

More gray-eyed children sprouted from the tall grass, many with slit throats. A familiar half-sagging face appeared from behind the trunk of an old growth fir. She vividly remembered how the Astra crushed the bones on his right side and shredded the clothing off his now gray, road-rashed body as it dragged him screaming along the brick-paved road. It was the gashes in his throat that killed him, though; the ones pumping black blood out onto his shoulder and down his side. His brother accompanied him next to the tree, dawning the same wounds on his neck. Nicholas had given them a matching set in a twisted act of fairness. *Bastard.*

She fought back a sob, but their names still managed to whisper off her tongue. "Hide. Seek."

They both pointed to the end of the driveway; gradually, they all did.

Cheyenne followed their fingers to the gap in the shrubbery at the end of the driveway. In the lot past the opening stood a pallid woman in a sodden sunflower dress which, oddly, did not drip. Her battered and scraped knees and shins oozed toward her mud-caked feet. The wind seemed to conspire to conceal her face behind a curtain of chestnut hair as she turned and pointed a bloody finger, with an upturned nail, to the left.

Cheyenne followed as far as the edge of the shrub, but the object of interest must have been obscured by the bush.

Were the dead upset she no longer bore their marks? Were they mad she found a way to escape them? Were they here to prove there was no escape? Why now? What was special about this place? The hairs on her body stood on end and her pulse drummed in her ears the further they progressed up the driveway.

"Is Nicholas here?" Jonny asked. "I don't smell him."

Cheyenne shook her head woefully saying, "Bad things happened here."

Jonny stopped the car. "What's wrong?"

"What's at the end of this driveway?"

"The house I survived in."

The Chevelle lurched forward.

Jonny mashed the brakes, but the car did not stop. He put Dolores into reverse and punched the gas pedal. The tires spun, flinging dirt and debris under the belly but the Chevy continued forward.

Cheyenne jumped, pulling her knees to her chest.

"What is it?" he asked.

She gawked down in the floorboard at the foggy eyes staring up at her. They belonged to the same little boy who avoided touching her in her nightmares, who never revealed how he died, who simply told her to *find him*. Was Jonny the *him* to whom he referred? Did Jonny kill him and now he wanted his story heard?

"Who are you?" she asked.

Jonny threw Dolores into park and locked the tires with the e-brake. The Chevelle continued to scrape along the gravel, undeterred.

"Who do you see?" he asked.

Cheyenne faced Jonny. Her voice but a whisper. "He says

he's Ralphie."

Jonny's eyes broadened. He held his breath and eyeballed the floorboard. "Why can't I see him?"

Ralphie reached upward for Cheyenne's wrist.

She jerked her hands in front of her face, screaming.

Jonny swatted at the air in front of her. "What should I do? I don't see anything!"

Ralphie held onto Cheyenne's knee, creaking and cracking up her body. He snatched her wrists one-by-one, and forced them into her lap. Small, dark-skinned hands emerged from behind Cheyenne's seat, pulling back her arms. Ralphie burrowed his fingers through the back of her hair. "Let me show you."

Cheyenne's body stiffened, her eyes rolled behind her head, and she gasped for air. She let out a loud exhale and her body went flaccid.

Jonny shook her shoulder. "Cheyenne!" He reached for her pulse, but he didn't need to feel for it; it throbbed visibly. He peeled back her eyelids searching for her pupils but her eyes hid behind her head.

Dolores came to a stop at the end of the driveway.

Jonny shifted the Chevelle into reverse and punched the gas; the tires spun in place. He put the Chevelle in drive and goosed it. Dolores acquiesced and lurched forward. He spun the car one-eighty and came to a sudden stop. Jonny floored the gas pedal, surrounding Dolores in plumes of dust and smoke, swaying her body from the torque of her big block. Roar as she might, Dolores advanced no further.

Jonny flung open the door and made his way through the dust to the passenger side. He grabbed the handle and immediately released it. He stood back, staring at his Chevelle, raking his fingers through his hair. He circled around to the rear, combing Dolores with his eyes. He walked up the driver side and back around to the passenger door. Imprinted in the dust on Dolores's body were several small handprints.

2

Cheyenne plunged into darkness and the rancid smell of decay punched her in the stomach. She wretched and dry heaved, falling to her hands and knees on what felt of gravel-riddled mud. The stench so strongly infiltrated the air, she could taste it and tried to spit the flavor from her dry tongue. Somewhere in the gloom, droplets plummeted into a pool drawing her attention; she desperately needed a drink.

She staggered to her feet and immediately tripped over a rod or bar, toppling into a solid construct with a dull, metallic thud. She glided her hand along the top edge; it had no lid. Maybe a tub or trough. Her hand rested over the rough ridge of the metal; she wasn't sure if she wanted to know its content.

"Je vais te tuer!" spoke a male voice with a southern twang.

The ire in his tone perked up her ears. She couldn't understand it but, it reminded her of Jonny's nightmare in the living room.

"H-Hello?" she called.

A child's softspoken voice responded, echoing in the darkness. "I'm going to kill you."

She spun around, with a gasp, scanning the blackness for movement; her breath trembling. "Who's there?" She held her hands out in front of her body and walked toward the child's voice. "Ralphie?" Her hand touched something hanging; she flinched and recoiled. "Please turn on the lights."

“Je vais casser ton cou!” said the angry southern twang.

“I’ll break your neck!” said the child.

Was he translating? He had to be; he only spoke after that man.

She palpated the foreign object swinging in front of her and felt a nose. She jerked her hands back. “Where am I?”

“Le temps me dure,” said another young voice, nearly pubescent.

“I can hardly wait,” the child translated.

“Ralphie, please, turn on the light!” Cheyenne placed her hands out in front of her and continued forward. “Jonny?” She ran into another hanging body. “AHHHH! Please turn on the light!”

“This was our friend’s life,” Ralphie said. “To understand him, you must experience what he went through.”

“Where are you?” She turned around in a circle. “Where am I?”

“Avan la nwit dési,” said the southern twang.

“Before the night is over,” Ralphie translated.

Fingers snapped beside Cheyenne’s head and she spun around. A pair of yellowish-green reflective discs greeted her. They reminded Cheyenne of cat eyes glowing in the dark.

“There,” Ralphie said, “now you can’t hear them.”

Cheyenne raised her hands and walked toward the dripping sound. “I’m thirsty. Please turn on the light so I can find the water?”

Ralphie closed his eyes, disappearing into the darkness. “Are you sure it’s water you hear?”

“What else could it be?” She turned. “Ralphie?”

Cheyenne’s head was on a pivot. She took several steps, homing on the dripping sound.

Sniffing and gnawing reverberated in the darkness; her breath quivered.

"To understand him, you must experience what he went through," Ralphie repeated.

"How can I experience it if I can't see?"

Ralphie opened his eyes; he was right in front of her.

Cheyenne jumped.

"The same way he did," Ralphie said.

"Tell me how he did it."

Ralphie shoved her to the ground and his eyes vanished into the gloom.

The darkness growled from multiple directions.

"Ralphie?"

A creature walked up her supine body and hovered, breathing on her chin.

Ralphie's eyes opened a few feet away from the top of her head. Was he going to let her get eaten?

"Jonny's an easy man to read," he said. "You wanted to play his game, remember?"

"I don't want to play anymore!"

"You don't have a choice; your life depends on it." He put his lips close to her ear. "What game is he playing?"

"I don't—"

"Nobody's life is at stake but your own." Ralphie stood, pacing above her head. "Maybe you're not the best player." He stopped and stared down at her. "You keep trying to take your life." Ralphie walked a circle around her body. "Sit," he said.

The invisible beast sat on Cheyenne's abdomen. It's warm, wet muzzle pressed against her cheek and sniffed. The tongue and breath that followed were laced with the scent of decay.

Ralphie stood above her head again. "Either tell me what game Jonny's playing or tell me how he survived."

Cheyenne held her breath.

The dog snapped at her face.

"It's a game of survival!"

"Whose survival?" Ralphie asked.

"His."

"WRONG!"

Cheyenne propped herself up on her elbows. "Yours?"

Ralphie used his foot and pushed her down into the wet dirt. "WRONG!"

She stared into the yellowish-green glow. "Jonny's son's; his family's?"

"WRONG and WRONG!"

The dog snapped its fangs in her face.

"Maybe he's not easy to read after all." Ralphie held her down with his foot. "Should I beat your chest and smack your face like you did him?"

Goosebumps washed her body and her hairs stood erect. "Nicholas," she said, sotto voce. "You must let me go. Jonny's in danger!"

Ralphie's glowing eyes turned away. "Go to him."

More pairs of reflective eyes populated the darkness.

Ralphie blinked his eyes, gazing down at her. "We're not finished."

3

The sun yielded to the moon hours ago, but the dense canopy shielded the forest floor beyond the clearing from the lunar light. Jonny returned to the camp with the last bundle of usable kindling he'd scrounged; it was too dangerous to venture into the dark woods for more. The batteries in his flashlight were nearly dead and the fire was delayed due to the lack of dry wood in the area.

He dusted the debris from his hands and lifted Cheyenne's eyelids; still rolled white. He tucked the blanket in tighter around her and re-centered her on the short grass bordering the gravel drive. He injected the Chevelle's cigarette lighter and removed Dolores's gas cap. He took off his shirt and tore it into strands, dipping two of them inside the gas tank. He stacked the leaves and kindling in the middle of the stone firepit he built from loose rocks. He needed to get the light going before Nicholas capitalized on the situation.

He would have preferred to tent in the car, but the cab light wouldn't run forever and push-starting a 454 in an inch-and-a-half of loose gravel is a tall order, even with two people.

Pop!

Jonny retrieved the lighter and returned to his burn pile. He placed the last of his dried moss against the glowing metal next to the shirt bomb and blew life into a flame.

The fire struggled to breathe.

"C'mon, grow bigger." He continued to blow and fan the miniature flame but it did not have enough energy to flourish.

He stayed close, gathering more dead leaves and twigs.

A rustle moved within the compost; he threw an ear in the direction.

The grind of bones and the squish of moist flesh accompanied every small movement. Rot and melted tissue now mingled strongly within the air.

Jonny focused on his depleting fire, then shifted his gaze to Cheyenne's motionless body; he couldn't outrun Nicholas. He brought his fists up to his sides and slowly backed toward his dying campfire. He scanned the vast blackness for the amber eyes and the silhouette but saw neither.

A cadence of heavy thuds accelerated toward them from the woods.

Jonny looked over his shoulder at the coughing, sputtering flame nearing its demise. Still, it was the only light he had for protection. He steeled himself; the thuds were nearly at his feet.

The fire crackled and whispered.

Jonny looked over his shoulder to see whisp of smoke fall into the smoldering embers.

The orange coals erupted into an intense blue flare bellowing outwards in all directions.

Nicholas's shadowy cloak could not veil him against the blinding indigo. He lurched forward, enduring the agony of the blue light, and roared in Jonny's face.

Jonny kept his tense stance but remained calm, studying his opponent.

Nicholas's frame was emaciated. If he had anything to fill his fire-ravaged skin, which was stretched over knobby limbs and crackling ribs, it would not have been much. Bits of exposed bone showed through his long-since, rotten face. Decayed blood oozed from his missing nose and from under his cheekbones. If he had any teeth, they were obscured by melted skin strung between where his upper and lower lips should have been. Steam smoked from Nicholas's face. The blood on his corpse sizzled. The hot glow of burning embers filled the blackened eye sockets.

The chair wreathed in flames flashed in his Jonny's mind. His eyebrow raised, and his head cocked to the side. He relaxed his arms and uncoiled his fists and took a small step forward. His upper lip peeled back baring his teeth. "You sonofabitch." His searing glare penetrated the glowing pits of Nicholas's eyes. "I know who you are."

Nicholas opened his mouth wide and shrieked. He turned and leaped back into the night.

Jonny turned somewhat, looking down at the base of the inferno, listening to the whispers emanate from the bonfire.

4

Ralphie snapped his fingers, illuminating a slaughterhouse of children hung, like deer, from the rafters. The drips emanated from a wash-trough catching blood from the slit throat of a small boy, near the opening of a homemade tunnel where a cart half-full of dead children partially protruded from the abyssal darkness.

"At the end of the night, the cart would be wheeled out and the bodies burned," said Ralphie.

Cheyenne's stomach soured at the realization she nearly dipped her hand inside that very cart. Some of the faces, and a few hanging from the beams, haunted her dreams. "What was the blood used for?" Cheyenne asked.

"You're not ready to know."

"The voices from earlier, who were they?"

"It was a conversation between Lee and Jonny."

"He told me what Lee did to him."

Ralphie led her by the hand to the cast-iron cage, flanked on either side by guard dogs. One chewed a small, severed hand and the other gnawed an ear between its paws.

Cheyenne wrapped her arms around her stomach. "They fed the dogs the dead children?"

They stopped in front of the iron tomb, where the past of Jonny demanding Ralphie to look at him played out.

She released Ralphie's hand and stepped forward. "That's you," she said, stating the obvious. "Why do you have blood dripping down your throat?"

"Because I obeyed him," Ralphie said, pointing to Jonny.

"He hasn't changed, just gotten older," Cheyenne said.

"They," Ralphie said pointing toward the two men, "wanted to teach Jonny a lesson."

"By hurting you?"

Ralphie looked up at her. "Torture isn't limited to inflicting pain on anyone person. Forcing you to watch what you could have prevented is worse."

Ralphie's statement reeled Cheyenne into an unexpected understanding of Jonny's earlier revelation during the drive. She digested both as she took a knee beside Jonny's afterimage. She examined his swollen eye, noting his grimace with each shallow breath. "I want to hear what's going on."

"Are you sure?" Ralphie asked. "This isn't Hollywood, this really happened."

Ralphie's doppelgänger gripped the cast-iron bars mouthing for his mommy.

Cheyenne pointed to the lanky man with black, snaggled teeth and a dangling, lit cigarette. She imagined if he laughed, it would mimic Goofy's *ah-hyuck*. His head and face were shaved and his clothes stained. "Who's he?"

"Lee," Ralphie replied. He pointed to the other man covered in Loa tattoos. "The other is Mickey."

She stepped in front of Lee. "So, you're the sick asshole who raped him."

Dead Ralphie walked alongside little Jonny, who army-crawled toward past Ralphie. "Mickey and Lee did far more than rape our friend." He snapped his fingers, freezing the past. "Last chance," he said. "Are you sure you want to witness what happens next?"

A prickly sensation ran through Cheyenne's spine. It wasn't the normal tingling she got before her body coated itself in goosebumps, this was different. She peered over her shoulder at a third boy who cowered in a ball, gripping the bars. His hands and arms hid his face but he stared calmly at her from the corner of his eye with a raised brow. She turned around, taking a few steps toward the kennel. "Who is he?"

"Jonny called him Al; he was a scaredy-cat."

Ralphie's tone struck her odd. It was the first thing he said that made sense for his apparent age. The thought took second stage to what Cheyenne observed from the still image of the boy in the cage. His curled body suggested a whipped dog, beaten into submission, but his face didn't agree. She knew the many faces of fear on children; Nicholas saw to it. Al seemed calm as he peered from the corner of his eye, mildly concerned maybe, but not afraid. "His body says scared, but it's like he's playing possum." She tracked his stare. "Or spying."

Ralphie pointed to little Jonny. "Do you want to continue?"

"Yes."

He snapped his fingers, and the past came to life.

Mickey turned, kicking Jonny in the side. "I said, stop coddling him!"

Jonny coughed and gasped but, still, he crawled toward past Ralphie.

Mickey swung back his leg, driving his foot into Jonny's face.

Jonny yelped and blood oozed from his mouth and nose, but he kept advancing.

Mickey laughed maliciously. "You're a stubborn shit, aren't you?"

Cheyenne charged Mickey to push him, but she went through him and slammed into the wall behind.

"You cannot change what has already happened," dead Ralphie explained. He helped Cheyenne to her feet and pointed to Jonny. "Now, watch."

Jonny lay on his back, tucking Ralphie's face in his chest. He spit the blood from his mouth. "You're nothin' more than a pussy preying on small children."

"Fine, you want to play big brother," Mickey said, walking

away. "If you win the fight, then the runt is yours to train, to clean up after, and to feed."

"Like a dog," Lee snickered. It wasn't the *ah-hyuck* Cheyenne imagined but more of a Sheriff Roscoe P. Coltrane's *gyuh, gyuh, gyuh* laugh.

"But," Mickey raised his pointer finger in the air and turned, "if you lose, he dies, and so does Al."

Al gripped the bars. "Me! What did I do?"

Mickey ignored him and continued with his terms. "Remember, our original agreement still stands. You lose, I pay a visit to your sister and brother."

Lee licked his blade. "Your sister gots to be fifteen by now." He fondled his manhood, closing his eyes. "I bet she's got the softest, perkiest tits." He opened his eyes, grinning at Jonny. "I can't wait to be balls deep in her again."

Jonny pushed Ralphie off and lunged.

Al jutted his arm through the bars, wrapping it around Jonny's chest. "Use your anger out there."

Jonny glared over his shoulder. "Afraid of dying?"

Mickey glanced at his watch. "Come on, hotshot. Time to deliver."

Jonny opened the cell door for Ralphie. "Go back inside."

"No, he's coming with us," Mickey said. "He needs to see what the rest of his life is going to be." He smiled. "If you win that is."

Lee snatched Ralphie's forearm.

"Owe, let me go!" he whimpered.

Lee slung Ralphie over his shoulder and pounded the barn door.

The door slid open and Jonny pushed past everyone, leading them to a crowd in the distance. He saw something he'd never seen before, men dressed in black surveilling the perimeter. Somebody important must be here. He stopped and asked, "Did a kid escape?"

"Nobody escapes." Mickey pushed him forward, "Nobody."

That wasn't true and they both knew it. Jonny helped several kids escape before Mickey locked him up.

5

The herd of criminals grew since Jonny's last fight. The majority of them wore camouflage hunting gear in case they were ambushed by a police raid; they could run into the forest and pretend to be hunters.

Silence befell the frenzied throng as they parted at Jonny's approach. Whispers spread through the horde like blades of dry grass rustling in a cold breeze.

"They know him?" Cheyenne asked.

Ralphie looked around the masses. "Everyone knew him; knew what he was capable of."

Mickey halted Jonny by the shoulders before a man in a pinstriped suit and matching hat, holding a golden cane topped with a large, garnet knob. A shirtless boy, taller and brawnier than Jonny by a margin, accompanied this godfather-esque figure; Jonny would have to fight smart.

Jonny focused on the man in the pinstriped suit. "Who you supposed to be, Al Capone?"

Mickey smacked the back of Jonny's head. "Ludvig, this is my fighter."

The man lifted his cane, poking Jonny's chest; he batted it away.

The boy standing next to Ludvig pointed at Jonny and moved his finger up and down, "*Eto shutka? Kto-to uzhe poveselilsya s etim.*"

Ludvig raised his hand, nodding his head. "Myrum says

he's insulted you would bring him used sheet."

Jonny leaned inward at Myrum. "I'm not your fuckin' dirty sheet."

Ludvig smirked, as did Myrum.

"Has he *always* been hot-tempered?" Cheyenne asked.

Ralphie squeezed her hand. "Pay attention."

"Your fighter has smart mouth," said Ludvig. He circled Jonny. "Boy, how many times you fight tonight?"

Jonny swatted Ludvig's hand off his bruised ribs and pointed his thumb. "Counting the beating Mickey and Minnie gave . . . " he paused, spitting, "three."

Myrum laughed. "*On umret s pervym udarom.*"

"He's right," Ludvig said. He stood before Mickey. "This would not be fair fight. Are you sure you want them to fight with the bid of two hundred thousand?"

"You haven't fed or allowed me to sleep in days and you have two hundred K to throw at a fight?"

Myrum's smirk vanished. He opened his mouth to speak, but Ludvig raised his hand.

"You beat your fighter, starve him, and torture him?"

Jonny spit the blood from his mouth. He glared at Mickey, with a sigh. As much as Mickey liked money and drugs, they were foreplay. Power and torture were the real aphrodisiacs. Win or lose, he was going into the ring; Mickey wanted to watch him suffer.

Jonny took measure of Myrum, gleaning whatever he could from his movement and attitude. The height difference was nearly six inches; how old was this kid? Was he chemically enhanced? Jonny felt like Rocky versus *The Russian*. Height, reach, and power, all out-matched. Jonny maybe had speed on him, but excessive movement with his shattered right side wasn't the answer against an unencumbered ogre. Usually, Jonny had the benefit of at least seeing the opponent fight before he faced them, but tonight, he would go in blind. He would have to learn Myrum's ticks and tells under fire. His only hope was to unsettle Myrum, either unnerve him or piss him off. *Let the mental warfare begin.*

Jonny turned to Ludvig. "What, you don't want the worms feasting off Drago?"

Ludvig whacked the side of Jonny's knee with his cane. "Be quiet, boy, and let the adults talk." He pointed to Ralphie. "Who is he, and what is he doing here?"

"Leverage," Mickey answered, "to make sure Jonny does what he's supposed to."

"They're gonna kill him if I lose."

Ludvig picked his cane up, connecting the gemstone to Jonny's jaw; his head spun, and he fell to the ground.

The corner of Mickey's lip pulled upward into a smirk.

"That brings you pleasure, me hitting your fighter?"

"He's always had a smart mouth but now, his mouth smarts."

"*Gyuh, gyuh, gyuh,*" laughed Lee.

Ludvig used his cane to roll Jonny onto his back. "Boy, it's because you have no idea who I am, I allow you to live." He inspected his cane. "Interrupt us again and I won't be as merciful." He shifted his eyes between Lee and Mickey. "Listen to crowd. They're not excited anymore. You know why?"

Mickey surveyed the whispering onlookers.

"Even the crowd is confused why this boy is back for another fight. So, I ask again, are you sure you want this fight at current bid?"

"He's never lost," Mickey said. "He'll fight, and he'll win." He locked eyes with Jonny. "He's got too much to lose."

Jonny picked himself up off the ground. His eyes toggled from Mickey to Ralphie to Lee. He needed to weaken Myrum, tire him out. With the condition of his ribs, Ali's rope-a-dope would be out of the question. He could possibly modify the technique. He was mostly ambidextrous, but his power was definitely his left side. *If I fake an orthodox stance, maybe.* He walked past his opponent. "If we're gonna do this, then let's do this."

"Wait!" Ludvig said.

Myrum grabbed Jonny's bicep.

Jonny looked down at his arm and the glared up at Myrum. "Get your fucking hand off me, Ivan."

Myrum looked to Ludvig and Ludvig waved his hand, nodding. Myrum released him without returning comment.

"Let's make things interesting," Ludvig suggested with a sly grin. "If your fighter loses, then I own him."

"No deal," Mickey said.

Ludvig leaned into Mickey's ear. "So, the boy means something to you?"

"Dollar signs," Jonny answered. "I'm nothing more than fuckin' dollar signs."

"He won't lose. Will you?" Mickey asked with stern eyes.

Jonny shifted his eyes to Ralphie then looked back to Myrum. "Let's get it over with and beat the fuck out each other."

6

Myrum and Jonny each moved to their respective sides of the hexagonal ring, demarcated by white-washed timber beams half buried in dirt. Parallel strings of barbed wire, stretched taught over metal fencing rods, restrained the crowd. Two bouncers guarded the open section of the ring, where fighters entered; they were as much to keep in the fighters as to keep out the crowd.

Jonny tilted back his head and closed his eyes, whispering inaudibly. He coughed and grimaced, forcing his arm to stay down; he didn't want Myrum picking up any weaknesses, though he knew it was a moot point. Myrum could see the purple bruising to his right side, the yellow-green smattering everywhere else, and the swelling of his right eye. He slid his left foot forward and raised his arms to his flanks, protecting his ribcage. He looked around at crowd; they were eager to see if he could pull off a miracle. Honestly, so was Jonny.

The crowd remained hushed when the bell rang; Jonny held his stance.

Myrum lowered his fists and circled Jonny wearing a cocky smile. Cocky worked. Cocky makes easy errors, errors Jonny could exploit; he focused on Myrum's face and shoulders for movement. Myrum came strutting with a puffed-out chest and balled fists.

Jonny steadied himself, waiting for Myrum to come within reach. His left sprung, connecting with a jab.

Myrum stumbled back but Jonny did not follow through with a combo. He needed to conserve himself until he learned Myrum's fighting style.

Myrum looked to Ludvig. The mafia wannabe waved him forward then whispered into a man's ear.

Jonny jabbed again but Myrum slipped the strike and countered with a volley to his abdomen and face. Jonny grunted painfully, from each blow, protecting his already battered ribs. He broke free of the onslaught and delivered a left uppercut. Myrum tucked his head between his fist. He was undoubtfully familiar with Tyson's hook, a hook Jonny did not throw.

Myrum's eyes raised and ran up and down Jonny; they were looking for answers to why Jonny had not pressed the assault. They settled on his ribs. The smirk Myrum wore dropped Jonny's heart. *Shit, he figured it out.*

Myrum offered up his ribs. So, he knew the rope-a-dope,

too. It stood to reason, but Jonny acknowledged the bait with a deceptive clumsy haymaker, leaving a small opening to his left flank. He watched Myrum's shoulder intently, awaiting the right moment. Myrum took the bait and Jonny shot his left through the narrow opening, punishing Myrum's ribs with four rapid blows. Jonny grunted painfully with each. Myrum's arm tucked back in, cutting off Jonny's barrage. Jonny followed swiftly with a heavy right-left combo. Myrum regrouped and Jonny tucked his right arm against his ribs.

Myrum spit blood from his mouth. He did not expect this fight in the *used sheet* they threw in the ring with him. Jonny was better than most of the other fighters he had already beaten, Possibly, even better than a few to whom Myrum had lost. His blood boiled with the thought of fighting Jonny in his prime, a *REAL* fight. But he had a job to do. He strode quickly up to his opponent, blocking Jonny's left strike, and grabbing his right hand. He lifted Jonny's arm, exposing the injured ribcage, and delivered multiple blows with his knee. Jonny's cries accompanied the crack of each rib beneath Myrum's knee cap. Myrum ended the onslaught with a backhand to Jonny's face followed by a punch to the jaw.

Jonny fell to the ground gasping for air, clutching his right side. He coughed, spewing blood from his mouth. Pain radiated through his back and chest. He crawled to his knees but Myrum kicked him back down. Jonny understood now; Myrum had been watching him, too. He assumed Myrum had been relying on his brute strength, but that was happenstance. Myrum was a true fighter; a warrior studying his art, learning Jonny's fighting style.

Mickey snatched Ralphie from Lee and wrapped his hands around Ralphie's throat.

Cheyenne covered her mouth, gasping. She grabbed dead Ralphie's hand, squeezing it tight. It turned out, Ralphie would show her his death afterall. "He killed you? Mickey?"

"Mickey killed all of us." Ralphie pointed to the fight. "Even our friend. Now, watch or I'll end it here."

Jonny rolled backward onto his feet, wheezing and watching the Russian man-child close in for a hard left. Jonny readied himself for a one-two counter combo, bringing up his right fist for the cross punch, but Myrum grabbed Jonny's fist and pulverized his remaining ribs. Jonny hooked with a desperate, off balance left.

Myrum swept his leg, throwing Jonny onto his back with a thud. "Hmph!" He sat on Jonny's chest and rained an assault upon his face. Jonny blocked and Myrum quickly attacked both sides of his ribs.

Jonny protected his ribs, taking each blow to the face. He took the deepest breath he could muster and blocked his face again and when Myrum went for his ribs, Jonny delivered four quick and painful punches to Myrum's face, followed by a liver shot, toppling Myrum backward.

Jonny lay on the ground a moment, racked with pain, struggling for each gurgling breath. He crawled to his feet, leaning unsteadily to the right, wheezing loudly. He glared at Myrum through his bloodied left eye; his right one long since swollen shut.

Myrum staggered to his feet, shaking his head.

Jonny was stunned the combo didn't work. His bag of tricks now lay empty. All he could do now was tuck his right side and deliver whatever dirty work he could with his left but even then, he knew the outcome. Worse, he knew the price for losing; his eyes welled at the thought.

Jonny had done many unthinkable things for which he would never forgive himself. Ultimately, his siblings would meet the same fate as the rest. To be forced to watch those sick fucks repeatedly rape his sister and torture his brother. He wouldn't be able to live with himself, knowing how they would end. He'd rather die now than bear witness. "COME ON!" he shouted, ignoring the tearing in his right lung, bringing his arm up for a final defense.

The mob whispered among themselves, rooting for Jonny even though it was clear he lost.

Cheyenne wiped her tears. "Why does he keep fighting?"

Ralphie looked up at her. "Lives depend on it." He pointed to the fight. "Last time I'll tell you, watch and learn."

Myrum blitzed with several jabs and Jonny could no longer bob and weave. Myrum came in for the KO, hooking Jonny's jaw. The agony shot up into Jonny's ear, followed by a loud snap. He fell to his back dazed, but lucid enough to process the severity of the moment. The fight was over and he knew it. He turned his head, searching for Ralphie.

Ralphie fought against Mickey's hands, his face already deep purple.

Myrum's blurry silhouette stood over Jonny and raised its foot. Jonny saw the foot come down, expecting his ribs to rip, crack, and tear. He was wrong. He lay on the ground wailing and cradling his arm in the fetal position. The bones of three fingers protruded through the skin.

The crowd profaned, spitting and booing. Some rushed the fencing, throwing debris into the arena.

Ludvig pushed his way to the front and waved aside the bouncers.

"Vy nikogda ne budete drat'sya snova," said Myrum.

"You will never fight again," Ralphie translated.

Myrum raised his foot.

Jonny rolled onto his back staring at the bottom of Myrum's blurry boot.

Ralphie snapped his fingers, pausing the past with Myrum's foot coming down toward Jonny's face. "That's enough."

Twenty-Six
The Doctor

1

Jonny lay under the blanket using his breath to help keep him and Cheyenne warm. His stomach rumbled again and he knew he could no longer ignore it. He pulled the blanket off his head and looked to Dolores slumbering in the gravel. Dew covered her body and streaked through the dust laden handprints. He thought about starting her up, but the last two days, all she did was whirl. Each day, he inspected her innerworkings and everything checked out. Most likely, it would be more of the same and he decided against it. He concluded they weren't meant to leave. Whatever supernatural phenomena created the indigo bonfire was also responsible for Cheyenne's comatose state.

Jonny's stomach growled even louder. His first day of sunlight, he gathered willow shoots and sticks, weaving a fish basket. It took him a day and half to finish, and late yesterday evening, he swam the snowmelt river. Most people secure their basket near the bank, but he knew these waters and the best catch swam the deeper parts. To prevent hypothermia, he removed his wet clothes and placed them next to the fire. It took two hours for his clothes to dry. The one saving grace was Cheyenne. She was feverish and her body radiated heat. When he thought about it, her having a fever seemed to be a side effect of her nightmares. When they picked her up to go to Boomer Hill, Cheyenne was feverish and again, when they rescued her. Was she having one now?

Borborygmus!

Damn stomach. He didn't want to leave the blanket. Even with Cheyenne as his heat rock, he spent all night getting his core temperature normal, which is difficult when the temperature plummets at night. Considering dew had cumulated on spiderwebs and the fog had not yet burned off, last night got pretty damn cold; *the river will be colder.*

He tore another strand from his shirt and poured the last of their water onto it. There was no way around it now, he was going swimming. He squeezed a little into Cheyenne's mouth and then wetted her lips. He peeled back her eyelids; still hidden.

He squeezed the remaining water from the fibers into his mouth and slid Cheyenne's head from his lap, tucking the blanket around her body. He opened the ice chest and dumped the melted ice. They had no food and now, no water. He sat on the ice chest and unlaced his shoes. One by one, he tied the water bottles together and slung them over his shoulder.

Already, the cold air nipped at his skin. He stood beside the fire procrastinating on what needed to be done. He stared vacantly into the indigo flames listening to the whispers die into the crackling bonfire which burned unaided. What created it? He turned, looking at Cheyenne. Are they linked? What he did know, the blue inferno not only kept Nicholas at bay, it hurt him. He assumed as long as the caerulean fire continued to burn, Nicholas wouldn't attack.

Borborygmus!

He looked down at his stomach. "I hear you. Let's get it over with." He snatched the other shoelace from the ice chest and hiked down the steep cliff face. Parts of the ground broke free under his weight, and he surfed some of the way down. It took him another fifteen minutes to reach the waterfall. He refilled the bottles and left them on the bank.

The frigid mountain air felt like sharp glass against is skin. He used his breath to warm his fingers, preparing himself for what needed to be done. He carefully waded into the water, slipping a few times on the algae covered bedrock. The snowmelt robbed him of what little heat his body retained. He took several deep breathes then dunked under, swimming for the rope he anchored to a tree trunk. He came back up, pulling in the line. Tied on the other end, a fish basket which captured two sturgeons.

Jonny made his way back to the bank and pulled out his pocketknife. He managed to behead the sturgeons despite the tremor in his left hand. He tossed their heads inside the fish basket and made a small opening in the female. He devoured some of her caviar then tied the tail ends with the other shoelace.

He warmed his hands again, staring at the water, thinking he didn't know how long they would be stranded. He dreaded it, but Jonny knew he had to go back in. He grabbed the rope and fish basket and headed back into the cold-ass river. He dove under, tying the line to the tree. He came back up for air and then swam back under, to the deeper end. He weighted the basket and then kicked off the riverbed.

Jonny's joints stiffened and his skin, drained of color, burned with pins and needles. He made haste to the bank, gathering his supplies, and hiked back up the cliff. The exertion warmed him some but not enough. He felt the hypothermia trying to take hold.

He placed his catch inside the cooler and undressed in front of the fire, scowling at the abandon house. He'd risk another Tillamook Burn razing it to the fucking ground before he'd shelter there. He wrung out his pants and underwear and placed them near the heat. He dragged Cheyenne closer to the flames before crawling under the blanket with her. He pulled her on top of him, siphoning her heat. He buried his head under the blanket and used his breath to help keep him warm. Like last time, he prayed Cheyenne wouldn't wake up with him under her and naked. He was certain she would give him a big fat kiss with her knuckles.

2

"No," Cheyenne protested. She entered the center ring and took a knee, reaching for Jonny's face, but her hands went through him. She recognized the future scars that now mangled his right hand. She understood why he withheld their origin, the layers of pain and anguish of which they reminded him daily. She could not hold the weight of the knowledge any longer, and neither could her tears. She took in the rest of his ruined body, little more than a corps, staring at the boot counting down his last moments. His face, it was not distorted in fear, it layered with shades of sadness, anger, regret. "I need to know what happened."

Ralphie stood next to his past self and stared into his lifeless eyes. "You need to figure out who's survival is important to our friend." He stared at her. "Watching the past play out won't tell you how he survived this nightmare."

"I want to know what happened."

Ralphie held out his hand and assisted Cheyenne to her feet. They stepped to the side, and Ralphie snapped his fingers.

"Ostanavlivat'sya!" said Ludvig

Myrum halted.

The man Ludvig whispered to earlier returned and now whispered into his ear.

Ludvig nodded his head, waving the man away. He kneeled beside Jonny. "Why you fight so hard? Why you so willing to die?"

Jonny turned his head away. Tears escaped, pooling on the ridge of his nose. His face grimaced as his breathing increased. His skin turned a blue hue.

Ludvig reached for Jonny's face and he rapidly grabbed Ludvig's wrist.

"I'm not your enemy, boy." He crawled on his knees, whispering into Jonny's ear. He stood and waved over the two men holding the makeshift cot. "Take him to the infirmary."

The men lifted Jonny onto the cot; he screamed in agony. A few men from the crowd stepped forward to help boost him.

One man began chanting Jonny's name, and slowly, the entire throng joined him. Their chanting could be heard everywhere within the compound.

Ralphie brought up his hand to snap his fingers but Cheyenne covered it. "No, I want to watch." She followed them into the infirmary.

The doctor tapped the steel table, "Put him here." He was in his early forties with salt-and-pepper hair and his clean-shaven face had few wrinkles. He wore an unbuttoned white lab coat over his clothes.

"Now, help me roll him so we can remove the cot," the doctor instructed. "No, no! Roll him to the left."

Jonny held his breath and grunted as they moved him; his

eyes watered.

The man standing in front of Jonny leaned forward, grinding his broken fingers into the table.

"AAHHH!!"

The man pulled away, snagging a protruding bone with his belt.

Jonny wailed and pounded the table with his left fist.

The doctor tucked the side of the cot against the child's body and then rolled him on his back, over the bundle. "Breathe, Jon."

He closed his eye, working through the pain. He breathed, wheezing through his nose; it hurt intensely. Jonny held each breath to ease the inhalation.

The doctor leaned over Jonny's torso making eye contact. "I will give you oxygen in a second. Right now, we have to roll slightly onto your right side to pull the cot out." The doctor looked to the men. "Let's make this fast."

Jonny moaned loudly. His wheezing became worse, and he struggled for air.

A man quickly grabbed the cot, sliding it out from under Jonny.

"Lay him back," the doctor commanded. He placed his stethoscope in his ears, listening to the patient's right lung. "You can all leave now," the doctor said. He continued his assessment of Jonny's condition, gliding his stethoscope from the right side of his chest to the left. "You took a good beating this time, Jon." The doctor removed his stethoscope from his ears and placed it back around his neck. "Did the morphine I gave you last fight help with the pain?"

He closed his eyes and bobbed his head.

The doctor inserted a cannula in Jonny's nostrils and cranked the oxygen to five. "How many times did they make you fight?"

Cheyenne walked around the doctor. “He cares for him.”

“He cared for a lot of us,” Ralphie said.

Jonny used American sign language to spell his responses.

She shook her head. “No, the doctor cares for him on a personal level.”

“So really, four fights?” the doctor asked.

Jonny nodded in agreement.

The doctor examined the patient’s mouth. “You’re signing, does it hurt to talk?”

Jonny pointed to his jaw. *Broken,* he signed.

“Let’s look.” The doctor examined his jaw and eyes. He removed the oxygen and examined around and inside his nose. “You lost?” he asked, replacing the nasal cannula.

Jonny nodded his head.

“That means your arrangement with Mickey is void. What will you do?”

Jonny did not reply. He lay there, staring at the lights above his table.

The doctor blocked the light with his head. “You know he set you up?” He stepped away, grabbing the sterile table, loaded with scalpels, clamps, and other utensils. He grabbed some sutures from the supply rack, elaborating on his statement. “No one makes a fighter fight more than once, let alone beat them before making them fight a third.”

Lee entered the room with a smug smile, tossing Ralphie’s lifeless body on the adjacent exam table like a hunter presenting his quarry.

Jonny stared at Ralphie; Ralphie’s empty eyes stared back.

Mickey rounded the doorway, stone-faced, holding a flip phone. He placed the phone on speaker and muted the microphone, and set it down between Jonny and him, as it chimed its distorted electronic ring.

Jonny could not break free of Ralphie’s glazed stare.

"Hello?" asked a garbled but familiar voice.

Red speckles of broken vessels ringed Ralphie's irises

"Jonathan, is that you?" the phone whispered.

"Is that Jonny? Let me have the phone. Jonny, it's me, Sandra."

The phone crackled and popped as they wrestled for it.

Ralphie, at least, could rest now. Mickey could hurt him no longer.

Dominick apparently won the phone. "I know you probably can't talk for whatever reason but know Sandra and I will be waiting for you tomorrow at our secret spot."

Jonny's tears squeezed free from his swollen eye. He longed for rest, too. How much more would he endure? How much would they?

Mickey ended the call. His upper lip curled, his nose and forehead wrinkled. His devilish voice spoke and spit sprung from Mickey's mouth as he shouted. "You have no idea how much you cost me tonight!"

The droplets wrested Jonny from his thoughts and from Ralphie's stare. He glared up at Mickey.

"I'm gonna hang that half breed, nigger brother of yours from the tree, leaving his body to rot." Mickey pounded the steel table with his fist. "I'm gonna harvest your sister's peach every damn day and night until she begs me to kill her. Your grandparents—"

Jonny raised up, screaming in pain and frustration, and connected his left fist to Mickey's face. He brought his elbow up and drilled it down forcefully toward Mickey's head.

Mickey slipped out of the way and grabbed Jonny by the throat, pushing him back to the table.

The doctor grabbed his scalpel and swiftly placed it against Mickey's throat. "I think it best you and Lee remember who I work for."

A small drop of blood pooled beneath the blade and squirmed down Mickey's neck.

Lee whistled, tapping the doctor on the shoulder with his knife. "And if I were you, Doc, I would remember who I am." He smiled, rubbing his blade up and down the side of the doctor's neck.

A metallic click emanated from behind Lee.

The doctor smiled. "Kto derzhit pistolet?" he asked.

"Who holds the gun?" Ralphie translated.

"Annika," the voice replied, pressing the gun barrel firmly against the back of Lee's head.

Cheyenne circled the girl in the white dress. "Is that—"

"No, it's not Sandra." Ralphie said. "You just heard her and Dominick on the phone."

"She looks just like her except, she has green eyes." Cheyenne stared at Jonny. "This . . . this is the girl." She focused on the doctor. "He's the one—"

"Shall I end this?" Ralphie asked.

"No. I just thought he made the story up."

Mickey released Jonny, and Lee handed Annika his knife.

The doctor removed his weapon from Mickey's throat. "I know who the both of you are. You, Lee, are a sick fuck who sexually abuses small children, getting off on the pain and torture before killing them. And you, Mickey—"

"Enough, Doctor Kirill." Ludvig appeared from behind the curtain of the adjacent room, accompanied by Myrum and a clean, clothed, and confident Al. If Cheyenne had not figured him out in the cage, she would have sworn he was merely a likeness to the scamp huddled in the corner of the crate.

"I knew something was off about him," Cheyenne said.

Annika pointed to Jonny. "On tot, kto spas menya."

"He's the one who saved me," Ralphie translated.

Doctor Kirill addressed Ludvig. "He doesn't belong here."

Ludvig closed his eyes, bobbing his head. He pointed to the two brothers.

Doctor Kirill addressed Mickey and Lee. "You two are to leave this room. I am to remind you both, Ludvig is not one to trifle with. He expects payment by the end of the night."

Annika wacked Lee in the head with her gun. "Move!"

Doctor Kirill pulled a chair out for Ludvig. He stepped to the side, giving his assessment of Jonny. "He has a punctured right lung, broken jaw and nose, a mild concussion, fractured cheekbone, and as you can see, three compound-fractured fingers on the right hand." He looked at Myrum. "I won't know if he has any other internal damages until I can get an MRI and I won't know how many broken ribs until I get x-rays but if I had to guess, he has at least seven."

Ludvig pointed to Ralphie's body.

Al spoke to Ludvig in Russian.

Ludvig listened quietly, watching Jonny. He raised his hand into the air, and Al stopped talking. He pulled his chair closer to the patient and pointed to Al. "My godson, Aleksei, says you protected him as you tried with that dead boy over there."

Jonny pointed at Ralphie, looked at the doctor, and manually dictated.

"They killed him," Kirill translated. "They're going after my sister and brother."

Jonny stared at Ludvig and continued his dissertation.

"He wants to know who we are," Kirill paraphrased.

"The less you know, the better you'll be," Ludvig answered. "Just know I'm powerful man with eyes and ears everywhere." He waved Annika forward. "I caught word one of my operations was being used to kill children, I injected Aleksei and a few other of my men to get truth."

Jonny signed, and Doctor Kirill translated again.

"He wants to know what truth you heard."

"A giant boy was unstoppable in the ring. This boy was killing children with one blow, and with each win, he and his two partners were making thousands of dollars in profits. How they took girls and raped and killed them for fun." Ludvig sat Annika on his lap. He caressed her face. "She belongs to me. Untouched until you."

Jonny began signing again, and Doctor Kirill signed back for verification on some misspellings. "He says, you're here now. What truth did you find?"

Ludvig chuckled. "I found a mouthy little shit whose emotions control him." He looked to Al. "That is why he can be nice and calm toward one and angry and vengeful toward another as you have reported." He played with his cane. "I answered your questions, now answer mine. What's the deal you made with those buffoons?"

Jonny grabbed his right side, trying to hold in a cough. He succeeded at first but when he relaxed, the cough came in full force. He grimaced, pounding the table with his left foot while holding his breath.

"I'm going to have to place a chest tube in the collapsed lung soon; fluid is building," Doctor Kirill said.

Jonny signed.

"He wants me to answer for him."

"You and the boy are close then?" Ludvig asked.

Doctor Kirill walked to the mini refrigerator, grabbing the morphine and a syringe. "Within the last four years, I have befriended him." He showed Jonny the morphine vial. "He has an older sister and brother. His mother went missing when he was two or three, leaving them in the hands of Mickey and Lee."

"So, one of those fools is his father?" Myrum asked.

"Jon doesn't know who his father is. Mickey has been training him and making him fight since he was four."

With each heartbeat, the morphine spread, washing away Jonny's pain. He relaxed, closing his eye.

Dr. Kirill turned Jonny's wrist over, checking his pulse. He patted Jonny's arm. "Good boy, sleep."

"You care for him," Al said.

"No, I—"

"Aleksei is right," Ludvig said. "You care a lot for this boy."

"No!" he answered sternly. "I have come to know him and respect him. Jon could have easily turned into a cruel, mean bastard like Mickey."

Cheyenne followed the doctor. "No, he loves Jonny; his eyes give him away."

Doctor Kirill cleared his sterile table and tossed the instruments into the sink. He walked over to the supply cabinet, gathering new tools and a chest tube.

"I don't remember how old Jon said he was, but he refused to fight once. Mickey and Lee repeatedly raped and tortured his sister. Beat, tortured, and sodomized his brother." He set up his workstation, waving everyone away. "These kids weren't even in their teens yet. Jon blamed himself for what they did and struck a deal with Mickey. He promised he would fight, and he would never lose, if Mickey promised to let his siblings go free."

Doctor Kirill placed a sterile pad under Jonny's hand and then poured saline over the fingers. He squinted his eyes, assessing the damage. "I can save his fingers, but I'm going to need to do surgery."

Myrum pointed at Jonny. "That kid never lost a fight until tonight?"

"Correct, and a good chance you would've lost if he hadn't already fought several times."

"How?" asked Al. Myrum is twice his size, stronger, and all most double his age."

"Jon is an ambidextrous fighter." He examined the little finger. "Most of his injuries were sustained on his right side, which tells me, he fooled Myrum into thinking his right side was his dominate." Dr. Kirill shifted his eyes to Al. "If I had to guess, he'd already sustained some injuries on this side, and needed his left to win." The doctor returned to his patient and relocated the little finger.

Jonny woke with a moan, gasping in short, painful breaths.

Doctor Kirill placed his hand on Jonny's chest and locked eyes. "It's all right. I only relocated your little finger. You're safe."

"There," Cheyenne said. "That's the same look Jonny gives Jacob."

Jonny held onto Doctor Kirill's hand, nodding his head, and closing his eye.

"He trusts you," Al said.

The doctor sat back down. "Like the boss said, Jon is a slave to his emotions." He picked the sutures up and poured the sterile water over the cut on Jonny's swollen eye. The doctor poked the needle through the patient's skin.

Jonny opened his eye, staring vacantly at the doctor.

"Can you feel the needle?"

He shook his head and signed; *O-K.*

Ludvig tapped Annika's hip and then slid his chair closer to the steel table. "You awake enough to understand me, boy?"

The morphine made Jonny sign slow and sloppy.

"Yes . . . in pain . . . but . . . listening," the doctor translated.

Ludvig glared at Annika. "You put your little cock in what's mine. My intentions were to have Myrum kill you tonight." He tapped his pointer finger on his cane.

Jonny signed.

"Then . . . why stop him?" Doctor Kirill translated.

"I watched and listen to the crowd. Some of my men made compelling cases for you, as did Aleksei." Ludvig glanced at Annika and used his head, waving her out the room.

Jonny signed again, and the doctor waited a moment.

Ludvig looked impatiently to Kirill, waiting for a translation.

Dr. Kirill hesitated then returned Ludvig's stare. "He says for a man with so much power, why'd his sappy story sway you?"

Ludvig stared at the ground. "Two years ago, my son, Sphen, was taken from me. He's same age as you." He tapped his cane. "This establishment is problem for me. Mickey and Lee are problem for me. You," he looked Jonny in the eye, "will be my solution." Ludvig stood. "Revenge is what you want, boy. I give it to you."

Twenty-Seven
Unsettled Dead

1

Cheyenne awoke beneath the great bows of an old oak, back-dropped by a serene, cloud-spotted blue sky. She recalled the cat story in which Dominick convinced Jonny to jump. She stared up into the sprawling limbs trying to envision a pint-sized Jonny gripping a branch in fear; it was difficult after witnessing a ten-year-old version, mouthy and fierce. At the base of the trunk leaned a photo of Dominick and a small organized pile of withering calla lilies, three dry and brown and one still bright yellow. It made sense. The cat story was personal, his sadness getting tangled in his throat. It must be where he goes to mourn, she thought.

She plucked out the leaves and brushed the grit from her hair, searching the yard and lawn for Jonny. Dolores was vacant and only the one blanket near the fire. Where could he have gone? Where were the children? Surely, she didn't image them.

She spotted the soaked woman from the end of the drive standing near the clothesline with her back to Cheyenne. She pointed to the house. Maybe a particular room? Whatever she was pointing at, Cheyenne was missing the heart of it.

Cheyenne ignored the woman and rose with the blanket. Over the curve of the lawn, she saw Jonny's head in the morning sun, staring out over the ravine. His arms pressed tight to his sides with his hand in his pockets, hunching his shivering, goose-fleshed torso. He turned his head slightly at the crunch and rustle of dead leaves and grass beneath her feet.

Cheyenne draped the blanket over his shoulders and stood beside him, taking in the greenery which captivated him.

"What happened to your shirt?"

He wrapped his arms around her, drawing her inside the blanket. "Used it to make the fi-fi-fire."

She pinched the blanket closed and leaned her back against his frigid chest. "Didn't think you ever got cold."

His teeth chattered. "It's colder in the mountains."

"How long was I gone?"

He pulled her tighter against his body. "Fiv-fiv-five days."

She turned around and wrapped her arms around him, rubbing his back. She inhaled deeply expecting his Old Spice fragrance, but became repulsed by the smell of old fish and BO. She turned her head, breathing fresh air, and stared at the white plume of smoke from the smoldering fire. "Why didn't you keep the fire going?"

He did not respond; his jaw bounced rapidly.

"What did you do for five days?"

"Survived."

She hugged him tighter thinking about Ralphie's question. *How did he survive?* "Ralphie took me to your past and at first, he kept me in the dark. He said in order to understand you, I must experience what you went through."

Jonny furrowed his brows. "I wouldn't wish that on you."

She took a step back and stared at the ground "When you started being me nice to me, I thought you were playing a game, trying to trick me again."

He pulled her back inside the blanket, siphoning her heat.

She hugged him, resting her cheek on his chest. "Part of me still thinks so."

"Life is nothing more than a game," Jonny replied through chattering teeth.

"I wanted to play your game, figure out what you were planning. When Nicholas attacked your son, I felt guilty, ashamed." She glanced up and saw the heavy red streaks in the whites of his eyes. He must have stayed awake all five days. Of course, he did. It's what he does, protects. Was he protecting himself or her? "Ralphie kept asking me what game you were playing."

"So, what game am I playing?"

Cheyenne shook her head. "I guessed a game of survival, but then Ralphie asked me whose survival."

He glanced down at her. "What was your answer?"

She shrugged her shoulders. "I don't know and Ralphie wouldn't tell me."

Jonny stepped away from her, taking the blanket. "If you only guessed it was a survival game, then maybe it's a trick question." He turned her around. "Close your eyes and tell me what you hear."

Cheyenne removed his hands. "I don't want to play."

He forced her to stay and he closed his eyes. "I can hear your breathing, the insects scurrying under the vegetation, the occasional popping coming from the dying campfire, the hawk in the sky, and the waterfall down below." He opened his eyes, glaring at her. "I can feel the morning sun against my back, the warmth of your skin on my palms, the cool air nipping at my body, the wool blanket scratching at my skin. I can feel your hair crawling across my hands."

"I don't know what you want," she said. She went to walk past him, but he held her firm.

Jonny took a deep breath. "I can smell the campfire smoke, the scent from your shampoo, your perfume, the Douglas Firs, the morning dew, the BO from my armpits, and even my breath." He brought his fingers to Cheyenne's nose, "I can smell my fish fingers. I can taste my morning breath and the remnants of old tuna fish sandwiches." He released her. "If you learn your surroundings, then you'll know when something's amiss." He walked away from her. "That's how I survived."

"Whose life is important to you?"

Jonny peered over his shoulder. "I'm an easy read; you figure it out." He faced forward, heading toward the campfire.

She rushed him, and he turned, pushing her to the ground.

"Whose survival is so important, huh?" She stood to her feet and pushed against his chest. "Who you trying to keep safe?"

He forced her wrist to her face. "You!" He threw her to the ground and stormed to the Chevelle.

Her? Why expend the effort on her? He had a son, a whole family to worry about. Why was he concerned about her?

"But if you don't value your life," he looked to the sky and threw up his hand, "then why the fuck should I?"

Jonny did care, though. He respected her sacrifices to protect those around her despite the extreme risks she represented. He related.

He jammed the key into the ignition and Dolores coughed and choked but turned over. He poured the last of their water over the smoldering woodpile and then, kicked dirt over the ashes. He grabbed the cooler and stuffed it in the back seat.

He plopped down in the driver's seat, slamming the door. He revved Dolores's engine, wringing the steering wheel. He took a deep breath and reached over, opening the passenger's door.

Cheyenne picked herself up off the grass. The dead woman by the clothesline was now joined by Hide, Seek, and the headless Ichabod; all of them pointed toward the house.

Cheyenne picked up the blanket and dusted it off. She clasped the top of the car door, taking one last look back. She was unsure if they wanted her to go inside the dilapidated house or somewhere behind it, but she had enough of Jonny's past.

2

Jonny babied Dolores through the potholed driveway and over the washboard roads. It took longer to reach the paved roads then it had to reach the land of the dead, but he needed time to cool his head. Since neither one was talking, he supposed she did, too.

He glanced at her. "Sorry if I hurt you, but you gotta stop attacking me."

She nodded once at him. He was blanketed in goosebumps so she turned the heater on and aimed the vents toward him. "When we met, I was covered in bruises."

"I remember." He glanced at her a few times but watched for wildlife on the road ahead. "Marked by the dead," he said.

"When I sleep next to you, the dead leave me alone and I sleep soundly."

Jonny propped his elbow on his door, resting his temple on his index finger. "When I sleep next to you, I don't have nightmares either."

"In my dreams, there is a little boy who never shows me how he died but always tells me to *find him*."

Jonny turned the heater up. "If you get too hot, let me know."

"The little boy," she said, "is Ralphie."

With the missing pieces found, things were beginning to look clearer to Jonny. He pulled over for gas. "The day you came to my shop, I saw Ralphie in my office. The night you hit your head, Jacob held your hand, and when I grabbed him." Jonny broke their conversation, telling the man at the pump to fill the car. He returned to their discussion, picking up where they left off. "Ralphie spoke to me."

The gas attendant handed back Jonny's card.

"What'd he say?" Cheyenne asked.

"*There you are.*" He opened his door. "Want anything from inside?"

"Sorry, Sir. No shoes, no shirt, no service," the gas attendant said.

Cheyenne held out her hand. "You want coffee?"

He handed her his card. "And a shirt if they have one, large."

3

Cheyenne pushed open the convenience store door and a cold rush of air washed across her face. She thought for sure the inside would be heated. She grabbed a hand basket and let it dangle from the bend of her elbow.

Inside the store, a giftshop capitalized on the tragic Tillamook Burn. One could buy ninety-year-old ashes for twenty bucks or an ashtray carved from burnt Douglas Fir trees. Postcards showcased the event as though it were art or a happy historical experience, none of which Cheyenne felt was in good taste.

Cheyenne didn't think she could ride home with Jonny reeking of fish breath and underarm. She stopped in the toiletry aisle and grabbed two toothbrushes, toothpaste, and deodorant. She ran her finger along the front of the shelf, searching for wet-naps but did not find any. She tossed a few bottles of hand sanitizer into the basket. She snapped her fingers; the wet-naps might be with the diapers.

Cheyenne felt something crawling within her hair. She threaded her fingers through it, making her way to the baby supplies. She tossed two packages of baby wipes into the basket; they would have to do. She felt a sharp prick on her scalp and reached for the back of her head, spinning around. No body there but her. She rubbed the back of her head and continued shopping.

She had the bare essentials but she still needed a shirt for Jonny and they could use coffee, breakfast, water, and maybe snacks. Afterall, the ride home was long.

The closer she got to the refrigerated drinks, the denser the atmosphere. She hadn't sensed Nicholas's presence since Ralphie sent those glowing eyes to aide Jonny. Was the air different because Nicholas was gone?

The glass doors to the refrigerated drinks were so frosted, she barely made out the blue waterdrop logo of the Smartwater. At first, she grabbed two but it was a long drive, so she grabbed two more.

She turned, allowing the door to close, and a reflection in the convex mirror caught her eye. Why was there a little boy in the aisle left unattended? What was the pouch he was playing with? She walked to the aisle in front of the refrigerated sodas. "Pardon me." She excused herself past a young man about to open the door to the sodas, and turned into the aisle.

It was empty.

She double checked the mirror, gone.

A glass marble bounced down the aisle and she chased it to the front of the row. As she bent down to catch it, another sharp tug stung her scalp. She grabbed the back of her head and looked behind her. No one there again, but the tile floor looked different. She had to squint to see them; small frosted footprints lead from the soda fridge to where she squatted.

"The heater's not working, Frank. My headlights are on high beams," stated the irritated clerk, as she rung up the young man with his sodas. "I know it's too warm to be cold."

Where was the boy? She searched around the store, in the mirror, and refrigerators. There was no one else but the three of them.

What in bloody hell was happening? She was awake; she was positive. She continued shopping, fidgeting with the marble: the weight, texture, temperature. She couldn't dream all of it, not in this kind of details.

She snagged a shirt from the gift shop. Was the boy trying to reach out to her? She grabbed random snacks, triple checking her memory's archives. She was certain she'd never seen him or his black velvet bag before. She retrieved two breakfast sandwiches from the convection warmer and then poured two cups of coffee.

"Damnit Frank, there's frost building on the windows. If it doesn't get fixed, I'm out."

A child's voice whispered behind Cheyenne. "I see you."

"Seek?" She spun on her heels and the lights went out.

4

Cheyenne exited with a bag on each arm and a coffee in either hand. She met Jonny's stare on the way to the Chevelle. He stepped out to help her.

"Everything alright? You look uneased."

"Yeah, the power went out is all. Why didn't you come in when the lights died?"

"I didn't smell anything. I figured you were okay. You are okay, aren't you?"

"Yes, here, take this." She handed him a coffee and one of the bags.

"What did you buy?"

She removed his card from her front pocket, giving it back to him. "Supplies, so you can take a PTA bath."

Jonny set the coffee on Dolores's hood and unfurled a large orange t-shirt with a bear silhouette outlined in pine trees above *Tillamook, Oregon* in forest green print.

"Hmm. Subtle."

"Shut it. What'd you expect from a convenience store in the woods. Besides, it was free."

"How'd you manage that?"

"The clerk was cold and Frank's a *corner-cuttin' asshole.*"

"Come again?"

"Just clean up and put it on."

They put their food and drinks in the car and walked around the side of the building to the bathrooms.

The smell in the women's bathroom 'bout knocked Cheyenne to her ass. She used the back of her hand to stop the smell of sewage from invading her olfactory. The humming of the fluorescent light created a dull ache behind her eyes and if she had been an epileptic, the flickering would have sent her into a seizing fit all over the filthy tile.

The rusty iron sink wasn't any better. A cockroach scurried amongst the leaves and dead mosquito hawks and disappeared down the drain. Cheyenne tried to turn the water on but couldn't turn the metal, star-shaped nob. She used both hands, struggling to open the valve, but it succumbed and thick, pudding like, muddy water oozed from the spicket. She turned it back off, reconsidering the idea of freshening up.

She hadn't noticed the spider-crack in the center of the mirror. She stared at the myriad tiny fragments, each showing their own tiny section of reversed reality. She narrowed her eyes, focusing on the section of mirror reflecting back the bathroom stall with the out of order sign. A pair of muddy bare feet stood behind the bathroom stall.

"Hello?" Her breath floated from her mouth. Her eyes locked on the ice crystals spreading outward on the mirror. The feet lifting upward behind the stall door drew her attention from the mirror.

She knocked on the stall. "Ma'am, are you okay?" She pushed open the door. A clogged toilet, overflowing with excrement, was the only occupant. Maybe the flickering lights created an illusion.

Cheyenne closed her eyes and held her temples. She didn't know if the annoying hum was getting to her, but an image of a tub full of water flashed in her mind's eye. The dull ache behind her eyes waxed into a throbbing rhythm, keeping time with the flickering lights. She opened her eyes and stepped to the next stall.

Sewage bubbled out of the toilet and used tampons decorated the stall walls. The throbbing behind her eyes pulsed and her vision tunneled. She felt nauseous, cold, and dizzy; she needed fresh air.

She turned around and found herself in a different bathroom. The sink was missing and the mirror lay shattered.

Mold grew in the grout and calking of the shower's tiles. Brown rings in the tub matched the stagnant water it contained. A single lit candle sat on the counter, projecting a flickering light show on the walls.

Cheyenne knew this nightmare too well. It was the first nightmare she had and it was the worse one of them all. How was it possible? She wasn't asleep, was she?

She needed out; she needed fresh air. The layout of the bathroom was a simplistic design and she didn't need a visual to remember where the exit lied. She strode through the imaginary wall, breaking the illusion of her nightmare. She jerked open the door and when the fresh air hit her, she upchucked.

Cheyenne wiped her mouth and peered back into the dim, flickering bathroom. Before the hissing door closed, Ichabod and the woman stood center; her fingers massaged two strands of auburn hair. Cheyenne grabbed the back of her head.

"Interesting," said the talking head. "If the Rosati brothers had succeeded in plucking more hair, we could have seen what she's scared of."

The woman turned to him. Her voice but a whisper, echoing off the walls. "Find the boy with the black bag."

5

Cheyenne propped herself trunk to trunk with Dolores and stared blankly at the open field littered with elk. She was so far lost in her thoughts; she didn't hear the rustling of the plastic toiletries bag Jonny tossed in the car nor the opening of the car door as he asked her if she was ready. It wasn't until he grabbed her arms and shook her a little, she blinked, bringing him into focus.

"You're pale. What's wrong?"

She looked into his green eyes. "The dead are stirring."

His eyes narrowed and his head titled. "What does that mean?"

"Before you took me to that place, the dead stayed in my dreams."

"Maybe you should sit down and breathe."

"I don't want to sit."

"Your face is drained of color. Do you feel like you're going to faint?"

Her head barely moved but she answered with a nod. "Everyone should stay away from me"

"I don't like the way you're talking."

"The dead are stirring; it's dangerous."

"Hey, I want you to look at me," Jonny said. "You're gonna stop talking like your about to off yourself. Remember, I'm going to help save you."

"Everyone tries to save me: you, my seanair, my best friend. Every time it's worse than before. My best friend ended up killing himself."

"I'm not a coward like your fri—"

Cheyenne pushed against Jonny's chest. "He wasn't a coward! He killed himself to spare me." She raised her hand, but Jonny grabbed her, pulling her into the comforting safety of his arms.

"Nicholas went after him," Jonny said.

She buried her face into his body and cried. "Death is all around me. It will come for you and your family."

"I'll kill you before I let that happen."

She looked up at him.

He stared down at her. “Not out of malice but because we’re friends.”

“Promise me. Promise, if Nicholas goes after Jacob or anyone else, you’ll end my life.”

He nodded.

“It’s not a promise unless you say it.”

“I promise,” he said. “But it won’t come to it. If you couldn’t be saved, then Angel wouldn’t be pushing so hard to save you.”

She took several deep breaths, calming herself. “Who is Angel?”

“He hasn’t said.” Jonny felt his answer was more truth than lie. “But he believes wholeheartedly you can be saved.”

Jonny cleaned her face with is thumb and it made him think of Jacob. “Let’s go. I’ve never been away from Jacob this long. I want to hold him.”

6

Jonny sat in the driver seat staring at a black velvet bag on the dash. It wasn’t there earlier when he tossed his toiletries into the car. When Cheyenne reached for it, he intercepted. He felt several smooth orbs and when he heard the *tinks* and grinding it made when he squeezed the bag, his eyes watered.

“Where did you get this?” he asked

“I don’t know, I didn’t buy it.”

“But you recognize it; I can see it in your eyes.”

“As do you,” she challenged.

His deal with Angel required him to open up about his past, but where did he start with this? Ralphie was painful enough.

“Jonny?”

“Before I was caged, I played chess to pass the time but I

didn't have a board."

"How'd you play if you didn't have a board?"

"Out of the earth. I used a stick to carve out the board in the dirt. I was still learning how to play so I also made the grid on the edges."

"Who'd you play?"

"My friend, Dr. Kirill. I couldn't keep going to the infirmary without causing suspicion so he used to slip his next move to some of the other kids after their checkups. When they brought my move back to him, he gave them a candy bar."

"What's the bag have to do with chess?"

"Fast forward some years and this little boy is brought to that hellhole. He didn't speak but if you touched him, he screamed bloody murder. Not one time did he ever cry."

"What was his name?"

"Finneas. Dr. Kirill diagnosed him with nonverbal autism."

Tears fell from Jonny's face.

"You don't have to talk about it," Cheyenne said.

"If I don't get it out now, I won't be able to revisit it again." He wiped his nose. "Finneas had an eidetic memory and he became the runner for our games. I grew close to him. When he died, I buried a bag of his favorite game piece with him."

"What was his favorite chess piece?"

"We used different kinds of marbles to represent the chess pieces. White cat's eyes for white pawns; black cat's eyes for black pawns; Ice Queen for white queen and the black queen was a Glitter bomb; and so on.

"Finneas loved the black night. I think he associated it with Batman because I use to read him the comics books. We used his favorite marble." Jonny pulled the drawstring and turned the pouch on its side, catching a palm-full of marbles. In each one, white, red, gold-yellow, and black swirled delicately through the clear, blue orbs. "Michelangelo."

Cheyenne pulled her marble from her front pocket. When I was in the store, I saw a boy in the security mirror holding the velvet bag. When I went to the aisle, he was gone but he left me this." She dropped the marble into Jonny's hand, restoring its rightful place with the others.

Twenty-Eight
Wreath of Flames

1

Breakfast in front of the grass field on the hood of the Chevelle proved more awkward than Cheyenne envisioned, even with the bright sun and blue sky. She only suggested eating before they left so they could clear their heads, but here she sat between a log cabin gas station full of ghosts and a melancholy Jonny full of skeletons. She was certain they were one in the same. One left a gift in the car for Pete's sake. She glanced sideways at him.

She was positive he hadn't told the whole Finneas story. She'd never seen him cry, not even when Nicholas attacked Jacob. She poked the last of her breakfast sandwich in her mouth.

Jonny gathered their garbage and tossed it without a word. He came back and opened her door. "C'mon, I'm ready to be home."

She grabbed their coffee from the hood and handed him his cup as she sat. She wasn't being honest with him either. He, inadvertently, hit the nail on the head when he accused her of hiding dark secrets. She knew, sooner or later, she would have to tell him the truth. Right now, wasn't the time. Really, when was it? Jonny had a temper and it scared her. Maybe she would hold off telling him the truth until it benefited her; when she needed him to keep his promise. Right now, he needed a friend to take his mind off Finneas.

She grabbed the velvet bag from the dash and hid it in the glove box. She took a drink of her coffee, catching his measuring gaze.

"Did Dr. Kirill teach you sign language?"

Jonny stared at her a moment longer and the cleaned his face. He answered but his voice crackled and faded at the end. "Yeah."

"I know sign language, too."

He cleared his throat and spoke softly. "Your uncle Rory?"

"Mm-hmm."

He wiped his nose and cleaned his fingers on his jeans. "I haven't signed since I escaped that place."

"I'm sure it wouldn't be hard to pick back up. If you ever wanted to, I wouldn't mind practicing with you."

He feigned a smile and stared ahead at the deep canyon of dense Douglas Firs. "Thank you."

She returned a closed lip smile knowing he wasn't thanking her for the offer but for the distraction. "You're welcome." She tapped her fingers on her coffee cup. "Is it okay to ask you a question about Dr. Kirill?"

He nodded his head. "Yeah."

"It's obvious to me, he cared for you. So, why didn't he grab you and run long before you escaped?"

He was silent for a long time and she didn't see his telltale signs of offering the truth.

"If you're not going to be forthright, then don't answer."

He stared at her, glancing at the road. "Do you have any

more questions?"

"Were you born there?"

"As far as I know."

"Did Dr. Kirill deliver you at birth?"

Jonny glanced at her and then propped his elbow on his door, resting his head on a closed fist.

"You don't know, do you?"

"No."

"Where is he now?"

"Next question."

"If you aren't going to answer my questions, then why allow me to ask them?"

"I said you could ask them, I never said I'd answer them."

She threw her hands in the air and let them fall to her lap. "More games. Surprise, surprise."

Jonny drank the last of his coffee and placed the cup between his legs. "I never met Dr. Kirill before he saved me from my OD. I don't know why he took a liking to me but, I wasn't the only one he took under his wing. I was the only one he educated, though. At first, he wasn't always around. I think I was seven when Dr. Kirill started becoming more of a permanent fixture. Now, you know all about him."

What he wanted her to know, she thought. "Why did he save only you?"

Jonny locked eyes with her. "We saved as many kids as we could."

So, that's why Dr. Kirill waited so long. She lowered her eyes and then turned, looking out her window. She brought her fingernail to her mouth and Jonny pushed it away.

"You lied to me."

He furrowed his brows. "About?"

"You said you survived by learning your surroundings." She

faced him; he had a bewildered look. "Dr. Kirill helped you survive."

Jonny merged onto the I-5 South. "Expand."

She looked out her window. "I don't think I need to."

Jonny stared at her with squinted eyes, bobbing his head.

They were silent for a while but Cheyenne had many questions. She cycled through them picking a few she thought he might actually answer, and out of those few, asking the one she was most curious about.

"Whatever happened to Mickey and Lee?"

"I took care of them," he answered. He took a drink of water struggling to put the cap back on.

She took it from him. "Did they suffer?"

He replied with a single nod.

She stared blankly out her window. "Good."

He glanced at her. "You get a glimpse into my past and that's enough to sway your opinion of me?"

"Anyone would have killed those sick, twisted bastards." She looked at him. "I think I'm beginning to understand why you're such an asshole."

He chuckled. "I'll take it as a compliment." His smiled faded. "I'm no saint."

"No one is," she said. "I'm sure you did horrible things, but who hasn't?"

Jonny shook his head. "Do not pretend to understand what you have no knowledge of."

She heard it in his voice; she struck a nerve. She had more questions and needed to tread lightly.

"Ralphie said Mickey killed you, how?"

"Figuratively not literally."

The irritation was still present in his tone. She overstepped her boundaries and whatever information she thought she could get from her line of questioning was now gone.

She reached for his hand resting on the horseshoe shifter, "Hey, I'm—"

Jonny tossed her hand off. "Don't do that."

"—I'm sorry if I offended you.

2

Dolores pulled into the driveway and Adélaïde was the first out the door. Everyone encircled Jonny, inundating him with questions. He pushed them aside and bent down, picking up Jacob. He held him tight, kissing him.

Jacob wrapped his arms around his father's neck. "Did you learn a lot?"

"I sure did." He carried Jacob up the first step and turned around.

Cheyenne walked down the drive in the opposite direction.

"You comin' in?" he asked.

Cheyenne turned. "I think I'll head home."

Jacob wiggled free of his father and ran to Cheyenne, grabbing her hand. "You're a part of our family now!"

"I wish that were true, sweetheart, but it's not. Besides, it's not safe to be around me."

"Angel says if you don't allow daddy to save you than your friend's death was in vain."

She looked to the porch. Everyone waited for her except Adélaïde, who walked back inside.

"Auntie Sandra and me made homemade stuffed manicotti and we used the marinara you and daddy made."

She kneeled, grabbing ahold of Jacob's shoulders. "Sweetheart, how do I speak to Angel?"

Jacob's eyes faded white. "You need to trust the boy's father."

The suddenness of the change unnerved her a bit. How quickly Jacob was gone, replaced by this . . . being, who refers to himself as a literal servant of God.

"Who are you?"

"A messenger. You want to be free of Nicholas, to live a real life, then you need to work with Jonny, not against him."

She shook her head. "None of them understand, nor you. I'm protecting them."

"It's you who doesn't understand. I protect them as I do this boy. If you truly want to end Nicholas and live the life you were robbed of, you'll go inside and join them."

3

After dinner, Jonny took a real shower. He walked into the living room, drying his hair. "There's plenty of hot water if you wanted to shower," he told Cheyenne. He carefully snatched the puppy from Jacob's sleeping body.

"I'll put him to bed," Sandra said.

"No, I'll do it when I come back in." He pointed outside. "Steven, wanna have a drink with me?"

"Sure."

Steven kissed Sandra's forehead and headed for the outside fridge, while Jonny set Phoenix down in the grass to play and potty. They met at the pergola where Jonny lit the gas firepit and Steven handed him a beer.

"Why'd you guys tape Phoenix's knees like that?"

"Sandra and I took her to the vet. I forget what condition they said it was but it's curable. Just gotta wrap tape around the knee, pulling the foot around. Then you sorta make a figure eight and grab the other knee, rotating the other foot forward."

"But only one foot is backwards."

"Yeah, the vet said it was odd. Usually both feet are turned backwards. So, the vet had to modify the wrapping technique to not affect the other leg. The vet guessed Phoenix's age to be around four to five weeks. She said since the bones and ligaments hadn't fused yet it should take a few weeks to correct itself."

"That's good to hear."

Steven took a drink and leaned back in his chair. "When you told us, you'd be back for dinner, I thought you meant that day."

"Unpredictable events occurred." He slouched, staring into the yellow-orange glow.

"You look like you went through hell. What happened?"

"I haven't slept in five days." He thought about it and really it was six, the day they left plus the five Cheyenne was absent. "I don't know what happened, but she became comatose." He took a swig. "She can see Ralphie."

"Well, that's something. Did she relay any messages from him?"

"No. She hasn't told me everything yet." He took a glug of his drink. "It's all twisting together: her, Ralphie, Nicholas. There's more to her than we'd thought." He raised an eyebrow. "Layers."

Steven placed his drink between his legs. "Have you asked her about any of it?"

He closed his eyes and shook his head. "I'll wait until she opens up to me."

"What makes you think she'll open up freely?"

Jonny opened one eye and glanced at Steven. "Have I ever opened up when forced?" He took another drink. "Some things take time."

"Where'd you take her?"

"Doesn't matter."

"It might," Steven said.

"The first night we were gone, Nicholas paid a visit. Something protected us." He narrowed his eyes, shaking his head. "I tried to start a fire, but the wood was too wet. When Nicholas attacked, the fire erupted."

"You took her camping?"

"Where I took her is beside the point. I'm telling you I couldn't get the fire to stay lit because everything was too wet. Then out of nowhere, fire erupted."

"Maybe it finally caught."

Jonny took a drink, shaking his head. "The fire burned blue. I never added kindling or wood, yet it kept burning until she woke. The interesting thing, the blue flames not only kept Nicholas at bay, they injured him." He locked eyes with Steven. "I heard whispers coming from the flames, telling me to teach her to survive."

"What do you think it means?"

Jonny shrugged and propped his elbow on the arm of his chair. He rubbed the stubble on his chin, zoning into the burning fire.

"Something else on your mind?" Steven asked.

A lot of things were on his mind but, the marbles and Cheyenne's ominous 'the dead are stirring' statement took the forefront.

Steven twirled his index finger. "I can see the wheels turning, Jon."

Jonny rested his temple on his index finger and his thumb under his chin. He stared at the fire and bobbed his head. "Obviously, I, nor anyone else, can see what Cheyenne sees." He broke his gaze from the fire and looked to Steven "I need you to help me keep an eye on her."

"What am I looking for?"

Jonny shrugged. “On the way home, something scared her. I’m talking full on color drain, tears-running-down-her-face, scared.”

“And you didn’t ask her what was wrong?”

Jonny frowned. “Course I did, I’m not heartless.” He took a drink. “She said the dead were stirring and that she’s ‘surrounded by death’.”

“Where did you guys go?’ Steven asked. “Something about the place caused a chain reaction.”

Jonny drank the last of his beer. “Stays between us?”

“You know it will.”

“If I tell you, you can’t ask me any follow up questions.”

“Jesus! You took her *there*?”

Jonny bobbed his head. “My deal with Angel requires me to tell Cheyenne about my past. I figured it might be easier if I took her there and told her. Less likely for anyone to eavesdrop on our conversation.”

“You didn’t tell her anything, did you?”

“I told her some. I even told her some things on the drive there. That prompted her to open up to me, which is what Angel said would happen.”

“What did she tell you?”

Jonny stood reaching for Steven’s empty bottle. “We can talk more tomorrow. I’m going to bed; I’m tired.” He reached for the gas nob.

“I’ll turn off,” Steven said. “I’m going to stay out here a little longer.”

4

Steven pulled out his cellphone and searched for Kowanta’s number. The phone rang and eventually went to voicemail.

"Hey Kowanta, I know it's late but I need your expertise. You majored in world religion, right? I'm not a religious man but, I've seen some things and heard some things I don't fully understand. Wanted to know if we could get together and talk. Call me when you can."

5

Cheyenne darted into Jonny's room wrapped in a towel. She didn't have any clothes of her own there and *if* she was going to stay, she would have to remedy the issue. Right now, the thought of reusing her undergarments disgusted her. She had no more of the clothes Sandra bought and there was no way she would fit any of Sandra's clothes; Sandra was a beanpole. Jonny, at one time, offered sweatpants and she hoped she could fit those.

She pulled a pair of gray sweatpants from the bureau. Apparently, Jonny liked his sweatpants baggy like his shirts. She couldn't imagine him wearing sweatpants, not when he's always warm. She put one leg at a time in and pulled them up under the towel. She dug back in pulling out a white undershirt. She couldn't help but smile at the irony.

Her eyes shifted to the rosary wrapped around the prayer hands. She flipped it over, running her thumb over the D-E-D.

"Those are my brother's initials," Jonny said.

"What was his middle name?"

"Ethan." He pointed at the undershirt. "I can get you a different one."

"It's okay. I find it almost comical now."

"Let me grab a pillow and the room's yours."

"You're not going to sleep next to me?"

Jonny pointed toward the living room. "I was going to—"

"Please? I don't want to see the dead."

He paused and then sighed through his nose, turning off the light. He cracked the door and pulled back the blankets, crawling into bed.

Cheyenne put the shirt on, sliding the towel out from under it. She crawled into bed and instinctively lowered her head toward his chest but stopped herself. "Is it okay to lay on you?"

He raised up his arm and laid it across her back when she hugged against his body.

She outlined one of his scars basking in his Old Spice fragrance; she missed it.

He grabbed her hand. "Why do you always do that?"

"I guess it helps me think." She propped herself up on her elbow, watching him try to sleep. "I know you said Lee pierced your body with hooks and suspended you in the air, but your scars have different sizes, different shapes. It makes me wonder what caused them and why you won't tell me."

He tapped her back, looking at her with a smile. "Tit-for-tat."

Cheyenne didn't know if it was the way he looked at her or his scent or his touch, but her face flushed. She ran her finger over his stubbled jaw feeling the whiskers prick her fingertips. She leaned inward to kiss him.

Jonny pushed her back and stood to his feet. "You and I will never be that." He snatched his pillow. "I apologize if I led you to think otherwise."

"Jonny, I—"

He halted in the doorway. "I don't have romantic feelings for you. You're a friend, nothing more."

6

A youthful Jonny slowly and painfully limped into the kitchen, bracing his bare purple and black ribs on the right side. The bones of his right hand still protruded from the first three broken, twisted, useless fingers. Both eyes were blackened, but his right completely swelled shut. Lava flows of blood cracked through the obsidian scabs encrusting his lips and broken nose. He retrieved a box of matches from the drawer by the stove and hobbled out the kitchen.

The house was trashed and mostly empty. Spray paint decorated the walls in satanic symbols depicting the loa Papa Legba and Baphomet. Paraphernalia lay scattered on the small table in the living room.

He picked up the bottle of lighter fluid as he passed the small, round coffee table and continued his slow, steady march down the hall over the creaking wooden floor. He looked in the open door on the left as he walked past.

Blood and brain matter spattered the blue walls and ceiling, speckling red the drawing of space-rockets hanging on the walls. Lee lay face down with his pants undone, in a pool of his blood, next to the bed, accompanied by a metal bat.

Jonny arrived at his destination and shouldered open the door on the right. The room was mostly empty except for a twin-sized mattress flipped on its side and leaned against the wall and, in the center of the room, Mickey.

Mickey was nude and tied to a chair. Drawn around the chair in cornmeal, was the symbol for Baron Samedi. On the wall behind the chair, painted in blood, was the sign for Damballa. Mickey fought against his restraints, jerking his head from side to side and up and down; his black hair danced in the air. His blue eyes wild and his lips curled as he screamed profanities.

"You can't kill me, you little shit. I'll come back for you and those bastards," he spat.

Jonny dropped the box of matches to the floor. He placed the bottle of lighter fluid between his knees and opened it with his functional hand. The hunching was nearly unbearable; the morphine was already waning. He drew in a breath, wheezing and gurgling, and limped toward the chair.

Mickey cursed in creole, flinging saliva.

Jonny could give a damn. He jutted the canister forward, and a stream of kerosene spattered Mickey's face. He paced in a small radius around the chair, dosing Mickey in repeated swiping motion. Jonny found amusement in the irony of the situation; all that was needed was to change the kerosene to holy water and to dress himself in an alb.

"I'm coming for you," Mickey taunted. "This isn't the end of me."

Jonny bent down for the matches, flinching and grimacing. He held the box between his knees and struck one, watching the flame flicker and dance. *We're finally safe.* He closed his eye and tossed the match.

Flames spilled onto the floor, swept up the chair, and engulfed its captive.

Mickey laughed. "I'm not done with you! I'm coming for you!"

Jonny opened his eye and turned, slowly walking out of the room.

As Jonny neared the front door, Mickey stopped laughing and started screaming obscenities. "JONNY! I'LL FUCKING FIND YOU!"

"JONNY!"

He stopped shy of the front door. The second voice was different. It was desperate, familiar . . . female.

Twenty-Nine

An Angel's Face

1

"All of your peaches, belong to me. I'll always find you; you'll never be free."

Sandra rolled over swatting the over-sized snooze button on the alarm clock. "Shut up," she murmured.

Steven spooned her, throwing his heavy arm over her body. "What's the matter, babe?" he asked still half asleep.

"The damn song's playin'." She sat up, yawning, to get a better look at the clock but the red LED display was blank.

"All of your peaches, belong to me. I'll always find you; you'll never be free."

Her ears rang and her breathing quickened. There was only one person who sang that rendition of "Peaches".

The last time she heard it, she was lying on top of Dominick hiding under a bed with her hand over his mouth. They tracked the heavy clops of boots synchronized to the creaks of dry-rotten wood rubbing against rusty nails. A metallic scrape against the walls, followed him as he sang: "Her peach is mine, just wait and see. Try as you might, can't save her from me."

The boots turned into the room and stopped at the bed.

Sandra snapped herself out of memories passed. It couldn't be him, Jonny said they were safe and he didn't lie. "Where's it coming from?"

"What?" Steven mumbled.

She shook him hard. "Where's the song coming from?"

Steven jerked up his head. He reached for their phones, but they were powered off. He crawled out of bed and flicked the light switch up and down a few times; nothing.

"Her peach is mine, just wait and see. Try as you might, can't save her from me."

Sandra curled up, sitting against the head of the bed and pressed her palms tightly over her ears. "Make it stop!"

Steven looked at the closet and crept forward, raising back his fist.

"All of their peaches, mine they will be. Open the door, and I'll make you see."

"Steven, don't open it!"

He stopped a little more than an arm's length from the closet door, staring at it.

"Babe, please don't!"

Steven shot his hand out and jerked back the closet door. Silhouettes of outfits hung quietly from the clothes rod.

Sandra caught a glint toward the bottom of the closet opening; inside the closet, the amber specs hovered near the ground.

"LOOK OUT!"

Faint amber dots flashed forward between Steven's feet, plowing his legs out from under him. Nicholas slammed Steven into the upper wall with his lizard like tail.

Sandra breathed as deeply as she ever had, "JONNY!"

2

A shrill cry startled Cheyenne out of bed. The same wail of small children screaming for their mommies and daddies when they skinned their knees. She stared at the open bedroom door. "Nicholas."

Her eyes searched the nightstand next to the bed. She needed something, anything to inflict pain. She snatched the lighter and flicked its flint, placing her hand above the flame. The heat intensified under her palm. She felt the blisters forming and smelled her flesh burning. She fought against her body's will to pull her hand away. Her face grimaced and tears fell from her eyes as she heard Nicholas yowl in pain.

Jacob charged into the room and pulled down the hand holding the lighter. "Stop hurting yourself!"

"It's the only way I know to stop him."

Jacob grabbed a candle from the nightstand. "Here, light this. Angel says to aim it at Nicholas and spray aerosol." Aerosol came out air-soul.

Cheyenne clutched her injured hand against her chest. "Where is Angel? Why isn't he protecting them?"

"Because I want to help keep them safe, like daddy."

"Sweetheart, this isn't a game, it's dangerous."

"But I want to help!"

A loud thud followed by Steven's grunt emanated from Sandra's room.

Cheyenne shifted her eyes toward the bedroom door, and saw Adélaïde run down the hall and then double back to Jonny's room.

"This is your fault." She grabbed Jacob and held him against her body. "How do I stop that monster, that demon?"

Cheyenne dropped the candle to the bed and flicked the lighter.

"No!" Jacob fought against Adélaïde's restraints. "GG, you're undoing everything."

Cheyenne placed her trembling hand back over the flame.

"What are you doing?" Adélaïde asked.

Cheyenne sucked her molars and grunted for the few moments she could withstand. Her cry was all but lost in the wall-rumbling roar from Sandra's room.

"You and that . . . thing are connected? I don't care what they say, I want you out of this house. Now, tell me how to destroy it."

Jacob broke free and tackled Cheyenne's hand. "Stop it!" He wrapped his arms around her giving Cheyenne a big hardy hug. "Please stop hurting yourself."

She hugged him back. "You want to help keep everyone safe?"

Jacob stared up at her. "Uh-huh."

"Then go to your room and wait for GG to come get you."

He pushed away from her. "No, you'll keep hurting yourself."

"I promise I won't, but the safest thing for everyone is for me to leave."

"You're wrong! GG's wrong!"

Another loud thud followed by glass shattering and a scream from Sandra.

Cheyenne caressed the tears away from his face. "Thank you for being so sweet to me. Now, go to your room and wait for GG."

He pushed her away. "No! Angel says—"

Cheyenne ripped Jonny's pocket knife from the nightstand and pressed the blade to her throat. Tears cascaded down her face. "Jacob! Go to your room or I'll end it right here!"

"Are you mad? You'll traumatize him!" Adélaïde chastised as she shielded his eyes.

Cheyenne flinched with each of Steven's grunts as he bounced off of walls and furniture across the hall.

Jacob's chin quivered as he pleaded, "Please, Cheyenne. Daddy can save you!"

"Go to your room!" Adélaïde commanded.

He spun, shoving Adélaïde. "It's all your fault! I hate you!" He plunged out the room, disappearing in the hall.

"Okay, he's gone. How do we kill it?" Adélaïde asked.

"You can't." Cheyenne answered as she leaped from the bed. "Angel might have stopped him, but it looks like he can't unless Jacob lets him." She unloaded the lighter and candle to Adélaïde. "Hold him at bay until I can leave."

Another crash and Steven's yowl swept through the house.

"Get hairspray and spray it through the flame." Cheyenne directed, as she swiped the Jeep keys and the bag of marbles from the bureau.

"You're stealing his car?"

"You want us both gone, don't you? I need to be far away to make him disappear." Cheyenne pointed to Sandra's room. "Go save your family and I'll do the same."

Adélaïde huffed. "Fine! Don't ever come back."

Cheyenne hurried down the hall to the living room past Sandra's door. She caught a glimpse of Steven crawling across the floor, grimacing and gasping, and Sandra rocking on the bed, huddled to the wall screaming for Jonny. Adélaïde wouldn't be fast enough. If Cheyenne didn't act now, Steven would haunt her for the rest of her days.

Jonny thrashed on the living room floor as Cheyenne emerged from the hall.

He might be the answer afterall. If she could wake him brusquely enough, maybe, just maybe.

She straddled Jonny, slapping his face viciously enough to hurt her good hand. "WAKE THE FUCK UP!"

Jonny continued to thrash beneath her, and another terrified screech stung Cheyenne's ears from the hall: "JONNY!"

3

Jonny stood broken and bruised watching the inferno lap hungrily at the doorjamb from where he sacrificed Mickey. The scream calling his name . . . it couldn't be Sandra, she should be safe at home, not in this hell, not after all he'd done to protect his siblings.

"JONNY!"

It was her. No mistake. It echoed so loud he could not pinpoint the source. That bastard lied! No, he knew she was safe, the phone call, he heard the call. His brother was there, too.

"JONNY!"

No. Dominick was dead, but not here. Jonny looked down at the photo of his dead brother. He didn't know how it got in his hand, but he looked at it anyways. This was some time ago, this house, the fire inching down the hallway; a nightmare.

The ache throughout his body vanished, taking with it the loud wheeze and broken bones, replaced instead by awareness of the weight on his chest and the sting in his cheek. He should be in his house; everyone should be safe at home. GG, Sandra, Steven . . . Jacob. Where was Jacob?

"JONNY!"

He turned and sprung for the front door. Fighting the weight on his chest felt like trying to run through deep water. The front door creaked open, unveiling a silhouette. "Mickey!" He charged headlong through the doorway at the ghastly figure blocking his escape.

4

Jonny held the blurry, wriggling figure down by the throat with one hand under his full weight. His other hand already cocked back, he prepared to drive his fist down for all he was worth.

The figure grabbed a handful of Jonny's dangling hair and pulled his head forward.

Jonny's fist swung for the blow when his sight focused in on his target. *Cheyenne.* He pulled the punch and nearly collapsed to the floor. Everything was still spinning and fading in and out, he could not get his bearings.

"Jonny!"

Sandra! She was screaming for him. Nicholas; Jonny needed to stop him, needed to save her.

He staggered down the hall, clutching his throbbing head. He entered her room and fell to his knees. His vision was a haze of the past and present. The Voodoo and demonic symbols of his childhood now tainted the walls of Sandra's room.

Adélaïde aimed the hairspray toward the ceiling through the teardrop flame of the raised candle. Her flamethrower sent a stream of indigo-fringed fire hurling into the upper corner where Nicholas hunkered.

Jonny could not unweave the overlapping imagery of the flames Adélaïde wielded from the ring of fire which cleansed the world of Mickey. Sandra no longer looked like the beautiful woman she grew up to be but the scared little girl who had just been raped.

Jonny's head hurt so bad he strained to lift his body from

the floor. He needed to stop Nicholas, needed to save them.

The glimmer in Nicholas's angry eye sockets dimmed. He looked around the room, searching; for what, Jonny was unsure.

Nicholas erupted in a frustrated caterwaul and dove headlong through the bedroom window and, literally, disappeared into the night.

Jacob entered the room and placed his hand on his father's shoulder. "Calm yourselves, he's gone."

Jonny met the white irises looking down at him.

"I'm here now, Jonathan. Close your eyes and go to your safe place."

Jonny's head plummeted onto the carpet as the world faded black.

5

Jonny blinked open his eyes. He lay in a vast wheatfield, listening to a child's laughter. He rose to his feet and looked over the hillside. Down below, Jacob played by a tire swing, hanging from the old oak tree, with Phoenix at his heels. A woman sat on a picnic blanket. Her back toward Jonny, she watched Jacob play.

The rustle of fabric against the wheat directly behind signaled Jonny. He tilted his head and threw an ear toward the source. He smiled and went back to watching his son. "It's about time you showed yourself."

"It's impressive, and unnerving, how you can hear so well."

"Coming from the man who turns my son's eyes ghost-white." His smile faded. "At one time, I had to depend on my hearing. Survival instincts don't disappear."

Jonny turned around and stared at Dominick's vibrant blue eyes which contrasted against his dark complexion. "I miss you."

They embraced each other tight.

"Quite the dream, Jonathan. Is this why you painted a mural of Van Gogh's *Wheatfield with Crows* on my fireplace?"

He shrugged. "Maybe, but I vaguely remember playing in a wheatfield when I was small. Maybe I never did, but as long as I can remember, I've dreamed of this place."

Dominick pointed. "Who is she?"

"Everyone has Hallmark dream. Mine is for Jacob to be happy, worry-free."

"The woman?" Dominick asked.

"I don't know. I suppose it's the woman I'll finally settle down with, the one Jacob will call mommy."

They walked down the hill toward the woman in the sunflower dress; her chestnut hair undulated in the breeze.

"I used to think it was Haven," Jonny stood in front of the her, "but she has no face."

Dominick stood beside him staring at the faceless image. "Perhaps she's doesn't have a face because you have not yet found the woman you seek." He snapped his fingers and the woman, the boy, and the puppy wisped away. He sat down patting the picnic blanket. "Jonathan, we have much to discuss."

"Is our sister safe?" Jonny asked.

Dominick opened the picnic basket and pulled out a bottle of red wine. "I promise she's safe." He filled their glasses. "It was a concerted effort, but everyone's safe for the time being."

Jonny sipped his wine. He had so many questions but he knew his dream was temporary; it was time to discuss business. "How do I kill Nicholas?"

"You can't, not by yourself. You need her help just as she needs yours."

"Is it because Nicholas is really Mickey?"

"I knew you would put two-and-two together. And to answer your question, yes; you're the only one alive who knows how he thinks."

"Why does Cheyenne call him Nicholas?"

"Because that's his name." Dominick swirled his wine, sniffing the glass. "When our mother disappeared, you were two years old. Every day, you'd scream and cry for her, for hours. Nicholas came into our room with his pointer fingers on the sides of his head, chanting his bastardization of voodoo and satanic prayers." Dominick brought his glass to his lips and held it there. "You laughed, calling him Mickey Mouse." He sipped his wine. "We were all little. Sandra was six, almost seven, and I was five. The nickname stuck."

"How is he connected to her in the first place?"

"Like you told Steven, she has layers of untold stories."

"Like the one where she can see the dead? Why can't I see them?"

"Only those who have died can communicate with the dead."

Jonny flung the wine from his glass. "She died?"

"Briefly, yes."

"Suicide?"

"Surprisingly, no."

"But if she's died, then why can I see Mick—I mean Nicholas?"

"Everyone, even nonbelievers, can sense and see evil. It's not that different from sensing danger."

Jonny shook his head. "I'm confused. If only those who have died can see the dead, then how come I was able to see Ralphie at the shop?"

Dominick raised an eyebrow. "You sure it was Ralphie?"

"I see, so it was Nicholas who attacked her in Idiotville?"

"No, it really was Ralphie, but he wasn't attacking her."

Dominick took a drink. “By the way, why’d you tell Cheyenne it was her life you’re trying to save? We both know that’s not completely accurate.”

“Is it not?”

“You can’t hide your thoughts from me, Jonathan. Everyone’s survival is important to you. Why toy with her?”

“Survival is like a game of chess. Success depends upon knowing the fate of every piece.” Jonny walked to the tire swing. “Cheyenne claimed she could read me. I needed to figure out how true her statement was.”

“What’s your conclusion?”

“She can only read my visual cues. It’s an advantage I can exploit.”

Dominick left his drink and stood beside Jonny. He interlocked his fingers and rested his hands in front of is navel. “Advantage how?”

Jonny leaned against the tree and sifted through his thoughts. “If I move my pieces right, I can chisel the mortar away from the bricks holding up her wall.”

“It’s a big wall, Jonathan, maybe bigger than yours. One wrong brick could bring it down and bury any hope of success.”

“I don’t have a choice with Mick—Nicholas always so close; I have to be subtle.” He exhausted all the tactical questions he could think of. The ones he had left were the ones pulling on his heartstrings. “How come I can’t see you in the real world?”

“Only the eyes of the innocents can see God’s messengers.”

“Children?”

“Yes.”

“Why does Jacob think you’re an angel? Why haven’t you told him who you are?”

“If you want him to know who I am, then it’s your responsibility to tell him. Until then, I’ll continue to withhold my identity and Jacob will continue to see me as he imagines."

Jonny bobbed his head. He knew exactly how he wanted to disclose Dominick's identity. For the time being, he had a few more questions to ask.

"When I grabbed Jacob, I saw the dead children who plague Cheyenne. How's that possible?"

"Because Haven was dying when she was pregnant with Jacob, he's unique. He's like a conduit."

"So, when I touched Cheyenne, Jacob was able to transfer her nightmare to me?"

"Basically."

"If children are the only ones able to see messengers, then how come I can see you now?"

"Am I really here, or am I an illusion of your dream?"

Jonny lowered his head. Those were questions he needed answers for but the real question he wanted to ask, made his heart accelerate. He wasn't afraid of the answer. He was afraid Dominick would end the dream without providing an answer. "How'd you die?"

"I wondered when you'd ask. You should return to church; they had nothing to do with my death."

"How'd you die?"

Dominick raised Jonny's chin. "Trying to save a life. Save Cheyenne, and I'll tell you everything."

The wind blew some wheat onto Dominick's cassock and Jonny brushed it away.

Dominick gently grabbed Jonny's face and kissed him on the forehead. He hugged him again, whispering into Jonny's ear. "I love you, baby brother." He held him tight and snapped his fingers.

6

Jonny flung the blanket aside and ran for Sandra's room. Dominick said she was unharmed but Jonny needed to see for himself.

Her room, a ruin of drywall and splintered wood, lay uninhabited. The support beams peeked out through the holes in the walls and ceiling. The closet door was crushed and imploded into the closet. The vanity mirror lay shattered facedown under the foot of the mattress, which hung half off the box springs.

He dashed to Jacob's room and it, too, was empty but untouched. Where was his family? He forged ahead through the living room.

"Daddy!"

Everyone sat gathered around the dining room table eating lunch.

Sandra stood; her eyes welled and her chin wrinkled.

He embraced her.

She cried into his shoulder. "You promised you'd always be there." She pushed off him and he reeled her back, holding her tighter. "You promised to always keep me safe."

"I tried, but I couldn't even stand. My vision wasn't right and my head throbbed."

Jacob lowered his head. "Daddy, it's my fault Uncle Steven got hurt."

Jonny shifted his gaze to Steven. He bore a cut under his eye, his nose broken, and his bottom lip split. If Jonny ever held doubts about Steven's devotion they were scoured from his thoughts.

"Thank you, Steven."

"Of course, they're my family, too."

"I'm sorry," Jacob said. "I just wanted to help save

everyone."

Jonny kneeled beside Jacob. "You know, you have a super power none of us possess. Your ability to communicate with Angel and to allow him to take control is helping to save everyone. Promise me, next time Nicholas attacks, you'll let Angel take over."

"I don't think there will be a next time," Jacob replied.

"What do you mean?"

Jacob looked to Adélaïde then to his plate of food.

Steven limped to the breakfast bar counter and retrieved an envelope. He handed it Jonny and sat back down. "Ryder stopped by this morning. Said Cheyenne asked him to deliver it to you."

Jonny stared at the letter. How could he forget? He nearly killed her and not once did he think to check on her. Maybe he really didn't care about her. Maybe it was all a façade. A pleasant lie he told himself, pretending there was a shred of decency remaining inside. "Where is she?"

"She took your car and left," Sandra answered.

Jonny gasped with wide eyes and a gaping mouth.

"Not Dolores," she corrected. "We don't know when she left or if she's coming back."

"What does the letter say, Daddy?"

Jonny removed a piece of paper from the envelope and unfolded it, reading silently.

> *I don't know where I'm going but when I decide, I'll leave your Jeep in a random Walmart parking lot and mail you the keys with the location.*
>
> *On our little adventure, I learned how hellbent you are to keep others safe. Even willing to sacrifice yourself. I don't know how that's any different from me taking my*

own life. What I know is, you'll stretch yourself thin trying to keep everyone alive. In the end, Nicholas will have everyone in a room asking which one dies. How will you choose between Jacob and Sandra's unborn child?

Don't beat yourself up over choking me. I only know one way to stop Nicholas, and that's to hurt myself. Jacob wouldn't let me, though. So, I tried to wake you hoping your violent response would be enough.

P.S. I'm sorry I crossed the line last night; I didn't mean to offend you. I don't know why I tried to kiss you, maybe hormones (who knows). Either way, it's my mistake and at least I know where we stand. Anyhow, I am glad we can at least call ourselves friends instead of foes.

There was a knock on the front door and Steven stood, wincing. "I'll get it."

"You, okay?" Jonny asked.

"Yeah, I'll be fine. Nicholas and I—"

The second knock was louder.

"We'll catch up later," Steven said limping past him. He stopped and took a step back, whispering in Jonny's ear. "About those blue flames."

"Later, we'll catch up, remember."

Steven gave him the single nod and headed for the front door.

"What does she say?" Adélaïde asked.

Jonny folded the letter and tucked it into his back pocket. He glanced at Adélaïde noting the feigned interest in the letters content. What the hell did GG do?

"Cheyenne says she's glad we can call ourselves friends now, but she won't be returning."

Jonny caught the faintest smirk cracking Adélaïde's otherwise emotionless face. He would have to put her in her place before he brought back Cheyenne.

"Did she at least explain why she stole your Jeep?" Sandra asked.

He placed his hand on her belly.

7

Steven peered out the sidelight. He surveyed the parking lot and spotted a Harley Davidson posed next to his Challenger.

Another heavy blow resonated from the front door.

Steven stepped back and swung it open.

An older gentleman dressed in black stood on the front porch. He chewed on the end of an unlit cigar, wearing a beret and round sunglasses which obstructed his eyes. His shoulder-length hair matched the whiskers concealing his face.

The man removed his leather, bike gloves, and tucked them in the pocket of his trench coat. He removed the cigar from his mouth asking, "Is Cheyenne here, Lad?"

Turn the page

For a sneak peek at

ARNDAS MARIE'S

Novel

Disturbance In The Darkness: Whispers Of The Dead

One

Faceless Danger

1

Cheyenne traversed the country backroads in the dense vines of fog blowing in from the nearby river. The headlamps were worse than useless in each bank, but required for the brief clear patches between. The sky glowed a soft blue-gray but it would be a while before the sun crested the horizon, especially in these steep ravines.

She actively scanned the ditches and tree line for movement and the fog bank for the telltale floating eyes; deer liked to surprise motorist along this stretch of road, according to her best friend.

Her original plan was to drive to Idiotville and find Ralphie, and perhaps Finneas, but she could not remember how to get there. Even if she remembered, she left her wallet on Jonny's bureau leaving her destitute.

She drove into another patch of thick fog and downshifted. She winced, glancing at her wounded hand. She needed to wash the bandage soon, the sebaceous fluid from the burn seeped through the cloth. The Tylenol she took was waning and she didn't have any more. She would have to pull up her big-girl panties and suck it up.

She emerged from the fog and ahead, a fir tree lay across the road butted against the trunk of another tree. She stopped and stepped out of the Jeep. She gave the tree a solid shove; it barely moved. She had hoped it was dry, but its sheer weight suggested a fresh fall; the wood would be too supple. Pushing through with the Jeep would only enfold it in a tangle of wet branches.

Cheyenne weighed her options. She was exhausted, driving all night searching for refuge. She was penniless, so a hotel was out of the question, and she could not return home because the DeLuca family would look for her there. She must continue forward.

She looked back at the Jeep's winch on the utility bumper. Nothing was preventing the tree from moving toward her and she didn't need to move the whole tree, only the skinny end.

Cheyenne unraveled a generous length of cable and tied off the top of the downed tree. She hopped in the Jeep and reversed, taking the slack out of the line. She engaged the four-wheel drive and spun the tires, scouring the gravel and debris from the moist soil. The tree eventually surrendered and hinged open at its trunk. She detached from the tree and climbed back into the Jeep and cradled her throbbing hand. She was almost to her destination and then she could attend to the wound.

The gravel drive veered left and descended toward a cattle guard perched above a small stream. A gazebo, battered by the seasons, peeked into view on the ascending hillside beyond the thick forest canopy. She neared the cattle guard and the arched boughs from the Douglas Firs unveiled a grand cabin. She crossed the cattle guard and ascended up the small hill.

The last time she was here, the yard to the right of the home was nothing more than mud. Now, it was a flat parcel of bright green grass. She shifted into neutral and stared at the home, listening to the Jeep idle.

The cabin could easily be featured on the front page of one of those country home magazines people thumbed through, fawning over homes they could never afford. The rustic cabin sat atop a gravel embankment butted against a steep hillside. The three-car garage entrenched into the slope allowed the second floor to be at ground level behind the house, and was overshadowed beneath a vast deck which connected to the great room. On the right side, a cat walk extended back from the deck, past the front door, to a wooden, split staircase which led out to the driveway and side yard. Large windows comprised most of the exterior facade, separated by heavy timber beams which appeared delicate against the gargantuan three-story building.

Cheyenne walked upstairs onto the sundeck and peered into the windows. The morning twilight made it too dark to see clearly, aside from the faint outlines of white covered furniture. Peeking into the home in all its grandeur was like a centerfold spread open, provocatively enticing you to enter.

She envisioned the vaulted ceiling shared by the living room and kitchen. She caught herself smiling, remembering how her best friend allowed her to pick the kitchen decor. The only rule, all material had to be recycled. Her fondest memory was the view. She remembered standing in the center of the cathedral-like great room and being able to see the surrounding woods from any point. She opened her eyes, scanning the house, barely spotting the piano to the right of the hallway. She smiled, wanting to play *that* piano again.

All of the doors and windows were locked. She remembered the woodpile under the deck by the garage doors. Mounted between a pair of support beams was a circular water trough with the bottom removed and corrugated steel welded longitudinally to sort chopped wood from kindling and starting materials. She removed a log and ascended to the deck. She prepared to hurl the log through the glass door, but could not bring herself to vandalize the home of her deceased friend.

Cheyenne decided to return the log and rounded the deck toward the stairs. The sight of deer tracks leading to the feed bin by the back fence distracted her. The first time she visited, her friend showed her the deer. They were wild but she could feed them from her palm. She followed the tracks for a long distance, but never found the deer.

Exhaustion was taking hold. She found a place to lie down and curled up in ball. It was cold and she didn't think she'd be able to sleep, but she closed her eyes and was out before she could take another breath.

2

The sun pierced through the narrow openings between the tree limbs and leaves, warming Cheyenne's face. She blinked her eyes open, but the intensity of the afternoon sun caused her to shield her eyes. She glanced at her watch; one-thirty. She scooted to the right, escaping the sun's view, and unwrapped her left hand. "You did it good this time, didn't you?" She would need antibiotics soon. She rewrapped her hand, planning her next move. There was no use staying at the cabin if she couldn't enter or, in her case, was unwilling to break in. At this point, she had no options, nowhere to go, no real way to get there. She could always camp in the woods, she supposed. It's not impossible. Jonny made everything seem like fight for survival. She heard his arrogant voice in her head, *"If you learn your surroundings, then you'll know when something's amiss."*

Fine then. She closed her eyes, took a deep breath, and listened. She heard . . . nothing; not even the wind blowing. This was stupid. In Idiotville, she could hear the hawk and the waterfall, after Jonny pointed them out that is. She remembered looking up at the hawk soaring in the sky while Jonny glared at her, smelly and stubbled-faced. His phantom whiskers tickled the ends of her fingertips. If only she hadn't ruined the moment trying to steal a kiss.

Dammit, focus! Jonny adamantly demanded she learn her surroundings; why? Sandra said he's careful with his words; what's so important? What did he think would happen to her?

She closed her eyes once more, took a slower breath, and quietly exhaled. She focused on the air escaping between her lips. She heard a rustle in the nearby blackberry thicket; lizards scampering through the tight brambles, maybe chasing insects. Overhead in the trees, a squirrel chirped and a gentle breeze tousled a strand or two of her disheveled hair which caressed her neck. She inhaled the rich scent of pine; she had taken it for granted this morning. She smiled at her miniscule accomplishment.

"Our friend needs you."

Cheyenne opened her eyes; Ralphie stood above her head. She rubbed her eyes and looked at him again and furrowed her brows. "I didn't think I relaxed that much."

"You're not sleeping."

Cheyenne sat. "Then, how are you here?"

Ralphie sat Indian-style away from her. "Bringing you to that place caused a chain reaction among those who died there."

She squinted her eyes. "How? Why?"

Ralphie let a salamander crawl up his leg and into his palm. He brought it up to his face and smiled. "Before, we were memories chained to Mickey." He placed the salamander back in the pine needle-covered grass. "Your presence allowed our energy to latch onto you."

"Why me, why not Jonny?"

"You've come back from death, he hasn't."

She reached for Ralphie.

He crawled away from her. "You mustn't touch me."

She stared at his neck, looking at the strangulation marks which took his life. "How'd you know I died?"

Ralphie averted his eyes. "Only those who have died can see the dead." He shifted his eyes back to her. "Jonny needs you; go to him."

She stood and walked away. "No, I'm a danger to everyone."

He pounded his fist on his legs. "But he needs you."

It was the second time Ralphie sounded more like his age. She looked over her shoulder, staring into his cloudy eyes. "That's the thing; he doesn't need me."

Ralphie stood. "You hate each other and want nothing more than to erase the other from your life. Yet, you both care enough about the other to keep them safe. You need each other, you just don't know it yet."

"I don't believe we hate each other. Not anymore." She looked through the leaves at the sky and smiled. "We bonded on the trip."

Ralphie shook his head. "Bringing you there released something more dangerous than Nicholas."

Cheyenne whipped her head toward Ralphie. "What do you mean?"

"When you're dead, you feel nothing, not even hunger." Thick, sappy tears escape from his dead eyes. "*She* makes us feel."

"Who are you talking about?"

"You saw her at the end of the driveway when you first

arrived."

"The woman in the sunflower dress? The one who kept her face hidden?"

Ralphie's chin quivered. "Jonny's trying to save you." He crossed his arms over his chest and puckered his lower lip. "Won't you save him?"

The more time she spent with Ralphie, the more childlike behavior he displayed. He was not the same little boy who revealed Jonny's past to her. Even now, she noticed the slow unraveling of his personality. "You're changing."

He lifted his head. His tears left a thick, yellow sebaceous residue down his cheeks. "The dead can feed off each other's energy. When we feed, our personalities merge. The stronger the energy, the stronger the personality."

She moved closer to Ralphie, and he stepped away from her. "Ralphie, I promise I won't touch you." She stepped closer to his side. "Once you consume the energy, how long does it last."

His brows wrinkled.

"When you talk, you go back and forth from child behavior to adult. I gather, the energy you consumed is fading."

He shrugged his shoulders. "I don't know."

If the energy he consumed was dissipating, it was best to treat him as a child. She sat on her knees and ran her hands down her quads. "Look at me, Ralphie. Whose energy did you feed off of?"

Ralphie sobbed to the point he had trouble breathing. "He made me."

She fought her instincts to hold and comfort him. She patted the ground. "Everything's alright now. You don't have to be scared." She waited for him to regain composure and then asked, "What's his name?"

He smeared his tears, staining his gray skin yellow-brown.

"He said his name was Quantrail."

She tilted her head so she could see Ralphie's face. "You never saw him before?"

Ralphie shook his head. "He's not attached to Nicholas like the rest of us are," he looked up at Cheyenne, "or to you."

Her brows furrowed; another damn puzzle piece. "Then why was he in Idiotville?"

The thick tears returned, coating Ralphie's eyes. He rubbed his nose with a balled fist. "Jonny killed 'im."

Her mouth fell open and her lungs held hostage her air. On their way home from Idiotville, Jonny told her he was no saint. Thinking back, when she tried to get him to kill her, Jonny admitted he had taken enough innocent lives. "Do you know how he died?"

Ralphie sniffled, shaking his head.

She squinted her eyes and frowned. "Sweetheart, do you know how they knew each other?"

He shrugged his shoulders.

Cheyenne tucked her hair behind her ears. "Where is Quantrail now?"

"I don't know." Ralphie's chin wrinkled. "I've never been alone before."

She raised her hand to touch him; Ralphie flinched. She lowered her hand. "You're not alone; I'm here." She interlocked her fingers and laid them in her lap. "I'll see you in my dreams, right?"

Wait, she didn't dream this morning. Her eyes scanned her body; she didn't have any cuts, bruises, or marks of any kind.

Ralphie sniffled, plucking blades of grass. "Quantrail saved me from the scary lady."

She studied his childish behavior. Perhaps this Quantrail character was not dangerous after all. "He protected you."

"The scary lady is gathering us."

"Like an army?"

He shrugged his shoulders again. "I don't know." Ralphie went back to plucking the grass. "He keeps five other children safe from her."

"Does the scary lady not consume his energy?"

Ralphie pouted. "I don't know. I don't know what's happening." He looked up at her. His bottom lip protruded outward. "What's heaven like?"

Cheyenne's heart plummeted. She wrapped her arms around him and pulled him in close.

"NO!" He fought against her and crawled away. His breathing labored and his eyes searched the woods in a panic.

She approached him and he crawled further away. "Ralphie stop!"

He jumped to his feet. "Run! Run away!"

The temperature in the forest dropped and the leaves rustled in the trees. The salamander and a myriad of his ilk scattered in all directions, vanishing into the hedges, holes, and under rocks. The dancing clouds of gnats swirled away in the wind, and the tree limbs above jounced under the leaping squirrels, sending pinecones thudding to the ground; the forest was afraid.

She held out her hand, "C'mon, Ralphie."

He shook his head. "Run!"

A headless body stepped out from behind one of the pine trees, his fingers threaded the matted hair of his head. It was the same boy Cheyenne saw at the entrance of the long, unkept, country driveway in Idiotville, the one she coined *the headless Ichabod.*

She shifted her eyes to Ralphie and saw a black spot with dark lines vining away on his back. She was certain it wasn't there in Idiotville, nor when he was alive.

"Whatever you're afraid of, it's too late." She stepped in

front of Ralphie, shielding him. Ichabod was harmless before. Was he still?

Ralphie hugged her legs, burying his face.

Hide and Seek stepped out on either side of a tall, thick trunk. More children appeared from behind trees and boulders and conjugated next to Ichabod.

A gnarled, gray hand slid into Ichabod's shoulder from behind. A woman, the one Ralphie referred to as the scary lady, rose from behind the gathered children. Her wet, chestnut colored hair continued to blockade her face. She stepped in front of the children and stood next to Ichabod.

"Run for the river," Ralphie said.

"Get on my back," she told him. Cheyenne could barely hold him with her injured hand. She kept her eyes on the dead woman. Like Ichabod, the woman did not pose a threat in Idiotville, she only pointed toward something. Cheyenne waited to see if she was going to point again.

"What are you waiting for? Head toward the river!"

She looked over her shoulder. "How do you and Quantrail communicate?"

"I don't know. He finds me."

Cheyenne boosted him up and regripped, wincing from the pain in her palm. She shifted her gaze to the tops of the trees; they were still. It was the calm before the tempest. She slid her right foot back. "You know how to get to the river from here?"

He wrapped his arms around her neck. "It's not far. If you listen, you can hear the water rushing."

Totally failed at learning the surroundings. The force of her heart beating against her chest and spine, jolted her thoughts back to her current situation. She knew how fast Nicholas was; she prayed they were not. "Hold on tight. If they catch us, I want you to save yourself. Do you understand me, Ralphie?"

He tightened his grip. "But Quantrail sent me—"

"Do as I said and save yourself." She glanced over her shoulder. "I'm not entirely sure they're hear for me."

"Huh?"

She bumped him up. "You said, Quantrail won't let the scary lady near you. This is her chance; he isn't here." She took another deep breath and bolted for the river.

Ichabod lifted his head; his eyes blinked. "Want us to bring them to you?" he asked the woman.

"Box them in," her whisper reverberated. "When you trap them, I'll come."

3

Cheyenne's lungs heaved under the exertion. She hadn't run this much since she was a child. She had to stop and catch her breath; her lungs expelled a cough. *Damnit, I need to exercise more*. The slant and bumpiness of the hillside terrain wasn't helping. She boosted Ralphie up; he was heavy for a boney, dead five-year-old.

"Keep going," Ralphie said. "You're almost there."

She looked behind them. *Hello Hide. Where's Seek?* She searched for his brother and found him to her flank.

Ralphie pointed in front of them.

She shifted her gaze and saw a different boy; one she had never seen before. He was a little Asian boy, with a swollen face, much like Jonny's when he fought Myrum. She turned right and charged in the direction of the wildlife.

For the first time, Cheyenne wanted, no, she needed, Nicholas's help but he was nowhere in sight; she couldn't even sense him. Cheyenne dared not look back; she needed to keep one foot in front of the other. The adrenaline blocked the pain in her palm and made her less aware of how heavy she was breathing.

Hide was five feet away, running parallel to them. She feared what might happen if the dead caught them.

"Hurry, Cheyenne!"

The hillside path, on which she fled was washed out a short distance ahead and the hill had become too steep to escape up or downward. Cheyenne estimated the gap small enough for her to jump. Her depth perception wasn't always accurate but there wasn't an alternative. "Hold on tight." She sped up and jumped, closing her eyes.

She reopened her eyes on the descent and found the scary lady waiting on the opposite ledge. Cheyenne landed, barely clearing the gap, and fell to her knees.

The dead woman reached for her.

Ralphie tightened around Cheyenne's neck and jerked her backwards. They both rolled down the sloped cliff like tumbleweeds during the Santa Anna winds.

The dead woman raised her hand, halting the children from their chase.

Cheyenne attempted to grab hold of the rocks and roots or to the trees to slow her momentum, but she was falling too fast to grip anything. "Hmph!" She came to an abrupt stop in the cradle of a tree trunk, landing hard on her ribs. She struggled for air and her body surged with pain, but she knew she couldn't dillydally.

The tree grew outward, away from the cliff, and then upward toward the sky creating a saddle. She slid her body off and dangled, eyeballing a landing zone.

"Hurry, jump!"

Of course, Ralphie would be unscathed, he's dead. She swung her legs a few times and then released, landing, ungracefully, on the large boulder below. She glanced at her throbbing, blood-soaked hand. The bandage was gone, likely caught on the bark of a fir tree or the thorns of blackberry brambles. The blister ripped opened and gashed well into the flesh. Infection would set in if she didn't clean it. She crawled down and splinted her ribs, limping her way to Ralphie.

They ran toward the clearing, leading to a paved road. Cheyenne saw an old wooden bridge suspended over the Umpqua River. "This is Tyee Access Road." She looked to Ralphie. "I know where we are."

He grabbed her hand and jerked her forward; Cheyenne winced, bracing her side. "We have to get to the river."

She limped behind him to the edge of the bridge and looked down. Snowmelt added to the already flooded Umpqua. The rapids raged over the large rocks creating whitewater.

"You gotta jump," Ralphie said.

Cheyenne shook her head. "There has to be another way; I can't swim." She turned around and gasped.

The scary lady stood in the middle of the bridge with her entourage.

Cheyenne pulled Ralphie behind her. "I won't let you have him."

The woman advanced forward.

Cheyenne stepped backward.

Ralphie held tight to Cheyenne's waist. "I'll fall if you keep going back."

The dead woman marched forward, her retinue of children behind her.

Cheyenne removed Ralphie hands. "Good." She turned and shoved him off the bridge. She turned back around and was face to face with the woman.

The wind blew, exposing bits of flesh under the dead woman's hair. Her lips were molded together, her eyes erased, and her nose melted into a pile of skin.

Cheyenne expected eviscerated remanence of a face beneath the wavy locks, but this made no sense. Where was her face?

Cheyenne had a more pressing question. "What do you want with all the children?"

The faceless woman silently brought up her hand.

Cheyenne stepped back a half pace, with no more ground to retreat.

The woman opened her hand, extending out the cracked fingertips, and lunged for Cheyenne.

The water below erupted upwards, launching a smoldering plume of black smoke toward the bridge. A claw escaped the plume, yanking Cheyenne backwards over the railing.

Cheyenne's fingers stretched outward toward the dead looking down at her descent; Ichabod grinned, waving goodbye.

The cold rapids of the Umpqua River knocked the wind out of her and the cascading whitewater consumed her eagerly as Nicholas pulled her, flailing, to its depths.

ABOUT THE AUTHOR

Ardnas Marie grew up watching scary movies and TV shows with her mother, Karen. She began writing at an early age as a hobby, and became a Stephen King fan after reading his book, *The Dark Half.* She published her first book, *Disturbance in the Darkness: A Fated Encounter* in 2019, while living in Salem, Oregon with her husband, Steven.

Made in the USA
Monee, IL
26 January 2022

fee79f88-524c-4e56-9983-2234560ca75eR01